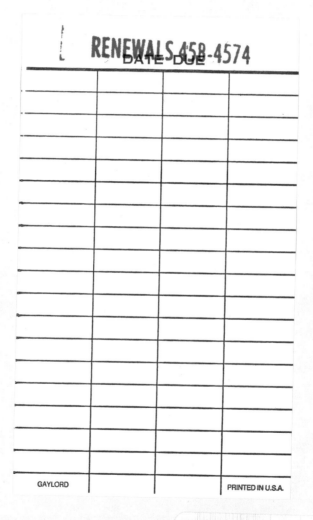

D0043534

RAINBOW

Voices from Asia

RAINBOW

MAO DUN

Translated by Madeleine Zelin

UNIVERSITY OF CALIFORNIA PRESS
BERKELEY   LOS ANGELES   LONDON

Rainbow is a translation of *Hong* (Shanghai: Kaiming Shudian, 1941).

University of California Press
Berkeley and Los Angeles, California

University of California Press, Ltd.
London, England

© 1992 by
The Regents of the University of California

Library of Congress Cataloging-in-Publication Data

Mao, Tun, 1896–
 [Hung. English]
 Rainbow / Mao Dun ; translated by Madeleine Zelin.
   p.   cm. — (Voices from Asia ; 4)
 Translation of: Hung.
 Includes bibliographical references.
 ISBN 0–520–07327–4 (cloth : permanent paper). — ISBN
0–520–07328–2 (paper : permanent paper)
  I. Title. II. Series.
PL2801.N2H813 1992
895.1'351—dc20   91–31273
                                                     CIP

Printed in the United States of America
9 8 7 6 5 4 3 2

The paper used in this publication meets the minimum requirements of
American National Standard for Information Sciences—Permanence
of Paper for Printed Library Materials, ANSI Z39.48-1984. ∞

Translator's Introduction

Shen Yanbing (1896–1981), better known by his pen name, Mao Dun, was born in Tongxiang county, Zhejiang, during the final years of China's last imperial regime. Mao Dun received a modern education, first at a middle school in Hangzhou and later as a student of literature at National Beijing University. In 1916, after three years at the university, financial difficulties forced Mao Dun to cut his academic career short and take a job as a proofreader at the Commercial Press (Shangwu Yinshuguan) in Shanghai.

Because he was born only two years before the 1898 reforms and China's abortive initial attempt at constitutional government, Mao Dun's early life coincided with the flowering of China's first cultural revolution and the beginning stage of the political revolution that would end in the founding of the People's Republic of China. The year he left school saw the death of Yuan Shikai, first president of the Republic of China, and the outbreak of the civil war among competing military governors known as the Warlord Era. Internal disorder, despair at the pressures exerted on China by the Western powers and Japan, and an increasing awareness of China's economic backwardness also gave rise to an intensified search by educated Chinese for the key to China's national salvation. The most influential group of intellectuals who addressed these problems were those dedicated to the complete overthrow of traditional values and the development of a "new culture" and "new thought."

In 1915, *New Youth* (*Xinqingnian*), one of the leading journals that provided a forum for the cultural iconoclasm and intellectual experimentation of the period, was founded in Beijing by Chen

Duxiu. Soon afterward, in 1919, Chinese outrage at the clause in the Treaty of Versailles that transferred Germany's Chinese concessions to Japan led to rioting in cities throughout China. The May Fourth Movement, named for the day on which the first of these anti-imperialist demonstrations took place, saw the joining together of patriotic fervor with the intellectual rebellion of China's youth and provided the inspiration for many of China's modern writers and poets, including Mao Dun.

Shanghai, where Mao Dun spent much of the 1920s, was a center for both political and cultural activism. Promoted to a position as an editor and a translator at Commercial Press, Mao Dun found ample opportunity to immerse himself in the works of writers such as Dickens, Chekhov, and Tolstoy. He was also one of the first Chinese literary critics to recognize the value of less well-known writers from both Western and Eastern Europe. In 1920 he founded the Literary Association, and in 1921 he helped reorganize the journal *Short Story Monthly (Xiaoshuo yuebao)*, acting as its editor until he stepped down in 1923.

At the same time that Mao Dun was developing his interests in a modern vernacular prose, his political and social concerns were drawing him to the growing body of socialist literature becoming available in China in the late 1910s. Political pressure in Beijing drove increasing numbers of radicals to Shanghai during the last years of the decade, and it is likely that Mao Dun joined one of the Marxist study groups founded in the city in 1920. Mao Dun's political activities appear to have taken precedence over intellectual pursuits during the early 1920s. He joined the Chinese Communist Party in August 1921, one month after its founding in Shanghai. Mao Dun participated in the party's efforts to organize labor during these years, both as a strike organizer and as a member of the worker's education movement. In 1923 and 1924 he taught at Shanghai University, a center for the training of party cadre, and in 1925 he played an active part in the anti-imperialist demonstration known as the May Thirtieth Incident.

For both communists and members of the Nationalist Party (Guomindang), the political goal of the mid-1920s was a joint northern expedition to overthrow China's numerous independent warlords and restore the beleaguered country to unified republican rule. In 1926 Mao Dun left for Guangzhou to join in this effort as a propagandist for the Political Department of the United Front government. And when the expedition's armies captured the strategic Wuhan cities in central China, Mao Dun remained in Hankou as editor of the newspaper *National Daily* (*Minguo ribao*). When the Nationalist government turned on the Communist Party in the spring of 1927, open political activity became more difficult, and Mao Dun left Shanghai for Japan in July 1928 and did not return until April 1930.

These years of political activism were a period of relatively sparse literary output for Mao Dun and even sparser results for the political movement he strove to serve. Nevertheless, out of the despair and disillusion these years spawned came the most compelling of Mao Dun's creative works. By 1928 he had completed his first fictional effort, a trilogy of three short novels—*Disillusion* (*Huanmie*), *Vacillation* (*Dongyao*), and *Pursuit* (*Zhuiqui*). Later published under the collective title *Eclipse* (*Shi*), they describe in vivid and depressing detail the events surrounding the northern expedition he had just lived through. These three novels served to establish Mao Dun's reputation as one of the leading writers of Chinese vernacular fiction and were soon followed by *Rainbow* (*Hong*), the first three chapters of which first appeared as a serial in *Short Story* in 1929. Mao Dun's best known works, *Midnight* (*Ziye*, 1933) and the so-called rural trilogy of short stories, "Spring Silkworms" ("Chuncan"), "Autumn Harvest" ("Quishou"), and "Winter Ruin" ("Candong"), continued his exploration of moral and economic bankruptcy in China in the midst of national crisis.

During World War II Mao Dun continued to write novels, short stories, and plays, including *Corrosion* (*Fushi*, 1941) and *Maple Leaves as Red as Flowers of the Second Month* (*Shuangye hongsi eryuehua*, 1943). But following the founding of the People's Republic of China, he was named minister of culture, and his creative work was largely replaced by his work as a bureaucrat and a leading cultural cadre in the new regime.

Mao Dun's mastery of descriptive detail and his objective representation of historical events have earned him praise as one of China's first "naturalist" or "realist" writers. In *Rainbow* we see a melding of several aspects of Mao Dun's creative genius. First, *Rainbow* takes its place with *Eclipse* and *Midnight* as a historical documentary of China's revolutionary process. The heroine, Mei, like hundreds of thousands of Chinese youths in the early years of the century, undertakes to travel the road from the limitations of traditional family life to the discovery of new, "modern" values of individualism, sexual equality, and political responsibility. These values were articulated in innumerable articles and works of fiction by the proponents of the New Thought Tide that flooded China in the wake of the May Fourth Movement. For Mei, the journey ends in political activism, as it did for Mao Dun himself. Indeed, the events of the last chapter are drawn almost entirely from the author's own experiences in the demonstrations that followed the 1925 May Thirtieth Incident.

Nevertheless, *Rainbow* is foremost a psychological novel, and Mei's travels are as much mental as physical. Through Mei's interactions with others and through frequent use of interior monologue, Mao Dun explores with impressive honesty the competing emotions and often selfish ambitions that motivate his heroine and the people she meets. It is with equal honesty that he unmasks the hypocrisy of a "new thought tide" that presents young people with the imperative to smash the old morality but gives them neither the tools to do so nor a safe haven when they are through. For Mei, as for many young people during this turbulent period in Chinese history, it is a quest for personal liberation, not a commitment to well articulated political goals, that leads to participation in the revolutionary movements of the 1920s. In *Rainbow*, the struggle has just begun.

This translation of *Rainbow* is based on the 1941 Kaiming Shudian reprint of the original 1930 edition. It began as a form of recreation and a way to expand my vocabulary while enjoying the art of one of China's foremost modern novelists. As a translator I have tried to remain true to the original. At times this was not easy. As the "Postscript" indicates, Mao Dun wrote this novel in self-imposed exile, in a mood of despair at the Nationalist betrayal of the revolution whose beginnings we glimpse in *Rainbow*. The tension Mao Dun describes between "the cause" and the personal problems of the individual is reflected in the increasingly disjointed way in which Mei's relationships are depicted in the second half of the book. And *Rainbow*'s intended place as the first book of a never-completed trilogy will undoubtedly leave some readers yearning to know what happens to Mei as she and the Chinese revolution achieve a new maturity at the novel's end. Inasmuch as Mei stands as a symbol for the youths, and particularly the young women of her day, I hope this will stimulate some readers to an exploration of the great variety of historical and literary works on modern China now available in English.

When the product of this exercise in translation ceased to be for my eyes only, a number of people kindly offered their advice and expertise. At the University of California Press I was fortunate to have the editorial advice of Betsey Scheiner, Marilyn Schwartz, and Jan Kristiansson. At Columbia, Shi Youshan, Tang Yiming, and Liang Heng each checked parts of the manuscript for accuracy of translation. Howard Goldblatt provided endless encouragement. He, David Wang, and the anonymous readers for the University of California Press checked the text against the original and provided valuable stylistic and editorial suggestions. To all these people I express my deepest gratitude.

Madeleine Zelin
New York, May 1991

List of Characters

Auntie Li	Mei's maid in the Liu household.
Auntie Zhou	a servant in the Mei household.
Chen Juyin	a male geography and history teacher at Lüzhou Normal School.
Chuner	a young maid in the Mei household.
Division Commander Hui	a warlord with progressive leanings who is in command of the Lüzhou-Sichuan region.
Dr. Mei	Mei's father, a practitioner of traditional Chinese medicine.
Huang Yinming	an unconventional young female family friend of Mr. and Mrs. Huang who later becomes Mei's roommate in Shanghai.
Lao Zhang	a member of the theater club at Mei's middle school.
Li Wuji	a Chinese language teacher at Lüzhou Normal School who becomes enamoured of Mei; he reappears in Shanghai.
Liang Gangfu	an arrogant male Sichuanese political activist living in Shanghai to whom Mei is physically and intellectually attracted.

Liu Yuchun	Mei's male cousin and proprietor of a dry goods store; Mei is promised to him in an arranged marriage.
Lu Keli	the male principal of the Lüzhou Normal School.
Mei Xingsu	always referred to as Mei; the heroine of *Rainbow*.
Miss Chen	a spinster teacher Mei encounters at the Zhiben Public School during her stay in Chongqing.
Miss Cui	the headmistress of Mei's middle school in Chengdu.
Miss Li	a member of the Shanghai women's association.
Miss Wu	a member of the Shanghai women's association.
Mr. Huang	a teacher and an advocate of the New Culture who moves next door to the Meis.
Mr. Tao	a teacher at the Lüzhou Normal School.
Mr. Xie	an elderly friend of Mei's father to whose home in Shanghai she moves temporarily after moving out of Provincial Department Chairman Liu's house.
Mrs. Huang	Mr. Huang's unhappy wife.
Mrs. Wen	a veteran suffragette and Mei's companion on the boat trip to Shanghai.
Pockmark Qian	a physical education teacher at Lüzhou Normal School and one of the instigators of the rowdy behavior at Mount Zhong.
Qiu Min	a married female friend of Mei's in Shanghai who is secretly a political activist and member of the newly formed women's association.

Wei Yu	Mei's male cousin, a victim of tuberculosis, with whom Mei is in love.
Wu Xingquan	a male physics and chemistry teacher at the Lüzhou Normal School.
Xu Qijun	Mei's best friend and student at the Yizhou girls' school in Chengdu.
Xu Ziqiang	Xu Qijun's young male cousin, first encountered in Chongqing and again in Shanghai.
Yang Qiongzhi	usually referred to as Miss Yang; her relationship to Division Commander Hui is ambiguous, although she appears to live at his official residence.
Zhang Dacheng	the husband of Qiu Min.
Zhang Yifang	also referred to as Miss Zhang; a provocative young teacher at the Lüzhou Normal School.
Zhao Peishan	a rather plain female teacher at the Lüzhou Normal School who becomes the object of rumors following a dinner at Mount Zhong.
Zhou Pingquan	a female teacher at the Lüzhou Normal School.
Zhu Jie	also referred to as Mrs. Fan; a female teacher at the Lüzhou Normal School.

Chapter One

The golden rays of the rising sun pierced the light smoky mist that hung over the Yangzi River, dispersing it to reveal the blue-green of the mountain peaks on either shore. The east wind played a soft, enchanting melody. The muddy waters of the Yangzi gradually plunged through the narrow gorges, now and then producing a bevy of small whirlpools in its wake.

An indistinct growl, like the roar of a great animal, issued forth from behind the wall of mountains upstream. After a few minutes it grew into a long, proud bellow, transforming itself into a thundering echo between the cliffs on the two sides of the river. A light green steamship burst majestically through the remaining fog, sailing effortlessly downstream. In an instant, the heavy rumbling noise of its engine swelled up on the surface of the river.

It was the renowned steamship *Longmao*, which plied the Sichuan waters of the Yangzi River. On this day it had pulled up anchor at dawn in Kuifu and was rushing to make the journey to Yichang by two or three in the afternoon. Although it was only eight in the morning, the ship was already packed to the rails with third-class passengers who had come up for a breath of fresh air. The passageway outside the dining hall on the uppermost deck was not as crowded. In fact, there were only two women leaning against the green iron railing, looking out into the distance at the magnificent, clear view of the Wu gorges.

They stood shoulder to shoulder, facing the bow of the ship. One, her body slightly turned at the waist, her left forearm leaning on the railing, looked about twenty years old. She wore a pale-blue

1

soft satin waist-length blouse, beneath which a long black skirt that billowed out in the wind accentuated the elegance of her slender and graceful body. She had short hair. Two jet-black wisps of hair brushed the cheeks of her oval face, complementing a pair of long, thin eyebrows, a straight nose, two teasingly beautiful eyes, and small, round lips. She displayed all the characteristics of a flawless Oriental beauty. If viewed from behind, she appeared to be the essence of tenderness. But her eyes revealed a vigorous and straightforward spirit. And her small mouth, which was usually tightly closed, gave proof of her resolute disposition. She was the kind of person who knew her goal and never turned back.

Her companion was a short, fat, middle-aged woman. Her face was not unattractive, but her thick lips drooped at the corners, imparting an air of gloom to her appearance. Her clothes were of high-quality material, but their style was old-fashioned. Her feet had once been bound but were now released from their confinement. Encased in black boots that were too large, their humplike deformity looked like two round balls. Next to the long, narrow natural feet of her young companion, they looked quite miserable and pathetic.

The two did not speak to each other. The grandeur of the scenery had long since cleansed their minds of all thoughts. Their hearts were empty, free of concerns, intoxicated by the vastness of the natural beauty surrounding them.

The boat's whistle shrieked once again. Far off in the distance a cliff intruded on the landscape, blocking the river and piercing the sky. The river cut through the tall peaks that lined both banks. They seemed to form two towering natural dikes, barring any possibility of continued forward passage. The sun shone like a ray of gold, sparingly clothing only the tops of the high peaks in its brilliance, leaving the mountain below a carpet of dark green. The boat continued to push unswervingly forward, its whistle blasting with ever more urgency. The cliffs that all but obstructed the river moved gradually toward the two women, higher and higher, more and more imposing, the luxurious growth of trees halfway up their sides becoming faintly visible.

"This is only the first of the twelve peaks of Wushan." The middle-aged woman, as she addressed her companion, nodded her head with an air of self-importance and such vigor that the large but loosely fastened bun anchored to the back of her skull bounced back and forth as if about to fall off.

The young woman replied with a smile, turning her head to avoid the foul odors that emanated from the large bun. Slowly she took a step forward, concentrating even more intently on the vista ahead. The precipice rushing toward her was now so close she could no longer see its tip. Clusters of jade-green cedars spread like a belt diagonally across the middle of the mountain. Below, thrust directly into the water, were reddish-brown rocks dotted here and there with climbing plants. All of this, this screen of mountains, grew slowly larger, moved slowly closer. Then, suddenly, it shuddered and gently turned around, as if to show off another aspect of its glory.

Bu...hong! The whistle gave a joyous cry, and the boat navigated the bend in the river. On the right the mountains that had been soaring to the heavens moved out of the way; once again the limitless waters of the Yangzi rushed between the mountain peaks.

"That's just like the Yangzi! From a distance it looks impassable. It's only when you get there that you see there's a way through. Who knows how many bends like this there are. Miss Mei, this is your first time. You must find it very interesting indeed!" the middle-aged woman called out loudly from behind. Unfortunately, the east wind was so strong that her words of experience were scattered with it. Mei, who was gazing absentmindedly at the eastward-flowing Yangzi, did not hear a thing.

The unbelievable beauty of the Wu gorges had deeply moved her. She thought of her own past. It, too, had been so treacherous, so quick to change. It, too, had had its dead ends and rebirths. Light and darkness were interwoven into the fabric of her life. She had already courageously made it halfway through. What would the rest be like? This puzzle called the future! Mei had no fantasies. Yet neither was she pessimistic. She was simply waiting, quietly, like a boxing master who has established his position and is waiting for his opponent. Hardship was deeply branded on this young life.

Quite a few people probably envied her life. But she herself still saw her past as worthy of the word "vicissitude." During the last four years she had begun to attract people's attention as a "prominent member of the nouveaux riches." In west and south Sichuan everyone knew of Miss Mei. She was no ordinary girl. She was like a rainbow. But she had never wanted her life to be like this, nor was she happy this way. She simply charged forward with the spirit of a warrior, doing what circumstance dictated. Indeed, her special talent was "charging forward." Her only ambition was to overcome her environment, overcome her fate. During the last few years her only goal had been to rein in her strong feminine nature and her even stronger maternal instincts.

On bright spring days and sorrowful rainy nights, she would occasionally feel the ancient legacy of being female stirring in her heart. At such times she would stare into space, immersed in a flood of loneliness and remorse. It was also at times like these that she fell to lamenting her unfortunate fate and conjuring up a million regrets about the vicissitudes of her existence. Nevertheless, her hardships had already cast her life into a new mold, and the whirlwind May Fourth Movement had already blown her thinking in a new direction. She could not look back. She could only strive to suppress and eradicate the traditional in her nature and adapt to a new world, a new life. She did not pause. She did not hesitate. She felt no contradictions.

The Yangzi was now struggling with difficulty to squeeze through the Wuxia Mountains. The river seemed a symbol of her past. But she hoped her future would be as open and surging as the Yangzi would be below the Kui Pass.

Mei could not suppress a smile. She turned her head and saw the middle-aged woman squinting at her, a reminder that the woman had been jabbering at her with that air of authority that older people so often displayed. Mei did not really like this companion, with her dejected look, but neither was she willing to needlessly offend her. Besides, as long as Mei did not have to smell that rancid hair, she didn't mind listening to the woman's pretentious din.

"Mrs. Wen, the wind is strong. Aren't you scared?" Mei spoke cordially. Stepping daintily inside, she deliberately took a position upwind.

"What hardships and bitterness haven't these old bones known? How could I be scared of the wind? This spring when we demonstrated for women's suffrage, the wind was stronger than this and there was a raging rainstorm, too. That didn't scare me. Without even opening my umbrella, I led the sisters to the provincial governor's office to make our demands."

Mrs. Wen spoke excitedly, the bun at the back of her head bobbing unceasingly.

Mei pursed her lips to hold back a smile, all the while feigning total admiration.

"Why didn't you participate then, Miss Mei? Oh yes, you're the governor's private secretary, the trusted lieutenant of the boss. You're already an official. But Miss Mei, being an official isn't the same as suffrage. Suffrage is . . . "

As she reached this point, the woman paused for a moment and moved a bit closer to Mei in preparation for an extended harangue. Mei took a half-step back to guard her position upwind and adroitly interrupted the other woman: "I'm only the provincial governor's family tutor. What's all this about being a private secretary? That's just a rumor started by people who want to ridicule me. And that's not all people have been saying. It's better to just laugh it off. Mrs. Wen, you lost your husband as a young woman. You of all people should know that people with loose tongues like nothing more than to insult a woman, to spread reckless gossip."

Mrs. Wen's jowls twitched, but she did not reply. Any mention of her youth always depressed her. Nevertheless, her days of "fearing rumors" had long since passed. She was now a wholehearted member of the movement for political suffrage. Yet on the day they had rushed into the provincial assembly and she had heard the guards cursing her as an "old tigress on the prowl," for some reason her ardent spirit had flagged. Subconsciously, she thought back to the past indiscretion that had cast a shadow over her future. She felt that as a woman, the only prerequisite for taking a role in society was that she be pure and above reproach. In believing that a woman should remain ever faithful to one husband and never remarry, she was of one mind with many of those who opposed the suffrage movement.

"The provincial governor advocates the new thought. On the question of relations between the sexes, he has some special views. No doubt Mrs. Wen has heard people speak of them?"

Seeing her companion's discomfort, Mei laughed and changed the direction of the conversation. But the term "relations between the sexes" was probably still very alien to the ears of this eloquent and ardent supporter of women's suffrage. She looked slightly puzzled at Mei and did not answer. Mei winked knowingly and continued, "This special viewpoint goes like this: a wife is a companion for life. A companion is a friend. The more friends the better!"

Suddenly the boat's whistle sounded again, two short spurts followed by a long, loud wail. The warning bell on top of the boat also began to clang wildly. Hiding in the hollows carved out of the hills on both banks of the river, local bandits had begun firing guns in the direction of the boat. This happened quite often. Suddenly the boat was filled with the chaotic sound of passengers' footsteps. By the time Mei grabbed Mrs. Wen and ran to the passageway in front of the dining hall, she had already heard the intermittent and then continuous sounds of gunfire coming from the left. The first-class passengers, who had already arisen, were now pushing and shoving to be first to squeeze down the narrow stairway leading to the cabins below. One of the crew gestured at Mei and her companion to go below as well. Without thinking, Mei took a step forward, but her nose was instantly assaulted by the stench of Mrs. Wen's hair. She stopped.

"I'm not going down. A boat moving with the current goes very fast. Even bandits' bullets won't be able to reach us," Mei said with a slight smile.

She did not wait for Mrs. Wen's reply but walked sprightly through the dining hall to her own cabin, lay down on the bed, picked up a book, and began to read. As it happened, her cabin was on the right-hand side of the boat. The reflection of the sun flashed across the window. Mei got up, thinking to pull down the curtains, when she saw a wooden junk on the water unfurl its sails. It moved along the edge of the cliff and in an instant was gone. She listened carefully. The gunfire had stopped. She returned to her bed, lay down, and yawned. Her nights had been filled with dreams, her sleep unsettled. Once again this morning she had arisen too early. She felt very tired. Folding her hands under her head, she lay back on the pillow and closed her eyes.

The doorknob to the cabin turned softly. Mei opened her eyes lazily and saw Mrs. Wen standing in front of the bed. She must have been jostled by the crowd, for her bun was about to come apart. It drooped limply down the back of her neck, and her temples were sticky with beads of sweat.

"How dare those gangsters even open fire on foreign ships. Ai-ya! But you're the bold one, Miss Mei. Bullets don't have eyes. It's not worth getting yourself killed." Mrs. Wen sank heavily onto the bed. She spoke breathlessly.

Mei smiled charmingly, sat up, walked to the window, and leaned over the dressing table. She considered advising Mrs. Wen to rearrange her bun, but in the end Mei changed her mind.

"The pity is it interrupted our conversation. Mrs. Wen, do you think what the governor said was correct?"

"Important people think differently from us common folk."

A casual observer might have thought that Mrs. Wen was just being polite, but her attitude was exceedingly earnest. Mei laughed faintly. She lifted her foot and lightly kicked the tassels on the lower part of the curtains with the pointed toes of her white leather high-heeled foreign shoes.

"But he said only that a wife is a companion for life, not that a husband and wife are companions for life."

Mrs. Wen opened her eyes wide in total incomprehension.

"He now has five of these companions for life," Mei quickly continued. "He treats them very thoughtfully and equally, but he guards them jealously. You'd almost think he used eunuchs in that famous garden of his. It's practically his Afang Palace."*

Mrs. Wen did not grasp the point of these words. But the number five conjured up rumors she had heard and aroused her interest. "I've heard that some are extremely ugly. Is it true?"

This time it was Mei who did not entirely understand. But just as she threw Mrs. Wen a startled glance, Mei realized what her companion was referring to. With a laugh, she stretched and coldly replied, "There was one who once wrote a poem containing the lines, 'I'd rather be concubine to a hero/than be the wife of a common man.' She'd probably qualify as the world's ugliest woman."

The sun's rays outside the window abruptly fell into shadow, as if the boat had entered a tunnel of some kind. Mei craned her neck to see but noticed only an exceedingly tall cliff slowly receding, its peak hidden from view. Suddenly, suspended before her eyes were row after row of trees, both tall and short, their trunks straight and thin like those of the hemp. Mei drew back her head and looked at

*The Afang Palace housed the harem of the first emperor of the Qin dynasty (221–207 B.C.).

Mrs. Wen's dazed expression. "One of the peculiarities of the general* of the Afang Palace," Mei added, "is that almost all his companions are kind of ugly."

A profound silence crept into the room. The normally talkative Mrs. Wen seemed to have been stricken speechless. She suddenly lay back on the bed and covered her face with her hands. Her fat, clumsy body and her unnaturally small feet all reminded Mei of that woman dwelling deep within the Afang Palace who would rather not be the "wife of a common man."

Images out of the past slowly began to congeal in Mei's mind, enveloping her consciousness like a veil of smoke. As in a dream, she was once again a family tutor in that large garden. She saw the familiar layout of manmade hills, the fish pond, and the Western-style gazebo. Ah! That unforgettable gazebo. It was there that she had refused the temptation of money and jewels. It was not that she did not like luxuries but that she valued her freedom more. Above all, she did not want to become a prisoner of the Afang Palace. It was also there that she had come to know the jealousy that had been bred in women by thousands of years of dependence on men. The vision of a small round face with a pair of fierce triangular eyebrows rushed into her mind. And then the smooth, shiny barrel of a Browning revolver, staring at her like the eye of some bizarre monster.

A barely audible snort of contempt rose up from deep within Mei, waking her out of her gloomy reverie. It was the same snort with which the *yuanzhu* bird in Zhuangzi's famous story replied to the owl who was cherishing his piece of rotting rat meat as if it were a precious jewel.** In fact, the last lesson Mei had taught as a family tutor was that very fable, "The Owl Gets a Rotten Rat."

A faint snoring arose from the bed. Mrs. Wen had fallen asleep. Mei glanced out the window and then walked softly out of the

---

*Mei refers to the governor as a general because most provincial governors during this so-called warlord period of Chinese history were powerful commanders of personal armies whose political role grew out of their military power.

**This is a reference to the section in *Zhuangzi* entitled "The Floods of Autumn" in which the philosopher chides the prime minister of the kingdom of Liang for fearing his job is coveted by the philosopher. He likens the prime minister to an owl who has just caught a rat and fears it will be stolen by the phoenix flying overhead. Just as the phoenix eats and drinks only the purest and most delicate foods and would not want the rat, Zhuangzi would have no interest in such a job.

cabin, back to the passageway outside the dining hall. She sat down on one of the rattan chairs.

On both banks of the river, mountains so tall they had never been inhabited jutted out of the muddy waves and pierced the sky like two high walls. The steamship *Longmao* puffed asthmatically down the middle of the river. Every once in a while a junk or two appeared on either side, but they clung so closely to the cliffs that it seemed as if those aboard could stretch out a hand and pick the wisteria growing on the rocks. Below the distant towering cliffs ahead were several small wooden boats. Crowded together as if immobile in the narrow pass, they seemed to leave no space for the steamship to squeeze through. But only a few minutes later, with a triumphant blast of its whistle, the *Longmao* was hurrying past. Only then was it clear that the Yangzi was really wide enough for four steamships. The wake created by the steamship's propellers dashed against the shore, and the snail-like wooden boats clinging to the cliffs swayed like a gathering of drunken men.

Mei smiled as she looked at the wooden boats. She admired the great power of this machine and had no pity for the snail-like objects being buffeted by the violence it created. She had complete faith in the huge monstrosity that carried her and was intensely conscious that this mammoth product of modern civilization would bring her to a new future. Although before her was a world unimaginably strange, it was surely more vast and more exciting than anything she had known. Of this she was firmly and unalterably convinced.

But she had no illusions. The experience of the last four or five years had taught her three lessons: never long for the past, never daydream about the future, but seize the present and use all your abilities to cope with it. Her past was just like a boat moving through the Wuxia Mountains. She often saw precipices blocking her path, convincing her that there was no way out. But if she bravely and resolutely pressed on, she would always discover that the road ahead was actually very wide. Then as she went a little farther on, the cliffs would again loom before her, and a way out would seem even more remote. If at that point she had looked back from whence she had come, she would have seen that the mountains were already hidden by clouds. To look back on the past was unbearable. The future was indistinct and full of hazards. She could only seize the present and press forward with both feet planted firmly on the ground. She was a "disciple of the present."

A hot wind passed over her. The sun's rays danced on the water like myriad specks of gold. It was almost noon. Mei leaned back in the rattan chair and felt her eyelids grow heavy. Although the scenery before her was fascinating, it now made her feel somewhat weary. The endless river pressed between the barren mountains, twisting and turning interminably as the torrents of water rushed ceaselessly forward, always promising new mysteries and yet always the same. And amidst it all, the ever present triumphant, yet mournful, sound of the ship's whistle.

She slumped down in the chair, letting herself drowse off to escape the monotony. No thoughts of the past disturbed her peace, and no thoughts of the future came to arouse her emotions.

A waiter arrived to call her to lunch. She found out from him that it would be around three o'clock before they reached Yichang and concluded that this so-called fast steamship was no better than a slow boat after all. She wished she could cross the Kui Pass immediately. The closer they approached the Sichuan border, the more her impatience grew. To Mei, everything about Sichuan was narrow, small, meandering, just like the river flowing before her.

After lunch, taking advantage of a reprieve from Mrs. Wen's incessant chatter, Mei withdrew into the cabin to take a nap. She had long since found this leading member of the women's suffrage movement boring. Now Mei had begun to hate her. She hated her vulgar manners; she hated her extreme narrow-mindedness; she hated the way she put on airs to mask her base nature; she hated her extremely muddled ideas on women's rights.

Half consciously, she compared herself to Mrs. Wen. Then, suddenly, Mei thought of what would happen after they reached Shanghai. She asked herself, "We are representatives, but as a group, what do we represent? How will we be able to accomplish our collective mission?" She could not but laugh. She admitted to herself that she had used her attendance at the National Student League conference as a pretext to evade the advances of that diminutive warlord. She knew if she did not escape now, it would be difficult to avoid being forced into becoming one of the ladies of the Afang Palace. As to whether her companion, Mrs. Wen, also had personal motives for attending, Mei was even less inclined to speculate.

All thought of sleep departed. From Mrs. Wen, Mei's mind wandered to recollections of other acquaintances. Xu, a good friend from middle school with whom she had kept in touch until two years ago, when she was a teacher in southern Sichuan, leaped into her mind. "She's in Nanjing," Mei thought excitedly. And with this a multitude of disconnected memories streamed into Mei's head, finally driving her from her bed.

A rumbling sound arose from the deck. From outside the window came the sound of swarming footsteps. Mrs. Wen stuck her head in through the window and shouted joyfully, "Don't you want to see the Kui Pass? We're almost there!"

Mei replied with a smile. The enthusiasm of the throng outside made her feel hot. She changed into a muslin blouse, wiped her face with a towel, and ran nimbly out to the passageway.

Lofty cliffs still stood on both banks, but now they were not so high and had begun to slope slightly. Behind them rose row after row of mountains, each taller than the ones before. The rays of the sun had now turned them a brilliant golden color. The wind had died down to a gentle breeze, as if it, too, had barely awoken from its afternoon nap.

The boat seemed to be moving more slowly. The splashing of the waves became more even. The whistle emitted a constant arrogant bellow like the cries of the heralds in ancient times who ordered the people to make way for an approaching official.

Many people were lined up along the railing, staring straight ahead. Mrs. Wen was among them. Mei stood in the passageway. She clasped her hands behind her neck and gently swayed her shoulders from side to side. Her short sleeves fell back to her shoulders, revealing her snow white arms like two triangles on either side of her head. The sight of her bare skin attracted quite a few sideward glances. Mei bit her lip and grinned as if no one else were there. Then, impulsively, she raised her eyebrows and skipped off, cutting right through the clusters of passengers to the door of the captain's cabin.

About one hundred feet from the front of the ship, two walls of stone jutted out of the water and faced each other across the river, so vertical and smooth they seemed to be sliced out of the rocks with a knife. There were no trees, no vines, no ferns, only the pitch black rocks looming majestically over the river like a monumental door frame without its top. Joining these two strange stones were row after row of undulating mountains. Each billowing wave of the Yangzi rushed to be first to reach the shore, crashing violently against the foot of the cliffs.

The boat's whistle once again let out a long ear-splitting shriek as the *Longmao* sailed into the great stone gateway. Mei craned her neck to see. The intensity of the sun made her dizzy. She felt as though the rapidly receding stone precipice was swaying, about to topple. Instinctively, she closed her eyes. She saw a flash of red light and then all was dark.

Mei buried her face in her hands and thought to herself, "So this is the Kui Pass. This is the great pass out of Sichuan. This is the demon pass* that separates Sichuan from the rest of the world!" These thoughts left Mei momentarily distracted, until the boat's whistle once again roused her. She lifted her head and felt a blinding flash from the returning sunlight. The Yangzi opened up before her, so broad that she could not see the shore. All that was visible were distant, smoky objects like the shadows of clouds lying on the horizon. As if a great weight had been lifted from her chest, Mei smiled, raised her arms high, and took a deep breath. She paid tribute to this glorious work of nature. It was only at that moment that she fully realized the vastness and power of the Yangzi River.

She turned her head to the right. The cliffs of the Kui Pass were still faintly visible. The pass itself now seemed but a crack among the myriad peaks, and within the crack lay a mysterious darkness.

"From here on you won't be seeing any more good scenery. Once you leave Sichuan the Yangzi is really quite ordinary. The Kui Pass is a natural boundary."

From her left came the sound of Mrs. Wen's voice. Mei turned her head and saw Mrs. Wen straining to move her small feet. As she nodded and walked away, Mei pursed her lips in a smile and called gently after her, "This is also the last time we'll be following a meandering, narrow, dangerous, mazelike route. From here on we enter the broad vast world of freedom!"

*This is a pun on the word *gui*, or demon, and the name of the pass as well as an expression of Mei's hatred of her isolation in Sichuan.

Chapter Two

When Mei was eighteen years old she was enrolled as a student at the Yizhou Girl's School in Chengdu. It was in that same year, on May 4, that the students of Beijing began their historic mass movement. Their initial attack on the Zhao mansion* gave rise to the raging tide of "May Fourth." The flames that burned through the Zhao mansion set fire to the zeal of young people throughout China.

Within a month this raging tide, this spark, had burst forth and spread all the way to Chengdu, that remote and enigmatic land on China's western frontier. Mei had gone to Shaocheng Park to witness the activity generated by a rally to boycott Japanese goods. The slogan of the rally was "patriotism." Of course, Mei knew that she should love her country, but the slogan was too general, too broad to arouse her enthusiasm. She remained only a spectator. At the time she was too caught up in her own personal dilemma, one that she could not resolve. Only three days earlier, without her consent, her father had betrothed her to her first cousin, Liu Yuchun.

When she returned home from the rally that evening, her father had himself just returned from getting drunk at the Lius'. He had apparently heard something at the Liu Dry Goods Store because instead of going straight to sleep as usual, he summoned Mei and began to rant, "So, this is our great republic! Students meddling in

*This was the home of Cao Rulin, minister of communications in the central warlord government and one of the three pro-Japanese officials who were targets of student wrath following China's mistreatment at Versailles.

13

other people's private affairs! They plan to go to the dry goods store to inspect it for Japanese goods. If they find any they'll confiscate them, and they even intend to impose a fine. It's ridiculous. It's impossible. I can't believe the *yamen** won't take any action."

Mei lowered her head and said nothing. The words "inspect the dry goods store" pierced her like a knife. The earth-shaking patriotic cries at Shaocheng Park, which had seemed so remote to her this afternoon, now turned out to be directly related to her personal problem. In the future she would have to be the proprietress of a store that secretly sold Japanese goods. This prospect intensified her misery. That day, when she heard people shout, "Patriotism," she hadn't given it a second thought, for she knew she had never sold out her country. Now her complacency was gone. Suddenly she felt like a notorious traitor.

"Heh! What they say *sounds* good enough. They say they want us to buy Chinese products. Well, I'm a genuine doctor of Chinese medicine, the real article. But in recent years look how unpopular, how poor I've become!"

Her father spoke wheezingly, filling the room with the stench of alcohol. From the students, he moved on to his usual routine of cursing his son. His tongue thick from drink, he laboriously recited the past events that Mei had heard so often before. How he had sold off family property to send his son to study in America. How, later, he had sold more family property to pull the right strings to get his son a job. How his son, who was happily living far away, never even asked whether his father was dead or alive. His eyes were completely red by the time he finished his tale.

"The year before last he was employed in the office of the Shaanxi military governor, but he still wired home again and again asking for money. Last year he became a magistrate and he stopped coming to me for money. But his telegrams and express letters also stopped. Ah! This is the way a son who studies abroad and becomes an official acts. The one with real promise is that child Yuchun. He was an orphan. I took him into our home only because he was related to us. Later, when I sent him to be an apprentice at the Hong Yuan Dry Goods Store at the Yuelai market, it was only so he'd have a way to make a living. And with nothing but his bare hands he turned around and made a fortune."

*A *yamen* was the office of the head of any administrative unit.

Her father closed his eyes and nodded his head in satisfaction. Then, abruptly, he opened them wide and shouted, "How dare those student bastards prevent people from selling Japanese goods!" Repeating himself once more with venom, Mei's father then staggered into his own room.

Mei watched his retreating figure and heaved a great sigh. If there hadn't been a maid still standing in a dark corner of the room, Mei would have already let the tears welling in her eyes pour out. Her eyes darted in every direction, like a drowning person searching desperately for something to hang on to. There was nothing, only the flickering flames of the kerosene lamp leaping toward her, the ancient wooden furniture gaping dumbly all around her, and the chill of a household in decline that pierced her to the marrow.

Biting her lip to hold back the tears, Mei fled into her own bedroom. Here the warmer atmosphere comforted her somewhat. On a delicate pear-wood table were arranged the mementos of the blissful days of her childhood: an exquisitely dressed doll; a red-lipped, white-toothed Negro figure with a small clock in its protruding belly; two peacock feathers inserted in a tea green triangular glass vase. These were all relics of better times, five or six years ago, before her mother had died. Mei, without a mother and without sisters, had used these toys to replace the intimacy of real flesh-and-blood relatives. Now she stared absentmindedly at these mute, though almost human, friends. Confused thoughts crossed her mind, but none took root in her consciousness. It was as though she were being assaulted by disconnected images—the dry goods store, Japanese products, cousin Liu, marriage, the rally at Shaocheng Park—each throbbing feverishly in her head.

Impulsively, she went to her bed and took out a small inlaid ebony box. She lifted the lid. It was completely empty except for a single photograph of the face of a slightly feminine-looking young man. Mei gazed at the photo for a few minutes, then closed the box and lay down on the bed. A vision of another man flashed before her eyes. On his round face were two broad, thick eyebrows and a pair of shrewd eyes. He was not basically bad looking. He just displayed too much of the vulgarity of the crafty businessman.

Mei buried her face in the pillow and gritted her teeth. How she hated that man! Her secret hatred of him was as great as her secret love for the other man. But it was not her secret love for the one that caused her to hate the other. She had hated him for a long time. Both were her cousins, but for some reason she had never felt as close to her father's sister's son, who had been raised in her own family, as she felt toward her other cousin on her mother's side. Although she did not want him to, the former continually pursued her. From the time Mei was barely old enough to know about sex, he, already an adult, had constantly looked for opportunities to flirt with her. She still had a scar on her arm where he had scratched her. This was something a proud girl like Mei could not tolerate. She carried in her bosom the secret of this humiliation. She secretly detested this man. Yet it had now been decided that she was to spend the rest of her life with this very person.

A feeling of having been vanquished, of having been taken prisoner, overcame her. Worse, there seemed no hope of escape. The marriage agreement had been concluded. The wedding would probably take place next year. What means could she use to resist? What means did she *have* to resist? Still worse, she had heard that the man she loved was also about to get married. At the latest it would probably be this winter. Last week when they had met and talked at the Wangjiang teahouse, had he not said to her, "Meimei,* circumstances demand that we part. Even if I was not engaged, would Uncle want a poor orphan like me? And even if Uncle agreed, I'm only a clerk in the army divisional headquarters. Could I make you happy? I know you're willing to suffer, but how can I bear to see the one I love sacrifice on my account? The doctor says I have tuberculosis. I probably don't have long to live. That's even more reason not to sacrifice your future."**

Two rows of tears streamed from Mei's eyes, but they were tears of happiness. She was glad she had tasted the bittersweet joy of true love. She sank once more into her memories, reliving that moment as if it were displayed before her like a motion picture. When her emotions had reached their peak, she had looked to see that there was no one around and pressed her face against her cousin's shoulder. Then slowly, half unconsciously, she moved her

*"Meimei" is a term used to address a younger sister. Here it demonstrates affection and the fact that the two are cousins.

**Traditional Chinese morality contained strong proscriptions against the remarriage of widows.

lips closer to his. A shiver ran through his whole body. He drew gently back and said in an unsteady voice, "Cousin, I have tuberculosis." Oh! Oh! Tuberculosis! Will it keep me from embracing this man while he is alive? Will it only let me cry at his grave?

A wild passion overtook Mei's heart. She did not blame her cousin for his seeming aloofness. On the contrary, she was even more grateful, felt even more respect and love for his pure and honest nature. She wanted to know only why she did not have the right to love the one she loved, why she was only worthy of being a prisoner, a piece of soft, warm flesh to be toyed with. She hated the teachers at school and the old revolutionary spinster headmistress, Miss Cui, for never having discussed problems of this kind.

These two questions went round and round in her mind, but she had no answers. Finally, her nerves, half numb with exhaustion, led her to that age-old explanation: an unfortunate fate. This simple answer wrenched her, tortured her, haunted her, gnawed at her until the chirping of the birds praising the dawn aroused her with a start. The sun shone obliquely on the eaves of the house. The clock in the belly of the Negro doll ticked steadily. All was beautiful. All was calm.

Mei rolled over and sat up. In a daze, she balanced herself on the edge of the bed. She could not believe a whole night had passed. She noticed mosquito bites all over her pale upper arm. Her neck also itched. When she walked toward the window to look in the mirror, she saw that there were faint blue circles under her eyes and that her cheeks were flushed blood-red. Putting down the mirror, she sank into a nearby chair and stared vacantly at the doll sitting atop the pear-wood table.

The big hand on the Negro doll's belly had marked the passing of a full ten minutes when Mei suddenly jumped up. She dashed off a short letter, combed her hair, changed into a pale lilac muslin skirt and blouse, and called one of the family's maids to bring her breakfast. Her lips had recovered their smile, and her eyes, which minutes before were suffering from lack of sleep, once again radiated determination.

Mei went to school as usual. As she dropped the letter into a mailbox on the way, an unconscious smile crossed her face. No formal classes were held that day. Yesterday's rally had already stirred up some of these normally sedate young ladies. Everywhere could be heard the buzzing of female voices absorbed in curious gossip. The old revolutionary, Headmistress Cui, suddenly became an object of great interest. Wherever she went, her long braid bouncing behind her,* there were always pockets of students secretly watching her every move. The reading room in particular was alive with activity. Group after group of students fought over month-old newspapers from Shanghai and Hankou to see how the students in Beijing had set fire to the minister's house and beaten up a high government official, to see how afterward they had taken to the streets to make speeches, and to see how several hundreds of them had been arrested by the police. A few of the more discerning girls went a step further and searched out five or six dusty volumes of *New Youth* magazine.** The whole school shook with nervous agitation.

Mei was no exception. But unlike the others, she was not absorbed in this intense research into recent events. Rather, she used it as a means to make the time pass more quickly. In reality, she was preoccupied with the date she had made with cousin Wei Yu for later that day. She was also afraid that she would hear people say things like "the dry goods store sells nothing but Japanese products." Whenever Mei ran into classmates who were talking about the boycott, she could not help feeling a bit jumpy, as if her own hidden sins had been discovered.

At ten past four Mei sneaked away to the Ziyun pavilion. A tall, emaciated young man was already there waiting for her. They smiled and stood gazing silently at one another, then walked slowly to a large *wutong* tree behind the pavilion, each deep in thought, as if pondering what to say first.

"Meimei, your letter gave me quite a scare." The young man spoke softly, his gentle eyes fixed on Mei's face.

Mei replied with a tender smile, "Why weren't you able to sleep well last night? You look pale and your eyes are a bit swollen. You were crying last night, weren't you?"

*Traditionally only young unmarried girls in China wore their hair in braids. Used by a middle-aged woman like Miss Cui, this hairstyle could become a symbol of feminism and the rejection of marriage.

**Founded in 1915 by Chen Duxiu, *New Youth* was one of the first of the new May Fourth era journals dedicated to, among other things, the promotion of vernacular literature, liberalism, women's rights, and the overthrow of Confucianism and traditional values.

The young man sighed faintly, hung his head, and allowed two imperceptible tears to drip down his cheeks.

Mei did not reply. Her lips drew together as if to speak, but she held back. She kicked a clump of grass at the foot of the tree with her toe and began mechanically fingering the hem of her muslin blouse. She hesitated for a full half-minute before she said calmly, "Cousin Yu, I don't know what was on my mind last night. But you needn't worry. It doesn't matter. Last night was nonsense, meaningless nonsense. But this morning I came to a decision. Let's work out a plan to go away."

Wei Yu raised his head in alarm and fixed his gentle gaze on Mei as if he had not understood what she meant by "go away." Nevertheless, a look of intense gratitude was revealed as his eyes slowly filled with tears. Mei smiled and added softly, "If we go away together, there might still be hope. If we split up, the future will be unendurable!"

Tears were his only reply. Two thoughts did battle in the mind of this overly sensitive young man. He could not bear to hurt her by saying no, but he felt he should not say yes. After a painful silence, he forced out these few words: "I am not worthy of such true love, Meimei."

This time it was Mei's face that turned pale. She began to have the uneasy feeling that the man she loved was a coward.

"I'm a sick man. At most I'll live another two or three years. I don't deserve to enjoy life. Even more, I shouldn't let the shadow hanging over my life blot out your chances for happiness. If you continue to think of me, then I will die with a smile on my face. Knowing that your future will be a good one, I'll be able to die content."

Although there was a slight tremor in his voice, he spoke these words with resolve. He had the aura of a martyr about to die for his principles. He shed no more tears. His cheeks were flushed with excitement.

Mei silently bowed her head. Then suddenly she spoke with total conviction: "My future most certainly will not be good."

"Huh?"

"Because I don't love him. I hate him."

"Do you hate him for the reason you mentioned last time? If he's too aggressive, it's probably because he loves you so much."

Mei could not but purse her lips and laugh. She shot a glance at Wei Yu and said with an air of disapproval, "When did you learn how to defend other people so well?"

"I'm not defending him. I'm just telling you the truth."

"You call that the truth?"

Mei spoke sharply. She was clearly angry. If this had not been her trusted Wei Yu, she would certainly have thought Liu Yuchun had bribed him to lobby on Liu's behalf. But coming from Wei Yu's lips this sort of talk was quite unexpected. She looked at him intently, waiting for an answer.

"Meimei, I was wrong. Please forgive me. Of course, I don't want someone else to love you. But at the same time I really wish there was someone who could truly love you and whom you could love in return." Wei Yu tried to dispel his feelings of guilt by defending himself.

"When did you start having such thoughts?"

"Since I found out that I had tuberculosis and knew I couldn't make you happy."

Again, tuberculosis. Mei's heart pounded. She sensed that the dark shadow of this disease would tear them apart forever. She wanted to curse this god-forsaken tuberculosis, but Wei Yu had already resumed speaking.

"Last year I didn't feel this way. Meimei, at that time we were both very shy. We never talked openly about our feelings. But in our hearts we both knew. We thought about each other all the time. At that time I hated myself for being too poor. I resented Uncle for not giving his consent. But recently I've been reading some stories and magazines and my way of thinking has changed. . . . "

"Now you just speak the truth, huh?" There was considerable dismay in her voice as she interrupted him.

"No. I've just come to realize that when you love someone it doesn't mean you have to possess her. To really love someone is to put her happiness ahead of your own. . . . "

"People only say that sort of thing in novels," Mei interrupted Wei Yu a second time. Clearly she was not pleased with what he had to say. Moreover, she did not understand what he meant by "possess."

"It's not from novels. It's philosophy—Tolstoy's philosophy," Wei Yu corrected her earnestly. But noticing Mei's exhausted appearance, he lowered his head and discontinued his argument.

There was a short silence. For the first time they heard the sound of the cicadas chirping among the leaves of the *wutong* tree. The breeze rustled Mei's muslin skirt. The sun shone obliquely on the sides of the pavilion. Mei wrinkled her eyebrows slightly and stared into space. In the end it was Mei who spoke first, her eyes gliding over Wei Yu's face. "That business of yours later this year, has the date been set?"

He replied with a resigned nod of the head. But after a brief interval, he began to defend himself: "It was all my uncle's idea. I told him that right now I'm not in a position to take care of a family, but he refused to listen."

"But did you bring up your tuberculosis and the fact that you have only three or four years to live?"

"No. It wouldn't have done any good."

"Then aren't you going to hurt *her* future?"

Wei Yu looked at Mei with a puzzled expression. For a moment he could not think of an appropriate reply.

"Do you think it's all right because you don't love her? But how can you know that she doesn't love you? How can you turn around and cold-bloodedly ruin the life of someone who loves you?"

"I can't worry about everything. Even if it will destroy her, it's my uncle who is the executioner. I'm only the sword. A sword can't move by itself."

"But when someone wants to throw herself on the blade of this sword, then it is able to come alive, isn't it? Then it is able to move out of the way!"

With this mild rebuttal, Mei turned her back on Wei Yu and began walking slowly toward the pavilion. She could no longer suppress the nagging suspicion, the uncomfortable sensation that gnawed at her insides. Her cousin was too passive, too timid. He was too lazy. Wei Yu only wanted to ensure his own immediate comfort. So much so that he was unwilling to brave danger for the one he loved. He placed his own comfort above all else.

By the time she stepped up onto the stone steps in front of the pavilion she could bear it no longer and turned around. But when she did, it was only to find that Wei Yu was right behind her. His feelings of apprehension brought her to a halt. They looked at each other for several seconds before Wei Yu spoke excitedly, "I'm a weakling, a good-for-nothing weakling. Meimei, you are wrong to love me. But you know what's in my heart. I worship you. To me you are a goddess. I beg you not to be miserable because of me. I beg you to forget me. I beg you to despise me. I beg you, just let me lock my love for you away in my heart; just let me repay your kindness to me with my tears. Ah! I might as well tell you everything. I'm an evil person. Two months ago, in the middle of the night, when I was thinking of you, I found myself hugging the covers passionately, squeezing them so tight, as if they were you. Oh, I'm a beast. It's only in the daytime, when I stand before you, that I become human again, an honest gentleman. I detest myself. When I read stories, when I look at magazines, it is in the hope of deriving some comfort from their pages, in the hope of discovering in their pages a way to save myself and save you. Now I've found it! A glorious ideal has relieved me of my agony, has made up for losing you. Now if I could only see you live a long prosperous life, I would be the happiest man in the world!"

Having said this, Wei Yu opened wide his troubled eyes and stared off into space. It was as if there, beyond the treetops, amidst the glow of the setting sun, was the new, glorious ideal to which he owed his salvation. As if there in the distance stood an infinitely compassionate, infinitely sympathetic sage, beckoning to him with a raised hand.

Tears the shape of pearls welled up in his eyes. Was this a natural expression of his humanity, or was it the last remnant of his desire? Wei Yu was not certain himself. He merely felt an extraordinary sense of relief, as though he had just spit out something that had been lodged in his guts a long, long time.

Mei leaned against a pillar of the pavilion engrossed in thought. She did not reply. After a while she turned around and, with a strained expression, said softly, "I know what is in your heart. It's not just fate that's brought us to this impasse, is it? Please don't worry. I understand what you're saying. But please, spare me the philosophy from now on. I also have principles. I refuse to be a prisoner. It's getting late, Cousin Yu. Good-bye!"

Mei turned and took one last look at Wei Yu, then followed the path on the right of the pavilion and walked determinedly away. Wei Yu followed slowly behind her. After about ten steps she stopped, turned around once more, and said to him, "Those stories and magazine you spoke of, I also want to read them. Would you send them to my house?"

Suddenly the evening breeze blew through Mei's muslin blouse, revealing the hem of her pale pink camisole. Like rosy clouds it dazzled Wei Yu's eyes and aroused his passions. Instinctively he rushed forward, about to press Mei to his bosom, but he instantly recovered his composure and stopped. In a daze, he nodded his head, turned toward a different path, and ran away.

Mei returned home bewildered. Her image of Wei Yu had begun to blur. She had always felt she understood Wei Yu completely. Now she was not sure. A few strange books had changed her Wei Yu. But how they had changed him, Mei did not really know. She just felt as though some kind of mysterious spirit had possessed Wei Yu, making his way of thinking different from other people's, different from her own. He had become even more cowardly, even more indifferent. It could even be said that he had become frigid and aloof. But that was not the whole story. Beneath his cowardice he had a new daring and determination; beneath that icy aloofness burned a passionate desire to sacrifice himself for the happiness of another.

There was only one thing of which Mei was still absolutely certain, and that was Wei Yu's faithfulness to her. This gave her incomparable comfort. In imitation of Wei Yu, she had come close to saying, "Even if my future knows no happiness, as long as there is someone who loves me with all his heart, my life will not have been lived in vain."

In such a mood Mei began to feel the days pass more easily. At the same time her native eagerness to explore new things encouraged her to devour the stories and magazines Wei Yu sent over. She thirsted for an immediate knowledge of the mysterious spirit that had changed Wei Yu.

As for the fervent activity of the "patriotic movement," she was still just a bystander. She could not get herself interested. Although the words "inspect the dry goods store for Japanese goods" occasionally upset her, when she thought of her decision "not to be a prisoner" she became inured, feeling that the matter of Japanese products at the dry goods store had, after all, nothing to do with her. She viewed the continued progress of this convulsive mass movement as she had before, as something totally unrelated to her own personal interests.

But the patriotic movement to boycott Japanese goods was slowly developing a new focus. The students of the city's highest educational institution, the Teacher's College, had proclaimed a new slogan: "Liberalize social relations between the sexes." Mei recalled that several of Wei Yu's magazines had mentioned this, but she had not paid it any attention. Following Wei Yu's instructions, she had read only the essays on Tolstoy. The stories were also by Tolstoy. In her excitement she had already read them twice, but they did not seem to say anything about open social relations. With a new curiosity and hope she perused them yet again.

One day on the way home from school Mei caught a glimpse of several eye-catching magazines arranged in the window of a bookseller's shop. Each and every one had the word "new" in the title. On the front covers were also prominently displayed article titles such as "The Cannibalism of Traditional Morality." She looked at them with surprise and joy and regretted that she was not carrying any money. The next day on the way to school she made a point of deliberately stopping in to buy one, but they were all sold out.

Dispirited, she went to school but was in no mood to listen to the lectures. Instead she daydreamed. She imagined that she saw a rush of powerful roaring waves rolling over all that was old and rotten. She was convinced that extraordinary and new things were spreading everywhere. Her small corner of the world was the only place they had not yet reached. And even if they did, she would never get her hands on them. Restlessly she gazed around the room. She despised her dull, lazy, torpid classmates. Then suddenly, unexpectedly, she saw a student, Xu Qijun, sitting not far from her, reading one of the magazines with the word "new" in the title.

After class Mei rushed over to Xu Qijun. Peering over her shoulder, Mei saw that this was the very magazine that had slipped through her fingers. "Ah. I never suspected you were the one who bought it," Mei called out gleefully. She turned half around and leaned on Xu Qijun's shoulder as though they were old friends. Xu turned her head, looked at Mei with dark, penetrating eyes, and said with a smile, "Are these also on sale in the city? Mine were sent to me by my brother in Beijing."

The two classmates, who had barely known each other by sight, suddenly began an intimate conversation. An indescribable but clearly sensed force drew them together. In the course of this animated discussion Mei again heard many strange new terms. Although she did not yet fully understand their meaning, each one gave her a feeling of rapture, of exhilaration. The two girls did not even hear the bell signaling the next class.

When Mei returned home that day she carried under her arm a bundle of magazines, all lent to her by Xu Qijun. Although the weight under her arm had increased, there was a greater spring in her steps. She felt that a new world had opened up before her. She had only to walk in and there would be happiness and light.

Her exploration of the new thought and the sudden acquisition of a new friend made Mei temporarily forget the anxieties evoked by her personal problems. From the crack of dawn when they went to school until the evening when it grew dark, she and Xu Qijun were inseparable. The two of them became a target of gossip at school. Some even suspected them of lesbianism. Summer vacation was near. The dates for final examinations had already been set. But Mei and Xu remained engrossed in the new books and magazines. The only time they opened their textbooks was in class, when they propped them up on their desks to fool their teachers.

Because of Wei Yu's original suggestion, Mei still concentrated on Tolstoy. But Xu seemed to be a disciple of Ibsen. Every other word out to her mouth was Ibsen. Each saw herself as the representative of her chosen writer. In reality, neither really understood the works of these two great masters. They had only a very vague idea of their meaning and even misinterpreted them in many places. But at the same time they shared a common conviction: Tolstoy and Ibsen were both new, and because they were new they were definitely good. This common faith strengthened the girls' friendship and brought their very souls together.

Examinations finally ended. On the evening of July 1, the first day of vacation, Mei's father suddenly took ill. The old man had returned home drunk at eight o'clock. At ten he started complaining of stomach pains, after which he threw up everything he had eaten. He wrote himself a prescription, which he himself prepared, but it had no effect. Mei did not sleep all night. She sat in her father's sickroom, wild and confused thoughts pouring through her agitated mind. Just before dawn her father seemed a bit calmer, but within half an hour he went into a rage over his son's lack of filial piety. Gasping, he jumped up and began ranting about dragging his son back and reporting him to the magistrate for disobedience to his father. All Mei and the maid could do was muster their strength to pull the old man back to bed. This melodrama lasted until eight o'clock the next morning, when the patient finally calmed down and Mei frantically sent for a doctor.

Later that morning, when the patient appeared to be resting easily, Mei returned to her own room to try getting a little sleep. But in her overly excited condition she could do no more than close her burning eyes and let her muddled thoughts overcome her. She pondered the fact that Xu Qijun would be returning home to Chongqing today. Mei's new friend had promised to mail her more new books, but Mei did not know when they would arrive. She also wondered whether her plans to spend the vacation reading would be upset and hoped her father would get well quickly. It also troubled her that Wei Yu had not been by all week. She turned these matters over and over in her mind. Time and again she rolled over to place her feverish cheeks on the coolest part of the mat.* Mei dimly heard the singing of birds in the trees outside her window. The voice of their servant, Auntie Zhou, drifted over from the living room, followed by the shuffle of footsteps. Finally, there was what sounded like a fly buzzing incessantly around her ear.

"Master Liu is here."

As the humming congealed into these words, Mei awakened from her exhausted stupor. She opened her eyes and stared vacantly in front of her. The maid, Chuner, stood grinning at the foot of the bed. Mei frowned and shook her head as if to say, "Don't bother me," then turned over and pretended to be asleep. She had expected him to come. She really had been hoping someone would come to drive away her depression. If only it had not been him! All thought of sleep departed. Mei jumped up and ran to the door to lock it but changed her mind. She left it half opened as before, walked to the window, and sat down in her chair. She spoke softly but proudly to herself: "Will he dare?" The small hand on the belly of the Negro doll showed that is was precisely three o'clock. The oppressive heat of the July sun muted all sound. There was only

---

*It is a common practice in parts of China to place straw mats on one's bed in summer to avoid the sticky heat of sleeping on sheets.

the chirping of the cicadas in the *wutong* tree outside the window. Mei sat stiffly upright in her chair, as if awaiting some grave omen.

Suddenly the door creaked. Mei watched, startled. The face of Chuner, her thick lips parted, peered in and then quickly withdrew.

"Chuner!"

Mei's stern shout drew Chuner back inside. She stood fearfully in the doorway. Her thick lips, which lent an air of stupidity to her face, were half opened, almost as if to smile.

"Has Master Liu gone yet?"

"He's gone."

"Is my father asleep yet?"

"Not yet. Master Liu and the old master talked a long time. First the old master was happy; then he got angry."

Mei cocked her head and hesitated. She thought this very strange and looked at Chuner's fat face with disbelief. She knew this tricky little girl would not stoop to lying, so maybe she was making a wild guess. But Chuner stepped closer and went on in a whisper, "Master Liu said to the old master that if he and the young mistress got married earlier, the old master could move into Master Liu's house. That way, if he got sick again in the middle of the night he wouldn't have to worry. Auntie Zhou told me your wedding will be next month!"

"Damn!"

Mei's color changed slightly, but she quickly recovered her air of indifference and scrutinized Chuner as if to test the reliability of her words. Then Mei laughed bitterly and asked, "And what did my father say?"

"The old master was very happy. Then I don't know what Master Liu said, but the old master started getting angry. The old master cursed the bastard student troublemakers and the *yamen* for not taking any action."

Mei closed her eyes and sneered. With the words "Button your lip" she ordered Chuner out, and holding her head in her hands, she sank into thought. She guessed what "Master Liu" must have said, but could her father really have agreed to carry it out next month? Mei was extremely upset. Although she had already decided on a way to deal with things, she had hoped they would not come to a head so soon.

That night Mei's father slept peacefully, and by the next day he had nearly recovered. While chatting with him, Mei tried to bring up the subject of her anxieties. Her father spoke to her with vehemence. "It was just some sort of bug, but everyone figured I was on my deathbed. Yuchun even wanted to rush the marriage without allowing time for the necessary arrangements. Heh! That youngster is really shrewd. I intend to live a few more years yet. I want to carry out your wedding with the full ceremony. With the students making such a fuss, who knows how much Yuchun will lose? Naturally, I would prefer that you wait until his business picks up before you get married. He sure knows how to talk. He said that I was getting old, that I was always sick, and that if you two got married soon, he'd have me live with you so he could look after me day and night. Ha! I, Dr. Mei, am not the type who follows his daughter to her husband's house just for a free meal ticket!"

Mei smiled. She knew her father intended to use all of this to get something out of the Lius. The severe criticism of "commercialized marriages" in her magazines immediately sprang to mind. But as long as her father's ideas helped further her own "delaying tactics" she was happy. She expressed the desire to "wait at least until I've graduated from high school," then quickly found a pretext to leave her father's presence.

"Worry about tomorrow when it comes. For the present, just walk the path that lies before you," Mei thought as she sat in her own room. She smiled as she picked up a copy of *Weekly Review*** that Xu Qijun had left and began reading it enthusiastically.

Before she had finished a page, she heard the sound of voices coming from the living room. She threw down the magazine and ran out. In the anteroom off her father's bedroom she saw a handsome young man in a military uniform. It was Wei Yu. He had come to inquire about Dr. Mei's illness and say good-bye.

"I've already seen Uncle. Tomorrow I'm leaving for Lüzhou." Wei Yu spoke these words rapidly, then looked intently at Mei. His eyes appeared moist.

Mei forced a smile and, acting the hostess, invited him to come sit in the library. This tiny side room had once served as Dr. Mei's

*Founded in Shanghai in 1919, this Guomindang, or Nationalist Party, organ was one of the most important new journals to appear during the May Fourth period.

examining room. Then it had been used as the classroom for the children in the family. Recently, it had been abandoned altogether, and although it was still kept spotlessly clean, it already showed signs of disuse. Mei had hurriedly thought of this place so they would not be disturbed.

It took ten minutes for Mei to find out that Wei Yu's unit was starting out for Lüzhou and could end up going into battle. She also discovered that Wei Yu had been promoted to lieutenant. She stared at him. He spoke with exasperating slowness. A million questions lodged in Mei's throat, waiting for a pause to burst out.

"It's because we heard there would be fighting that a lot of the men who managed the division's paperwork resigned. So they promoted me a grade. Of course, I don't know how to fight, but when you think about it, it's not so terrible. If I'm killed, that's okay. If I'm lucky enough not to be killed, I'm hoping the experience will improve my health. I think this should stir up my spirit. You see, Meimei, I'm wearing a uniform now. If I can't be a healthy person, I might as well die. This is my last act of courage, my last hope. But there's an eighty or ninety percent chance I'll die. If we lose the battle, I won't be able to escape, someone like me . . . "

Wei Yu stopped abruptly. Although he felt the iron hand of fate tightly gripping him, the new books and magazines he had been reading of late kept him from letting the final words of self-denigration escape his lips. He cast his eyes downward, then glanced once more around the room. It was still the same old library. Events of ten years ago rushed into his mind. Back then his parents were still alive. Back then he had studied in this very room, sharing the same desk with Mei. Back then they had often pretended that they were bride and groom kneeling before the altar on their wedding day. It was also back then that their two hearts had become inextricably intertwined, inseparable for eternity. Now, now the two hearts were still the same, but everything around them had changed. He had to acknowledge the power of reality. He had to sever the feelings of love he had harbored for ten years. He could not hold back his tears.

Mei did not share his feelings of sorrow. She had been waiting patiently for Wei Yu to continue speaking. When it seemed likely that there would be no more, her questions began pouring out. "When will you be back? Do clerks also have to go to the front? It will take about ten days to get to Lüzhou, won't it? When you're traveling by land, they'll have to give you a sedan chair, won't they?"

This string of questions interrupted Wei Yu's train of thought. He smiled at Mei and replied as slowly as before, "There's no telling with the army. Maybe once we get there we won't fight. Right now no one knows. Even if we do fight, of course they won't send me to the front. But if we lose I'll need two strong legs to escape. I'd rather get shot at! When will we be back? That's even harder to say."

For a moment it was silent. They exchanged glances. Then Wei Yu laughed bitterly and added, "This could be our last good-bye. I pray, Meimei, that you will have a peaceful and happy future."

Mei smiled knowingly and said with gravity, "I hope when you get to Lüzhou there is a battle. I hope you win. I know you are going to win. I have faith that this will be the beginning of your career. When that happens, when that happens, everything will be different. I'm waiting for that moment."

Smiling again, Mei stood up energetically, like a brave woman seeing her sweetheart off to war. Suddenly she remembered something. Staring strangely at him she whispered, "You probably won't get back this year. What about that matter of yours?"

As he replied, Wei Yu stood up and straightened his uniform. "If we don't return there is nothing they can do about it. They can't send her to Lüzhou, can they? Anyway, who says we'll stay in Lüzhou. When you're dealing with the army, who knows what will happen?"

A sudden gust of wind blew open the glass doors. Outside was a small courtyard with several stalks of bamboo and a flower bed covered with dense moss. Beside the flower bed stood a few broken flowerpots filled with scraggly weeds. Mei walked woodenly over to close the doors, then turned and faced Wei Yu. He stood in the doorway, about to leave. She could not help smiling. It was a smile that said, "Our hearts are one," a comforting smile, an approving smile. It was also a smile of hope.

Chapter Three

Summer vacation passed quickly. It was early evening, just after a rain shower, and the air was cool and refreshing. Beads of water dripped from the leaves of the banana trees. Several earthworms emitted their long faint squeaks from beneath the rocks at the foot of the *wutong* tree. Mei bent down and selected from a bamboo chest the textbooks and lecture notes she had not touched for nearly two months. A girl sat in the rattan chair by the window. She wore a white linen dress with green glass buttons, light green stockings, and yellow shoes. Her face was slightly square, with lively eyes and thin brows arched in a manner that was delicately feminine. But there was something masculine about the curve of her jaw, displaying a vigor that demanded both fear and respect. Her soft, short black hair was parted in the middle and arranged neatly on either side, partially covering her ears.

It was Mei's friend Xu Qijun. In her hand was a paper fan, which she waved lazily in front of her and occasionally in the direction of Mei, who was still stooped over the bamboo chest.

"You think I've put on some weight? Well, maybe I have. I'm all right, no problems. Except at times I thought I'd almost die waiting for your books and letters." Mei spoke quickly, as she leafed through a set of mimeographed lecture notes.

"Now that you mention it, I'm really ashamed of myself. I wasted the whole summer and never got through one whole book. My big brother always says it's useless to constantly bury your head in books. You have to know how to use your eyes to observe, how to use your brain to think. So I listened to him and just took it easy.

Just sitting around chatting every day does make the time pass quickly. But if you think about it, real intellectuals don't have to bury their heads in books. They already know how to use their eyes and how to use their brains. I'm not one of them! Mei, am I right?"

"I agree one hundred and twenty percent."

Mei straightened up and sighed. She pushed the bamboo chest up against the wall with her foot, walked over to Xu, leaned on the arm of the rattan chair, and scrutinized Xu's head of short jet-black hair. "Sister Qi, do a lot of girls in Chongqing have short hair?"*

"Not many. My older brother insisted that I cut it, so I cut it. My mother said it was a pity, that when I got to Chengdu people would make fun of me. Really, Chongqing is more liberal than here, more progressive."

Xu Qijun unconsciously stroked her own hair, then looked up at Mei. Gazing at her intently, she smiled as she suddenly remembered something. "When I arrived a while ago I saw a man. Your maid, Chuner, called him 'Master.' Mei, is he your fiancé? Why didn't you ever mention him?"

Mei shook her head, half as if to confess and half as if to deny it.

"That Tolstoyite that you're always talking about, Wei . . . Wei Yu. Is that him?"

"No!"

With this simple denial Mei hastily turned away and looked out the window. The two tiny round buns at the back of her head glistened before Xu Qijun's eyes, emitting a fragrance of rose blossoms.

Mei turned around. There was something slightly uneasy in the sound of her voice. "But Sister Qi, how come you're back? Didn't your brother want you to go to Nanjing to study?"

"He did at first. Then he found out that beginning this term Yizhou will also undergo reform. So he said I might as well not transfer to another school. Really, Mei, the school has changed enormously. Several of the new teachers they've hired are my brother's classmates."

And so the conversation turned to school. Each vied with the other to express her views on the subject, to anticipate the joys of

*Traditionally, Chinese women did not cut their hair. The movement to do so was part of the women's liberation movement that emerged during the larger May Fourth era.

the school days about to begin. Xu's loud, distinct, laughing voice and the clear, soft tones of Mei's words filled the space below the flower-patterned papered ceiling of the small room. Then it was silent again. They both smiled and looked at each other.

"Mei, your cousin, Wei . . . Wei Yu, is he still in Chengdu?"

Xu's tone was filled with curiosity as she returned to the topic they had dropped so inconclusively a while ago. This time Mei did not offer a one-word answer. Largely because the joyous expectations they had just voiced had aroused her enthusiasm, she briefly told her friend the story of Wei Yu's life. Although she had spoken only in general terms, Mei's tone of hidden concern made a profound impression on Xu Qijun.

"Then who was it that Chuner called 'Master'?" Xu candidly pressed further.

"This, Sister Qi, this you will know soon enough. I'm not as fortunate as you. It's difficult for me to talk about my personal life. It's too depressing to think about, so I don't. Worry about tomorrow when it comes. For the present, just walk the path that lies before you." As she spoke a bitter smile crossed her face. She grabbed the paper fan from Xu's hand and began fanning herself vigorously.

"Oh, but you have to have a plan for the future!"

Having quietly expressed her opinion, Xu questioned Mei no more. The purple of twilight had already begun to diffuse through the banana leaves outside the window. The chirping of the crickets gradually became more rapid. The two girls chatted a while longer. Then Xu said good-bye and left.

Mei felt overcome with a sense of loss, but after a short while she recovered. The dreams that had been nourished in her soul a month before when Wei Yu had come to bid her farewell had long since been shattered. There had been no fighting in Lüzhou. Wei Yu had continued to live the monotonous life of a clerk. They had written to each other three or four times, but their letters contained nothing more than idle chatter about their mundane lives and inquiries after each other's well-being. There were no signs of progress toward a common future. So when Xu Qijun said, "You have to have a plan for the future," Mei felt it was totally inapplicable. What sort of "plan for the future" was there? And even if there was one, would it work? From the beginning Mei had felt that dreaming about the future was meaningless. She still believed that for the present you should "just walk the path that lies before you."

School reopened. This was Mei's present. She accepted this present with her entire body and soul. Just as Xu Qijun had predicted, the school had taken on a whole new face. On the first day of school Headmistress Cui, her long braid dangling behind her, addressed the student body with these impassioned words: "In the past, when we overthrew the Qing dynasty, men and women party members worked hand in hand. While male revolutionaries fired their guns and set off their bombs, female revolutionaries smuggled those guns and bombs to them. Now, as we build the Republic of China men and women must again work hand in hand just as we did when we overthrew the Qing. At present there are those who shout, 'Women's liberation.' But I say, 'Women do not need anyone to liberate them. We can strike out a new path for ourselves!' " These words pierced Mei's heart and set it afire. She was exhilarated. Some of the new teachers also spoke. Everything they had to say was fresh, was new, was intoxicating like a fine wine.

On the first day of class Mei was in a serious mood. Her Chinese teacher was new. His lecture was on the colloquial language used in the "new" magazines.* Her history teacher was also new. He mounted the podium without any notes and expounded on "social progress" and the "discovery of man." Mei listened with rapt attention and threw herself into the task of reading about these new subjects.

Within two weeks the school had undergone a complete transformation. A student council had been founded and held frequent meetings. Preparations were underway for a theater group and a mimeographed weekly newspaper. Reading novels no longer constituted a violation of school rules. The Chinese teacher even lectured on novels. A new air of expectation spread over the whole school.

The last innovation to arrive was the "movement for short hair." That came a month later. Talk of haircutting had already been circulating for some time when one day it suddenly became a reality.

*Until the 1910s, most Chinese literature was written in unpunctuated, classical Chinese. One of the major achievements of the May Fourth period was the development of the vernacular literary form, both for use in fiction and in scholarly, journalistic, and official writings.

Several students active in the Student Council were the first to take the plunge, after which they stalked the school lopping off the hair of others. It was in this fashion that Mei lost her own two small buns. Laughing all the time, Xu Qijun evened out Mei's remaining hair and parted it in the middle.

Just as the legends of some primitive tribes hold that a person's good fortune resides in the hair, Mei found that her hair now brought her unanticipated problems. When her father first saw her that night, he simply frowned and accused her of recklessness. After she explained what had happened, his anger ceased. "For daughters to become sons is not really such a bad thing. It's just too bad that in the end they can't take the place of a son," was all he said. But several days later the old doctor's attitude changed, and his conversation began to return again and again to the subject of Mei's short hair. His ceaseless admonitions were peppered with phrases such as "What's all this about equality between the sexes?" and "People will look down on you." Mei could only lower her head and smile. She understood her father's ramblings.

What troubled her more was the young hooligans on the street. Every day on the way to and from school a few impudent youths would follow her. At first they just shouted from a distance, "Look at the student with the short hair!" But later on they began to hurl obscenities at her. There were few girls in the city with short hair because Mei's short-haired classmates all lived in the dormitory and rarely went into town. Therefore, the curious eyes and insolent tongues concentrated on the person of Mei, who had to walk these streets twice each day. Like her own personal bodyguard, Mei was always surrounded by four or five drooling, leering young hooligans. The whole city knew of the dazzling, short-haired "Miss Mei." Each day she attracted a number of men who waited on this or that street corner just to catch a glimpse of her walking by.

Mei's newly found reputation was extremely upsetting to Liu Yuchun and Dr. Mei. One night, after the two of them had discussed the matter, Dr. Mei unexpectedly said to his daughter, "I've decided to schedule your wedding for this winter, after all. It won't be long now, so you needn't go to school anymore."

Mei was flabbergasted. She looked at her father and spoke falteringly, "I won't graduate until next summer. Father, didn't you promise that you'd at least wait until after I graduated?"

"That was before. After all, it doesn't make any difference whether you graduate. Your brother graduated from an American university, which sounds wonderful, but what good has it done the family?"

Dr. Mei launched into yet another tirade against his son. He cursed him as a bankrupt would curse an overnight millionaire who owed him an ancient debt but absolutely refused to pay it back.

"Of course Brother's conduct is improper. But parents send their children to school in the hope that they will prosper, not as a loan to be repaid." Mei could not resist applying some of the new thought that she had been introduced to recently to her own desperate situation.

"Ah, just wait until you have children of your own. Now . . . well, you've been in school for six or seven years. Tomorrow you needn't go to school anymore!"

"Father, I wish you would remember your promise."

"That was then. This is now. Don't be like your brother and make your father angry."

"Father, why won't you keep your word? I'm only asking for one year! Anyway, Father, you said you wanted to wait until Liu's business was improved before my wedding. Why have you changed your mind? The boycott of Japanese goods in Shanghai and Hankou has intensified. The city is in an uproar. Father, why don't you consider this carefully?"

Old Dr. Mei's face showed a slight hesitation. In the end he appeared to give way. "The date for your wedding has not been set yet. I haven't made any preparations. Let's say we drop the subject for the time being. But I won't permit you to go back to school. I don't like what people are saying."

"What are they saying?"

"You mean you don't know? It's all because of that haircut of yours. You practically look like a Buddhist nun!"

Mei could not resist a smile. So that was it! There was now a target for her attack. Very tactfully, she explained that rumors were meaningless and pointed out that all she would have to do was live on campus. That way she would not be traveling back and forth on the streets every day, and these annoying slanders would soon cease. Dr. Mei hesitated for some time, but finally agreed to Mei's request.

When Xu Qijun heard why Mei was suddenly moving to the dormitory, she became extremely agitated and gave Mei two pieces of advice: establish a definite objective and prepare for the future. She vigorously criticized Mei's philosophy of living for the present as virtual resignation. Mei's only reply was a smile. Six months ago, if someone had spoken to her of objectives, she would have had some to talk about, but recently they had begun to seem increasingly futile. She now felt that Wei Yu's "philosophy of nonresistance" was merely a narcotic with which he soothed his coward's soul. Of course, she still respected his sincere nature. It might even be said that she still loved him, but this so-called love had already become no more than an abiding sympathy for the man.

Filled to overflowing with negativism and depression, Wei Yu's recent letters had made Mei unhappy. She was convinced that her first love would fade before it ever had a chance to blossom. At the same time she thought of eventually being married off to Liu Yu-chun and became disgusted. Mei did not feel that she had failed in love but instead felt a sense of having been conquered, of having been taken prisoner. Emotionally she erected a towering barricade of hatred. From the start she could tell that Liu Yuchun would be unable to respect her, unable to love her for herself. This, too, had evoked in her feelings of true friendship with Wei Yu that went beyond the bounds of mere romantic love. In such a complex state of mind, Mei simply could not articulate what her goals were, much less speak of any "preparation for the future." All she could do was deal cautiously with the present.

The lively atmosphere at school also left her no free time for idle fantasies. Time passed quickly. Double Ten, the anniversary of the founding of the Republic of China,* would soon be here. A theatrical performance had been arranged in celebration of the event, but although Ibsen's A Doll's House had been chosen as the play, no one was willing to take on the central female role of Mrs. Linden. Until three days ago each of the girls in the newly formed theater group was still making excuses why someone else and not she should take the part. Mei had not actually joined the theater

*Double Ten refers to the tenth day of the tenth month on the Chinese lunar calendar, the date of the Wuchang uprising, which marked the beginning of the 1911 revolution establishing the Republic of China.

group, but at the time she could not resist commenting, "Lao Zhang, you've always had such a passion for acting. How come you'd rather sacrifice the opportunity to go on stage than play the part of Mrs. Linden? Isn't it just acting? What's the big deal?"

"I'm willing to play any other part. I just won't play Mrs. Linden. She's a woman who loves a man and then abandons him and a widow who remarries," Zhang said angrily, her lips pursed in contempt.

"Then it's her behavior you object to. Well, I disagree. I think Mrs. Linden is the best character in the play. She's a woman who doesn't let herself be controlled by love. In the first case, she drops Krogstad and marries Linden because Linden has money. He can take care of her and her younger sister. She sacrifices herself for the sake of her mother and younger sister. Later, when she marries Krogstad, it is because she wants to save Nora. That's the kind of courageous and decisive woman she is!"

"Since you endorse her behavior, you play her!" Zhang maliciously cornered Mei. The onlookers clapped and shouted their approval. Mei smiled noncommittally but did not reject the idea. It was decided: Mei would play Mrs. Linden. And so they managed to get through the Double Ten performance.

Mei took advantage of this opportunity to make a thorough study of *A Doll's House*. Originally, she had worshipped the character of Nora, but now she felt that Nora's situation was actually very commonplace. When she realized that her husband regarded her as a mere plaything, she decided to leave him. Was this so extraordinary? Mei began to feel that every aspect of Nora's life was no more than a reflection of the attitudes women had held since ancient times. When all her options were cut off, Nora took advantage of her beauty to get what she wanted. She affected an air of gentle sweetness and femininity to borrow money secretly from Dr. Rank, but when her flirtatious games threatened to turn serious, she retreated. To the very core of her being she was conscious of being a woman. Although her actions were taken to help others, she still could not use her sexuality as an item of exchange. Mrs. Linden was completely different. Twice she bartered her sexuality to help others, with no regrets. She was a woman for whom being female was no longer of primary importance.

Ideas of this sort took root in Mei's mind, and as they slowly matured, they came to influence her own life. She gradually began to view her own pending marriage as insignificant. She prepared to devote her life to some great purpose, though the outlines of this so-called purpose remained quite blurred.

Just before the arrival of winter vacation Wei Yu suddenly turned up. His unit had unexpectedly been transferred back to Chengdu and was stationed in the Qingyang temple outside the city. He had already aged considerably, and his expression was even more melancholy than before. He stammered as he told Mei that he could no longer avoid getting married, his voice filled with the fear that she would get angry.

After listening to Wei Yu's explanation, Mei spoke openly, almost laughingly, "Though I don't believe in fate, it certainly seems that destiny has already had its say in this."

"Then, Meimei, what about you?"

"Me? I've also decided to await the command of fate. Please don't worry about me."

With this simple, ambiguous answer, Mei changed the topic of conversation. She asked him about the scenery in Lüzhou and told him about events at school. Her pretense at happiness left Wei Yu with a peculiar feeling. As he looked at the dimples that appeared as Mei smiled, he thought to himself that this was not the same girl she used to be. This new Mei was hard to understand.

Mei's feelings were the exact opposite. She was aware of the conflicts in Wei Yu's timid heart. She now found it rather too easy to laugh at his surfeit of contradictions and kindheartedness. But for some reason she also felt an inexpressible sense of melancholy. After Wei Yu left, she returned to her own room and sadly lay down. She dimly heard the chatter of her classmates outside the window. Although she could not make their words out clearly, they seemed to be talking about the male visitor who had just gone. She also recalled the wistful look on Wei Yu's emaciated face. She visualized him in his wedding clothes and herself being pulled this way and that by so many people, always against her will.

"Hey, what are you doing hiding in your room?"

The sound of Xu Qijun's voice suddenly shattered Mei's solitude. She opened her eyes for a moment and then shut them again. She imagined herself being led from the wedding hall to the bridal chamber. So many noisy, jostling people, some familiar, some unfamiliar, their faces all wearing an expression of pity. Finally, Liu Yuchun, like a wild animal, pinning her beneath him . . . She began to tremble. The images dispersed at once. But there remained the distinct feeling that her body was being crushed under a warm mound of flesh. She opened her eyes with a start and saw that the person grinning before her was, in fact, Xu Qijun.

"You must have been daydreaming," Xu said gaily. But the look in her eyes was quite serious. Seeing that Mei, who was blushing, had looked away without answering, Xu pressed her further, "I assume your guest is gone. What happened? Instead of coming to tell your older sister, you go and hide in your room and drift off into a dream world. You should be punished! Come on, hurry up and tell me everything."

"What happened? It's very simple. Wei Yu has come home to get married. Everything is proceeding as arranged. Everything is as it should be. Everything is fine. Nothing's happened." Mei's tone was unexpectedly calm, almost as though she were talking about someone else's life.

"Well, what do you intend to do?"

"Naturally, I'll go ahead as planned. There's nothing unusual in that either."

"You! Are you saying you plan to marry that Liu fellow?"

Mei responded with a smile.

Xu Qijun straightened up and sat down on the edge of the bed. Gazing at Mei, she sighed. It was a sigh of indignation but also a sigh of regret.

Mei felt compelled to explain further, "I don't think there's any reason not to marry. . . . "

"But there isn't any reason to marry him, either," Xu Qijun cut Mei off angrily. "Anyway, didn't you already say you don't love him?" She stood up, took a few steps, turned and looked, and waited for the rest of her reply.

"Do you think it's an unforgivable sin for a woman to marry a man she doesn't love?" Mei asked. "That once married she can't get divorced? Do you accept the old moral proscription that says, 'A wife must die faithful to one husband'?"

Mei's demeanor was calm. But as she watched Xu shaking her head in disapproval, she became somewhat agitated and quickly added, "Please don't suspect me of lusting after other people's money. I'll tell you the truth, Sister Qi—my father's aim is money. And Liu is using money to tempt him. I can understand my father's motives. But I can't forgive Liu for taking advantage of the power of money. I want him to lose both me and his money. I want to teach him a lesson. You think that by getting married I am walking into a prison, but I'm not afraid. I want to walk into the prison, look around, and then fight my way out."

"Ah . . . well, you've thought it all out, but I'm afraid that when the time comes you won't succeed. Not only that, it's too great a sacrifice of your individual free will. I never expected you to change into an old-fashioned filial daughter—a filial daughter who sells her body to save her father!"

"Maybe I'm still not able to break out of the traditional relationship between father and daughter, but I believe that my actions are genuinely in accordance with my free will," Mei said confidently as she jumped up from the bed.

"In any case, I don't approve of sacrificing love, whatever the reason."

"I don't have any love to sacrifice."

On hearing this unexpected response, Xu's eyes opened wide with astonishment. She looked at Mei's tightly pursed lips and gleaming eyes and, after a moment's hesitation, said, "That man . . . who just came . . . I feel sorry for him."

Mei smiled. She walked over to Xu Qijun and grasped her hand. Smiling again, Mei said softly, "Didn't I already tell you? He's come home to get married. He believes in nonresistance. Long ago he decided to submit to fate, and he advised me to do the same."

There was a brief silence. The two girls looked at each other for several minutes. Then Xu spoke solemnly, "Mei, you'd better be careful that your own plan doesn't turn into nonresistance. You shouldn't take this prison too lightly. If this Wei person really loves you and you really love him, you should find a way to pluck out his nonresistance so that the two of you can search for a solution together. You shouldn't just sit by and watch him sink into the suicidal trap of nonresistance."

The earnestness with which these words were spoken moved Mei. She was deep in thought and had not yet responded when a classmate ran in; their conversation could not continue.

The second installment of their argument over this issue began that night after they had gone to bed. Generally, the closer pairs of students slept together in one bed. Mei and Xu were no exception. Under the cover of darkness their discussion became freer and bolder. Gradually, Mei revealed to Xu all the complexities of her past, forcing Xu to concede, "The way you're talking, Wei Yu has turned losing his love into something to be happy about. No, you can't even say it's losing his love. It's stranger than that. Nevertheless, if he saw you actually married to this Liu fellow, wouldn't he be sad?"

Mei laughed but did not answer.

"Someone who is that incorrigibly weak can really be depressing. But it's also that kind of person who often meets a tragic end— for example, by committing suicide. Mei, you must be careful not to unintentionally destroy this person."

Stroking Mei's face, Xu casually pushed her argument to its conclusion. Suddenly she giggled and, pressing her lips to Mei's ear, whispered, "What if the person sleeping next to you wasn't me but that Liu person? What would you do then? How would you avoid becoming a prisoner?"

"What would I do? I'll decide that when the time comes."

"By that time it won't be so easy for you to be in control of the situation. You will have already lost your freedom!"

"At that time I will definitely be in control. I refuse to believe that I can't handle a philistine."

"But a philistine can sometimes be very aggressive."

"There are always ways to make him not dare to be aggressive. Anyway, as long as he's willing to come to terms with me, accede to my conditions, what difference does it make if I have to let him have what he wants? We've already broken through the old moral attitudes about virginity, right?"

Xu sighed and said nothing. She never dreamed that her companion would harbor such notions. She could not concur with these ideas, but neither could she think of an appropriate rebuttal. After a brief pause she changed the subject and said sarcastically, "Your terms, your conditions. Are you going to wait until then to decide on those, too?"

"Maybe. But I can tell you the general principle behind them right now: to make him *my* prisoner." As she spoke, Mei put her arms around Xu, hugged her, then laughed easily.

"Who would have thought that you were the kind of ambitious person who thinks only of the ends and not the means, a real heroine?"

As soon as she spoke these words Xu began to laugh so wildly she could not catch her breath. Mei's hands had begun to assault her most ticklish spot, under her armpits. The sound of laughter and struggling took the place of their muted whispers and spread throughout the small four-bed room. As usual, two of the beds were empty. The girls sharing the other bed, who had themselves been in the midst of chattering, giggled and shouted at them, "Lovers. Be quiet! Or we'll have the headmistress in here!"

Xu parried Mei's attacking fists, rolled over, and tucked her arms tightly against her sides. "Don't bother me anymore," she said, and pretended to snore. After a while she dozed off. But Mei, her mind filled with wild and confused thoughts, was unable to sleep for a long time.

What would Wei Yu's future be like? Would he really meet with a tragic end? Gradually the new issue raised by Xu began to press heavily and persistently on Mei's mind. When she sat quietly alone reading her books she often saw Wei Yu's sunken gray cheeks and gentle, inquiring eyes drifting between the lines.

Mei was alarmed by her sudden nervous state but could not dispel the pressure on her soul. She carefully reviewed Wei Yu's attitude from beginning to end and recalled the minute details of their childhood at the family school. She admitted that a love that penetrated every bone of their bodies had already joined them closely together. But now Wei Yu was acting like a deserter from battle, like a soldier who, desiring to avoid the fight, commits suicide as a form of passive resistance! Of course, Wei Yu's motive for acting this way was Mei's "happiness." But this only made Mei feel more responsible. Enveloped in her despair, she came to hate Wei Yu. Finally, she wrote him a letter indignantly criticizing him for his improper attitude, the way a stern father would reproach a profligate son.

Wei Yu's reply came in the form of a heartbreaking meeting between them. He defended himself in an unsteady voice and wished Mei a happy future. Again and again he said that as long as he was in her heart, he was supremely content. As for committing suicide, he utterly denied any such intention. But he repeatedly brought up the subject of his tuberculosis.

That day after class Mei, breathing heavily, told Xu Qijun, "If what I have been experiencing is the pain of love, then it was not because other people obstructed that love; it was because we had no way of realizing our love. That Wei Yu, I don't know how to get through to him. Sometimes I hate him, but I also pity him, love him, respect him. Maybe the thing that most makes women suffer is men like him! He keeps saying he has tuberculosis. The earlier he dies of it, the better!"

She sighed, lowered her head, and shed two tears. Xu Qijun found it strange, for it was the first time Mei had cried over this affair. But when Mei raised her head she was smiling again. She linked arms with Xu and ran all the way to the athletic field to watch their classmates play ball.

Exams were soon upon them and stretched out over a period of two weeks. After her Chinese exam Mei took advantage of some free time to return home. It was only then that she discovered that on the day of his wedding Wei Yu had coughed up blood and had been confined to bed for three days. According to the maid, Chuner, in his delirium Wei Yu had called out Mei's name.

Mei's heart skipped a beat as she thought of Xu Qijun's prediction. She made up her mind to go visit him, but after careful consideration returned to school and forced herself to get through her exams. She related this news to Xu, but between them they could not decide what to do.

The short winter vacation passed in gloom. That Xu Qijun did not return home somewhat eased Mei's loneliness, but the news about Wei Yu kept her constantly depressed. Following his wedding, Wei Yu's whole personality had changed. When he was not mechanically going about his job, he spent his time sitting or lying down, staring into space. Anyone speaking to him at such times could be sure to receive no answer and might even arouse his temper. Every day he ate less and less. His face grew ashen. His eyes lost their gentle, laughing glow and became as vacant and dispirited as a zombie's. He often stood absentmindedly in the icy wind and freezing rain. When it grew cold he did not put on more clothing, and when it got warmer he did not take any off. He was slowly but steadily killing himself. He would often close his door and write. But when he was through he would laugh bitterly, tear what he had written to shreds, and burn it.

When Mei finally heard about Wei Yu's condition, she became despondent and could no longer concentrate on her school work. She found an opportunity to see Wei Yu and ask him about it face to face, but he denied everything, claiming that what she had heard were the exaggerated ramblings of idle gossips.

After the onset of the spring term, the New Thought Tide began to disrupt the schools even more violently than before, for the first time affecting people's personal lives. Dr. Hu Shi's call for "more study of problems and less talk of isms"* suited the times and soon became very popular. Mei felt that Wei Yu was among those who had been poisoned by an "ism," the poison of nonresistance. But when she tried to treat her own circumstances as a topic of study, she once again became lost in a sea of contradictions. She did not know where to turn and blamed herself for not having sufficient knowledge. Her determination to drink in all the new thought intensified, and she decided never again to allow her practical problems to agitate her mind.

The new books and magazines were now available everywhere. Individualism, humanism, socialism, anarchism, every shade and color of competing ideologies could be found in a single magazine, each praised with equal enthusiasm. Mei accepted them all without the slightest discrimination. Essays that attacked traditional thought elated her. Essays that advocated individual rights stimulated her. Those written like promissory notes of a future society of happiness and prosperity gave her a sense of intoxication. Under the influence of this passionate current of "new thought," Mei's anxieties about Wei Yu decreased, and she forgot her own as-yet-unresolved problems.

*Hu Shi was one of China's leading twentieth-century scholars. After receiving a B.A. at Cornell and a Ph.D. at Columbia, he returned to China to teach philosophy at Beijing University. A disciple of John Dewey, Hu Shi pioneered the use of the vernacular in literature and was a major advocate of liberalism. His article entitled "More Study of Problems, Less Talk of Isms," published in July 1919, marked the beginning of a split between those May Fourth intellectuals who favored a pragmatic approach to China's social problems and those who were developing a commitment to Marxism.

Mei passed several months in the grip of this delusive idealism. But in the end, cruel reality once again knocked at the door of her life. Her father told her that her wedding day had been set for September.

It was finally coming. Mei was not a bit surprised. She had long since thought of a method of handling the situation and really did want to give her father this opportunity to have her fiancé clear his debts. She was also confident that there was a way to subjugate that philistine she was to marry. And yet, and yet, a new consideration had for a time slightly shaken her convictions. On this point Xu Qijun's lively argument had been quite persuasive.

"I have disapproved of your plan from the start. Looking at your actions just as they affect you, you are unnecessarily risking making a complete fool of yourself. And you may bring serious trouble to someone close to you. Have you forgotten your nonresister? Isn't he already distraught, nearly to the point of killing himself? This proves he really cannot forget his feelings for you. So I fear that your marriage will be his death sentence. You admit you love him, but in actual fact it is you who are killing him!" Leaning against a willow tree in a corner of the athletic field, Xu spoke coldly, her eyes focused on Mei's face.

"But he's already slowly committing suicide. He's determined to do so." Mei offered a feeble defense and sighed. Staring fixedly into space, she added with loathing, "I want with all my heart to do something of benefit to others, but the result is always the opposite. Do you mean to say I'm some kind of monster who can only hurt people?"

The realization of her human responsibility shook Mei's soul as if she had been struck by lightning. Suddenly she embraced her friend, pressed her head to Xu's shoulder, and cried. But the toughness of her nature immediately pierced through the sadness. She interrupted Xu's gentle words of comfort, raised her head, and said, "I don't think there's anything that can be done to save that situation. I've decided first to help my father repay his debts."

"Then you're saying you still plan to risk entering that prison?" Xu asked somewhat incredulously.

"Yes. This is my final decision. There are many types of prison. I'm not afraid of a prison of willow branches.* I don't want to talk about such unpleasant things anymore. Sister Qi, tell me about your plans for after graduation."

Regaining her composure, Mei changed the subject of their conversation. Their graduation was imminent. Xu naturally wanted to continue her studies, but she had not yet decided which school to enter.

"Me? I don't have any great plans. My elder brother wants me to go to Beijing. He says Beijing University is going to lift its ban on admitting women students. But my mother thinks that Beijing is too far, and even though my brother is there, he'll be graduating next year. So maybe I'll go to Nanjing. I have some relatives there, but Nanjing has no good schools. Tell me, which place is better?" Xu spoke slowly. She reached out and broke off a willow branch, revealing the extent of her distress.

"Any place is good as long as it isn't Sichuan," Mei promptly replied. A new feeling came over her. She sensed that even someone like Xu Qijun, whose life was so free of troubles, had many unresolved longings, that although numerous promising paths lay before her, she still had to choose the best one. She was determined to arrange her life in the manner most in accord with her ideals. When compared with someone who had only one path to travel, and that path covered with brambles, the difference was vast indeed. These thoughts brought Mei to the verge of tears. Her resolute manner of a moment before withered. She smiled bitterly and added, "I'm just afraid it will never be like this again, when we can be together all the time."

"I'll definitely come home on summer vacations to see you," Xu comforted Mei with genuine sincerity. But in Mei's mind, Xu was already in some school in Beijing or Nanjing. Mei glanced at her companion and smiled.

That night Mei thought about her situation for a long time. She considered how she would play the inevitable game scheduled for this September. She thought about how she would escape, what pretext she would use to escape, and after her escape how she

*This is a pun on the surname of Mei's fiancé, Liu, which means "willow."

would live. The more she thought, the more uncertain she became. She had no means to reach a solution. In the end the magic formula "Worry about the future when it comes" dispelled these idle thoughts. A fearless smile of self-confidence appeared on her lips and she fell asleep.

Chapter Four

Mei had lived these past three days as if in a dream. Until the eve of her wedding she had been very brave, very calm. She had concocted a number of strategies for dealing with her future husband, but when the curtain was raised for the final act, she was as panic-stricken as an actress mounting the stage for the first time. Her well-laid plans, her ideals, in the end all came to naught.

The atmosphere in the wedding hall had been suffocating, had made her feel alone and helpless. But the atmosphere in the bridal chamber made her lose all sense of herself. She became an object, a thing. Her intelligence, her quick wit, her ability to manipulate others, everything that had been so well ordered in her mind became utterly useless at the crucial moment.

At first she had believed that as long as her opponent remained under her control, it would not matter what he did. Because of this, she had prepared several "conditions" for him. But later she had read Yosano Akiko's essay "On Virginity" in *New Youth,* and her beliefs had changed.* Her self-respect as a virgin would not allow her to casually relinquish her chastity to a despicable man. Wei Yu's pitiful condition also gave her new resolve. Two days before her wedding day she had secretly written Wei Yu a letter. In it were written only two lines of poetry: "The silkworm produces its

*Yosano Akiko was a well-known Japanese poet, a portion of whose essay "As a Person and a Woman" appeared in translation in the May 15, 1918, issue of *New Youth.*

49

silk until it dies / The candle sheds its tears until it turns to ash."*
At the time she herself did not really understand her change of
heart. But whether for Wei Yu's sake or for the sake of her own pu-
rity, she was motivated by a powerful desire not to let this philistine take advantage of her.

In the end she failed. Three days after her wedding, a mood of
indescribable depression, inner rage, and remorse and a feeling of
dazed confusion enveloped her, as though she were dreaming.

The autumn wind rattled the window. The sky was overcast. Mei
looked out the window for a moment, then leaned against the
mahogany daybed. The cold, hard wood supporting her limp,
exhausted body was exceptionally uncomfortable. She stood up
again, frowned, and walked aimlessly over to the bed to lie down.
But the warm, thick, embroidered bedding also seemed to have
changed. As it supported her back and buttocks, it only made her
ache. She wanted to sit up again, but her head was suddenly seized
with dizziness, and she slumped back onto the pillow. "Why am I
so weak?" Mei wondered. Such extraordinary fatigue was a new
phenomenon. It added to her depression.

Her life these past three days could be described as a constant
struggle. She was always on the alert. Whenever night drew near,
she became irrationally frightened. Actually it was not fear; it was
disgust. It was the feeling of uneasiness that might attend seeing a
revolting insect. Although Mei was well aware that this nervous
state was ridiculous, she deplored her own weakness. She was
forced to acknowledge that her original ideal had been no more
than a naive fantasy. Although on the first night she had been
forced to submit, she had come up with a rationalization: "All
things considered, Xu Qijun's prediction was correct. But wasn't
this because at the last minute my resolve had weakened, and I
had let myself be trapped? I can't believe I won't eventually be
able to remedy the situation." At that time she had appeared to be
defeated, but her spirit was still quite strong. But after three days,
what had she remedied? All she had was her weakness. Her intellectual and emotional contradictions had been completely exposed. By now even the strength to comfort herself had dissipated.

*These two lines appear in a famous Tang dynasty poem by the poet Li
Shangyin (812?–858). The theme of the poem is thwarted love.

All that was left were fear, depression, inner rage, and remorse combined together in a deep melancholy.

The event that she did not want to remember but could not help but remember once again rushed into her consciousness. It had been a typical wedding, the guests raucously teasing the bride and groom in the bridal chamber. She had taken on the frigid attitude of one who would not allow herself to be violated. She slipped under the covers and turned her body to the wall. The strategy she had worked out was to ignore him no matter what he did. But when his warm, strong body came at her from behind and hugged her, she could not keep her heart from racing. Where he showered her neck with kisses, she began to feel a tingling sensation. At the same time a hand began to stroke her breast. As she felt her nipple being squeezed, she considered struggling. But the lightning fast movements of her opponent left her defenseless. In a sweaty daze her body was kneaded and twisted. She felt faint. Perhaps she could have cried out, but what use would it have been? It would only have made her the butt of people's jokes the next day.

Originally she had thought there would be more talking, more imploring. She never expected him to pounce on her like that. It greatly damaged her self-respect but also forced her to admit that her fantasies had been naive, that failure had been inevitable. From then on her attitude was to let him do what he wanted. She would never again put up a useless struggle. In fact, she could not. Every time he grabbed her breasts she became numb, as if a strong electric current had passed through her entire body.

Mei listlessly got out of bed, walked over to the table in front of the window, and absentmindedly pulled open one of the drawers. It was filled with Liu Yuchun's things. Mei rifled through them until she came upon an envelope hidden beneath several account books. She picked it up and tried to feel what was inside. She was about to toss it aside when she saw reflected in the dressing mirror a movement in the screen hanging over the door to the room, revealing Liu Yuchun's smiling, round face.

Seeing the envelope in Mei's hand, Yuchun's expression changed. He rushed forward and stood opposite her. He stuck out his hand as if to seize the envelope but then drew it back and only said coldly, "Don't go through my things. Those are important invoices!"

A flash of heat poured from Mei's heart and flushed her cheeks. She riveted her eyes on Liu Yuchun's face and replied sharply, "I'm not going through your things! Why get so unpleasant about it!"

She laughed coldly and threw the envelope onto the table but quickly picked it up again. As she tore it open she said even more willfully, "As you say I'm going through your things, I'll go through them a bit."

Liu Yuchun could not restrain himself from grabbing for the envelope again. But Mei agilely evaded him and ran around a small square table in the middle of the room. She fished photographs of two fashionably dressed young women out of the envelope, then kept the square table between her and the pursuing Liu Yuchun, holding the two photographs high and laughing haughtily.

"Don't tear them up!" Liu Yuchun gasped. Seeing that he would probably not be able to snatch them back, he now stood still, separated from her by the square table. He concentrated on Mei's movements, his eyebrows arched in an expression of great dignity.

Mei said nothing. She laid the pictures out in her hand and looked at them once more. Then, with a mean laugh, she threw them in Liu Yuchun's face and added icily, "Who gives a damn! I wouldn't tear them up if you asked me to!"

A triumphant smile spread across Liu Yuchun's tense face. He carefully picked up the two photographs and gazed at them with squinting eyes. Mei walked proudly over to the dressing table, sat down in front of the mirror, and brushed her hair. A contemptuous smirk flickered across her lips. But from deep within her she felt the rising of intense disgust.

"What do you think? Which one of them is prettier?" Liu Yuchun said, turning his drooling face toward Mei. She continued slowly brushing her hair as though she had not heard the question. Liu Yuchun laughed with embarrassment, then came up behind Mei. Staring at her image in the mirror, he insistently and mischievously repeated his question: "Which one is pettier? Tell me!"

Mei suddenly stood up and threw down her brush. She turned toward Liu Yuchun and stared at him angrily. Her face turned white, but her eyes were completely bloodshot. A broad grin on his face, Liu Yuchun took a step toward her, his arms open wide as if to take her in his embrace. Mei instinctively drew back, then suddenly sprang forward in attack. *Ba!* A sharp slap landed on Liu Yuchun's cheek, and a red mark instantly appeared on his greasy fat face.

"Demon! Monster!"

Teeth clenched, Mei cursed and flew past Liu Yuchun. She stopped in the doorway, straightened up, and panted lightly. The disgust swelling in her breast now became a fiery, burning sensation, causing her bosom to tremble involuntarily and making everything before her eyes appear surrounded by a faint haze.

"I meant well. Why are you so angry?" Liu Yuchun turned around and spoke with his eyes opened wide. His thick eyebrows gave him a ferocious appearance, but Mei was not intimidated. On the contrary, her fury was aroused even further, and she replied sharply, "Go ask your dog-meat friends! Don't babble at me anymore. Get it straight! Dog, monster!"

To her surprise, Liu Yuchun laughed coldly. He shook his head in disdain and said with pouted lips, "I've already got it straight. Do you suppose I don't know? I've just kept it to myself."

"What do you know?" Mei interrupted. Her long eyebrows twitched and there was an unconscious quiver in her voice.

"You know what I'm talking about!"

"I don't know. You had better explain yourself."

Liu Yuchun gave another sly laugh. He scrutinized Mei's face. Slowly he stood up, then sat down again, his fingers tapping the two photographs. He spoke evasively: "Why did you cut your hair? Why was your name on someone else's lips? Why, when he was sick, did he keep calling out for you? Heh, you can't hide anything from me! But we're relatives. Your father had recently fallen on hard times, so I didn't pay these things any mind. I thought you were smart and figured I could let you come to your senses on your own. I never suspected that you were such an incorrigible snob, with your nose in the air, so arrogant. You're getting jealous for no reason at all! The photographs are of two local prostitutes. Gambling and visiting prostitutes are my pastimes. Even my mother couldn't do anything about it, so what are you planning to do?"

Mei turned pale. There was a roar in her ears and black stars danced before her eyes. She barely heard the last part of what Liu Yuchun said. It seemed to reach her as though the two of them were separated by a wall. Her bosom heaved violently beneath her silk dress. She closed her eyes and bit her lip forcefully. The pain snapped her out of her daze. She stared resolutely at Liu Yuchun as she spoke. "Okay. Since you've brought it up, let's talk about it. Up until now I've despised you, even hated you. Your damned tricks deceived my father. Now that you've achieved your goal, you think I'll be your possession forever, don't you? No! No! No! You want to talk about Wei Yu. You're right. We do have feelings for each other. But our actions have been honest and proper. He isn't shameless and low-down like you!"

Suddenly she lowered her eyes and stopped. An idea had dawned on her, but she could not immediately find the words to express it. The room instantly grew silent, so silent they could almost hear their own heartbeats. Liu Yuchun stared at her in alarm, beads of sweat forming on his brow. He had not expected this courageous declaration. He hesitated, unsure of how to respond. Mei took a step forward and launched another attack: "If you can prove any improper behavior on my part, feel free to sue for divorce. Otherwise, I want you to apologize to me publicly and acknowledge my freedom, my personal independence."

For a moment he did not reply. Two pairs of hostile eyes stared at each other. Mei's excitement had caused her cheeks to sparkle with a captivating red glow. When this was combined with the beautiful curves of her trembling breasts, Liu Yuchun could not control his emotions. He suddenly came to a decision. With a smile on his face, he said softly, "I never meant to imply that you had done anything improper. Why are you so tense? I'm no bookworm. If a woman does something improper, she can't hide it from me. The way you acted that first night, I knew you were a good girl."

Mei shivered and her face turned a deeper shade of red.

"I don't doubt you in the least. There's no need to get all worked up. We're both at fault for what just happened. Let's forget it. I have some work to take care of at the shop."

Liu Yuchun laughed dryly once again and hurried out without waiting for a reply. Mei stared angrily after him, then slowly walked over to the window and sat down. Cradling her head in her hands, she sank deeply into thought. Intermittent, confused images of her past and present life turned over and over in her throbbing head. She could not concentrate. She had no regrets about the struggle of moments ago, nor did she feel any pain. She had already anticipated the inevitability of conflicts between them, but there was one thing that she had not anticipated: that Liu would be so vicious and calculating. She had previously underestimated this "prison of willow branches." Now she recognized that the willow branch was an unbreakable stem of thorns with which she would have to deal with the utmost care. Her thoughts were in disarray, her face covered with gloom.

Her fat personal maidservant slipped noiselessly into the room. Mei raised her eyes and sensed the awkwardness of the smile on the maid's face. Ah! That fat pig. What has she come in here for? To spy on me? A feeling of restlessness suddenly crept over Mei's whole body. The two photographs of the prostitutes were still lying on the square table. The fat maid walked slowly over as if to clear them away. Instantly Mei's stern voice stopped her: "Auntie Li! Has the young master gone to the shop yet?"

The fat maid seemed startled and drew back her hand, looked at Mei, and replied, "I just saw him leave the house. He was probably going to the shop."

"Go call him back. I forgot to tell him something important. Quickly!"

The maid half smiled, then turned and walked out. Mei stood up, walked over to the table, picked up the two photographs, and hid them on her person. She hesitated a moment, then quietly walked out of the room that she had regarded as her prison for these three days.

Mei deliberately took a circuitous route to her parents' home. It was almost noon and Dr. Mei was there, reading a newspaper. The sudden return of his daughter surprised him somewhat. Mei calmly explained the circumstances of her quarrel with her husband. Pulling out the two photographs and placing them on her father's knee, she added seriously, "Wei Yu is my cousin. Ever since we were small we studied together in this house. Is it so strange that we are rather close? He kept making those ludicrous accusations. He's the one who visits prostitutes! When I saw the photographs I didn't say a word, but he began to attack me in order to defend himself. He even said he hadn't made anything of it because we are relatives and he felt pity for you because you had recently fallen on hard times."

Dr. Mei frowned and said nothing. He looked at the photographs, then back at his daughter. Indignantly, he threw the newspaper to the floor and said unexpectedly, "What a mixed up world! What kind of damned 'tide' is this, stirring up all this trouble?"

Mei looked at the newspaper on the floor. It turned out to be the weekly *Student Tide* to which she had subscribed. Now, at least, what her father was saying made sense to her. She looked at him out of the corner of her eye and could not hold back a smile.

"But what did you come back for?" Dr. Mei added, as if he had just woken up.

"I don't want to go back to the Lius'. I don't want to live with him. I'll take care of you."

Mei's words were spoken with such determination, yet such ease, that Dr. Mei raised his eyebrows in amazement. He laughed dryly and said, "You're joking! Even if Yuchun is a philanderer, how can you spend your life in your parents' home?"

"For now I can take care of you. Later I can go and teach in a school or become a nun."*

Dr. Mei closed his eyes and shook his head in disbelief. He doted on his daughter. Then, too, her statement that Liu Yuchun had had the audacity to express pity over her father's poverty also displeased him. And there was the evidence of the two photographs. He felt he had to deal with this matter fairly. Sighing softly, he said, "I'd really like to start my life over and be a child again. You young people really have it easy. All you know how to do is indulge yourselves. As long as you're here, you might as well stay a few days before going back."

Mei returned to her own room, from which she had been parted these three long days. She felt unusually close to every item in the room. It was like a reunion after a long separation. She leaned against the small square pear-wood table by the window and, one by one, picked up her cherished possessions—the tiny doll, the Negro figurine with the clock in its protruding belly, the two pea-

*The term used here refers to Buddhist nuns. Few options were traditionally opened to the Chinese woman who wished to refuse marriage or leave her husband's home. Only men were entitled to demand a divorce, and paid employment for women, as opposed to part-time handicraft work, was virtually unknown. As a result, a respectable woman in this position would occasionally enter a Buddhist nunnery as an alternative to family life.

cock feathers—looked at them carefully, then put them back where they belonged. She also checked to see that none of her magazines had been gnawed by rats. At last, quite satisfied, she lay down on her own little bed.

In the afternoon, as was to be expected, Liu Yuchun came by. Mei stayed in her room and would not go out to see him. But she put her ear to the door and listened quietly to what he and Dr. Mei were saying. She could catch only a word here and there. She guessed at the rest and felt somewhat ill at ease. At last there was a knock at the door. It was her father.

"Liu Yuchun was so rude. He ridiculed me to my face. Okay, you stay here. Let's see what he can do about it." Dr. Mei spoke angrily. He was wholly on his daughter's side. Mei, who found it all very amusing, became more convinced than ever that her own small room was the most comfortable place in the world.

But that evening, the murky yellow glow of the kerosene lamp made her feel quite alone. The crickets in the small courtyard outside the window chirped mournfully. The cold rays of the crescent moon fell on the gauze covering the windows, reflecting the shadows of the trees like some treacherous figure in the night. Mei opened a copy of *Student Tide* but could not concentrate. Suddenly her thoughts turned to those two photographs. She wondered whether Liu Yuchun was carousing with the two prostitutes right now. Who knows? He might even be telling them about his "new bride." With this thought Mei once again smelled the putrid, suffocating stench in her guts. She felt as if she had been stripped naked before the two prostitutes and was being forced to suffer their ridicule. She threw down the magazine and chastised herself, "He's enjoying himself as usual. Why, why should I have to endure this loneliness!"

The fire of rebellion burned in her heart. She thought again of Yosano Akiko's "On Virginity" and of the romantic adventures of the heroine in one of de Maupassant's short stories. She admitted to herself that if any man had walked in at that moment, she would surely have let him do as he pleased, not for love but for revenge against Liu. She felt feverish all over. She opened the buttons on the front of her blouse and let her breasts be caressed by the rays of the moon. She felt that her breasts had grown larger. They seemed to be squeezed tightly into her cotton undershirt. She suddenly recalled the day before yesterday. A feeling, half numb, half despondent, poured into her mind.

The sound of laughter emanating from the neighboring house was so near it seemed to be coming from just below Mei's window. The loud voice of a young man intoned, "Enjoy life while you can. Don't raise an empty goblet to the moon."* His words were followed by the sounds of a man and woman chatting and laughing together to the accompaniment of the clear tones of the *huqin*.** Its melancholy notes made Mei's heart pound.

The family next door had moved here quite recently from Hubei. The young man appeared to be a teacher in some school. One of the women was his attractive young wife, while the other was a lively girl of seventeen or eighteen. Mei ran into them frequently and would exchange polite words of greeting. There was nothing extraordinary about them, but at this moment Mei felt considerable hostility toward them. They were people rather like herself. What right did they have to be so happy? The man who was the teacher was probably pontificating about "the new thought," "the philosophy of life," and relations between the sexes; he was offering this melancholy glass of wine to the young in return for his daily bread, blithely chanting, "Enjoy life while you can," with no regard for how the young might solve their depressing problems.

In her soul the irate Mei suddenly felt that the "new culturists," like everyone else, were sacrificing people to enrich themselves. People always preyed on each other like this, using every device at their disposal. Intimidation, smiles, even tears. And she, why was she always the victim? Mei could not hold back her tears.

The sound of the *huqin* ceased, but the chatter of voices continued for some time. Then, suddenly, the gentle tone of one of the speakers turned to cries of woe, like the laments sung by a wife weeping to her husband in the traditional opera. In the bracing air of autumn the cries were carried directly to Mei's ears. Her heart skipped a beat. Mei was confused until she heard the sound of a laughing female voice shouting, "Seventh Younger Sister! Shame on you. People will make fun of you."

*These lines are taken from a poem by the Tang dynasty poet Li Bo (701–762).
**The *huqin* is a two-stringed Chinese violin used especially in Beijing opera.

It was the voice of the young wife. Mei recognized it clearly. It was followed by a burst of laughter; the sounds of weeping were no more. The sharp, distinct laughter of the women and the guffaws of the man mingled together for a while. Only then did Mei realize that even the sounds of weeping were all part of a game. For happy people, even sad things can become the ingredients for merrymaking, just as these happy people were taking another's agonies as their own way to "enjoy life while you can." But the virile voice of the young man suddenly interrupted her train of thought: "Smash the hypocritical old Confucian morality! Long live freedom and equality!"

Mei could bear it no longer. Smash! All he did was yell, "Smash"; he wouldn't think of helping people figure out how to smash it! Here she was, suffering from the privations of the old morality, and all she could do was quietly listen to her neighbors having a good time shouting about smashing the very thing that imprisoned her. Mei jumped up and ran to the bed. She pulled the covers tightly over her head and rolled back and forth in agony.

She cursed, she wept, she clenched her teeth until her temples ached. As a result, she came down ill the next day. Dr. Mei took her pulse, then examined her tongue.* His head dropped to one side as he considered her condition. Finally, he asked her gently, "You haven't slept well these past two nights, have you?"

At first Mei stared at her father, not quite comprehending the question. Then her face suddenly turned red and she turned away, shaking her head.

"Come now. What's it all about? You don't have to be afraid to tell your father."

"He—he's all over me all night long. I never really sleep. Yesterday I felt dizzy. When I walked around, when I sat down, whatever I did, it was as though I was in a fog," Mei replied hesitantly, before pulling the covers back over her head.

The illness lingered. Mei lay patiently in bed, often listening to Chuner gossip about the neighbors. Issue after issue of *Student Tide* arrived, but Mei refused to look at them. To her, their ever so satisfying, and ever so pleasantly sounding words were only suitable reading for carefree people of leisure who just wanted to kill

*Taking the pulse and examining the tongue are the basis of traditional Chinese medical diagnosis.

time. Reading them was like drinking a cold bottle of soda on a summer's day. For people with problems, the more they read, the more troubled they became.

Liu Yuchun came by several times, ostensibly to inquire after her health. He brought her many presents and made small talk, but Mei just pulled the covers over her head and ignored him. Wei Yu also came, but he did not go into her room. He only told Chuner to go in and say hello for him. Mei closed her eyes and nodded her head, thinking to herself resentfully, "You poor timid man! You're even more careful now to avoid suspicion. You may not prey on other people, but all you care about is yourself!"

During her solitary illness, Mei's cold and disdainful philosophy of life ripened. It was like a towering ladder, supporting her high in the heavens. From her lofty vantage point she looked down on the world, despising everything, contemptuous of everyone. Gradually she began reading the latest issues of her magazines again. She read them in a mood of scorn and sarcasm. But one day in a very thin magazine she came upon several sections of translation from *Thus Spake Zarathustra*. She completely agreed with it and read it over and over, reciting key passages aloud. It seemed to satisfy her, to comfort her.

It was late October. Mei had already recovered her health. Liu Yuchun stepped up the intensity of his campaign to get Mei to return home. He had not only approached Dr. Mei on the matter but had also pleaded with Mei to her face. On one occasion he even shed tears, saying, "Both my parents died when I was young. I was raised entirely by your father. Your home is my home. I've loved you ever since I was ten years old. I'm a boorish man who hasn't had much education. I'm not able to express myself very well. Since entering the world of business I've become utterly vulgar. I know I'm not worthy of you. But the timber has already been turned into a boat. I am what I am. I just yearn for the day when all of us can live happily together. Let's just say it's my way of repaying you and your father. I don't think I'm stupid. I want to learn from you, so I can make you happy."

Mei was silent for a while, then responded with one languid sentence: "You're wasting your breath."

"I'm not just saying this. I genuinely want to learn. However you want me to change, I'll do it," Liu Yuchun blurted out in his defense. His attitude was one of complete sincerity. Mei quickly looked up and stared sharply at him. After a few minutes she spoke, seriously and with complete frankness: "You've misunderstood me. That isn't the issue. You've hurt me. There's already a gap separating us, a gap as wide as the ocean. There's no way to fill it in. Let's just say I've been sacrificed, that I'm dead. If you have decided to be a virtuous man from now on, I'm happy for the sake of your dear departed mother and father, but it has nothing to do with me. It doesn't change anything."

Liu Yuchun opened his eyes wide as if he had not understood what had just been said. But his alert mind had grasped the general meaning, and he saw clearly that these were not angry words spoken in haste. She would not change her mind. His sharp businessman's eyes had recently come to see that Mei was no ordinary girl. He knew that Mei's every word bore the weight of truth. He absentmindedly got up and took several steps, then turned abruptly and stood facing Mei. His skin was drawn tightly across his face. His eyes flashed red with anger. He spoke quickly and loudly: "You have your reasons. I'm not saying you're wrong. But look, am I to be blamed? At twelve years old I became an apprentice at the Hong Yuan shop. I never had enough to wear or enough to eat. I swept the floors, drew the water, cleaned out the toilets. I was beaten. I was cursed. I experienced every kind of hardship. I was subjected to a trial of fire and bore it with patience.

"And what could I hope for? I thought, 'I'm human, too. I have a nose, eyes, ears, hands, and feet just like everyone else. I'm entitled to some happiness, like other people.' I relied on my own two hands to bear this suffering. I used my own two eyes to see. I wondered if I was doomed to be an apprentice all my life. Whether I'd be poor all my life. At times like these, when I was beaten and cursed by day, at night I would dream of opening my own shop, of marrying a nice girl, of enjoying life like other people.

"I earned my fortune with my own bare hands. The store I've opened is bigger than the Hong Yuan. I did all of this with my own sweat and blood. All I lacked was a nice girl. I have no parents, no brothers, and no sister. Even though I was rich, I was a man completely alone. I longed for a nice girl to share a little happiness with me. From the first time I saw you I knew you were just right for me. Half a lifetime of suffering had not been in vain.

"But now it seems as if it were all a dream. I am also made of flesh and blood. Do you think I don't feel pain? Other people want something and they take it. I'm no different. I'm not greedy or lazy. Have I asked for too much? Sure, I've gone to prostitutes, and I've gambled. But who hasn't? Do I deserve this kind of punishment? Even someone who has committed the greatest crime in the world is still allowed to repent. Is even that to be denied me? You say you've been sullied. Well, what about me? Am I happy? You're an intelligent person. Tell me. Can it all be my fault?"

This last sentence echoed though the room like the sound of ripping silk. Mei could not keep her heart from pounding. Liu Yuchun took a step back and sank heavily into a nearby chair, his flashing eyes still studying Mei's face. Mei returned a stern glance, then gave him a reply that was straightforward but spoken with gentleness: "You have the right to promote your own happiness just like everyone else, just like me. Your present dream has been shattered, but you can dream another. You should know that 'you cannot relive old dreams.' Even if you force them to come true, they won't bring you happiness. "She sighed softly, casually picked up a copy of *Student Tide*, raised it to her face, and said no more.

Dazed, Liu Yuchun nodded as though he had only barely understood the meaning of Mei's words. A bitter smile appeared on his face, and, teeth clenched, he uttered the words, "We are brought together again to repay a debt from a former life,"* before rushing out. In the doorway he turned his head and glanced once more at Mei, his face as pale as a sheet of paper.

"We are brought together again to repay a debt from a former life." His words echoed in Mei's ears and then were gone. She tried reading an article in the journal, but the words jumped mischievously about the page. She felt something in her eyes blurring her vision. Instinctively, she raised her hand to rub them. Unexpectedly, two pearl-shaped tears fell from her fingertips onto the

*This quote from the famous eighteenth-century Chinese novel *The Dream of the Red Chamber* refers to the hero's, Baoyu's, act of benevolence toward the heroine, Lin Daiyu, in a former existence. Baoyu, a heavenly servant, waters Daiyu, a crimson herb. The developing love between them is discovered, and the two are banished to life among the mortals of earth. There they again fall in love, but their dreams are shattered when Baoyu is tricked into marrying another. The parallels to Mei and Wei Yu would be apparent to Chinese readers, especially as Lin Daiyu, like Wei Yu, was dying of tuberculosis.

page and then disappeared. Mei furrowed her brow in surprise, then smiled at her foolishness, threw the journal aside, picked up a piece of note paper, and wrote:

Elder Sister Qi,

It really fills me with anxiety when your letters take so long to arrive. You said that to hate everyone is really the same as not hating anyone, that it is a kind of mental illness. I agree. But there is nothing here that can make a person happy. I want to leave here right away. What about the job I asked you to find for me? I'll even take a job as a fourteen-yuan-a-month elementary school teacher. You said I should bring up the subject of divorce immediately. I've given it a lot of thought and I cannot do it. As soon as I mention divorce, I won't be able to get away. Every day I hope for a letter from you. You are the only one I can rely on. I detest this inconvenient method of communication.

Mei hid the letter and lay on the bed, for a moment letting her confused thoughts envelop her. She was soon overcome by one concern, the question of money. Xu Qijun had said it would cost at least one hundred yuan to travel from Chengdu to Nanjing. This was no paltry sum. Mei had only half that amount, and it had been given to her by her father on the day of her wedding as pocket money for expenses. Fifty yuan would probably take her only as far as Chongqing. Mei jumped up and hurried over to the square table to add a postscript to her letter:

I'm still short part of the travel expenses. Please enclose a letter to your family saying that I would like to borrow fifty yuan from them when I get to Chongqing. I'll use your letter to introduce myself.

Mei put down her pen and sighed. Her situation made her heart ache. It was not the uncertainty of her future that concerned her but the unbearable cruelty of her present. She muttered to herself, "Fifty yuan. My fate hangs on another fifty yuan. Can it really be possible that it hangs on just another fifty yuan?"

Two or three days passed. For Mei, the hours just crept along. Every day at twilight she thought anxiously, "How can there still be no letter? Why hasn't her letter arrived yet?" To while away these gloomy hours, she became friendly with the Hubei people next door. The man, named Huang, was a teacher at the Normal College and a very outspoken person. Often he would shake his head and lament, "Oh land of plenty, heaven on earth, yet so filled with chaos. Anyone who lives here for a year would burst from anger and frustration. Such a great and beautiful land, yet it cannot produce outstanding youths. There are no brave generals willing to storm the enemy's position, only privates who wave the flag and shout."

He was a classmate of Xu Qijun's brother. It was said that he was actually present when the Zhao mansion was burned. His wife did not talk much, but she was lively. The one who interested Mei the most was the younger sister of the family. Although she was only a girl of sixteen or seventeen, her deep, dark eyes disclosed the experience of a person twice her age. Her habit of always wanting to be the first to speak and the mischievous way she behaved were in every sense childlike and naive. But the meaning of what she said was so incisive. She was precocious, a girl who had seen much, heard much, and experienced much. She and Mr. Huang were not brother and sister by birth. Her father was a minor official in Beijing, and her mother had died when she was young.

As Mei got to know them better, she came to envy the happy life of this little family. They also seemed to know a little about Mei's own past and her present situation. That strange little sister frequently baited Mei with short, needle-sharp questions, but Mei always gave an evasive response. On one occasion, when Mr. Huang was once again lamenting the backwardness of this "heaven on earth," Mei said to the little sister, "Yinming, your father is in Beijing. That's the center of the New Culture. Wouldn't it be better to study there. Why come all this way to study at the Girl's Normal School?"

Huang Yinming cast her small eyes upward, pursed her lips slightly, and answered with a question of her own: "Why didn't you go to Beijing to study instead of getting married?"

Mei was silent. The question displeased her, but Huang Yinming continued: "Modern women shouldn't rely on their fathers. And Beijing schools aren't necessarily good. Learning depends entirely on oneself. What does the school matter? Besides, I have Elder Brother to teach me!"

Mei smiled as though she did not want to argue the point. Turning her head, she noticed Mrs. Huang's sad eyes focused on Huang

Yinming's face. They seemed to conceal considerable disapproval. A flash of suspicion leaped across Mei's mind. She remembered Chuner's frequent gossip about the Huang family. It confused her somewhat. But the sound of Mr. Huang's loud voice suddenly burst forth: "A great and beautiful land like this cannot produce any outstanding rebellious youth! It's true. Chengdu is on a plain, and the people of Chengdu are very common and self-indulgent."

Mei's ears burned. She felt that the words of this brother and sister were aimed directly at her. She felt she had been done an injustice, and her heart recalled her feelings of that night when she had heard them laughing with joy.

Xu Qijun's long-awaited letter arrived at last, but it was not her most recent reply. The letter bore the postmark October 30, so, of course, there was no mention of the job Mei so desperately wanted. Mei calculated the days and, realizing that her problem could not be solved for at least a month, relaxed a little. At times she thought about how, in the future, she would escape, how she would make her way to Nanjing, but then she would immediately laugh at herself and think, "Isn't it retrogressive to be so absorbed in fantasizing about a future that may never materialize?"

Liu Yuchun still came by every other day. Sometimes he only chatted for a while with Dr. Mei and left, and sometimes he looked in on Mei. But he no longer raised the subject of Mei's return. Dr. Mei, however, mentioned it to his daughter several times, but Mei never expressed her true feelings. She just skirted the issue by talking about other things. She knew her father was still somewhat angry with Liu Yuchun and so was letting her have her way. She guessed that the old man was probably giving Master Liu a hard time by saying such things as, "I already gave her to you in marriage, and you turned around and messed it up. There's nothing I can do about it!" But one day as Mei was about to go next door to chat with Mrs. Huang, Dr. Mei suddenly stopped her and said, "Yuchun says you seem to have fully recovered, and he wants to take you home to celebrate the first day of winter. How about it?"

"I'm not going."

Dr. Mei frowned, then lowered his voice and said, "All right, you win this round. But in the end you'll have to go back. At the latest you'll be able to put it off only until the end of the year. At first you were sick. Now you're well and you frequently go out. When people see you, they're shocked."

"Then I'll wait until the end of the year to go. Or how would it be if I stayed sick in bed like before?"Mei giggled as she spoke. She understood her father perfectly and knew that playing up to him was the only way to deal with him.

"Ha, you're joking!" Dr. Mei's voice became somewhat sterner, and he furrowed his brow more tightly. Seeing his teasing but miserable daughter standing there before him, he suddenly felt an inner sorrow. He shook his head and said mournfully, "I've spoiled you and now I'm paying the price. But that's all right. Yuchun once asked if he could move in here, but I didn't agree. Now I think it would probably be best to let him come. But you mustn't be so temperamental."

"The room on the east side of the courtyard that we once used as a library is empty, isn't it?" After a moment's hesitation, Mei smiled, made this brief comment, and flitted out of the room. This new turn of events, so sudden, yet to be expected, at first left her quite uneasy. "How can I deal with him? What if he comes after me again?" Such questions pressed on Mei's mind and were difficult to drive away. At the same time her sexual instincts began to stir and reach out into her conscious mind.

But after his arrival, Liu Yuchun was surprisingly well behaved, staying in his own room like a guest and even telling Mei candidly, "Please don't be suspicious. I don't have any ulterior motives. After you left I did visit prostitutes again, but they could not dispel my loneliness. I have no interest in doing anything. I seem to be happy only when I see you, and the only reason I moved here is to see you as often as I can."

Every day at twilight he returned home carrying a large package of fruit or snacks, which he would send to Dr. Mei's room. Another small package he would deliver personally to Mei's room, silently placing it on the table before leaving. Once in a while he would sit and chat briefly with her, but always about unimportant things. He often bought books for Mei, purchasing any book or magazine with "new" in the title, which was why books such as *A New Introduction to Hygiene, New Methods for Playing Baseball*, and even *A New Approach to Sexual Intercourse* were mixed in with the pile of *New Youth* and *New Tide*. This always brought a smile to Mei's lips. Probably because he saw Mei subscribe to *Student Tide*, he suddenly rounded up every book published by Commercial Press and China Publishers that bore the word "tide" in the title, put them all in a straw bag, and, his face dripping with sweat, placed them in from of Mei, saying, "Look. Among all of these there must be one or two you'll like!"

Mei feared this attentiveness on Liu Yuchun's part. She feared it more than the oppressive treatment expressed in his angry outbursts and harsh talk, especially when she sensed that he was at least somewhat sincere and was not trying to trick her. She sank into a state of anxious indecision. Mei felt as though his new attitude was an indestructible web of silk binding her heart, a heart that so wanted to break free and fly away. But she had no way to free herself from this encirclement. She was shackled by the same traditional weakness that had plagued women for thousands of years: she was easily moved by emotion. She was fully aware of this defect but could neither rid herself of it nor control it. What could she do! She wanted to tell him honestly of her plan, but she did not think it was safe. If she divulged her intentions, she would be pronouncing an irrevocable death sentence on herself. Her father would never allow her to leave. She waited even more anxiously for Xu Qijun's letter, but it never came.

These new problems brought her even closer to her neighbor, Mrs. Huang. If she did not come to Mei's house, then Mei went to hers. The two of them met to chat at least once a day. Mrs. Huang had studied at the Girl's Normal School in her own province and was very familiar with the city of Hankou. This was just what Mei was interested in. She inquired in detail about the transportation between Chongqing and Hankou, the schools in Hankou, and what old acquaintances Mrs. Huang had there.

Mrs. Huang, however, wanted to know about Chengdu. Her questions were strange, often going beyond the scope of Mei's knowledge. For example, she asked, "Does Chengdu have any charities set up by foreigners to help women and children? Are there any church convents? Are there any quiet Buddhist nunneries?" Neither of them spoke of personal matters. It was as though something were blocking the way, keeping them from talking freely. But when their small talk about local customs had been exhausted, talk of their personal lives finally came out.

"Mr. Liu may be a businessman himself, but he certainly pays a lot of attention to buying books for you," Mrs. Huang said with envy as she looked at a newly arrived package from Yuchun. Mei smiled but did not reply. Mrs. Huang stared sadly at the package for some time, as if something had touched her heart. Then, with a light sigh, she unexpectedly asked, "Sister Mei, have you ever experienced the feeling that when you look at things from a distance they generally seem okay, or even rather good, but when you get up close they change, they become surprisingly bad? Why is that? Is it because we originally misjudged them, or is it because later the things actually turn bad?"

"I suspect it's a bit of both," Mei replied casually, although her answer frightened her companion. Mrs. Huang's face suddenly turned pale. She lowered her head, her chest heaving almost imperceptibly. Then she raised her head and looked straight at Mei. She spoke excitedly, a hint of despair in her voice: "You think so, too? I've asked so many people and they all say the same thing! Turn bad? There is nothing in this world that isn't constantly, in ways we never expected, turning bad! Is there nothing we can do to prevent it? Man lives in this world, and everywhere there is misfortune. Where is the enjoyment in life? I think that if these misfortunes were my own fault, if I had misjudged people, then at least I could chalk it up to experience. I'd still have the courage to find someone else, retaining the hope that I would not misjudge the second time. But everyone says that things turn bad as inevitably as vegetables will rot during the rainy season. So what can we do?"

As if drunk, Mrs. Huang abandoned her usual taciturn demeanor. The change nearly left Mei dumbfounded. As she listened to Mrs. Huang, Mei conjured up an image of an unhappy married life. She understood what Mrs. Huang meant when she said that things "turned," but Mei could not agree with such an objective philosophy of change. She believed implicitly in the individual's subjective power to transform the environment. But Mrs. Huang's sad remarks pressed on Mei's heart like so many pieces of lead, causing her to grow irritated and impatient. She thought to herself, "She's another Wei Yu. How unfortunate, yet how loathsome!" Mei shook her head placidly, still saying nothing.

Her eyes red, Mrs. Huang sighed and finished her speech. "Right now all I want to do is lead a life of solitude. I'm willing to go anywhere, a Buddhist nunnery, a Christian church, no matter how poor and simple."

Forgetting herself, Mei raged at Mrs. Huang. "How can you say that?" An acrid lump of anger exploded in her belly, shaking her whole body. Her eyes fixed on Mrs. Huang's face like two sharp swords.

"If you were in my place, you'd be thinking the same way!" Mrs. Huang raised her sad face and protested weakly.

"I most certainly would not! Why must you escape to a nunnery? Wouldn't you rather go into the world to seek an independent life? Wouldn't you rather resist by finding yourself a lover?"

Mrs. Huang was silent. After a few moments she lowered her head and said softly, "He won't let me go. He says I'm needlessly suspicious, that I'm overcome by blind jealousy. Ha! You don't know how indescribably complicated our relationship is. In your wildest dreams you could not imagine such a disgraceful affair. You judge me unfairly."

"I don't want to know. In any case, you're useless; you're too weak. It serves you right!" Mei lashed out at her neighbor. In her fevered mind she had already mixed Mrs. Huang's problems together with her own recent miseries. She herself did not know if her present outrage was due to Mrs. Huang or her own situation. Mei resembled a defeated revolutionary who, to keep herself from sinking into pessimism and inactivity, is forced to curse her frowning, weeping fellow sufferers. But in the depths of her heart, she was also bleeding.

Mrs. Huang was not angry. Instead she looked sadly at Mei and slowly replied, "That's easy to say. But it's not that simple. You haven't seen how intimate they are. Right in front of me. Yinming deliberately asks me, 'Sister-in-law, you're not jealous are you? Elder Brother and I are in love!' Ah, how many people have told me I'm being overly suspicious. No one understands me. I've been wronged. Am I being too suspicious? I've seen it with my own eyes. I haven't wronged anybody. If I leave, no one will believe me; not a single person will sympathize with me. On the contrary, they'll all say I lack virtue, that I'm heartless and unfaithful. If you were I, you would definitely say that the only place left to go besides a nunnery is to your grave."

"I most certainly would not!" Mei hissed these words, but this time with more despair than anger. Staring dumbly at Mrs. Huang, she felt as though a boundless veil of darkness and cold had swallowed them both.

For a while all was quiet. Then, suddenly, a burst of laughter emanated from the next room, followed by the lively sound of Huang Yinming's voice. Mrs. Huang shuddered, then slumped up against the table and wept uncontrollably.

That night Mei planned to write a letter to Xu Qijun, but she could not get started. The face and voice of Mrs. Huang kept enveloping her mind like a dense fog. In the past she had thought that Mrs. Huang was happy. Only now did she know this was not so. Was there no such thing as true happiness, especially between husband and wife? If it was man's fate that he pass through filth and suffering right up to the grave, then wasn't struggle useless? Was man suited only to the blind pursuit of sensual pleasure, swallowing his own kind or being swallowed himself? In the end was man worthy of holding onto any lofty goals or ideals? Mei suddenly let out a fierce laugh. She stood up and gently swayed her hips from side to side, thinking excitedly, "Did heaven give me this body just to provide pleasure for others? If so, then I intend to live for my own pleasure. I will not be used!"

This idea wrapped itself around her like a poisonous snake. A feeling of sexual passion drove her forward. She opened the door to her room and stared out into the darkness beyond. A cold wind blew from the courtyard, whistling as it threaded its way through the side door. Softly, Mei stepped out and walked over to the eastern wing of the house. There she stopped, cocked her ear, then pressed her face against the door, peering through the cracks in the boards. The glow of the kerosene lamp revealed the figure of Liu Yuchun, seated at his desk, a pile of account books in front of him. He appeared to be thinking about something, facing the window, as he scratched his head. Then he stood up and began pacing. Just as he reached the door he stopped as if about to open it.

This so startled Mei that she nearly lost her balance, her shoulder accidentally bumping against the door. Suddenly she wondered what she was doing here. Like someone awakened from a dream, she hurried to see that no one was around and was about to run off when the door opened. Liu Yuchun stood stiffly in the doorway, too startled to speak.

They stared at each other for a few seconds. Then Mei turned and ran back to her own room. She wondered, "When did I go out? What was I doing standing outside Liu Yuchun's room?" She slumped down in a chair and buried her face in her hands.

When she looked up, she was surprised to find Liu Yuchun standing before her. An unusual but not unpleasant palpitation of her heart left her speechless. Only one thought turned over and over in her mind. Something is going to happen. Mei felt her hands being grabbed as she heard Liu Yuchun say, "I guess our un-lucky star should have receded by now. A fortune-teller told me, 'On the first day of winter, when the sun rises, happiness will de-scend on the entrance to your house.' The day after tomorrow is the winter solstice, isn't it?"

Mei could not keep from giggling. She suddenly felt sorry for Liu Yuchun and, in such a mood, accepted his embrace.

Five or six days passed. By then, relations between Mei and Liu Yuchun had become quite good. Liu Yuchun had really become much gentler, and Mei let her relationship with her husband con-tinue to develop. Occasionally she even felt that Liu Yuchun was not all that bad. Compared to Mr. Huang next door, he was much more open. Who didn't want a life of happiness and contentment? As long as one did not hurt others, one had the right to seek one's own ultimate good fortune! Mei even went so far as to reason that if Liu Yuchun could agree to her going away and would not keep her from pursuing her dream, she would readily satisfy his imme-diate desires; in fact, she would be positively pleased to do so.

Mei continued to wait every day for a letter from Xu Qijun. And she continued to make her secret preparations. She did not totally reject Liu Yuchun's requests, but she refused to return to the Liu house.

Expectation and contentment, like two large wheels, carried Mei through this monotonous period. Mrs. Huang still came over often to chat. Like a magician, each time she came over she pulled many strange things from her mouth: the secret love affair between sister and brother, Buddhist nunneries, graves. Each time they aroused in Mei feelings of irritation, loathing, sympathy, disdain, and alarm. They always left her with a foul taste in her mouth and beads of cold sticky sweat on her brow. After Mrs. Huang de-parted, Mei always felt as though a bush of thorns had been thrust into her heart. She despised the pitiful Mrs. Huang, but when a day passed without seeing her, Mei felt bored.

From the start, the wildcat Huang Yinming had not made a good impression on Mei, but now she began to interest her. To Mei, Huang Yinming's way of thinking and personality were incomprehensible. If she were to say she was seeking her own happiness, what happiness could she derive from her alleged affair? Perhaps she was too young, too irresponsible, too moved by emotion. But she also seemed so experienced, so able to cope with everything. Perhaps she was muddle-headed, completely unaware of the effects of her actions. But then again, she was full of the New Thought and she knew what love was. Insidiously, these enigmas drew Mei and Huang Yinming closer together. But in the end even more puzzles emerged. For when Huang Yinming spoke of her elder brother, she often seemed somewhat contemptuous of him.

Her conversations with these two women formed a maze of suspicions in Mei's mind, which she abstracted and wrote about in a short essay. Mei sent the piece to *Student Tide*, which was just then engaged in discussing the issue of love. Her essay was published, and the editor even added a note, courageously calling for the overthrow of the old morality and stating that the bitter pain of love described in this essay had also been brought about by the old morality. Mei was not at all pleased with this incongruous note. To her, it seemed that every kind of evil was blamed on the old morality, while at the same time every kind of evil paraded under the banner of overthrowing the old morality. This was the glorious and fashionable New Culture Movement!

Three days after the essay appeared, Huang Yinming came over to Mei's house. An unfriendly expression was on the face of this feral young girl, and a fierce look was in her eyes. "My sister-in-law often comes to complain to you, doesn't she?" Huang Yinming asked frankly and directly.

"She's never talked about anything specific." As Mei offered up a strident denial, she wondered how Yinming had the nerve to bring this up.

"Mei, you needn't deny it. Your essay is proof. But I haven't come to argue with you. I'd like to be your friend. You're not one of those useless young master's wives. And you're not one of those young people whose sole concern is to be popular. That's why I want to be friends with you. I don't want someone I respect and care about to misunderstand me."

Huang Yinming smiled as she spoke, grasping Mei's hand warmly. Her words assaulted Mei's mind, and she felt embarrassed at the deceit contained in her denial of a few moments ago. Her face flushed, but Huang Yinming had already resumed speaking.

"When you said I was incomprehensible, you misjudged me. I'm not a ghoul; I'm an ordinary person. I can think, I can feel, I have a temper, I want happiness like everyone else. What makes me different from other people is that I won't pretend. More than that, I deliberately set out to destroy other people's pretenses.

"It's because of this that I couldn't live in my father's house any longer and came to live here with my cousin. Who could know that this would arouse my sister-in-law's jealousy? Mei, I'm human. I can get angry, very angry. I told myself that as long as she insists on being jealous for no reason, I'll really start up a relationship with her husband and see what she can do about it. So I did. I never took possession of her husband. Her husband is still hers, the same as always. He's not missing an arm or a leg or anything.

"Mei, you can say it wasn't necessary for me to do this. But I haven't hurt my sister-in-law one bit. Sure, I know that if I had pretended from the very start, that if I hadn't been so intimate with my cousin, that incident would never have occurred and my sister-in-law would not have become jealous. But why should I pretend? I absolutely refuse to pretend!" Looking at Mei with wide-open eyes, Huang Yinming seemed to ask, "You see what I mean, don't you?"

"But at the time you probably never thought that it could have such tragic consequences, did you?" Mei replied quietly after a brief pause.

Seeming not quite to understand, Huang Yinming's frowning eyes quickly scanned Mei's face. She laughed loudly and responded in disbelief, "What tragic consequences?"

"Your sister-in-law said that if she doesn't go to a nunnery, she'll go to her grave!"

"If she doesn't go to a nunnery, she'll go to her grave? Ha-ha, ha-ha!" Huang Yinming laughed maliciously.

Frightened by the terrible sound of this outburst, Mei inadvertently shivered. Her previous good feelings toward Huang Yinming dissolved into thin air.

Huang Yinming stopped laughing and spoke sternly: "If she had such a low regard for her right to live, why did she get jealous in the first place? Especially when she had absolutely no reason to?"

"Because she's also human, with feelings and a temper. And because she's a woman, with the weakness passed on by women for thousands of years." Mei's tone was gentle as she delivered this sharp refutation.

"She should overcome such weaknesses," Huang Yinming shouted angrily, as if she were a third party, as if she had nothing to do with the events currently under discussion. Mei smiled and asked casually, "Then you were just joking and didn't really love him? But once your joke became reality, didn't you feel any regrets?"

These remarks caused the feral Huang Yinming to bow her head. With a sigh, she lowered her voice and replied, "Because I'm also made of flesh and blood. I'm also controlled by physical desires. I also have sexual urges. I stumbled into it. But I have no regrets. I never placed much importance in the matter. I just hate myself for being too weak, for being unable to use my will to control my emotions, and for letting a momentary fit of passion overcome my will! Now I think it's time for me to extricate myself, not because I feel any pangs of conscience but because I don't like being involved in such a quagmire.

"But Mei, mark my words, my sister-in-law won't be happy. Her kind of person can't possibly get along with that kind of husband. Maybe you'll soon have a opportunity to see this."

Huang Yinming left as suddenly as she had come. Stunned, Mei leaned against the table, wondering if this had all been a dream. Her ears still echoed with the words "I just hate myself for being too weak, for being unable to use my will to control my emotions, and for letting a momentary fit of passion overcome my will." After a long while Mei lazily stood up. A resigned grimace appeared on her lips as she tore up the issue of *Student Tide* in which her article had been published.

A feeling of uncertainty, restlessness, and dejection welled up in Mei's heart. Her self-confidence and optimism had already faded. She despised all people. She despised herself. She sensed that ultimately men were not their own masters, that against their free will they were constantly being compelled to do the most contemptible things. Was this what was meant by fate? Mei did not believe in fate, but she had to admit that there was a force, an invisible thread, making them act contrary to their desires.

All people had two natures, two contradictory natures. Since her marriage, Mei had frequently sensed this contradiction in human nature. But it was only after hearing Huang Yinming that she understood the essence of that contradiction. "A momentary fit of passion overcame my will!" That was it precisely. Twice already she had sunk in the mire of passion. Now she was sinking deeper still, and somehow she had lost the courage to pull herself out. Mei felt that the people of this world could be divided into two types: one was animal in nature, fierce, and cruel; the other was human in nature but was weak. She herself belonged to the latter category, and in her depression she began to think, "In the long run, weak people cannot overcome their environment, even if that environment is composed simply of willow branches."

Mei's formulation of this theory was soon followed by a letter from Xu Qijun reporting the hopelessness of finding Mei a job. Together the two events pressed heavily on Mei's soul. The most important section of the letter read:

There is no hope of fulfilling your request to find you a job. Even for a fourteen-yuan-a-month elementary school teaching position there are more applicants than openings. When we were at Yizhou we thought the world was so vast. It is only now, since I have been running around several days for you, that I realize how unbearably constricted it really is. Even to get your foot in the door is not easy. Mei, for the time being you had better put your philosophy of "living for the present" into action! Next summer vacation I will definitely come back to Sichuan. Then we can talk about this in more detail.

Reading and rereading these words, Mei felt as though her heart had been doused with ice water. Yet in the midst of this frigid despair, she also became more clearheaded. For the first time she recognized the true nature of the world outside. At the same time she realized that she was not only weak but too naive, overestimating her own power and underestimating the power of her environment to obstruct her.

Everything she had seen, heard, or experienced during the last three months welled up in Mei's mind. She compared herself to the others in her life. They were all lined up in her imagination: Mrs. Huang, Huang Yinming, Liu Yuchun, and herself. She could hear Liu Yuchun angrily detailing how he had struggled to overcome life's difficulties. She could also hear Mrs. Huang's words: "Turn bad! There is nothing in this world that isn't constantly turning bad. . . . I haven't the courage to try again. . . . The only place left for me to go besides a nunnery is my grave." All of them lived in pursuit of something, but none of them seemed to obtain even a part of what they were after. She envisioned herself alone, suspended in the air, cut off from everything. In the end it was Huang Yinming's malicious laugh and angry cries that blotted out all else: Mei had to overcome this weakness!

Raising her head abruptly, Mei noticed the setting sun outside her window and thought to herself, "Huang Yinming knows her own weaknesses. Liu Yuchun struggles patiently. Why can't I? No doubt things will take a turn for the worse. What's there to be afraid of? I should have the courage to try a second time, and a third time, an infinite number of times!"

Nevertheless, for the moment Mei had no choice but to follow Xu Qijun's advice and "live for the present." Liu Yuchun wasn't treating her all that badly. They were still getting along pretty well. This was Mei's "present."

The earth had put on its winter garb. Most of the trees had lost their leaves, and most of the birds had already escaped to some unknown destination. The whole world had entered a period of hibernation. Mei's emotions had done the same. She passed her days tranquilly, one by one, feeling free of the need to rush after something better. Thus, when the first snowflakes floated down and Liu Yuchun once again proposed that they return home, she agreed, although it made her slightly uneasy. Two weeks before the Chinese New Year she returned to the Liu household and the bridal chamber she had once lived in for all of three days.

Nothing had changed since her departure, except that strange looking, fat-faced old maid was no longer there. A simple, honest country girl had taken her place. Liu Yuchun was swamped with year-end shop business and often did not return home in the evening. As a result, the place didn't seem to Mei to be much worse than her father's. She didn't know when it had begun, but she had come to feel that if she and Liu Yuchun were together only occasionally, he could even be pleasant to be around. It was the idea of being together every day that was loathsome. Mei hoped that the end of the year would stretch on forever.

The ones who were upset by the move were Mrs. Huang and Huang Yinming, who could no longer see Mei very often. Mei didn't much like either of them, but now, separated by such a distance, she began to feel a sense of loss. She was so anxious about the activities of the sisters-in-law that she went to her father's house nearly every other day so as to call on the two women.

The new year arrived. Mei, who, according to local custom was still considered a new bride, was extremely busy. It was just at that time that she discovered that Huang Yinming was returning at once to Hankou. When Mei rushed over to see her one last time, Huang Yinming told her, "Everything nearly blew up the day before yesterday. Sister-in-law tried to kill herself!" Mei turned pale. Before her eyes floated the image of Mrs. Huang's ashen face.

"So tomorrow or the day after I have to return to Hankou with Sister-in-law. Elder Brother still refuses to give his permission!"

With these words, Huang Yinming left, giving Mei no opportunity to acquire more details. The next day Mei went looking for the two women but missed them. Later she heard they had already departed.

The incident helped Mei pass a good many idle hours. She tried to figure out how this surprising occurrence had come about. She wondered why Mr. Huang had been unwilling to let his wife return to Hankou. She concluded that Mrs. Huang must have met with misfortune on the road. And so she went on speculating, with neither indignation nor sympathy, as though her feelings were already numb. But once her meditations had run their course, once she had turned the incident over in her mind a few million times and had begun to tire of it, Mei's life became more unbearably dull and isolated than before.

Xu Qijun's letters were Mei's only comfort. But they were too infrequent, too slow in coming, and too short. Reading could not dispel her boredom. She did not find academic articles interesting, and stirring essays always reminded her of Mr. Huang and the way he had shouted, "Smash the old morality." She even considered seeking some pleasure from Liu Yuchun. She longed to hear him speak with indignation, as he had after their last fight when he told her he was not at fault. But he did not. Recently his attitude had been one of submissiveness and caution, lest something he said once again be misinterpreted and lead to trouble. He went to great efforts to buy Mei gifts and books, as though this were the only way he could repay the sexual pleasure she gave him. Yet when, on the days after their revelries, Mei saw Liu Yuchun bringing her gifts, her heart overflowed with a perverse sense of shame and disgust.

She saw something of a change in Liu Yuchun. He himself had said he had improved, but even the new Liu Yuchun was revolting to her. Previously he had viewed Mei as his exclusive property. Now, however, he felt he had to win her heart with money. Previously he had thought like a feudal landlord. Now he had simply become a capitalist businessman. Thus, as much as Liu Yuchun tried to win Mei's affections, her feelings of loneliness and desolation intensified daily.

So as to have someone to communicate with, Mei had begun corresponding with Wei Yu again. When she had seen him once over New Year's, he was as gentle and melancholy as before. He said he was now reading Buddhist sutras and happily recited a passage from the "Sutra of a Hundred Parables." Mei had absolutely no interest in Buddhist sutras, but the look in Wei Yu's eyes revealed an exceptional sense of contentment and satisfaction.

Mei was seized then with thoughts such as "Ah, you weakling. You sure know how to delude yourself. You sure are adept at seeking your own happiness!" Although she would not acknowledge it, writing to Wei Yu had become for Mei an exercise in how to numb her mind, how to divert herself so as to pass the time. But when she received his replies, she was disappointed. Wei Yu's letters were filled with sadness and sentimentality, only increasing Mei's own sense of desolation. She angrily tore the letters to shreds, thinking to herself, "Well, it looks like I'm going to die of loneliness! Even Wei Yu can't understand how I feel."

Mei had no clear idea what it was that she actually wanted. Like a peevish child awakened too early from her nap, she was dissatisfied with everything; the whole world provoked her enmity.

Gradually spring returned and with it the passions of youth. Mei was like a discarded soul; her days were filled with disappointment and boredom. Of course, the spirit of spring moved her. She needed some activity, some outlet, but she had no object toward which to direct her energies. Because business was slow, Liu Yu-chun was frequently at home. He, too, noticed her depression and tried to think of a way to make her happy, but to no avail. On the contrary, Mei was annoyed at this disturbance of her solitary despair, particularly as he now slept at home every night. His powerful passion, his insatiable demands, really frightened Mei. Each time they made love, her feelings of passivity, of being a mere sexual object, grew stronger. Each time he held her these feelings swept away all her sensual enjoyment. In fact, whereas before, when her breasts were stroked she had felt a pleasant tingling sensation like an electric current passing through her, now it only made her skin crawl. Having endured this for about ten days, Mei finally had to sternly refuse his advances: "No more! I can't stand it. You've got to let me get some rest!"

The next day nothing happened. But on the third day his demands became even more violent. Mei was in the mood to go along with them, but the outcome was as bad as before. There was little else she could do but seek refuge in her father's house. Liu Yuchun followed her there, apologized, and swore he would not force her in the future. Finally, he begged Mei to come home.

From then on, Liu Yuchun often spent the night at his shop. Mei felt somewhat less disturbed, but snippets of disagreeable news continued to reach her ears. Even Dr. Mei alluded to them once or twice, apparently blaming his son-in-law's renewed visits to prostitutes on his daughter's inattentiveness toward her husband. Mei merely bit her lip and smiled. She felt it was just as well like this, each going his or her own way. When she left she would have even less to worry about. She counted the days. There was still a month and a half until the summer vacation. If all went well, then, in two months Xu Qijun would arrive. But when Mei thought about it, two months was a long time off.

Every two or three days, Liu Yuchun came home to sleep. There was always a scene between them. Imploring, coaxing, cursing, and once again imploring, Liu Yuchun seemed to go crazy. The whole time Mei maintained an icy silence, although in the end she gave in. She was like a child teasing a cat with a ball of wool. She would not give in to him until she had seen him leap and pounce to her satisfaction. That way she could have the pleasure of believing she had the upper hand. But when he held her tender body in his strong arms, she suddenly realized she could not escape having the filth of other people's bodies transplanted on her own. She could not keep from trembling, an inexhaustible hatred rising within her.

Such experiences repeated themselves with great regularity, renewing her depression and giving her a feeling of suffocation. In a letter to Xu Qijun she wrote, "I do not know how to describe the last six months of my life. My mood has changed an infinite number of times. I might as well admit it. My 'presentism' has been broken down. Now even this road is blocked! Sister Qi, hurry, hurry, hurry back!" Nevertheless, on the surface she continued to appear relaxed and unperturbed. In fact, even in her letters to Wei Yu she never revealed her distress. She felt it would be best not to air her grievances to this fragile being. But Wei Yu seemed to know everything. On the day of the Dragon Boat Festival* he came to Dr. Mei's home to pay his respects and took the opportunity to speak to Mei: "I'm sorry I didn't listen to you. I never expected that you couldn't be happy. . . ."

Mei glanced at him and smiled.

"I also never expected that I'd still be alive," Wei Yu added, choking back his sobs.

"There are too many unexpected things in this life. That's why I used to warn you not to think too far ahead. In any case, right now I'm doing fine, except that I've developed a bad habit of forgetting. I forget today what happened yesterday. Tomorrow I'll probably forget what happened today, much less what happened last year or the year before. So I say I'm doing fine. When you think about it, a bad memory isn't so bad. Ha-ha!"

Mei laughed dryly, turned around, and walked away, furtively glancing back once more at Wei Yu. He nodded his head dumbly as though pondering the full meaning of her words. He then rushed forward and grabbed Mei's sleeve. His voice shaking, he struggled to speak: "You're lying. You're just saying this to trick me, to console me. It makes me even more miserable! You can't forget. I can't forget either. If you were happy, I know I could forget everything. Right now, the opposite is true. As long as I live I cannot rest easy. As long as I live I cannot forget. As long as I live I cannot forgive myself for not listening to you."

*One of the four major holidays of the Chinese year, the Dragon Boat Festival falls on the fifth day of the fifth lunar month.

Mei turned her head and stared straight at Wei Yu. After a few seconds she sighed and said softly, "You still have a chance to listen to me. Hurry up and forget everything."

A flush of excitement appeared on Wei Yu's ashen cheeks. He replied with determination, "Never! Not while you're still suffering."

Mei laughed unexpectedly. A feeling of exhilaration like the sensation from eating hot peppers came over her. After several months of being immersed in a stifling atmosphere, for the first time she felt a breath of fresh air. This was precisely what she craved: to cry out in angry rejection of everything! Happily, as though hinting at something, she said, "No! You still have to listen to me. You can't? I'll teach you how. I'll teach you to forget everything. Why do you come to see me so infrequently?"

"Then I definitely won't go to Chongqing," Wei Yu blurted out, almost as though he were talking to himself. But when he saw Mei's startled expression, he went on to explain, "At first it wasn't certain. I'd heard reports that the unit headquarters was being moved to Chongqing. Now that we're really moving there, I won't go. I'll resign."

Chongqing! Could it really be Chongqing? A new plan floated into Mei's mind. She looked at Wei Yu sternly as she spoke, almost as though issuing him an order. "Go! You must go to Chongqing!"

This time it was Wei Yu who was startled. He stood, mouth agape, not knowing how to reply.

"You must go to Chongqing! Listen to me. You must go! Didn't you just say you regretted not listening to me in the past? Well, listen to me now! In Chongqing we'll be able to see each other again." Mei spoke these last few words softly but with such conviction that Wei Yu's heart pounded. She smiled and glanced captivatingly at Wei Yu, then left.

From that day on a state of nervous excitement swelled in Mei's heart. Up until then, she had seen no sign of hope, nor had she contemplated any concrete future plans. In fact, when she had said to Wei Yu, "In Chongqing we'll be able to see each other again," it had been no more than a flash of poetic inspiration, not the result of careful thought or consideration. She had merely sensed that there should be a change in her life. It did not matter whether it was good or bad as long as it helped her break out of her present depressing circumstances. This vague feeling turned into a sense of excitement. Like someone half drunk, a rosy cloud was suspended before her eyes. The ups and downs of her present existence became irrelevant. As though waiting for some development that had to emerge, she simply longed for the days to pass a bit more quickly.

Mei had urged Wei Yu, once he arrived in Chongqing, to write to her describing in detail the route between Chengdu and Chongqing. This letter finally arrived, but three days later another letter came, and, unfortunately, it was seen by Liu Yuchun. This letter, which was only half a page long, merely related the hardships of the trip and how Wei Yu had suddenly become ill and was feeling totally alone. Liu Yuchun hesitated for a moment, then looked at Mei and said, "Cousin Wei's health is terrible. Since I'm sending a man to Chongqing to buy some goods, I'll tell him to stop by unit headquarters and give Wei Yu our regards. Wouldn't you like to buy something to send to Cousin Wei?"

Mei knew that there was more to these harmless sounding words than met the eye, that some ulterior motive lay behind these words, and she became restless and impatient. Instead of replying, she hurriedly wrote a few lines and handed them to Yuchun. "Have him take this reply with him. Whether you want to buy anything is up to you."

That afternoon Mei went to visit her father. Afterward she stood absentmindedly in her own small room for a few minutes, laughed grimly, and returned to the Liu home.

Although the weather had suddenly become swelteringly hot, Mei frequently found herself shivering with cold. She felt surrounded by spies, and that Liu Yuchun came home more frequently seemed to confirm her suspicions. June was nearly over, and there wasn't even a hint of a change or of the great explosion Mei had expected. Wei Yu had written again. He was still sick, but he seemed troubled more by an abnormal frame of mind than by illness. His letter was full of resentment and a censorious attitude toward Mei he had never before expressed. His concluding words were, "In the past I wanted to die. Now I want to live! I want to live! Every day only one sentence goes round and round in my mind. In Chongqing, we will be able to see each other again! But the days pass and still you don't come! You tricked me! If only I could see you once more, I would be content to die. You're not coming, are you? Then I'll return to Chengdu to see you!"

Mei tore up the letter and bit her lip in outrage. She threw herself down onto the bed and asked herself over and over, "Did I trick him? Did I trick him?" Her whole past flashed before her. As she looked back on her life, it all seemed like a poorly executed woodblock print on which everything was off center. Why was it that in the past Wei Yu had been so cowardly, so set on denying his own right to live? And now, why had he suddenly become so assertive? Mei could only conclude that love was the answer.

She recalled that she had promised to meet Wei Yu in Chongqing, but somehow things had just not worked out. Now if he were to come back while he was still sick, there was always the possibility that he might die. One thought, long buried in the dust of Mei's memory, suddenly leaped into her mind. "With all my heart I've wanted to do good for people, but the result has always been bad. Am I the kind of monster who can only hurt people and can do no good for herself?" This notion, this self-conscious sense of responsibility, exerted an irresistible pressure on her, making her sink into an unprecedented state of helpless, mournful tears.

That night when Liu Yuchun returned home, he saw that Mei's eyes were swollen and red and that her face was unusually pale. He stared at her inquisitively, trying to find the words to ask her what was wrong. Mei leaned listlessly against the back of her chair, her chin resting in her left hand, looking exhausted. But just as Liu Yuchun approached and was about to speak, Mei suddenly straightened up as though startled and spat out, "Tomorrow I'm going to Chongqing to call on an old classmate."

Although somewhat taken aback by this outburst, Liu Yuchun had been prepared for something like this for a long time. He glanced at Mei and muttered, "Couldn't you postpone it a few days?"

"No," Mei declared with uncompromising determination.

Liu Yuchun nodded his head without any hesitation, laughed shrewdly, and said, "In that case, why don't I go with you?"

"I'd like nothing better than to have you along," Mei immediately responded with a smile. A thought flashed through her mind: "You're quite the smart and cunning man; let's match wits and see what happens."

As though suspecting nothing, Liu Yuchun didn't even ask who the old classmate was; instead he chatted gleefully about the dangers he himself had encountered while traveling the "Great Eastern Road." His eyes sparkled at Mei as if to say, "This is why I'm worried about letting you go alone." To these words, the meaningful look in his eyes, Mei gave only partial heed. She was too busy thinking about other things. Her heart, so easily moved by generosity, was suddenly filled with contradictions, with the stirrings of good feelings toward Liu Yuchun. She felt that this man, who had climbed above his humble origins, did indeed have some good qualities. His present situation was worthy of some pity. If over the last two years inexplicable events had not, like some mystical wind, blown people's thinking in a new direction, then the two of them might have loved each other. But the dots had all been misaligned, like the mah-jongg tiles of some very clumsy gambler!

During their days on the road, thoughts like these came to Mei ever more frequently. She did not know why. Liu Yuchun handled everything with great skill, and because they had not brought a servant along, he had more opportunities than ever to demonstrate his thoughtfulness. The night they stayed in a hotel in Yongchuan Mei, locked in Liu Yuchun's passionate embrace, almost cried. She cursed herself. She despised herself. She wanted to tell him everything. She wanted to say, "I shouldn't make you suffer like this. I only want to go to Chongqing to take care of Wei Yu for a few days. He's dying. Afterward we can devote ourselves to living a good life together."

But in the end she said nothing. A strange force took control of her tongue. She could console herself only by promising to tell him everything once they reached Chongqing. And for the first time she voluntarily satisfied all of Liu Yuchun's physical desires.

The next afternoon they arrived at the Hutu Pass. The cruel July sun was poised above the horizon, dumping its broiling heat onto the earth. Each rock, each grain of sand, seemed to be panting. The sedan-chair carriers rested in front of a tea booth, wiping handfuls of sweat from their brows. After drinking her tea, Mei leaned back in the sedan chair and closed her eyes. She knew they were only fifteen li* from Chongqing. In an hour they would be there and she would see Wei Yu. After that . . . Her feelings of the previous evening pressed on her heart, disturbing her greatly.

When she opened her eyes she saw a sedan chair stop off to their left. The broad, reddish-brown back of the sedan-chair carrier moved aside, revealing the face of his passenger, so haggard, yet so gentle and feminine. Wei Yu? Startled, Mei leaned over to get a better look. The man also noticed her. Opening wide his weak eyes, he stared vacantly ahead. The corners of his mouth trembled as though he were about to call out. "If it isn't him, who could it be?" Mei wondered. But the sound of Liu Yuchun shouting, "Let's go" had already broken the silence. The figure of a man passed before her as her own body seemed to float high in the chair. She saw the tea booth and the trees quickly recede into the distance as the hot air rushed toward her. For some time Mei was in a daze, which was followed by regret over not having stopped the sedan chair to make certain of the man's identity. But now it was too late.

They arrived in Chongqing just before nightfall. After settling into the hotel, Liu Yuchun ran into some friends, who proceeded to drag him off. Mei was exhausted. She sat down in the room and tried to sort out her suspicions about what had happened. In her confusion she could come to no conclusions. All she could do was imagine that haggard, gentle face, those eyes opened wide, floating before her. Suddenly, a sharp ringing sound roused her from her thoughts. Instinctively she pushed open the door and looked outside. When she saw the telephone on the wall in the corner, she relaxed and smiled.

After finally getting through to unit headquarters, she asked for Wei Yu. At first she was told that there was no such person there; then she was told he wasn't to be found. Just as she was about to inquire further, she heard a click. They had hung up.

Disappointed, Mei returned to her room and lay down on the bed. A combination of depression and fatigue drove her to sleep. Innumerable confused dreams helped her pass the short summer night. In her slumber she felt as though something were pressing

*A li, a traditional Chinese measure, is approximately one-third of a mile.

down on her chest, making it hard for her to breathe. She did not know when Liu Yuchun came home, but she awoke to see him fully dressed, standing before the bed.

"Ten days on the road really tired you out, didn't they? Last night you slept like a corpse. You kept snoring even when I hugged you. Nothing I did woke you." Liu Yuchun smiled as he spoke.

Without responding, Mei turned over and shut her eyes again. After a long pause, Liu Yuchun said quietly to himself, "I had originally planned to see Cousin Wei today. Who would have thought that he would have returned to Chengdu yesterday?"

The words "returned to Chengdu" woke the sleepy Mei like the stab of a sharp needle. She raised her head and asked, "Who?"

"Wei Yu. Yesterday I saw a man at the Hutu Pass who looked exactly like him."

Mei sank back down on her pillow. It was all too clear. At the time Liu Yuchun must have recognized Wei Yu. That was why he shouted for the sedan-chair carriers to leave so quickly! Perhaps he had used some sinister plan to lure Wei Yu into leaving Chongqing in the first place, like sending a telegram under her name. How deceitful! How cunning! And just the night before she had actually considered being totally frank with him! A chill passed over Mei's body. A bitter sense of having been tricked, of having been manipulated, combined with her hatred and fear of Liu Yuchun, pressing on her numb nerves so that she completely forgot about Wei Yu. She felt no anxiety over where Wei Yu was, as if he were already dead, murdered by one of Liu Yuchun's schemes.

Seeing the expression of bitterness on Mei's face, Liu Yuchun changed the subject. "What street does your old classmate live on? Shall we go visit her today?"

"I still want to get a little more sleep," Mei replied, turning toward the wall. For a long while she heard nothing, saw nothing, and thought of nothing. She floated in a strange, giddy state. Later, she raised her head and glanced around the room. All she saw was the mute, silently squatting furniture. At the head of the bed was a note left by Liu Yuchun saying that he would not be back before evening. Mei held the note in her hand as she read it. Suddenly she laughed. She leapt out of bed and got dressed, found Xu Qijun's address in a notebook, and glided out of the room. On her face was a look of complete calm and determination.

Chapter Five

At Mei's insistence, Xu Qijun kept everything a secret, even though she did not approve of Mei's methods. At any rate, she felt that Mei was acting strictly out of emotion without any firm objective. On the first day they had a long argument. Mei adhered stubbornly to her point of view.

"There's no way I can bring up divorce right now. All I have to do is mention the word and they'll be so panic-stricken, they'll rush out and try to find me. Right now the best I can do is run away without giving any reason and leave the rest for later. Please don't worry. Just let me hide out here for a few days. I'll think about how to handle the future when it comes."

Xu Qijun closed her eyes and shook her head. After a long while she asked, "And if you just run away without saying anything, then they won't come looking for you?"

"Of course, they'll still look for me, but they'll look in a different way. They might think I met up with bandits or drowned in the river or . . . "

"Or ran off with another man," Xu Qijun added with a giggle. This brought their argument to an end.

Because she was in hiding and could not go out, Mei helped pass the long summer days with afternoon naps. Xu Qijun's bedroom seemed to her to be a refuge. Xu, however, was suffering from unbearable anxiety. All day long she ran around looking for so-called news, but with no results. All she discovered was that Liu Yuchun was in contact with some petty leaders of the *Hong*

87

*bang** whom he had asked to help him find his wife. On the fourth day she saw an anonymous notice in the *New Sichuan News*. Xu Qijun gleefully awoke the sleeping Mei, handed her the paper, and sat by her side, intently watching her face. The notice read:

Dear Su,**

You have not returned for three days. Am extremely worried. If you are in any difficulty, quickly write Jinjiang Hotel. There is nothing that cannot be worked out.

Signed,
Chun

Mei scanned it quickly, then opened the paper to read the news. Suddenly she flipped back to the notice, laughed faintly, and threw down the paper, closing her eyes.

"Well? Shouldn't you send a letter?" Xu Qijun asked impatiently.

Mei shook her head in reply, then jumped to her feet, ran over to Xu Qijun, throwing arms around her neck as she said with an innocent smile on her face, "You'd think you were Liu Yuchun! Do you feel sorry for him? There's no need to pity him! In the daytime he may publish a notice saying "am extremely worried," but at night he still sleeps with prostitutes, happy as a clam! Why should I send a letter. Of course, I'll write to my father. But that will have to wait until later, until I've found a job. Hurry up and help me find a job. Let Liu do what he wants. You'll see. After he's sick of hanging around Chongqing, he'll head back to Chengdu." With another laugh, Mei suddenly got out of bed and began to swagger proudly about the room, looking very pleased with herself.

Xu Qijun gazed at Mei for a while, then said slowly, "Do what you like, but you must also promise me one thing."

"What's that?"

"Not to take any more afternoon naps."

*A secret society, also known as the Triad Society, the Hong Bang was established in the early Qing dynasty (1644–1911) to overthrow the Manchu rulers and restore the previous Ming dynasty. By the republican period this group, sometimes called the Red Gang in English, was involved primarily in smuggling and other activities associated with modern gangsterism.

**Mei's given name is Xingsu.

Mei fluttered her fetching eyes naively, then pursed her lips in a smile. She understood what Xu Qijun meant. After a moment's hesitation she answered with another question: "It's been four days already. It's time to wake up. Starting tomorrow we'll get a group together to play mah-jongg, okay?"

Four more days passed, hot and sticky days. Xu Qijun often went to the Jinjiang Hotel, and each time she saw the three big characters "Liu Yu Chun" still written on the guest roster in chalk. This disturbed her. She felt she bore a great responsibility as Mei's protector. Thus, although Mei was able to play mah-jongg and take her daily nap without a thought or a care, she, Xu Qijun, could not feel so free and easy. The family maids were also beginning to whisper. Could they have heard some news from outside? Could they be having suspicions about this young guest? Thinking about it depressed Xu Qijun, but she couldn't bring it up with Mei. She knew this adherent of "presentism" would never waste her time with such "idle speculations."

Xu Qijun's mother and sister-in-law appeared to be bitten by the same bug as the maids and started asking all over again about Mei's background. But what embarrassed Xu Qijun the most was her cousin Ziqiang, a cunning sixteen-year-old middle-school student who said to her with a smile, "That friend of yours, I have a feeling I've seen her some place before. Her name isn't Zhou, is it?"

"Nonsense, and don't ask silly questions." Xu Qijun promptly denied his accusations, but she had already begun to blush.

"Ha! Why not tell me the truth? I can keep a secret. Wouldn't it be better to have one more person to help?"

Xu Qijun stared wide-eyed at Ziqiang for a moment, then smiled faintly before turning around and walking off. But Ziqiang followed her, saying softly, "Why don't you two go to Jiangbei to Zhiben Public School for an outing? It's quiet and safer than here—it'll do you good."

"Thank you for your 'good' intentions. Now please stop meddling in other people's affairs!" Qijun replied casually. Ziqiang followed Xu Qijun with his eyes and winked slyly. Suddenly he laughed loudly, folded his arms in front of his chest, and ran off greatly satisfied.

As suggested, the next day Xu Qijun and Mei went to Jiangbei. Zhiben Public School was already in recess for the summer, but there was a woman teacher named Chen who had remained at the school during the vacation and was an acquaintance of Xu's. As a result, Xu Qijun and Mei were able to stay. Although the area was only separated from Chongqing by a river, it was completely rural. Mei was satisfied with everything, except for a feeling that the woman teacher was a little too sophisticated. Miss Chen was probably older than thirty, and although she claimed to believe in celibacy, she still enjoyed discussing other people's marriages and romances. She seemed to have had a great deal of experience in matters concerning relations between the sexes. On Xu Qijun's orders Mei had little to do with this extremely worldly old maid and used preparation for the coming college entrance examinations as an excuse to remain in her room reading. But Miss Chen never passed up an opportunity to stop by for a chat. One day, seeing that Xu Qijun had gone back to Chongqing, she dropped in.

"Oh, are these the books they're using for the entrance exams these days?" Miss Chen asked with surprise, noting that Mei's desk was covered with novels and magazines.

Mei merely laughed gently.

"I used to enjoy novels, too. But no longer. Miss Zhou, when you get to be my age you won't want to read them either." Stopping abruptly, the old maid glanced at Mei, as if to say, "You don't believe me? Wait and see!" Then she continued, "Many people read novels as a pastime, but not me. I've been looking for a companion in novels. I want to find someone in them who, like me, is also an advocate of the celibate life. Do you think I've found anyone? I have not. That's why I don't read them anymore. Have you read *Dream of the Red Chamber?* I've read it twice."

"What about Miaoyu, the one who became a nun? Didn't she embrace celibacy?" Mei said, feeling a bit embarrassed at not having contributed anything to the conversation. She did not expect Miss Chen to be so shocked. An indistinct red flush spread over the tips of her eyebrows. She turned her head and laughed dryly, then began to argue, "How can you mention her? That's too far-fetched. Celibacy is a noble ideal, not a phony affectation. So many people misunderstand."

Mei nodded her head, pretending to concede. At the same time she was struck by a new thought: apparently people's points of view don't come on them suddenly. Each had its origin in personal experience. No one's life was as simple as it appeared on the surface. Everyone had a secret, and other people were always coming across these secret scars, almost as though they were a delicate provocation.

But Miss Chen was again excitedly expounding her exalted ideals. "There are people who, because they are dissatisfied with marriage, figure that they might as well seize on celibacy as a refuge. There are also people who cannot get married because their expectations are too great or because their own characters are too base, and they seize on celibacy so as to escape ridicule for being old maids. Then there are those for whom celibacy becomes a shield because they cannot stand to have men chase after them. There are even people who hang their celibacy out like a sign waiting for the highest bidder. Lately many of the women here who advocate celibacy have done so for reasons such as these. They all misunderstand the real meaning of celibacy!"

"In that case, Miss Chen, you must have more enlightened reasons for embracing celibacy." Mei was deliberately tactful in her choice of words but could not help glancing sharply at Miss Chen.

"Oh? Well . . . only because it's a lofty ideal." Her response slipped out swiftly and with little thought. It was vague but blocked all further dialogue.

The topic of discussion shifted, and Miss Chen went on to curse her life as a teacher. To Mei she seemed like an experienced merchant relating the hardships of his profession to a future member of the trade as a kind of surreptitious intimidation to guard against business competition. Mei had no choice but to listen patiently, hoping something would happen to cut short this repugnant conversation.

Walking in the fields beyond the campus became Mei's way of escaping the garrulous old maid. Whenever Xu Qijun had to return home, Mei would walk outside with her. Mei could pass the better part of a day sitting with a book under the shelter of the *huangzhuo* tree beside the small stone bridge. She watched the tanned, half-naked country children wearing the huge palm-shaped leaves of the *huangzhuo* tree as hats, in imitation of "long hairs" at war.* They also rolled the leaves into tubes, putting them in their mouths and blowing them like whistles. Sometimes they blew on three of them at once, producing a deep mournful sound like the howling of a wolf. Mei had never known how many uses there were for *huangzhuo* leaves and found it all most interesting. She, too, made a whistle and blew on it gently as she read.

The weather became hotter. Now not even in the early morning or late evening was there a trace of wind. Xu Qijun fell ill from the intense heat and did not come to Zhiben for three or four days in a row. Mei was bored. At the break of day she ran down to the large *huangzhuo* tree on the bank of a small stream to cool herself in the shade. After arranging some leaves into a soft seat, she leaned against the trunk of the tree to watch the fish swimming by. A school of tiny fish near the bank was aligned in such neat rows that they seemed to be participating in a military inspection as they wriggled past. Suddenly a willow fish darted over from the middle of the stream and scattered the file of tiny fish. But in an instant they had lined up again, nearly as orderly as before.

Mei was watching them with delight when suddenly from behind her came a sharp humming sound. It startled her. She turned her head and saw a youth squatting behind her, laughing, a *huangzhuo*-leaf whistle in his mouth. It was Xu Qijun's cousin, Ziqiang.

They did not speak. A current of uneasiness flowed between them. "Qijun can't come today. I've come to take her place." Smiling, Xu Ziqiang introduced himself as Mei stood up.

She replied with a gentle nod of the head.

"That man at the Jinjiang Hotel has left already," Xu Ziqiang added softly. His triangular face revealed a look of extreme contentment. He gazed at Mei with his long narrow eyes set beneath a broad forehead, waiting to see what response his powerful words would elicit. But Mei offered only a bland reply: "Is that all?"

*The term *long hairs* refers to the Taiping rebels whose Taiping Heavenly Kingdom challenged the Qing dynasty from 1851 to 1864. The long hairs were noted for their practice of letting down their hair in defiance of the Manchu Qing order that all Chinese shave the front of their heads and wear their hair in a queue.

Xu Ziqiang's elation instantly vanished. The long speech he had prepared turned out to be useless. He had to devise another plan on the spot. With the back of his hand he wiped the beads of sweat from his brow. Kicking at the grass with his toe, he examined Mei's face out of the corner of his eye.

"Surely Sister Qi had some other message?" Mei asked, adding a warm smile.

This emboldened Xu Ziqiang to speak up. Taking a step closer to Mei, he spoke with wild excitement: "Actually, Sister Qi didn't send me. She wouldn't talk. She didn't tell me anything. I told her I can keep a secret, but she didn't believe me. But I did some checking around on my own, and four or five days ago I figured everything out. Sister Qi went to the Jinjiang Hotel every day, but all she did was take a look in the door. But I would go right in, and I even saw him once. You see, I can keep a secret, can't I? As soon as I found out this morning that he had definitely gone home, I rushed over to tell you. Sister Qi still doesn't know about this development!"

Mei smiled again. She felt very agreeably disposed toward this young man's expressions of loyalty and his self-satisfaction at having succeeded in his mission. She had never before come across a man whom she barely knew who was so concerned about her, who was so ardent toward her, or who would work so hard to please her. Because she couldn't think of a way to thank Xu Ziqiang for his thoughtfulness, all she could do was incline her gentle eyes in the direction of his sweaty face.

"I heard he went home because a relative had just passed away in Chengdu." Xu Ziqiang completed his report. He leaned casually against the tree trunk, like a low official who had just reported to his superior on an accomplished mission and was awaiting his reward.

"What relative? Was his name Wei?" Mei asked urgently, as if she already knew of the event and was now only waiting for confirmation.

"I think he was named Wei.* I didn't think it mattered, so I didn't ask about the particulars. Do you want to know precisely? I can give you the details tomorrow."

*The two surnames, although identical in sound, are represented by different characters in written form.

Mei sighed, lowered her head, and, as though talking to herself, said, "So, he's died at last! Why would he rush back? But Mr.* Xu, please don't make any more inquiries. Ask Qijun to come over when she's well!"

The tone of these last words was stern. Moreover, the brow above her long eyebrows was slightly furrowed, and her lovely mouth had lost its smile. Xu Ziqiang did not understand. He swallowed the words that had been waiting in his throat.

Then, in what seemed like only an instant, he gathered up his courage and said, "Maybe she won't be able to come tomorrow. Is there anything I can do for you? You can still trust me, can't you? There's so much I've wanted to say to you, but Qijun wouldn't let me come to see you. She treats me like a child. But heaven has eyes and has made her sick these past few day. Now if you like, we could sit here and chat. I have so very much I want to say."

Mei did not answer. She was too preoccupied with thoughts of Wei Yu, Liu Yuchun, and her father to digest Xu Ziqiang's words. She glanced at him absentmindedly and sat down on her thick cushion of *huangzhuo* leaves.

Of course, to Xu Ziqiang this was a signal that she wanted to talk. He could not keep his heart from thumping or his face from turning red. From his inexperienced mouth he spat out those clumsy and innocent three little words: "I love you!"

Mei opened her eyes wide in amazement. The young man of medium height standing before her suddenly grew taller, as tall and as broad as the *huangzhuo* tree. His triangular face, flushed with embarrassment, revealed an air of guilelessness and unease. Those abrupt words, "I love you," echoed in Mei's ears, rushed into her heart, and made it beat faster. In that instant, her cynical laughter shattered all illusions.

She gazed into Xu Ziqiang's face and asked in a sincere tone of voice, "When did this start? And why? Have you ever been in love before? Do you know what love is like? I'll bet the only things you know about love you got from novels."

Her string of questions confused Xu Ziqiang. In other areas this sixteen-year-old middle-school student really did have considerable experience, but in matters of relations between the sexes, to

*Here the author uses the transliteration of the English word *Mister* for the first time.

say he was unsophisticated was an understatement. He was totally untested. Even in his dreams he had never imagined how complicated the heart of a woman is.

Mei smiled again. Without thinking, she grasped the hand of the red-faced youth and said frankly, "You've almost made a fool of yourself. But I don't blame you. I know you are sincere. I also love you, but only as a younger brother. You probably haven't given much thought to whether it would be good for you if I loved you, much less what effect it would have on me. You'll run into a lot of girls to fall in love with. When that time comes, you can remember what I said to you today."

Mei stopped suddenly. She saw Xu Ziqiang staring with curiosity and greed at her breasts, which were covered only by a thin gauze. She also felt his fingers scratching lightly and timidly at her wrist. At almost the same moment she heard the sound of approaching footsteps. She instinctively let go of Xu Ziqiang's hand, jumped up, and saw Miss Chen no more than ten steps away. After several seconds of awkward silence, Mei smiled and said, "Xu Qijun still hasn't gotten over her cold!" But before Miss Chen could respond, Mei turned her head and solemnly said to Xu Ziqiang, "If she's still running a fever tomorrow, please come and take me to her."

The three of them left the riverbank. Quite out of character, Miss Chen did not speak and deliberately kept to the rear. Only after Xu Ziqiang had left did the "old maid" rush to Mei's side. Laughing, she slyly accused Xu Ziqiang of being a "freak." Mei only smiled.

In the afternoon it rained. Because Mei could not go out, she took the opportunity to nap in her room. In her dream she was once again under the tree by the riverbank. Xu Ziqiang was squatting opposite her, blowing madly on a whistle of five or six *huang-zhuo* leaves. Its strange *pu...pu* sound made her dizzy. All went blank. Suddenly she felt herself locked in an embrace. She struggled. Water soaked through her clothes. Then she heard a fierce shout, as if Wei Yu were saying, "You said we would meet again in Chongqing, but you tricked me!"

Mei opened her eyes, but still she saw Wei Yu's pallid face covering her own like a large sheet of white paper. A driving rain was falling outside the window, and the water pouring off the eaves made a sound like firecrackers. She lay distracted, her mind unable to focus on any one thought, until her sweat-drenched gauze shirt was once again dry.

As night began to fall, Mei left the school and returned to Xu Qijun's house. While crossing the river, bathed in the crimson glow of sunset, she observed the reddish hue of the river water and thought, "How can I live such a drab life amidst such beauty? Is it fate? Then I will struggle against my fate and go forward!"

Xu Qijun's illness continued to hang on. Mei took on the role of nurse, closeting herself all day in Xu's bedroom. Although she was bored, the days did pass, one after the other. She was not bothered by any worries or anxieties, but neither could she arouse any lively enthusiasm. The heartsick tears of her miserable past had already been baked dry by her fiery wrath. Even if thoughts of the past accidentally caused a wave of old regrets to overflow from deep within her heart, they would immediately be suppressed by her ruthless intellect. She had already used the sharp blade of her will to cut her ties to the past. But what of the future? Her dreams of the future had always been vague. Recently there had been none at all. Thus, she was unable to lull herself into a false sense of happiness. She had only her monotonous, colorless present. She could only let her present become the past and relegate it forever to oblivion.

Xu Ziqiang continued to make occasional passes at her. In the end he poured out quite a bit of the "so very much" he had wanted to say. But to the "present" Mei, this, too, seemed utterly boring. What love? Hadn't she already experienced it? And hadn't she already seen so much with her own eyes? Besides, she had not forgotten the cruel lesson Liu Yuchun had taught her. She was like a person eating fish for the first time who did not savor the true taste of fish but had her appetite spoiled by the foul smell. In her confusion she had come to this realization: the difference between friendship and love was sex, and sex was no more and no less than the one-sided gratification of the lust of Liu Yuchun. This she had been taught all too often. The very thought of it disgusted her.

Nevertheless, deep in her heart, beneath the hard shell of emptiness and boredom, was still concealed a blazing fire from which a pale blue flame from time to time pierced through. At times like these she felt an unbearable anxiety. She worried. She agonized.

And in the end all her anxieties congealed in one specific question: what was life going to be like from this point on? But in a fraction of a second her innate openness, decisiveness, and self-confidence would dispel all these useless, self-inflicted fears.

And so the time passed, until it was the middle of August. Xu Qijun overcame what turned out to be a bout of malaria. Even before her recovery she had written several letters to her brother asking him to help Mei look for a job. Two replies arrived, but neither provided any definite answer. Xu Qijun often agonized over the possibility that she might fail, at the same time feeling angry at Mei's indifference and her refusal to take responsibility for her own future. They disagreed over this frequently. Like a stern father encouraging his indolent son, an enraged Xu Qijun asked, "Don't you care at all? You act as if it has nothing to do with you. What if nothing at all comes of it? What are you going to do then?"

Mei only smiled. She understood her good friend's eagerness. Warmly grasping Xu Qijun's hand, she recited, "There's no point in getting anxious. In life there is no such thing as a dead end. It really is a big wide world out there."

"You still feel that way? At Yizhou you said nothing bad would happen to Wei Yu. You also said you weren't afraid of a mere prison of willow branches. Now what's happened? Everything—your intelligence, your courage, your unscrupulousness—has only served to hurt you. And still you trust in heaven. Still you believe in a world of opportunity. You—you really make me furious!"

Shaking her head angrily, Xu Qijun pressed her point sharply. But an innocent laugh was the only response she received. After several seconds Mei suddenly stopped laughing. Getting to her feet with a solemn look on her face, she clenched her teeth and said, "I trust only in myself."

The last word, "myself," was spoken loudly and with a tone of sadness. Xu Qijun was startled, but Mei suddenly laughed loudly and dashed over to hug her friend. Pressing her lips to Xu's ear she said softly, "What do I intend to do? I intend to find a lover!"

Xu Qijun could not help but laugh as well. It was a laugh of disbelief but one that also seemed to ask the question, "Why do you want to degrade yourself?" At the same time something occurred to her; turning her head, she looked straight into Mei's eyes and asked, "The man you have in mind wouldn't be Xu Ziqiang, would it?"

"What? Absolutely not. Why would I want to ruin that child? Besides, why do I have to have someone in mind beforehand? Can't a person who has sunk to the bottom still have beautiful dreams? But I definitely won't make the same mistake twice."

After a brief silence, Xu Qijun slowly asked, "Why so grumpy? After all, the world is full of opportunities!" In spite of her calm, in her heart Xu Qijun felt twice as nervous as before. She imagined all the worst possible outcomes. She now realized that Mei's superficial coolness was not the product of laziness or of a lack of responsibility but of a determination to "take calculated risks." This discovery made Xu Qijun tremble and raised doubts in her mind about the New Thought, something in which she ordinarily believed. When people were awakened, when they were summoned forth, it was not into the light that they moved but into the darkness. The people of lofty ideals who sounded the battle cry to awaken youth did not prepare a bright and happy world to receive these refugees.

The end of August was soon upon them. An eye-catching missing persons advertisement appeared in the *New Sichuan News* along with a photograph of Mei. When Xu Ziqiang ran in all out of breath and opened the newspaper, the two girls turned pale. The three of them exchanged stares without saying a word.

"If I stay here any longer, you'll become implicated. I'll go back to Chengdu and negotiate with them myself! Otherwise, I'll have to run away, to Hankou, Nanjing, or Shanghai. Things will work out somehow. I can't believe I'll just starve to death!"

Mei spoke calmly, but Xu Qijun and her cousin both shook their heads. Lowering their voices, they began arguing in earnestness. Mei's final proposition was that Xu Qijun raise one hundred yuan for her. Then she would immediately leave Sichuan. Xu Qijun felt it was still too early to take such risks. Besides, one hundred yuan was not that easy to come by. She said that her family would not notice the advertisement and that the situation was not yet desperate. Moreover, if she tried once more, perhaps she could find Mei a teaching position nearby. Then Mei could clear things with Liu Yuchun, using the excuse that she had become bored at home and wanted outside employment. This would work for the time being.

Xu Ziqiang, of course, approved completely when he heard that this plan would enable Mei to remain in Chongqing. Given Xu Qijun's tenacity, Mei said nothing more but just smiled as usual.

Several days flew by. Xu Qijun went to a number of places and spoke to quite a few people, but all to no avail. Nearly giving up hope, she was about to scrape the money together when some unexpected news arrived. A certain Mr. Lu, with whom she had a passing acquaintance, had just been appointed principal of the Lüzhou Normal School and had fired all the old teaching staff. It was possible that there was an opening for a teacher in the elementary school run under his supervision. After some discussion, Mei decided to go to Lüzhou to try her luck. Xu Qijun accompanied her there.

Chapter Six

Xu and Mei arrived in Lüzhou just as the Normal School was preparing for the ceremonies opening the new term. All the necessary teaching staff had already been engaged, but Mei managed to achieve her goal and to involve Xu Qijun as well. This was because Principal Lu, a young adherent of the New Thought, felt compelled to find a way to help a talented person such as Mei. Therefore, he divided the sixty students in the first and third grades at the elementary school each into two classes. After Mei was hired, the school was still short one teacher, so at the last minute he persuaded Xu Qijun to trouble herself on their behalf by staying on for a fortnight or perhaps a month.

On the evening before the start of the term, some three days after Mei and Xu arrived, Principal Lu arranged a tea party to help the new teachers get to know one another. The party was held in the sitting room. The white porcelain shades of the overhead lamps scattered pale yellow rays of light. Because there was a wind, the flames occasionally flickered, changing the room from light to dark and back again. The mottled rays cast romantic shadows on the dark yellow wooden walls.

In this atmosphere of hysterical anticipation a bewildered Mei listened quietly as the ten or so male teachers engaged in polite small talk with their five or six female counterparts. Opposite Mei was a girl of no more than seventeen or eighteen. She was wearing a bright apricot blouse and had a narrow chin and dark eyes. Every now and then she glanced at Mei, her sharp gaze conjuring up the image of Huang Yinming in Mei's mind. The lingering memory of this wildcat of a girl wound round Mei and dragged her away from reality so that she was not paying attention when Principal Lu said, "As for the elementary school, we plan to experiment with the new theories of teaching—starting this term. Fortunately, we have found Miss Mei Xingsu* to take on the responsibility for this new task."

Everyone fell silent. Even the sound of the mosquitoes could be heard. All eyes turned to Mei. Xu Qijun gently nudged her distracted friend with her elbow as a bright clear voice burst out from the group of male teachers: "Would Miss Mei tell us these brilliant new ideas on education?"

The not-too-friendly tone of these words annoyed Mei. She calmly glanced at the crowd and blurted out a response: "Everyone, you mustn't laugh at me. This is my first job as a teacher, so I can't pretend to have any brilliant ideas. . . . "

The girl opposite her suddenly lowered her head to hide an irrepressible smile but not soon enough to hide it from Mei. Her whole body bristled, and she felt alert, as though her nerves were charged with electricity. The words that she had only dimly heard Principal Lu speak a moment ago leaped forth from deep in her subconscious mind and compelled her to suspect that remarks such as "Fortunately, we have found" were meant to be sarcastic. This flash of displeasure struck her dumb, but in an instant she found her voice again, each word louder than the last: "Each of you is an erudite and experienced person, engaged in the glorious task of the educator. For someone like me, without experience and with no learning, to come here as your colleague is truly shameful. I am not worthy of the principal's praise. I imagine that each of you already knows why I came here, why I forced my way into a position in this school.

"But I don't intend to treat this as just a livelihood or to just go through the motions. I believe in two maxims: learning is the accumulation of experience; ability is the patience to endure hard work. I can be patient, but I want to get experience. This is my goal. You are all advocates of the New Thought and want to smash the hypocritical Confucian ethical code, so I naturally assumed that you also disapproved of polite social conventions. Therefore,

*As a demonstration of his progressive leanings, the author has the principal use the English word *Miss*.

when I heard you wanted me to talk about my 'brilliant new ideas,' I must say I was overwhelmed by the irony of it. Tonight is the principal's tea party. Tomorrow school begins and we will all go to assume our individual posts. I hope to get to know each of you.

"I'll start by introducing myself. My name is Mei Xingsu. I graduated from the Yizhou Girl's Middle School in Chengdu. As I did not want to stay at home and live the idle life of a 'young mistress,' I have come to try my hand as an elementary school teacher."

The entire assembly was silent for several seconds. Then someone began clapping. Others followed and amidst their applause was heard the sound of muted laughter. As the applause began to subside, Principal Lu's voice broke through: "I approve of Miss Mei's suggestion. I will also introduce myself. My name is Lu Keli. I'm a graduate of the education department at Nanjing University, and this is my first job as an educator."

The girl in the bright apricot blouse sitting across from Mei suddenly giggled and whispered something to the female teacher seated next to her. She then cast another glance at Mei with those dark eyes. By now others were following the principal's lead, each vying to be next to introduce himself. Mei watched and listened intently. Some only told their names; some told jokes. Soon it was all over but not before Mei discovered that the girl who had so attracted her attention was named Zhang.

At this point people began to pair off and engage in loud conversation. Xu Qijun and a round-faced male teacher discovered that they were distant relatives and began talking enthusiastically. On Mei's other side was another female teacher with a flat face who kept her head lowered as she cracked watermelon seeds. Miss Zhang, in the apricot blouse, occasionally stole a glance at Mei, but whenever Mei returned Zhang's gaze, she turned away. Sitting across from Mei was a male teacher with disheveled hair and a cigarette hanging from his mouth who did not take his eyes off Mei. She recalled that he was a teacher in the Chinese section of the education department, a man named Li who had described himself as a "high-class reptile." But they were too far apart to speak to each other.

The mosquitoes under the table seemed to increase their activity. Other people's fans were engaged in a continual effort to beat them away. In a moment of carelessness, Mei let hers fall to the floor. When she bent down to pick it up, she noticed through the darkness that the leg of the person opposite her, clad in high-heeled shoes and white silk stockings, was resting gently on the leg of the man in the white suit seated to her left. Shocked, Mei quickly raised her head, just in time to receive a look of utter contempt from Miss Zhang. A peculiar feeling of isolation swelled in Mei's breast.

The tea party ended at last. After they walked back to their room, Mei heaved a sigh and said to Xu Qijun, "The atmosphere here is depressing. If you actually leave in two weeks I'll die of loneliness."

On the next day the opening ceremonies were held and the school was especially lively. Mei was assigned the task of greeting visitors, which just happened to put her in the same group as Miss Zhang. The young woman was dressed even more attractively on this occasion, but the look of ridicule that was always in her eyes made Mei doubly uneasy. By about two o'clock the guests and students had all squeezed into the auditorium, but the bell had not yet rung to start the assembly. When combined with her bad mood, the stink of sweat and the clamor of voices made Mei dizzy. She fled the auditorium and stood dumbly for a moment beside the wooden railings in front of the terrace, mechanically mopping the perspiration from her face with her handkerchief. Miss Zhang walked toward her with a sexy swaying of her hips. She smiled and cast a coquettish glance at Mei as she walked into the makeshift lounge next to the auditorium.

Li Wuji, the Chinese-language teacher with the disheveled hair, suddenly appeared before Mei and said gently, "Miss Mei, you must be worn out. Why don't you step into the lounge and have a cool cup of tea?"

Mei blinked. Dazed, she responded with a smile. She was momentarily speechless, as if in the midst of distress she had come across a dear old friend. She turned away from Li Wuji's intensely penetrating gaze and stared into the distance at the disorderly jumble of human shadows in the doorway of the auditorium. Li Wuji turned to follow her gaze, then looked back and continued in a friendly tone, "The guests have just about all arrived. Now we're only waiting for the guest of honor, and the principal can take care of him. So there's nothing to keep you from resting a bit, Miss Mei. Look, the entire welcoming committee is in the lounge."

Someone called to him from across the way. Li Wuji looked back at Mei, then turned and walked into the auditorium. Mei instinctively left the railing and cautiously approached the door to the lounge.

It was very lively inside. Miss Zhang was seated in a large rattan chair, her legs crossed, one propped high above the other. She seemed to have just finished speaking and was munching zestfully on a piece of watermelon. Three or four of the female teachers were giggling, but when Mei's face appeared in the doorway, their laughter stopped. A look of surprise and embarrassment crossed their faces. Obviously they did not welcome a stranger bursting in on their cozy little surroundings. Mei stopped short and swallowed hard. Pretending to be looking for someone, she merely peered into the room, then turned around and walked away. But she had taken no more then ten steps before a roar of boisterous laughter once again burst forth from within the lounge, piercing Mei's ears like a sharp knife. Through the laughter she could hear Miss Zhang saying, "Look at her, she . . . " Mei's heart pounded and her face turned beet-red. She spun around and ran back into the lounge, a brave, cold smile of indifference on her lips.

After a moment of suffocating silence, Miss Zhang squinted at Mei. Deliberately to put her off guard she said, "Miss Mei, aren't you going to stand there to welcome Division Commander Hui?"

"Weren't there originally four or five people assigned to welcome guests?" Mei replied with equal sharpness. Just then two questions raced through Mei's mind: What division commander? Is that why they were secretly making fun of me?

There was another long silence. The noise in the auditorium resembled the croaking of distant frogs, the sound rolling in and out like breakers on the shore. The flat-faced Miss Zhao, who had not yet talked to Mei, suddenly spoke: "We're country folk who don't know how to treat a man of means. Division Commander Hui belongs to the New Thought faction, the only New Thought general. Only a pretty, new-style person who has overcome all obstacles to leave home could suit his tastes."

One or two of the girls issued joyful laughs of approval. But Miss Zhang did not seem to agree. She gazed at Miss Zhao's flat oval face and said coldly, "Our general in the New Thought faction! What's the big deal? What does he know about the New Thought? To tell the truth, I have only contempt for him. But Peishan, you forget that Division Commander Hui has shown a preference for bizarre looking people, which means you are also qualified to welcome him. Ha-ha!"

Zhao Peishan's face turned bright red. She looked around awkwardly with the air of one who dares to be angry but dares not show it in words. Mei stood off to the side with a smile on her face. She understood the favorite tricks of these petty young women.

"It's nearly three o'clock and he's still not here. They must be waiting for him to arrive before starting the assembly. That's really too much." Miss Zhang's constant companion, Miss Zhou, quickly interrupted, wanting to change the topic of conversation. One or two others grunted in agreement. Miss Zhang smiled and turned to Mei, as though she had something to say. Suddenly the sound of Xu Qijun's voice came from the doorway: "So this is where you've all been. The assembly is about to start. Come on."

The sound of the army band began with the eruption of the loud, clear sound of the trumpet, accompanied by the beat of the cymbal. Suddenly the sound filled the lounge as though the military band were right outside the door. Each girl instinctively stood up. Mei turned and looked at Miss Zhang, who was hurrying along, clicking her high-heeled shoes. She laughed and said softly, "Miss Zhang, even I would fall in love with that pair of white legs you're always so fond of raising up so high!" Without giving her a chance to reply, Mei laughed and skipped out the door, caught up with Xu Qijun, and pulled her across the winding, covered walkway. At that moment the bell chimed in the suddenly silent auditorium behind them.

Mei understood now that some strange and complex experiences lay in her future as a teacher. She did not know when it had started or why, but these five or six women teachers bore a hostility toward her as though by some secret pact. It was a hostility that combined a variety of emotions—jealousy, disdain, suspicion, and more. At first Mei thought it was no more than narrow "exclusivism" because they were all graduates of the Second Girl's Normal School in Chongqing. But when she saw how friendly they were toward Xu Qijun, she had to look for another reason. A powerful unhappiness gradually built up in Mei's heart.

When she told Xu Qijun how she felt, Xu unexpectedly accused her of being overly sensitive. Overly sensitive? Mei refused to admit it. She saw clearly that other people were trying to squeeze her out, and she wasn't about to show any signs of weakness. Why should she? If there were people who opposed her, there must also be people who supported her. Only the most commonplace people evoked neither praise nor condemnation. Beginning on the day of the opening ceremonies, her unhappiness turned to anger. She was prepared to deal with her enemies with force, even if it meant confronting them head on.

But once school started, everyone was busy with class work, and the tension gradually subsided. Mei's primary responsibility was the new students in the first grade. The class had girls of sixteen and seventeen* as well as seven- and eight-year-old children. During class either the older girls were sleeping or the younger ones were making a racket. It was impossible to make everything she said suit the interests of each and every student. Mei felt that if even one student did not have her eyes opened wide and fixed on the teacher as she spoke, then it was a great professional defeat. She stood anxiously at the podium, frequently glancing outside the classroom as if she had committed some heinous act and was afraid of being found out. As for her resolve not to show weakness before her colleagues, this, too, began to waiver. "Could it be that, at least when it comes to teaching, I'm not as good as the others?" Such terrifying thoughts were unbearable.

When she had no classes, Mei secretly observed how her colleagues taught. They were doing every bit as badly as her. She also inspected the work of the teachers in the education department. What really startled her was that several students in the back row were playing poker. Her own habit of secretly knitting during lectures when she was a high school student leaped into her mind.

*Until the turn of the century it was quite uncommon to send girls to school. The teenage girls in the elementary school were mostly likely the daughters of parents who were only convinced of the propriety and necessity of providing girls with a modern, formal education under the influence of the so-called New Thought Tide.

"Wasn't I just as guilty of not listening to the teacher as they!" Gradually she stopped worrying about these normal-school students. But then, when she recalled that it was only in the classes of senile, old-fashioned teachers that she had knitted or secretly read other books, her emotions rose again. She felt that this normal school was not worthy of the reputation of being a school that had undergone a thorough reform, one in which all the teachers were members of the New Thought faction.

Realizations such as these destroyed Mei's illusions about her own vocation. At the same time they enhanced her courage. She disdained her male and female colleagues. She even disdained the determined new-style principal. At the same time this "disdain" exacted a large price from Mei: depression and loneliness. Xu Qijun was her only friend. Her other colleagues had all become imaginary—and not merely imaginary—enemies. Although the Chinese teacher, Li Wuji, displayed friendship on numerous occasions, her response was always aloof.

But Xu Qijun would soon be leaving. On September 12 the two good friends went to Longma Lake. They sat in a small boat on the clear-green autumn waters and were filled with emptiness, the emotions of parting pressing on their hearts. For a long while they said nothing. The little temple-studded island in the middle of the water was still blanketed with luxuriant vegetation, the green cloak of midsummer. Around the edges were several maple trees already turning yellow and red. Beams of sunlight shone on the white walls of the temples, glistening brightly, like flowing beads of water, making the island's landscape appear from a distance as a lotus leaf about to wither. From time to time a golden carp leaped up from beside the boat, raining drops of water on it. From among the reeds near the sandy bank of the island came a swoosh; several white seagulls emerged on the wing. They circled the water for a while, then dove past the prow of the boat, plunged into the gentle waves that had been turned silver by the sun's rays, and disappeared. In the background stood the quiet mountain peaks, slowly spewing out a purple mist.

Mei watched in a trance. She felt overcome by gloom. All that this beautiful scenery gave her was a suffocating sadness. She sighed. Turning her head, she suddenly felt as though a flash of light had appeared before her eyes. The undulating mountaintops in the west were now balancing the setting sun like a giant fireball, painting the pointed peaks on this side a deep crimson.

"Such a drab life amidst such beautiful scenery!" As she dramatically spoke these words, Mei felt somewhat relieved. It was as though some foreign object were striking her from within her heart. She had to say something. She had to pour out her feelings. A tide of red arose on her cheeks. She was obviously excited, but in her eagerness she could not construct a coherent sentence. Instead, she just squeezed Xu Qijun's hand tightly as a substitute for words.

In the end it was Xu Qijun who spoke first. "Mei, there's been something strange about you lately, hasn't there? You could probably say it's depression, yet somehow it doesn't seem like it. Or you could say it's melancholy, but that doesn't seem quite right either. To tell the truth, you don't seem as lively as you used to. What do you think?"

She did not turn her gaze from Mei's face, focusing on her bright and animated eyes. Mei laughed faintly but did not reply right away. Slowly their small boat reached the shore of the island, brushing over a clump of water plants. Mei stretched out her hand and plucked a stalk of candle rush. Holding it in her mouth, she chewed on it lightly, then spat it out.

Glancing casually at Xu Qijun, she said softly, "What do I think? I know in my heart what's wrong, but I can't express it. Sometimes even I find it strange that I'm no longer as resolute and bold as before. Instead, I'm always so languid and indecisive; that's right, languid and indecisive. At other times I feel I'm the same old me, that I haven't changed a bit. Sometimes I feel that my heart is empty. Like a blank sheet of paper. But at other times I have the vague sense that it is a crumpled sheet of paper and not so very clean. It's like turning over a multicolored plate—everything is wrong; everything's gone wild! Discontent, worry, rage, it's a bit of each of these. In a word, of late I've come to recognize even more clearly that on the painting that is my life all the colors are mismatched. Take the present, for example. I have to admit that once again I've rushed through the wrong door; once again I've fallen into an unsuitable environment!"

"You still feel that way!"

"Am I being overly sensitive?" Mei quickly asked in response, a smile on her lips.

"What else? It's precisely this newfound oversensitivity of yours that's changed you recently, changed you so that you're no longer open and determined but are always languid and indecisive. Yes, languid and indecisive."

Mei lowered her head and did not speak. She dangled her left hand over the side of the boat and let the spray splash against it. It seemed to her that her behavior had been completely misunderstood and that there was no way to defend herself. Xu Qijun felt at once that her tone had been too harsh. She grabbed Mei's hand forcefully and continued with more tact, "I'm not saying this is a good job because I helped you find it. It's just that society has not yet prepared an ideal place for us. You say the teachers here don't like you. But you should also realize that there is no place in the world where people get along with each other perfectly. You say the Second Girl's Normal School group is exclusionist, but they say you're too arrogant, too caustic. I know you're not like that, but because you try too hard to show how intelligent you are—like, for example, what you said the other night at the tea party—naturally people might get that impression.

"I'm leaving tomorrow, and it will be a fortnight before we can receive letters from one another. I'm very worried about your situation. We're old friends, almost like real sisters. I urge you to be a bit more easygoing. Try to get by for six months, and then we'll think of something else."

Suddenly the boat lurched and a spray leaped up, splashing Mei's sleeve. Cursing, the boatman used a paddle to push off from an old mangled tree stump on the left to avoid an oncoming boat. A set of neatly laid out stone steps appeared before them, part of a pier leading to a temple on the island. A couple was walking up the steps. Mei craned her neck to look at them, then smiled and turned back to Xu Qijun.

"Whatever you say. I don't really agree, Sister Qi, but I'll do whatever you say, okay? Don't worry. I can survive in this world. I won't collapse. Nevertheless, Sister Qi, after you leave I'm afraid I will change even more; I'll change into someone completely different from what I was."

Suddenly a dark shadow covered her face. Mei threw herself on Xu Qijun's chest, pressed her face to Xu's breast, and held her tight. Xu seemed startled, but she also felt deeply her friend's unspeakable sorrow. Gently stroking Mei's hair, Xu racked her brain for some way to console her friend. But Mei raised her head first and, laughing innocently, said, "I've always thought my 'present-ism' was an irrefutable philosophy of life. Okay. Let's look for something we'd like to do at present. Let's go wander around the temple."

Mei's liveliness returned, as if she had turned into another per-son. Tugging Xu Qijun by the hand, Mei rushed into every door she saw. After running once around, their faces were covered with sweat, and their muslin shirts were soaked through to their backs. Finally, they sat down in a small pavilion near the water. It was a four- or five-room one-story building shaped like the character *ao*,* each room separated by a wooden partition. During the three months of spring visitors would come here with wine and delica-cies to "visit scenic spots," and this would serve temporarily as a private dining room. But now the silence was broken only by the intermittent sound of aquatic birds preening their feathers.

A monk from the temple brought over some tea, and Mei unex-pectedly asked, "Do those two visitors who just walked by come here often?"

"The two just now? Our small temple is much obliged to you la-dies and gentlemen for livening things up."

It was a shrewd, flattering answer. Mei glanced sharply at the monk, then sat down in a chair by the window and gazed at the vista outside. She seemed preoccupied and merely responded po-litely to Xu Qijun's pleasantries about the scenery before them. But when Xu worked her way back to the subject of school and Chengdu, Mei cut her off. "Sister Qi, you really worry about me like a mother hen. What about Chengdu? I've already put it com-pletely out of my mind."

"But others aren't willing to forget. One of these days you are going to have to settle this matter."

Mei laughed. She stared at Xu Qijun for a while and then said slowly, "What am I, an official who has to wrap everything up be-fore leaving office? Sister Qi, you really are like a mother hen. Okay. Tomorrow I'll write a letter saying that for the time being I'd like to teach and tell him not to worry."

"Without telling him why you left without saying a word?"

*The character *ao* is written like this: 凸

"Yes. If I bring it up it will only complicate matters. It will confuse everyone, all for nothing."

"You're always putting things off. You are never willing to make any comprehensive plans."

Mei laughed again. A room opposite them on the left side of the pavilion suddenly attracted Mei's attention. She bent forward to get a better look. Behind a low-hanging bamboo curtain she made out the shimmering shadows of two human figures. Suddenly a lovely milky-white arm emerged from below the curtain. Mei drew back, as though shocked, and frowned.

"You're just not willing to take the time to think about the future," Xu Qijun pressed further.

Mei shook her head aimlessly and her expression instantly turned serious. With a hint of excitement in her voice she replied, "It's not that I'm unwilling to think about it. It's just that something unanticipated always gets in the way and makes me feel it's futile to plan. There was a time when I thought far into the future. I made plans to bring Wei Yu's wife and child here, to help them work out a life for themselves, and to find a school for the child. But Sister Qi, do you think this plan is feasible? Or maybe you feel I was being too impractical. This was a problem that would affect the entire future of several people. I thought it was far more important than anything concerning Liu Yuchun or my father. But what good were my plans? Who knows what will happen tomorrow or the next day. Apart from this, I can't see that anything is worth worrying about."

"What about your own problems? Your marriage?"

"The key to that problem lies not with me but with him. I would really like to think about what to do, but what good would it do? Isn't it a waste of time; isn't it just asking for trouble?"

Xu Qijun could not suppress a sigh of despair and said no more. She still did not approve of Mei's plan. It was as though she could already see that Mei would end up wasting her life. Xu suddenly thought of what Mei had said: "Nevertheless, Sister Qi, after you leave I'm afraid I will change even more; I'll change into someone completely different from what I was." Change! Was she consciously trying to change? Was something forcing her to do so? Xu Qijun's expression was one of gloom. All the events of the past reappeared before her. She thought about Mei's manner and what she had said as she hid in Xu's house, unable to find a job. She could not even raise her head to look at her friend.

But Mei was once again leaning casually in front of the window. As though deep in thought, she stared into the distance at the bamboo curtain. The cold wind blew gently. A thin, silken veil now enveloped the mountain peaks of Longma Lake, mixing together the red of the mist and the white of the smoke from kitchen chimneys. The sky appeared as if it were about to darken.

The gentle wind carried the sound of soft, bewitching laugher so clearly that it seemed to be just outside the window. Xu Qijun was startled out of her pensiveness and threw Mei an inquiring glance. Another burst of laughter and this time there was no mistake. With an air of amazement, Xu rushed to confirm her suspicions: "Isn't that Zhang?"

"Lu is there with her. When we were on the boat I spotted them standing on the stone steps," Mei said, still looking in their direction. But the others seemed to be spying on them also. Mei suddenly drew inside and, staying clear of the window, walked cautiously over to Xu Qijun. They stared at each other for several seconds, then left the pavilion.

On the way home Mei chatted and laughed in a carefree way. Xu Qijun, however, felt somewhat agitated. The sound of that soft, bewitching laughter still echoed in her ears. She formulated various explanations and made a number of assumptions, which increased her feelings that given Mei's original nature and her present state of mind, she did not belong in such an environment. It was extremely worrisome.

By the time they reached the school, the lamplights were already shining through the darkness. The school's caretaker was looking everywhere for Principal Lu, saying there was important business for him to take care of.

After Xu Qijun's departure, Mei's room was changed to a small, poorly lit chamber that could be reached only by passing Miss Zhang's. Because it was a private room, Mei was still content, but that she could not avoid the increased contact with Miss Zhang was somewhat annoying. Zhang's attitude was more friendly than before. Petty everyday matters such as borrowing a book, sharpening a pencil, or showing some new little item she had purchased all became an excuse for her to run over to Mei's room. These visits were always short, never consisting of more than a smile, a nod, or, at most, an exchange of a few pleasantries.

But those sidelong glances as she was about to leave, so seductive, so deep, and yet so sharp, as if they contained at infinity of hidden meanings, always confused Mei. She did not know whether she wanted to pull this eccentric young girl back to kiss her or to bite her. Watching her delicate, lively image as she walked away, Mei frequently could not help but think, "She's lovable, but she's also detestable—what a monster!" Then all at once Mei would recall that glimpse of Zhang's leg under the table at the tea party celebrating the opening of school and the laughter in the pavilion at the temple on Longma Lake, and Mei would begin to sense that behind the strange look in Zhang's eyes lay a background of fear, suspicion, and a distrust of people.

At times like this Mei felt sorry for Zhang and wanted to say to her, "I'm not so unfriendly. You can trust me. Don't worry. Let's be friends." But she never had the opportunity to express such sentiments. Time and time again Zhang's evasive manner made it difficult for Mei to express the generous feelings of amiability that she had been storing up for so long.

Nevertheless, on the surface they became closer every day. Just a week later, Zhang, on her own initiative, addressed Mei familiarly and said with a giggle, "Why be so formal? It's always Miss this, Miss that. Call me Yifang. Better yet, just call me Yi. My sisters and I share the character 'fang' in our names. My younger sister's name is Shufang. I plan to stop using this character."

Mei smiled. Her mind turned to those words she had long wanted to say. But Zhang had already stood up and was speaking. "Tomorrow I'll show you her picture. She's very pretty. As pretty as you."

In a slightly teasing manner, Zhang Yifang took Mei's hand and touched it to her lips, then giggled and walked away. An intoxicating fragrance drifted from Zhang's pale blue dress.

The flat-faced Zhao Peishan lived next door to Mei. The windows of both rooms faced the same direction and looked out on a tiny courtyard. The two women could carry on a conversation leaning out their windows. But if either wanted to go to the other's room, she had to walk some distance around the corner. Miss Zhao was probably about twenty-five or twenty-six. You could tell she was a mediocre person at first glance. On her plump, flat face two deep wrinkles ran from the sides of her nose to the corners of her mouth, giving her a mournful appearance that was depressing to look at. Her roommate was a married woman named Zhu Jie whose home was in the city. Although she was ostensibly living on campus, in reality she went home every night to sleep. In the quiet hours of evening until well after eleven o'clock Mei could always hear Zhao Peishan bustling about her room like a rat building a nest. How different from the Zhao Peishan who never made a sound in crowds.

Mei had no interest in this flat-faced young woman. So even though they were the closest of neighbors, they rarely conversed. The person Mei felt most inclined to befriend was Zhou Pingquan, Zhang Yifang's constant companion. She now lived in the room Mei had once shared with Xu Qijun in the westernmost part of the women's dormitory, right across the covered walkway from the second-grade classroom. During the first few days after Mei changed her accommodations, she often went to Miss Zhou's room out of habit, as a result of which they had had several long talks. Miss Zhou was not more than twenty-two or twenty-three, neat and smart, just like her personality. Because she was also the head of the elementary education division, Mei's contacts with her were naturally frequent. In addition, there was another woman teacher who did not live at school and two male teachers who had just graduated from the Teacher's College. But in the four weeks since school started, Mei had yet to meet them.

Mei gradually became accustomed to her narrow new surroundings. Although she felt somewhat lonely and bored, the exchange of pleasantries and smiles with the people she met made her life there bearable. Almost imperceptibly another month slipped by. From Chengdu Dr. Mei sent a castigating letter, the closing words of which read, "What's done is done. But at the end of this term you must quit and come home." Liu Yuchun also sent someone with clothing and money. Mei returned every penny of the money, but after this her fellow teachers began to question her openly about her past. Mei only smiled and did not reply.

A dense cloud of conjecture and rumor gradually accumulated around Mei. She became the target of gossip for the whole school. The male teachers from the Teacher's College were always coming over to chat with her on the slightest pretext. Li Wuji, who had displayed a certain amount of friendliness toward her from the start, was particularly attentive. The whole school was busily preparing for the Double Ten lantern parade. Li Wuji's job was to compile a "Double Ten special edition," but as of the 9th he had not yet begun looking at the drafts of the articles that had been submitted. The cold rays of the moon shining on his face, he ambled back and forth along the corridor in front of the elementary education division classrooms, wondering why there wasn't a single female teacher in sight.

Faint peals of laughter, rising and falling like waves, reached his ears. "It must be coming from the athletic field," was the thought Li Wuji's confused mind dimly conjured up. He threw back his head—this was the only way he could toss back the hair that fell down over his eyebrows—and instinctively began walking.

Hundreds of red lanterns twinkled on the broad, pitch-black field. The shrill tones of a whistle sounded regularly. The physical education teacher, Pockmark Qian, was rehearsing the student body in the new routine he had "composed." It had been in preparation for a full two weeks. At a certain command these four or five hundred lantern-carrying students could arrange themselves into the characters for "Long Live the Republic of China." It was because of this small skill that Pockmark Qian had become the star of the evening, attracting the attention of everyone in the school.

Li Wuji let a bitter laugh escape his lips, then opened wide his narrow eyes to scan the crowded field. A group of people stood out on the diving platform beside the swings. Beneath the clear light of the crescent moon he became aware of several round protruding breasts and slender waists. Li Wuji sighed, then rushed impetuously past the rows of lanterns to the platform.

"There's no room for you!"

This shout emerged from the middle of the platform. Li Wuji recognized the voice of the physics and chemistry teacher, Wu Xingchuan. It truly was packed to capacity. The highest level of the platform was occupied by five or six women, almost all the women teachers in the school. Even Zhu Jie, who was now Mrs. Fan, was there. A male teacher was already standing on each of the lower steps. Only the two lowest steps remained empty, but you could not see the lantern routine from there.

"You should all be punished for running over and sitting so smugly here without even calling me! Hurry up and make room for me!" Li Wuji said, raising his head.

"At first we thought of calling you. But then we were afraid we'd interfere with your work in compiling the 'Special Edition'!" This time it was the history and geography teacher, Chen Juyin, who spoke. He and Li Wuji shared a room, so he knew for a fact that Li Wuji had not even glanced at the pile of drafts.

"That's for sure! If you don't let me have a good look at Pock-mark Qian's routine tonight, there's no way I'll be able to put pen to paper and describe it."

He was answered with a burst of laughter. Li Wuji was already standing on the lowest level of the platform, calculating how to push his way up, when Principal Lu Keli, who was squatting on the middle level, spoke: "Okay. In that case I guess you qualify to come up."

"No way! Add one more person and no one will be able to see," someone chimed in.

"He's too tall," someone else said.

"It must be possible to make room for one more on the top level," Chen Juyin slowly tried to mediate. No one seemed to hear him, as there was no response. Perhaps it was because everyone was too busy watching to pay any attention. The lanterns in the middle of the field had just transformed themselves from a long snake into a square. The best part of the performance was about to begin. Li Wuji took this opportunity to push his way up. But just as he reached the uppermost level, Zhang Yifang's voice seemed to leap out and stop him. "What? You want to come up here with us?"

"You've got lots of space up there. Where else should I go? You don't want me to stand on people's heads, do you? You call this open relations between the sexes?"

A burst of laughter rose up from among the female teachers. Li Wuji straightened his shoulders and stood at his full height in front of Miss Zhang. As usual he tossed back his head to clear the hair out of his eyes, then added with a smile, "It wasn't easy climbing up to this sacred place of yours!"

"In that case, please squat down. You're too tall. We can't see." The voice belonged to Mei, who was standing in the rear off to the right. Because she had changed into a dark-colored outfit, Li Wuji hadn't noticed her when he arrived.

Now the flickering red square was swaying once again. Suddenly, as if a door had opened, three red streamers rushed out from the middle of six neat rows of stars. They shot out twenty feet or more, then rolled into a pile, like a huge charcoal brazier, a living charcoal brazier. Each red element shimmered brightly, forming a number of vertical and horizontal streaks. Then a flame-like point came spewing out of the upper end. At the same time the remaining three sides of the square revolved around at lightning speed, until they formed three parallel rows like the wicks of three large candles.

"South Sichuan."*

No one knew who had shouted these words, but they were immediately echoed by everyone on the athletic field. The pattern formed was precisely these two Chinese characters. The people holding the lanterns had arranged themselves in just that way! From the tier of seats above him Li Wuji heard someone let out a loud cheer of admiration. He turned and looked behind him and was able to make out the vague outlines of the smile that had appeared on Mei's face. Unable to restrain himself, he gnashed his teeth and muttered, "Wow. Tonight really belongs to Pockmark Qian."

All around him Li Wuji heard nothing but expressions of joy and surprise, but he kept his eyes fixed on Mei's beautiful face. Suddenly, the gaze of a pair of light, limpid eyes poured down like a clear spring and washed over Li Wuji's burning stare. Li's heart pounded. With great effort he said, "Just look how easy it was for Pockmark Qian to create a bright and promising South Sichuan."

That special look of Mei's, a smile on her lips, and her eyes dazzling could be seen distinctly through the twilight. Taking her expression as a silent reply, Li Wuji continued: "But the gloomy darkness over there, like an ancient temple, that's the real South Sichuan!"

"You and your grumblings again!" It was not Mei's reply but Zhang Yifang's jeering remarks that had so rudely interrupted him. Li Wuji laughed weakly, then suddenly stood up, faced Mei, and, looking intently at her, said softly, "Miss Mei, what is your opinion?"

Mei only smiled gently. Her lips quivered as though she were about to say something, but the deafening screech of the whistle

*This is the name of the school at which they teach.

beat her to it. The lanterns that had formed the two words shuddered like ripples on a pond, then quickly dispersed. When he finally heard the long measured tones of her reply he could not believe his ears.

"Please squat down like before, okay? You're blocking our view."

By now the lanterns had again taken up the shape of a long snake. The whistle sounded loud and clear. Numerous flashes of red gradually assembled close together in the form of the pyramids. Suddenly, as if breaking apart, they became six groups of double oblique lines. Faster than the eye could see, they wove in and out. From afar they looked like six wriggling caterpillars. Then, to the hurried but rhythmic sounds of the whistle, the six groups of lantern lights passed in succession, like waves pushing toward the shore, down to the last group, until all was still.

Li Wuji stared straight ahead, but he saw nothing. Only one thought kept going around and around in his mind: "Is she so shallow that she likes this kind of performance?"

The thunderous sound of applause cut short his musings. Somehow these six groups of lanterns had lowered themselves and distinctly revealed six large characters: Long Live the Republic of China!

The rehearsal was over. Amidst the clamorous sounds of praise Li wrapped his arms around his head, drew his body in close, and squatted there high up on the platform. In his confused state he heard someone say, "Don't call him. Let him reflect quietly so he can write this all up for the 'Special Edition'!"

Li Wuji laughed coldly to himself and remained squatting motionlessly, sunk in an unspeakable depression. Finally the sound of voices vanished completely. The plaintive cry of crickets echoed intermittently. Only after a blast of cold wind gave him goose bumps did Li Wuji stagger down the platform, reluctantly dragging his heavy legs along.

He instinctively walked up the path leading to his room without running into a soul. Then, quite unexpectedly, in the courtyard outside the classroom of the first-year normal-school students, he noticed Mei leaning beside a large raised flower bed, staring into space. Li Wuji hesitated a moment, then quietly and resolutely walked over to her. When they were less than two feet apart, Mei suddenly turned around and cast him a smile, as if to say, "I knew you would come!"

For a moment no one spoke. Mei waited, while Li Wuji struggled to figure out what to say. Moonlight dappled their bodies, shining into Mei's unlined silk dress. The blouse fluttered imperceptibly as though the moonlight were about to open it and reveal Mei's breasts. Her eyes were clear and still as always, but more lustrous. At last Li Wuji decided how to open the conversation: "You see, doesn't this place remind you of an ancient temple?"

"Oh. But you don't like ancient temples, do you, Mr. Li?"

"That depends," Li Wuji said in the same tone he used in the classroom. "At first I didn't like the school. I absolutely detested it. I thought I'd come to the wrong place. Everything is so gray, as though a Confucian academy had hung out a new sign to call itself a modern school. All you have here are old things dressed up in new clothes. People who are always talking about the New Thought Tide are even worse than the real old-fashioned teachers. But now I feel a ray of bright light has penetrated this ancient temple. If only this light would be willing to shine on me, even this ancient temple would be transformed into a brand-new structure."

Mei lowered her head. After a short pause, she said slowly, "I'm afraid it's probably no more than the faint glow of the firefly."

"If it alights on my eyelids, it will become the sun!"

Mei did not reply. An uproar reached them from the direction of the student dormitories, as if the entire student body was still up and about. But here there was nothing but the cold moonlight and a silence above which one could even hear the beating of a person's heart. Li Wuji stared intently at Mei, parting his lips slightly as if waiting for a response but also as if he himself had more to say. After two or three minutes Mei raised her head and spoke gently but sternly: "Mr. Li, I hope that with your help I can illuminate this ancient temple. It's getting late, and I suspect you still haven't compiled tomorrow's 'Special Edition,' have you? I'm looking forward to reading it as soon as possible. Good-bye."

She departed slowly, leaving only a gentle smile to comfort the dazed and despondent Li Wuji. When she reached the walkway to her dormitory she found Misses Zhang, Zhou, and Zhu discussing Pockmark Qian's display. Miss Zhu said loudly, "We ought to be the stars at tomorrow night's lantern parade!"

"Unfortunately, the Number Three Memorial Archway is too narrow. I'm afraid we won't be able to perform."

Feigning great enthusiasm, Mei entered the conversation. At the same time she carefully scrutinized the facial expressions of Zhou and the others. Nothing unusual there. Obviously they had occupied themselves wholeheartedly with Pockmark Qian's display since leaving the athletic field. After chatting for ten minutes or so, Mei returned to her own room. She lay down on the bed, where she tossed and turned for some time, her mind cluttered with thoughts. Finally, biting her lip, she said to herself, "To heck with it! I'm going to continue being a firefly that flies about in space for all to see. I do not intend to alight on anyone's eyelid and become the sun." With that she heaved a deep sigh, closed her eyes, and, before long, fell asleep.

The next day Mei awoke at six in the morning. The whole school was suffocatingly still. She wanted to go back to sleep, but the events of last night—Li Wuji's fixed stare at the top of the platform, the conversation under the moonlight beside the flower bed—one after the other, they all violently assaulted her mind. She forced herself to lie in bed another half hour, then got up and went outside to find a maid to bring her water to wash up. To her surprise, even the door to the maid's quarters was tightly shut. She paced back and forth in front of the corridor for a while out of sheer boredom, then followed her toes to the western end of the corridor. She noticed that not a sound was coming from Miss Zhou's room either. It really was too early. Everyone must have gone to bed late last night, and, as today was a holiday, it might be nine o'clock before anyone got up.

Discouraged, Mei headed back, but as she passed by Zhang Yifang's room she heard some noise. Mei was as happy as someone who has "heard footsteps in a deserted valley." Recklessly, she rushed up to the door. Seeing that it was opened a crack, without a second thought she pushed it in. Mei was speechless. She saw a sexy-looking Zhang Yifang, dressed only in panties and a camisole and bent over in front of the wash basin, suddenly turn around and look at her in alarm. She also caught a glimpse of a pair of men's shoes in front of the bed. From behind the mosquito netting over the bed she heard a voice intimately call out, "Yifang."

She bolted out of the room and fled back to her own, where she threw herself down on the bed, her heart pounding so wildly she could hardly breathe.

In this hysterical state one thought kept turning over and over in her mind: "What rotten luck. Three times I've caught her at it. This will only make trouble for me. Of course, I'm not afraid, and I don't regret having seen them. I just feel uncomfortable that my burden has been increased for no reason, as if some invisible monster were toying with me."

She did not know how long she had lain there in this reverie when suddenly the door opened and she saw Zhang Yifang standing in the doorway, already neatly dressed, a smile covering her face.

"Mei, I thought I heard you up long ago. How come you're still lying in bed?" Zhang Yifang spoke these words quite naturally, then walked over to her bed and tugged affectionately on Mei's hand. A mood akin to remorse floated into Mei's heart. She felt she might have been too suspicious, too ready to view others in a bad light. With this, she laughed sincerely and squeezed Zhang's hand tightly. Zhang continued with animation: "Hurry and get up. There are no classes today so we're going to Mount Zhong. You've already been to Longma Lake. They say the scenery at Mount Zhong is even better than there."

Mei readily agreed. Zhang Yifang ran out to call for water for Mei, then hurried back and sat to one side watching Mei comb her hair and wash, noisily helping her pick out her most fashionable clothes and enthusiastically matching their colors. The sincere friendship with which all of these actions were imbued made Mei extremely uncomfortable. Her heart, which was easily moved by honest trustworthiness, compelled her to shed a secret tear. Her tender gaze fell on Miss Zhang's face, and Mei decided that when they arrived at Mount Zhong she would definitely explain everything to Zhang Yifang.

At the last minute they were also joined by Zhou Pingquan. The flat-faced Zhao Peishan seemed eager to go as well, but Zhang Yifang pretended not to notice. With a word she hurried them all off, heartlessly abandoning Zhao Peishan. Mei smiled, more certain than ever now that Miss Zhang had something in mind when she suggested today's outing.

As they walked they chatted about this and that. Mei was already looking for an opportunity to express her true feelings. To their surprise, several shops on the road had hung out Chinese flags. A five-colored banner hung in front of the door of the Popular Lecture Society, and below it several people were huddled together, noisily reading what appeared to be some sort of proclamation. There seemed to be an unusually large number of people on the street today, and the spirit of national celebration permeated everywhere. Mei and her companions attracted even more attention than usual. A group of older children followed behind them engaged in an animated debate about whether Mei was an actress.

With some difficulty they passed through the west gate and before them loomed Mount Zhong. The majestic sound of a steam whistle bellowed from across the mountain. Although muted, the whistle was still quite deafening. When they were halfway up the mountain, they could see the Yangzi. A steamship pushed its way upstream through the muddy waters, issuing now and then a long triumphant cry. Mei, feeling unusually happy, ran energetically ahead of her friends.

"Mei, try not to be too happy. By the time you get to the top of the mountain your clothes will be soaked!" Miss Zhou called from behind. She and Miss Zhang had linked arms, propping each other up as they staggered along. Miss Zhang looked particularly exhausted.

At last they reached the top. They stopped to rest on the imposing stone steps outside the gate of a large temple. Before them flowed the Yangzi, embracing the mountains like two strong muscular arms. Off to the left myriad mountains rose and fell. Lüzhou city lay dusty and dark in the middle, sunken among them like a scar. The temple, too, was extremely majestic. Its soaring eaves pierced the deep blue sky. The broad steps that had been so tiring to climb were spread out neatly before them like a huge white face. Mei gazed around greedily, then shouted to her companions, "It's magnificent! Longma Lake was delicate and beautiful, but this place is simply magnificent." But Miss Zhou and Miss Zhang were completely exhausted, so they just sat there, shoulder to shoulder, panting shallowly.

Although it was late autumn, the weather was still very warm. All three women had worn lined clothing, so before long even Mei was willing to leave this scenic spot and follow Zhang Yifang into the temple. Miss Zhang was feeling somewhat better by now, and with a nod of her head she led the others across a large courtyard to the tastefully decorated monk's dining room. "Okay, let's stop here and have a vegetarian meal," Zhang said.

Zhang Yifang gave a relaxed sigh and threw herself into a black sandalwood armchair. But suddenly, reminded of something important, she straightened up, looked back, and said to her friends, "Ping, could I trouble you to go ask the monks to set up a vegetarian meal? Mei, this meal is on me, and I insist."

Mei smiled and nodded her head, saying nothing. As she watched Zhou Pingquan step through a side door and disappear among the cluster of columns supporting the long promenade, it occurred to her that this was the perfect opportunity to talk. She walked gracefully over to Zhang Yifang. Allowing her gentle gaze to fall on Zhang's face, Mei considered how to begin. Zhang, who probably already had an idea of what was on Mei's mind, returned the look with a meaningful glance of her own. After a few moments, just as Mei was about to speak, Zhang Yifang suddenly laughed and tweaked Mei's chin.

"Mei, you are really beautiful," she said. "No wonder someone has you on his mind!"

Mei blushed slightly, but her color quickly returned to normal as she replied with a smile, "What about you? If I were a man, I would surely be in love with you."

"Then you should also say you'd let me alight on your eyelids and be your sun—it was the sun, wasn't it?"

These words caught Mei totally by surprise and left her stunned. Zhang Yifang laughed even louder. Suddenly she stood up and gave Mei peck on the cheek, before quickly continuing, "I'll tell you the truth. I heard everything that was said between you and Li Wuji. Last night when we left the athletic field I noticed you were deliberately lagging behind, so I had an idea: wherever you went, I would follow you. While you were standing beside the flower bed, I was squatting behind the large goldfish bowl to the left. When I heard you say, "Good-bye," I ran away, so I'm still not clear whether it was really 'good-bye.'"

"Believe me, we immediately said good-bye."

Somehow the situation had been reversed and Mei was on the defensive. She felt confused. Suddenly she realized that this attractive and mischievous young woman was not as naive as Mei had imagined. At the same time she sensed that the words she herself had prepared last night to "speak frankly and sincerely" were now not very appropriate. "Maybe she doesn't care about what happened this morning." This notion struck her mind like a flash of lightning. She hesitated, deep in thought.

"But Mei, you are being too cruel. Li Wuji is a good man, isn't he?" As she spoke these words Zhang Yifang's attitude became stern, without a hint of sarcasm or playfulness.

"Whether he's a good man or a bad man makes no difference. I have no need of love and no interest in it."

"Then why did you cast off your husband?"

Mei smiled. Before she could answer, footsteps could be heard from outside. The sound of Zhou Pingquan talking with another girl cut short their discussion. Mei did not know this other girl. She was petite and delicate in stature, with an attractive but unexceptional face. Her clothing was in the height of fashion, and she could not have been more than seventeen or eighteen. Although she had the look of a student, under Mei's sharp scrutiny she appeared somewhat out to the ordinary.

Zhang Yifang greeted the girl, calling her "Miss Yang," and introduced her to Mei. The usual pleasantries dragged on for more than ten minutes. Miss Yang's gaze fell frequently on Mei, as if she hoped to penetrate below the surface to discover the real nature of this new acquaintance. A neatly dressed high-ranking monk brought in a tray of tea. He glanced at Miss Zhang and the others, then turned, bowed slightly, and spoke in a tone of extraordinary deference, "Miss Yang, the guards ask for instructions. . . . "

"Instruct them to return without me! The sedan chair can wait at the foot of the mountain!" Miss Yang interrupted the monk impatiently.

"Understood. And the young lady's lunch?"

"She'll eat here," Zhang Yifang answered for her. The monk looked at Miss Zhang in amazement, uneasily said, "Understood," and withdrew.

For a while the three did not speak. Mei gazed at an ancient pine outside. Thoughts of her unfinished conversation a moment ago with Miss Zhang saddened her. But when she turned back and noticed that Miss Yang was staring at her again, her sadness turned to a somewhat nervous bewilderment.

"It's certain to be very lively tonight," Miss Zhou said, searching for a new topic of conversation.

"Five schools. At the very least there will be more than two thousand people. It will really be breathtaking. I hear that Division Commander Hui is planning to send a battalion to participate in the lantern parade. Can this be true?" Zhang Yifang continued with great interest, looking at Miss Yang.

"He'll most likely send them," Miss Yang replied with indifference, without taking her eyes off of Mei.

"It would be best if he did send them. Xianzhong is still vying with our school to head the parade. We might as well ask the army to march first. That would be one solution. Of course, South Sichuan would be second. If Xianzhong insists that they should be first because they have more people, then . . ."

Zhou Pingquan's argument was suddenly cut short by a loud "Aha!" from Miss Yang. Even Miss Zhang and Mei were somewhat surprised. Miss Yang, her face beaming with joy, said to no one in particular, "I remember. Yes, I remember now. This is the Miss Mei who ran away from home and whom everyone is talking about."

The three companions laughed; the sound of their laughter faded slowly like the faint echo that lingers when a lead pipe is dropped on a hard floor.

"How did you know about this, Miss Yang?" Mei asked, still maintaining a calm and natural demeanor.

"It probably spread from your school. You needn't worry; you're safe here. Division Commander Hui is an advocate of the New Thought Tide and is in favor of women's liberation. If you go to the Daoyi Prefectural Commissioner's Office and request a divorce, I guarantee it will be granted immediately."

Mei smiled. At last she felt relaxed, as though she had acquired an additional safeguard. The conversation gradually turned to Division Commander Hui's promotion of the New Thought Tide. Zhou Pingquan, who was very well informed about local conditions and Division Commander Hui's new governmental policies, recited them as though she had memorized them from a book. She seemed to feel that because Mei was curious about her new and unfamiliar environment, it was her duty to act as Mei's "guide." From time to time Miss Yang supplemented what Zhou said. This made Mei even less able to fathom the motives of her new acquaintance. All she could conclude was that she was not altogether unlikable. Although her speech carried a certain air of arrogance, it also revealed an open and innocent disposition.

"No matter what you say, I still think the force of tradition is firmly entrenched here." Zhang Yifang, who until now had remained silent, suddenly dropped this bomb.

"What firmly entrenched forces of tradition?" Miss Yang countered disapprovingly.

"In the minds of the average person. Take our school, for instance. This year we accepted some slightly older girls, and everyone on the outside is talking about it. They say we are a boy's school. The normal and the elementary school are in the same compound, so how does it look, letting in sixteen- and seventeen-year-old girls?"

"Oh that! That's ultraconservatism. That's why Division Commander Hui has started the popular lecture societies."

"But the only ones who come to hear the lectures are students! And they have an ulterior motive. Most of them use this as an excuse to come to look at the night market!"

Silence followed. A look of excitement and tension crept over the faces of the two debaters. Mei sat on the sidelines and smiled. Suddenly she remembered Li Wuji's grumblings last night about "old things dressed up in new clothes" and could not keep from joking, "Yifang, your goal is to change yourself from the inside out, to become a perfect human being. If you can't, then you won't even wear a suit of new clothes."

Stunned, the three stood staring dumbly at Mei's grinning face. Then, suddenly and in unison, they burst into roars of comprehending laughter, especially Miss Yang, who grasped Mei's hand warmly and laughed until she could not catch her breath. More serious in tone, Mei clarified her point of view: "I'm new to this area and not very familiar with things here, so I really have no right to speak up. But whenever I go out I always run into people, eyes gawking, looking at my 'nun's head' in the same way that they would watch an acrobatics performance. So I understand a little. I think it's going to take a lot of time and energy to get this gray town of Lüzhou to wear a suit of fashionable new clothes."

"Right! First we must make some new clothes for it to wear!" Miss Yang jumped up and shouted, after which she proceeded to spew forth a stream of "new clothes" that were being planned: Division Commander Hui was about to recommend short hair for women and careers for women. Division Commander Hui was also planning to confiscate all the temples in the city and turn them into popular lecture societies and libraries. Division Commander Hui was also thinking about going to Shanghai and Beijing to invite several New Culture Movement activists to come and hold a large-scale New Thought Tide symposium. Division Commander Hui also approved of the "new village movement" and planned to erect several right here at Mount Zhong and Longma Lake. Division Commander Hui . . . " At this point a monk came in bearing their meal.

The four girls chatted exuberantly as they ate, then went back down the mountain. By this time Miss Yang had become quite intimate with Mei and insisted on dragging her over to Division Commander Hui's official residence to meet the new-style master of Lüzhou. Mei declined a number of times before Miss Yang reluctantly agreed to postpone the encounter by taking Mei to the commander's headquarters to view that evening's lantern parade. "The lantern parade will assemble in front of the headquarters building. Division Commander Hui will probably appear in person to make a speech," Yang said seriously as they parted.

That Zhang Yifang and Zhou Pingquan had not been invited as well made Mei feel somewhat uneasy. Zhang Yifang did not seem to mind, but Zhou Pingquan's face briefly revealed a look of anger. Mei thought it best to pretend not to notice. Under the circumstances she did not feel right about asking Zhang and Zhou the questions that had been bothering her since Miss Yang's appearance—what kind of person was Miss Yang, and what was her relationship with Division Commander Hui? Mei did not want to be misunderstood or to be taken for one of those self-satisfied people who had really never experienced life.

She decided to avoid all mention of Miss Yang. She would ignore this new friendship that had fallen into her lap. She also decided that when Miss Yang came for her tonight she would excuse herself from going so as to show people that she was not one of those stupid people who got all excited just because they met someone of high status.

Mei's thoughts expanded and matured on the road back to school. By the time she and her companions had reached their destination, Mei had nearly forgotten that the incident with Yang had occurred. She rested a while in her room, then went to the faculty recreation room to pass the time. The physics and chemistry teacher, Wu Xingchuan, was playing Ping-Pong with the history and geography teacher, Chen Juyin. Li Wuji sat off to the side, his head in his hands. Clearly he had something on his mind, and watching Ping-Pong was only a cover. In a corner of the room Zhang Yifang and Zhou Pingquan were engrossed in a game of Chinese chess. When Mei entered it was like a flash of lightning, causing everyone to blink as a strange look passed over their faces.

What could be called a bashful smile involuntarily appeared on Mei's lips. She walked straight to the chess table, leaned on the back of Zhang Yifang's chair, and concentrated intently on the game.

"Is that you? Aren't you going to get dressed up?" Miss Zhang said softly without turning around as she moved her "chariot" to "eat" her opponent's "horse."*

"Why should I get dressed up? But Yifang, you'd do better not to take that horse," Mei responded nonchalantly, even though she felt she was about to choke.

"Why? . . . Aiya. Okay, I'm returning your horse. I won't take it after all. Yang Qiongzhi will be here in half an hour."

"Oh, that. Let her come. I have no intention of going."

Zhang Yifang put back the horse and grasped her own chariot in her hand, unable to make up her mind what to do. Zhou Pingquan stretched, raised her head, glanced at Mei, and added somewhat sarcastically, "You already agreed. Anyway, it will be fun!"

"Fun? That's of no concern to me! Yifang, why don't you move that cannon!"

Sensing someone standing behind her, Mei swung her head around just in time for Li Wuji's burning gaze to fall directly on her face. A stream of soft but excited words poured from his lips.

*Chinese chess is similar to Western chess. It is played with round markers on which are embossed the Chinese characters for different pieces. Among them are horses, chariots, foot soldiers, guards, and generals.

"Good. The very fact that Yang Qiongzhi is so anxious to drag you along means you shouldn't go."

"What exactly is Yang Qiongzhi's story? I'm still not very clear," Mei said frankly, straightening up as if to say the reason she was not going was not simply because of that Yang girl. The two chess players looked at each other and smiled. Forgetting that she was still holding a chariot in her hand, Zhang Yifang proceeded to move her cannon.

"You should know what's going on. In name, she's Division Commander Hui's adopted daughter. In reality, who knows! But everyone says that she is in charge of finding lovers for Division Commander Hui. There's no doubt about that!"

"Oh, I see," Mei responded dryly. She turned her attention back to the chess game, but in her heart she could not repress a feeling of gloom. Not yet noticing that Zhang Yifang's side was short a chariot, she shouted in alarm, "What's up? What's up? Disaster! Yifang, you're going to lose!"

"She's still going to come looking for you. I hope you understand the dangers involved," Li Wuji pressed urgently. Apparently upset with Mei's casual attitude, he raised his voice somewhat.

The steady *cong-cong* of the Ping-Pong game suddenly fell silent. The atmosphere in the recreation room became unusually menacing. Although she was still looking at the chessboard, Mei could sense the eyes focused on her person. Danger? The danger of being seduced, the danger of moral degeneration, no doubt. Nonsense! Mei's native self-confidence suddenly erupted in her mind, causing her entire body to shudder with indignation.

She swung around and faced Li Wuji. Staring at him earnestly she said coldly, "Thank you for your concern. But I simply do not see what the danger is. Mr. Li, I'm opposed to prejudices like yours: treating women as so fragile that all you have to do is bump into them and they will break; as so morally deficient that they will fall into degeneracy at a moment's notice. It seems to me there must be some women who are neither fragile nor so easily ruined!"

Never expecting such an adverse reaction, Li Wuji turned slightly red. But he still managed to say, "But you must take every precaution!"

Someone nearby snickered. Mei noticed a furtive look of disapproval on the face of someone beside the Ping-Pong table. What was the problem? Li Wuji seemed to be proclaiming himself to be Mei's protector. This nearly drove Mei crazy.

She stood up straight and, to a room full of doubting eyes, proclaimed, "Originally I had decided not to go. Now I think I'll go to see just how fragile I really am."

Mei glanced calmly at her wristwatch and headed toward the door. But before she got there, someone burst in. It was the very subject of conversation, Yang Qiongzhi, carrying her shoes in her hands. She had rode over on a horse.

"Great! Everyone's here. Let's all go together!"

Without waiting for an answer, Miss Yang hurried Zhou Pingquan and Zhang Yifang out of the recreation room like a brood of chickens. She ran in front of them all the way to the school gate, where she turned around and, in the tone of a command, said to Zhang Yifang, "I've brought horses. You've ridden before, so you help Zhou Pingquan. I'll take Miss Mei. We'll eat dinner at headquarters!"

This strange procession headed into the cold evening wind, rushing toward the Number Three Archway. But when they reached the street on which the Popular Lecture Society was located, Miss Yang suddenly stopped her horse. When she saw the bodyguards outside the Lecture Society, she knew that Division Commander Hui must be inside. Just as she was guiding her three companions in, Division Commander Hui, who had been toiling at the podium, was enjoying the brief respite granted by a thunderous round of applause. As the applause gradually abated, Miss Yang whispered a few words in his ear and he continued, "Equality between the sexes has been written into the provisional constitution. Women's liberation is part of the New Thought Tide. It is my responsibility as division commander to support this. Today I will set an example by asking a certain Mei—Miss Mei—to speak!"

Mei, who was standing on the side of the podium, suddenly jumped in alarm. The applause started up again. As if in a trance, Mei was pushed up to the podium by Miss Yang. As Mei bowed instinctively to Division Commander Hui and turned her face, now flushed with excitement and fear, back to the podium, the applause seemed to billow forth like a storm, and the podium beneath Mei's feet appeared to shake ever so slightly.

Chapter Seven

By coincidence, Xu Qijun's third letter since leaving Lüzhou was written on Double Ten and reached Mei on the 28th. It was a long letter, three pages of tiny characters composed on narrow-lined paper. Mei read it twice, but only one phrase caught her eye: "I worry about you!" Had her best friend written a letter from several thousand li away to arrive on that very day just to waste so much ink on the transmission of a platitude such as "I worry about you"? Of course, Xu Qijun had been motivated by a pure and honest sense of friendship, unlike the people here who were also always saying, "We worry about you," but Mei's reaction was the same.

Lazily, she tossed the letter aside and sighed heavily. The petty and vulgar events of the last month of her life unfolded chaotically in her mind. Yesterday she had got drunk at the Hui mansion, learned to ride a horse with Miss Yang, fired a pistol, and hit a wild dog; the day before yesterday she had seen Li Wuji complaining, cursing, and even crying; the day before that she had refrained from laughing and had listened quietly to compliments from Zhou Pingquan; and the day before that? Five days, six days, a week ago? Jealous, envious eyes; small pouting lips; the intimacy when she and her colleagues were face to face, the cold laughs behind her back; drawing near to flatter her; surrounding her to shower her with adulation; their conflicts among themselves; the stares of people on the street; rumors filling the air like a dense fog; so many faces, so many voices, so many grasping arms, so many fawning smiles. Like an old photographic negative, everything was blurred. At the last came a scene that was sharp and clear and whose colors would never fade: the evening of Double Ten! Everywhere cheers rose up like spring thunder. Everywhere adjutants from headquarters were saluting. Everywhere the fine, polite phrases of Division Commander Hui were heard.

Wishing to remember no more, Mei shook her head, as if to drive away these images. Clearheaded, she stood up and paced slowly around the room. She felt she had run to the top of some cone-shaped object. Heaven knows, she had not intended to run that way. But wouldn't any intelligent, attractive girl in her situation who had met with the same series of coincidences have had to do the same? In playing this dangerous game, she entertained none of the concern that others had felt for her. She trusted the strength of her own legs. She would tolerate no speculation that damaged her self-respect—even if it was offered in a friendly spirit of protectiveness. But she was not devoid of anxiety. How long could she live up there on the top? She wished that someone would come and talk to her about this problem. But all Xu Qijun said was, "I worry about you." How maddening!

In her anger Mei had lost all sense of time. She even forgot that when Xu Qijun had written her letter, she had no idea of the new turn Mei's life had taken. Mei simply assumed that Xu had a low opinion of her, like everyone here—male teachers, female teachers—and that at most she felt a kindly concern for Mei and no more.

"There still isn't a single person who really understands me!" This sense of despair began churning violently in Mei's mind. She paced the room more quickly. Then, suddenly smiling as if she had forgotten all her troubles, she left her room and went looking for Zhang Yifang to have a chat.

According to Mei's detached observations over several days, Zhang Yifang was still the most deserving of being called a friend. She did not harbor—or at least had not revealed—the prevailing attitude of concern that Mei might do something bad. But for some reason, the normally lively Zhang Yifang had recently begun to look worn out and depressed. Whenever she lay sprawled out on her bed and she saw Mei enter her room, she blinked her eyes in recognition but said nothing. Before her was a pile of letters covered with stamps.

"Are you busy?" Mei asked casually as she seated herself in a chair by the window. She could not avoid a sideward glance at the pile of letters next to Zhang Yifang. They were obviously all express letters, and none of them appeared to have been opened.

Zhang Yifang smiled and shook her head in a passive gesture of welcome. Mei watched the clouds outside the window meander across the sky like white sheep, then added slowly, "Aren't we all supposed to be going to Mount Zhong tonight to have dinner and to view the full moon? But it's getting so cloudy. I'm afraid it won't be possible."

"I'm not going!"

"Why? How can *you* not go? This was Mr. Lu's idea!" Mei involuntarily emphasized the word "you," and although she immediately tried to soften the effect of what she had said with a gentle smile, the damage was already done. Zhang Yifang jumped up as though she had been stuck with a pin and with a tone of urgency refuted Mei: "Why must *I* go? Why is my not going so strange? Mei, you are such a . . . conformist."

Mei looked at Zhang Yifang apologetically, searching for an appropriate way to explain her remarks. But before Mei had a chance, Zhang uttered another extraordinary comment that made Mei's heart leap: "Just because I decided not to go, he threw all these letters in my face. What do you think of that? Isn't it ridiculous?"

These letters? Whose—her letters? Mei suddenly remembered that someone, she could not remember who, had once mentioned that Zhang had sent an express letter to the principal once a week all the way from Nanjing. Until now Mei had always thought it had been gossip started by some busybody, but now here was the proof. She thought she understood now why Zhang Yifang had been so depressed lately, but what could Mei do except offer a look of sympathy?

Zhang smiled again uneasily. She walked over to Mei and said softly, almost to herself, "Who has the patience to read these letters? Might as well rip them up and be done with it!"

"Isn't there another way?" Mei said without thinking. She never expected the reaction she received.

"Another way? I'm tired of hearing that. Do you want me to find one? Hm! No way! Do you want him to find one? Here you see his solution. He hid the letters without even opening them. He falls in love with any girl he sees. While he loves you it's fantastic. He doesn't let you out of his sight. When I said I wasn't going to the dinner party, he practically got down of his knees and cried. Then as soon as he left, he forgot everything and just went looking for a big box to put these express letters in! It's infuriating. People who write express letters are really stupid!"

Having said this, Zhang Yifang could not but laugh. She turned around and lay down on the bed. With a flick of her hand she pushed all the letters onto the floor. One after the other the thick letters fell in a heap on the ground. As each one hit the floor it issued a sound like a feeble sigh, then lay there, immobile.

Mei watched in amazement. In her mind's eye she imagined a worried face, its tear-filled eyes opened wide, gazing at Zhang Yifang on her bed. Then suddenly it moved toward Zhang Yifang and the two faces merged. Zhang Yifang's sparkling dark eyes were indeed moist. This illusion—perhaps it was a reality—moved Mei deeply. She walked slowly toward the bed, pondering what to say, when suddenly the "sincere sentiments" she had been storing up for so long rushed into her mind. Realizing that this was a rare opportunity and unable to think of anything better to say, she began to speak tactfully: "Maybe it won't come to that. But as a third party, I can take only a third party's point of view. Yifang, I assume you've also heard the gossip going around the school. Of course, it's not worth taking to heart. But the truth of the matter is, first, your position here looks strange to people. Second, this is a school dormitory, which in the final analysis is a public place.

"Because we live near each other, a lot of people come to me with strange questions. Each time I warn them not to spread nonsense. People with nothing better to do like to wag their tongues. Lately, I've also become one of their targets, but I don't pay any attention. In any case, what I do can't hurt the school.

"But you two are somewhat different: I think it would be more suitable if you rented a place outside the school. Don't misunderstand me. I sincerely want to be your friend. With you living here, we can talk any time we want. Of course, I prefer that. But we have to take the long view. Please trust me, Yifang. I would never say anything bad about you behind your back."

For a moment all was silent. Zhang Yifang's luminous black eyes remained fixed on Mei. Then Yifang lowered her head and, laughing softly, grabbed Mei's hand and squeezed it tightly, as if to say, "I understand you." By now the yellow light of evening had crept into the small room. A crow stood cawing on the ridge of the roof-top outside the window. Zhang Yifang suddenly stood up and said, "Forget it! I might as well go along to Mount Zhong. It's already getting late."

"It's late. Everybody's ready to leave!" someone echoed from outside. Mei turned around and saw Zhou Pingquan, followed by Principal Lu. The not-very-tall young man was astonished at the sight of the express letters on the floor, and a faint reddish hue rose on his cheeks. Mei stood to the side and smiled.

When they arrived at Mount Zhong, the full moon had already forced its way through the floating clouds. The food and drink brought in from the city filled six baskets borne on poles. Even in the relatively large Tihu pavilion all the teachers and staff of the school, close to thirty people, were squeezed in so tightly they could barely move. Because Zhang Yifang had decided at the last minute to come, Principal Lu was so happy that his raspy voice bellowed almost nonstop throughout the room.

From the start of the party the main topic of conversation was a case of adultery that had recently occurred in the city. Of course, because all present were all in favor of smashing the old Confucian morality, none of them held back. But once they became tipsy, the discussion grew even more uninhibited. The physical education teacher, Pockmark Qian, was said to have seen the "immoral couple" tied naked together, so the physics and chemistry teacher, Wu Xingchuan, urged him to give a full report. Four or five people grabbed Pockmark Qian and shouted wildly, "If you won't speak you'll have to drink one jug of wine as a penalty. Does everyone agree—agreed?"

"Agreed! Give him three minutes to decide!"

"Just talking about it is no good. He has to act it out! Everyone knows Pockmark Qian is a star performer!"

Acting it out? Interesting! Pockmark Qian's eyes, red with drink, became even more luminous. He laughed wantonly and sneaked a peek at the group of women teachers. But he was greatly disappointed because their previously smiling mouths were now tightly shut. Moreover, he had not heard anyone clap at the suggestion that he "act it out." "Oh, that bunch of hypocrites! Those phonies!" Pockmark Qian thought angrily. Without being aware of it, he picked up his wine cup and downed a large mouthful.

Li Wuji happened to be sitting next to Pockmark Qian. He sneered and said in a low voice, "It's not even been three minutes! Are you paying your fine already?"

"Besides, you have to drink at least a jugful!" Wu Xingchuan added, reaching over to snatch Pockmark Qian's cup from him.

"Humph! Only bastards have to pay a penalty by drinking. What's so interesting about talking? Because you all rely on your mouths to earn a living, you should be the ones to talk. Acting is my thing. I won't do the talking. To drink is to admit I'm a bastard! Find someone to act it out with me. Then I'll do it."

At first everyone was shocked; then they burst out laughing. Immensely pleased with himself, Pockmark's gaping drunken eyes prowled in the direction of the red lips and soft breasts. Each pockmark on his face glistened as though it had been rubbed with oil. At last Principal Lu said sternly, "Whose idea was it to act it out? Let that person be his partner."

No one remembered clearly who it was, but everyone began shouting the name of anyone they thought might have made the suggestion. Those whose names were called yelled back in kind. A cacophony of voices collided with each other amidst roars of silly laughter that grew louder and louder like a howling storm. Suddenly someone picked up a chopstick and began drumming madly on the edge of the table. It was Li Wuji. Startled, everyone stopped talking and turned their eyes toward the young man with the disheveled hair. But an authoritative shout from Pockmark Qian once again threw everyone into a crazy mood: "I remember. It was Miss Mei! She suggested it!"

Like an echo there immediately arose random shouts of "Miss Mei" interspersed with strange lecherous noises. A wine cup fell to the floor. A chair overturned. No one paid any attention. It was almost as though the eyes of everyone in the room were focused on the supple body of Miss Mei. The flat-faced Zhao Peishan lowered her head and smiled, seeming to take pleasure in Mei's misfortune.

Mei, however, was unusually calm. She put down the apple she was paring, glanced sharply at the crowd, smiled, and said nothing. Amidst roars of laughter, the shouts of her colleagues fell on her face like drops of rain.

"Everyone has agreed on it, so don't play dumb."

"If you don't perform, you have to drink a penalty of wine!"

"Who says she can drink wine as a penalty? We want her to perform!"

"Perform? Ha-ha-ha, that should be good!"

Several of the more "well-behaved" men said nothing but sat on the sidelines laughing merrily and helping out by hissing as an audience would to hasten the raising of a theater curtain. Some people stamped their feet under the table, the tapping of their shoes increasing the frenzied mood of the group. Suddenly Pockmark Qian let go a wild scream. With both hands he smacked the men seated to either side of him on the back, leaped up onto his chair, and began to shout, "Rah-rah," waving his arms like paddles. Incomprehensible shouts and hoarse laughter filled the room.

About half the group had risen from their seats and gawked with bloodshot eyes, each vying to have his own words heard through the mad confusion. Suddenly from one seat away someone—she did not know whom—placed a hand on Mei's shoulder and shook her, and a cheer shot up from the floor, rattling the dishes and cups on the table.

Zhou Pingquan, who was seated on Mei's left, sighed as she leaned over and said, "They're really wild! Mei, this time you won't be able to escape!"

"Escape what?"

Her response hit the room like a clap of thunder. The clamor stopped abruptly. An exchange of astonished looks seemed to ask, "What did she say?"

Smiling, Mei repeated in clear, round tones, "Escape what? This is an unprecedented undertaking. I'm just sorry there isn't a reporter here to record it all for tomorrow's *New South Sichuan Daily*, to open the eyes of all Lüzhou and let them know how unconventional the behavior of the new man is that he can have such marvelous notions of how to respect women!" Smiling gently, Mei gracefully left her seat and walked outside to the courtyard.

The rays of the full moon seemed to be hanging from the branches of the pine trees. The cold wind blew in gusts. The Tihu pavilion was quiet as a tomb. Gradually the noise from inside returned, but it could no longer compare to the din of a while ago. Were these blustering gentlemen really acting like fools only because they were drunk? Unprecedented deeds would never be accomplished by the likes of them.

On reflection, Mei realized that it was all too laughable, even though she felt a tinge of sadness as well. Were these upstarts riding on the crest of the New Thought Tide worthy of the task of reforming education, of remolding society? They made a living off of "overthrowing the old Confucian morality" just as their ancestors had made a living off of "quoting the Songs and the Analects"* or as our division commander, who "bore the responsibility to support the New Thought," was still living off of warlordism. Mei utterly despised these people. But what about herself? By living among them, wasn't she also just trying to make a living off of something? She could not deny it, but neither did she want to accept reality. She breathed a sigh of despair and thought, "I came to escape, to watch the show!"

But this explanation only made her more upset. Her original goal was not simply to make a living or to watch a show. What ideal, what yearning, had driven her to leave her family? There was no clear, conscious reason, but there was a force that at some point in time had taken possession of her entire soul. Perhaps it was just a recognition of her self-worth; perhaps it was just a quest after the meaning of life that caused her to be discontented with her surroundings and made her charge forward. Right at this moment she was already charging ahead, but everything before her was gray and barren.

These dark thoughts surfaced in Mei's consciousness for only an instant. Less than a yard away from her, a new disorder roared forth from within the Tihu pavilion. The sound of clapping literally forced open the door and rushed out, drawing with it the sounds of laughter and conversation. Mei turned around and before her eyes was the terrified flat face of Zhao Peishan surrounded by groping arms about to envelop her and devour her whole. This time these gentlemen, crazed by drink, had found a target that could not resist. A fiery indignation suddenly exploded in Mei's breast. She charged forward like a warrior rushing to the aid of a comrade. But

*The Book of Songs and the Analects of Confucius were part of the five classics and four books that made up the Confucian canon in traditional China. Together they formed the basis for education and intellectual discourse in the late imperial period.

at the door she bumped into someone. A mop of long hair brushed against her face. Mei knew immediately that it was none other than Li Wuji.

"Don't go in! They've gone crazy in there," Li Wuji said, obstructing the doorway as if to prevent Mei from subjecting herself to any danger.

"Out of my way! Teasing that pathetic creature is going too far!" Mei spat out angrily, her sharp gaze focused on Li Wuji's face. All of this immediately attracted the attention of those inside. Their mouths snapped shut, and only the sound of Zhang Yifang's fatuous laugher reverberated through the air. Zhao Peishan availed herself of this opportunity to escape, but in her haste she bumped into Li Wuji, smashing her large flat face up against the tall Chinese teacher's chest. She quickly recovered her balance, but the roars of laughter coming from inside seemed to startle her again. Suddenly she screamed hysterically and collapsed in the doorway.

Even Mei could not refrain from laughing. As she lifted Zhao Peishan up, Zhou Pingquan and Zhang Yifang also came running over, followed by Principal Lu. Zhao Peishan buried her face in her hands and said nothing, refusing under any circumstances to raise her head.

"There will be no more of this unruliness—no more. Miss Zhao, come inside, come inside, won't you? It'll be all right, I promise," Principal Lu said urgently. Several male teachers who had already crowded into the doorway echoed the principal's sentiments. They hung around playing the role of her defenders until they finally succeeded in getting Zhao Peishan to remove her hands from her face. Only then could they see that the black eyebrow pencil she had applied heavily had been smeared all over her forehead.

Everybody felt overstuffed and exhausted, and before long the entire group returned to the school. Along the way Pockmark Qian resumed his roars of "rah-rah," while the others continued to laugh and talk energetically. Mei, however, felt extremely uncomfortable. She said nothing until they were about to enter the city gate, when she suddenly turned and smiled at Li Wuji; as though she knew that this man, who had been following her like a shadow, had somehow been watching her expression, she addressed him in a whisper, "Don't waste your time writing me anymore of those letters. The surging of life's great wave has forced me to walk the narrow road in front of me. Most likely all I can do is continue to charge forward! You think I am in danger, but it's really Zhao Peishan who is in danger. If I had met you two years earlier, perhaps my answer could have satisfied you. But now, no! It's not because I'm interested in someone else; it's just a simple no! I've made up my mind to wander this world alone!

"Please understand that I am a strong-willed person who likes to walk the road she herself has chosen. Only in this way can our friendship endure forever. Please don't waste your time writing anymore of those letters. Concentrate on studying your history of Chinese literature instead."

Seeing Li Wuji standing there with his head lowered and making no response, Mei's heart softened. But she bit her lip, forced out a bitter laugh, and added softly, "It's too bad I don't have a sister! Otherwise . . . " Suddenly she stopped. As if unwilling to look at anything sad, she turned quickly away and ran ahead to join Zhang Yifang and her group.

Zhao Peishan was whispering something in Zhou Pingquan's ear; when she saw Mei approaching, the conversation stopped abruptly, and the corners of Zhao's eyes revealed a look of suspicion and fear. Zhou Pingquan also had a strange smile on her face as she lowered her head and kept walking. Mei looked at them carefully, then drew up close to Zhang Yifang. As if trying to break through the gloom, Mei laughed and asked, "Do you smell that? It's awful."

"It's probably the stink of sweat. While we were eating a while ago, it got terribly hot. I always sweat."

Mei laughed loudly. She sniffed Zhang Yifang's collar and said in a loud voice, "I don't believe it. I'd heard your sweat was sweet-smelling, but I . . . Why does Zhao Peishan smell so bad?"

The latter part of this sentence was spoken softly, but it shocked Zhang Yifang nonetheless. She leaned toward Mei, looked at her for a moment, then said candidly, "Timid people are always like that. Mei, you needn't concern yourself."

"I am concerned because she seems to be afraid of me. I wonder what else has frightened her."

This time it was Zhang Yifang who laughed loudly. She grabbed Mei's hand and squeezed it tightly, then said slowly, "You are precisely what frightens people! Didn't you say it was a pity there wasn't a reporter present? She was afraid you might have gone ahead and done it. She was afraid she'd get dragged into the middle of it and everyone would laugh at her."

Zhou Pingquan, who had been walking a few steps ahead, drew close and added, "Let's get this out in the open. Zhao Peishan felt that tonight's events would influence her reputation. Although it's all over now, she's still afraid you will tell people on the outside. She said that if what happened tonight gets around, she would be too humiliated to teach here anymore."

Her voice was very low and she frequently looked at Zhao Peishan, who was walking anxiously in front of them. A feeling of scorn mixed with pity and a touch of sadness turned Mei's smile to a frown. She laughed coldly, saying nothing, then offered a serious reply: "Is that what she's afraid of? Tell her not to worry. But I can't promise that others won't talk about it."

No more words passed among them. By now they had reached the downtown area to the left of the Number Three Archway. The crowd of male teachers walking ahead of them also maintained a dignified silence, striking an air of "models of virtue." Mei looked up at the moon and moved her legs mechanically forward, choking down a hopeless, cold laugh. She knew the philistines all around her were not worthy of her disdain. At the same time she thought of how, in this strange environment, she had come to be considered a "dangerous figure," everywhere the object of groundless envy and suspicion; she also felt a sense of frustration and despair.

The days passed numbly by. Somehow rumors of the events at Mount Zhong spread and grew among the entire student body. Zhao Peishan's fears became a reality. Perhaps Zhao Peishan was glad things turned out that way, for the frightening rumors did not focus on her alone but were diffused to encompass the whole school. This "confusing the issue" bothered some people.

One afternoon, while Mei was lying on her bed resting, she heard some chattering coming from the next room. She could make out two voices, and from the disconnected words that reached her ears it was obvious that they were discussing the gossip of the past few days. Impatiently Mei jumped up and took several steps over to the connecting wall. The chattering stopped.

Outside the window the sun's rays slanted slightly to the west. Blown by the wind, several autumn leaves floated into the courtyard from the other side of the wall. Mei suddenly remembered she had a date with Miss Yang. She took a quick look through her handbag and was just about to leave when she heard a voice booming from the next room as if intended for her ears: "Wasn't the trouble stirred up from the inside? Of course, it was her! Her reputation was too good to begin with. Within a radius of a hundred li who hasn't heard of the illustrious . . . what does she have to worry about? Dragging everyone down with her is just one of her tricks. I'm really thinking of quitting at once. It's not worth suffering for someone else's bad reputation."

She heard each word distinctly. Moreover, she was certain it was the voice of Mrs. Fan, formerly Zhu Jie. Mei smiled, turned around, and left. She recalled that Zhu Jie was not even present the night of the dinner party. For her to be so angry the rumors must be terrible indeed. How shocked this feeble band of self-proclaimed liberated women must be. Mei suddenly felt a kind of perverse pleasure. Other people's slander of her—their insistence that it was she who started the rumors—did not bother her at all. She was certainly not so shallow as to become angry over something like this.

With these thoughts in mind, Mei walked to the western end of the walkway outside the dormitory. Someone called to her from behind. It was Zhou Pingquan, a stern look on her face. Zhang Yifang was also in Zhou's room. Apparently they, too, were concerned about the rumors. Mei laughed to herself. She entered the room and spoke simply and directly, "From the looks of it you two are also worried about these rumors, aren't you? The best way is not to pay any attention to them! In a few days they'll disappear by themselves."

Zhou Pingquan and Zhang Yifang looked at each other and smiled but said nothing. Nevertheless, Mei could guess from their eyes what they were thinking: "How? I knew all along she'd say that!"

Feeling slightly impatient, Mei added, "No doubt the male teachers are feeling a bit apprehensive as well. If they were so concerned about what people would say, why did they make trouble in the first place?"

"It's not as simple as that." Zhou Pingquan slowly spit out these provocative words.

"Not simple? Sure it is. It all comes down to the fact that there are still people who say that these rumors started inside the school and were spread to the outside and that I am the suspect!"

Mei's anger was beginning to show, so Zhang Yifang had no choice but to explain herself: "Don't misunderstand me. I don't suspect you. And if these were run-of-the-mill rumors I wouldn't even pay any attention to them. But there is a story behind these rumors. The person who made them up had a definite purpose in mind. There's an element of struggle between the old and new in this. People who oppose our school are planning to use this to get rid of us all!"

"It's precisely because they want to get rid of us all that these bizarre rumors are being concocted. Believe it or not, they are saying that we all spent that night at Mount Zhong!" Zhou Pingquan added. Whether out of excitement or nerves, her voice trembled slightly.

Seeing that Zhou had finished, Mei added indifferently, "Is that all? There's nothing special about that. You still should ignore it."

"If someone attacks you, do you ignore that?" Zhou Pingquan countered.

Such moral indignation was unusual for her, but on this occasion the only impression it made on Mei was of disgust. She recalled that when Pockmark Qian was stirring up trouble that night, Zhou was among those sitting on the side egging him on with hisses and shouts. At the time she probably never anticipated the embarrassment she was experiencing now. Mei could not help but smile. She looked sharply at Zhou Pingquan and, as if disinclined to argue anymore, answered with a question of her own: "How about this— do you wait until someone attacks your person before you take any precautions?"

Seeming to not quite understand, Zhou Pingquan opened her eyes wide. Mei laughed and continued, "It's already history, and the rumors have already spread throughout the city. What's the point of getting yourself upset over nothing, of making a big deal out of this? Especially when it was the men who acted irresponsibly in the first place. If anyone is going to set things right, they should be the ones to think up something. Who told them to have such a good time? Excuse me, I have to be going."

After a brief silence, Zhang Yifang suddenly added sternly, "But now it's everybody's problem. We're all part of the same school. We should take the attitude that we must act in solidarity, as though our interests were all the same."

Mei, who had already turned to leave, stopped in her tracks. She glanced at Zhang Yifang's pointy face, which had become very solemn, and said excitedly, "What solidarity? When did we ever feel solidarity? When the men wanted to take liberties with the women, maybe they thought we were one, but when that failed, then we split in two. I completely disagree with such pleasant-sounding phrases. 'Group.' 'Society.' Those words look great on paper or sound wonderful in speeches, but I have received only ostracism from the group and the cold shoulder from society. When I ventured into society, did it welcome me?

"Of course, there were those people in society who put on smiles and tried to get close to me, but in the end they all had ulterior motives. I never asked anyone to agree with me. Nor do I intend to force myself to agree with others. If everyone thought the way I do, this whole thing would never have happened. Even if we had spent the night on Mount Zhong, what business is it of theirs! Excuse me. I really have to be going. We can talk more when I get back."

With a gentle smile still on her lips, Mei hurried out, leaving Zhang Yifang and Zhou Pingquan behind; they frowned and looked at each other, remaining silent for some time. Finally, Zhou Pingquan sighed and said dejectedly, "So it is hopeless to try getting her to look to Miss Yang for a way out."

Zhang Yifang laughed coldly and shook her head. Then suddenly she jumped up and said through clenched teeth, "We'll see!"

"We'll see! Every man for himself. I'm sure the day will come when she will come crashing down in front of us," Zhou Pingquan echoed, perking up again. The conversation now turned to Mei. As if she could not dispel her own unhappiness without berating someone else, Zhou Pingquan recounted, item by item, everything being said about Mei both inside and outside school. She did so with more skill than a student reciting her lessons. In their eager, animated conversation, Mei became an intriguer; a selfish, vile character; a slut—in short, the epitome of shamelessness. Peals of laughter filled the room.

In the midst of this gay conversation a maid came in to ask them to go to the principal's office for a meeting. Both girls pouted, for they were reminded of the reality on which the fate of the whole school rested. Who wanted to go to a dumb meeting just when they were really beginning to enjoy their conversation? But they had to attend.

When they arrived at the principal's office, Pockmark Qian was already barking out his opinions. His short, clipped, incoherent phrases were becoming so unbearable for those present that as the lovely images of the two young women flashed in the doorway, all heads turned and saluted them with their eyes. Wu Xingchuan quite rudely cut off Pockmark Qian and put forward an impromptu proposal: "That's enough of Old Qian's speech. Let's hear Miss Zhou's report on the results of her consultations."

Pockmark Qian did not go along. Face flushed, he said even more loudly, "There's one more thing. It's the county middle school. There's proof. They are, without question, the ones who started the rumors and made the trouble."

"Everything you've said we already know. Please take your seat! Time is precious!" Wu Xingchuan called out loudly. Pockmark Qian thrust out his neck, ready to argue. Fortunately, he was forcibly pulled into his seat by the teacher next to him, thereby giving Miss Zhou a chance to make her contribution in a sweet, delicate tone of voice. With some exaggeration and much cursing, she reported on Mei's attitude, implying that Mei was an accomplice in making up the rumors and was therefore already an enemy of the school.

An unusual silence followed. Not one male teacher expressed any pleasure in Zhou Pingquan's self-satisfied exposé. On the contrary, they seemed to feel sorry for Mei. Moreover, it depressed everyone that Mei, who had played such a leading role in the New Thought Movement, could undergo such a negative transformation. A few minutes later Li Wuji's unhurried voice broke through the silence. In essence what he said was this: From what he could see, Mei had nothing to do with the rumors. Moreover, she was not necessarily unwilling to help out. Even if she had said what Zhou Pingquan reported, she was only letting off steam because from the start she had not approved of the reckless behavior of that night at Mount Zhong. Besides, she herself had been humiliated that night. It was unavoidable that she still had something of the spoiled disposition of a young girl. Her present attitude was at most one of haughtiness, not deliberate opposition or indifference.

Li Wuji's opinion was immediately endorsed by several of the male teachers. After all, if a lovely girl like Mei were ostracized as an enemy, from then on it would be impossible to get close to her. This was something none of the male teachers wanted to happen. They would rest easy only after they had preserved her former position as "one of us."

The history and geography teacher, Chen Juyin, supported Li Wuji even more openly, stating frankly, "I propose that we elect someone to earnestly discuss the matter with Miss Mei one more time."

Zhou Pingquan, her face red with rage, was about to voice her violent opposition when suddenly she heard someone say, "That's too tall an order!" It was Wu Xingchuan.

"At least we should apologize and admit that we got too rowdy with her that night," Wu added.

Unexpectedly, people began to clap and laugh lightheartedly. Unable to bear anymore, Zhou Pingquan looked angrily at Wu Xingchuan and said, "So you want to make up to her, huh? She has nothing but contempt for you rotten bunch of men."

"Not only that, when she gets an idea she sticks with it. When she says she won't do something, she won't do it. Every word of what she just said to us came from the heart. It was certainly not idle grumbling, and it was most particularly not mere haughtiness!"

Seeing that Zhou Pingquan was getting carried away, Zhang Yifang had quickly jumped in as a means of getting the argument back on track.

"Right! It is precisely because Miss Mei is a person who stands up for what she believes, not some muddleheaded type, that I absolutely cannot believe she would express sympathy for those diehard elements on the outside," Li Wuji said in refutation of Zhang Yifang.

"There's no use in discussing it anymore. Let's wait until after we send someone to confer with her," another Chinese teacher named Hu interjected loudly.

"Oh no, oh no! I can't agree to that under any circumstances!" Zhou Pingquan said, wild with anger.

"Suppose for the time being that we let someone go to confer with her. If she is still unwilling, won't you two have won anyway?" a teacher named Tao who was seated across from Zhao Pingquan said in a conciliatory tone. But Zhou Pingquan paid no attention to him.

At that moment all decorum was abandoned. What had been a discussion became a chaotic shouting match, each person saying whatever he or she wished. Principal Lu, who all along had been listening quietly, just stared at one face after the other. Zhao Pei-shan shrank off to a corner of the table for fear that someone might once more recount the events of that night at the Tihu pavilion. Pockmark Qian began shouting commands again. No one listened and no one stopped him. Thus was the tragic fate of this solemn meeting to discuss "the matter of the survival" of the whole school.

It was finally decided that Principal Lu would once again ask Mei what her attitude was and report it at the next meeting. Only then did everyone breathe a sigh of relief, as if a major problem had been solved. With the meeting room calmed down a bit, there should have been other matters to discuss. But the dinner bell rang and no one wanted to sit any longer, so the meeting was adjourned.

After dinner Li Wuji, his head hanging low, lingered beneath the *wutong* trees in front of the school gate. With a swooshing sound, the wind swept away the last remaining *wutong* leaves. All else was silent. He glanced frequently at his wristwatch and looked down the stone path that threaded its way from the school gate through clusters of humble homes. He was filled with confused emotions, but not one of them remained in his mind for more than a few minutes. The autumn wind blew his disheveled hair over his eyes. Again and again he tossed back his head to flick it away, the motion only intensifying his feeling of light-headedness. He really would have been more comfortable going back to lie down on his bed, but he preferred to stand like this, exposed to the autumn evening wind. Something drove him out of his room and made him come to this spot outside the school gate.

He leaned against a *wutong* tree and peeled away the rough bark of its trunk with his fingernail. He asked himself why he felt so disturbed but quickly rejected each reason that came to mind. But there was something that he kept locked away in the deepest recesses of his heart and that did not even enter his thoughts at this time. Nevertheless, it was precisely this that had caused him to be depressed. He had not yet seen Mei today. Lately he had been exerting a constant effort to keep himself from thinking of her too much. He rallied all his strength to control himself, but in the end all he succeeded in doing was giving himself a case of heart palpitations. At that very moment, in fact, he was again suffering from that affliction.

A gust of wind made him shiver. He moved over to a spot beneath one of the larger trees and continued to struggle against his nervous condition. The cold wind seemed to clear his mind, allowing him to concentrate for a full ten minutes. He was thinking about a short story he had just read when he was suddenly awakened by a loud noise. Two horses galloped toward him and stopped. Beneath the light of the moon he saw the rider of the first horse purse her lips in a smile. It was Mei!

The bodyguard who had escorted her home led the riderless horse away. Mei walked over to Li Wuji and glanced at him warmly. A slight panting sent the sweet smell of alcohol in Li Wuji's direction.

"Who would have thought that you would be standing here? It just so happens that I have something I want to tell you."

Although the smell of the alcohol troubled him a bit, Li Wuji merely nodded his head as usual. It wasn't that he did not like alcohol; it was that he did not like the source of the alcohol. He knew where Mei had just been.

"The rumors about the school have already reached the ears of Division Commander Hui . . . "

"Mei, how about talking about something besides Division Commander Hui?" Li Wuji interrupted. He could bear no more. The mere sound of that name broke his heart.

Mei had never been reprimanded in this way before, but she was not angry. She smiled understandingly and said no more, merely focusing her frank gaze on Li Wuji's face.

"I also have something to say to you. If . . . you . . . " This time Mei nodded her head and smiled. From his hesitant tone Mei guessed that he was about to repeat those words he had uttered more than once before, words she had more than once expressed an unwillingness to hear. Nevertheless, this time she decided to listen patiently.

"If you're drunk I can wait until tomorrow to tell you. . . . You're not the slightest bit drunk? Okay! Then please answer me this: is our school worth preserving or should we just let it go? In other words, is there any point to what we are doing here?"

"What made you suddenly think of that? Oh, you're also worried about the rumors, that there are people who want to use this to take over the school, just as Zhang Yifang and the others have been saying. You people really worry too much. No one can take over your school."

There was a slight quiver in Mei's voice as she spoke these last few words, and her unusual smile made Li Wuji feel awful. He frowned and stared at Mei, the muscles at the corners of his mouth twitching slightly. Mei did not notice. Seeing that he was not going to speak, she continued calmly, "A moment ago I said I had something to tell you, but you wouldn't listen. You're like an old-fashioned father who gets upset when his daughter comes home late. Ha-ha! You don't want to hear anything about Division Commander Hui, but I have to say this. He has already heard these rumors, and he knows that people from the county middle school are behind them. He does not approve of the county middle school. All we have to do is publish a notice refuting the rumors, and he will be able to silence their slanderous remarks. So, you see, is it or is it not the case that no one can take over your school?"

As if trying to avoid any direct response, Li Wuji merely snorted and, as was his habit, tossed back his head to fling the hair off his face a bit. After a while he finally said slowly, "Let's put aside the rumors for the time being. Hypothetically speaking, what do you think of what I just said?"

"I have only ambivalent feelings. I feel if someone else came to do what we are doing, they would not necessarily do a worse job."

"Then you're saying you could support the opposition?"

"Not necessarily support. All I am saying is that basically there's not much difference between us and the opposition."

Li Wuji's face changed color. He never expected to hear anything like this. Even though he was always complaining, and had called his school an "ancient temple" and an "old thing dressed up in new clothes," he would never admit that there was little difference between it and the opposition. He glanced sharply at Mei, then called out as if to echo her, "Not much difference?"

"Yes! Haven't you heard what people are saying on the outside? They say that our curriculum is the same as the county middle school's and that our textbooks are the same as well. The only thing that's different is that our male and female teachers go to Mount Zhong to drink and spend the night.

"Of course, this was meant as an insult, but we ought to take the time to examine ourselves. Besides a new style of relations between the sexes, what is the difference between us and the county middle school? If you say that what we have set up is the new mode of education, isn't theirs, too? We use the Dalton system; so do they. You say we not only have the form but the spirit, too? Okay. Our students are able to doze off in class and secretly write personal letters. We even have students who play cards in class. In reality, there is nothing special about us, except that Pockmark Qian can arrange lanterns on Double Ten."

"And that Miss Mei has access to the divisional headquarters!" Li Wuji added with a malicious laugh. Instantly recovering a dignified demeanor, he continued, "Your criticism is partly correct. But it is precisely because we have a new style of relations between the sexes that the work we do is entirely different from theirs. In setting up a new system of education it's not enough just to switch to a new curriculum. You still need a new life-style to act as a practical example. If you don't have this new life-style, then everything you have done is just for show."

Mei smiled and shook her head, then lightly bit her lip with her pearly white teeth.

"Take you, for example. Without your new philosophy of life, your recent actions would be meaningless, utterly meaningless!"

Mei was stunned. She felt his mocking remarks like the sting of an insect. Her face became flushed, but she still smiled as she replied, "There you go, worrying about me again!"

"I won't dare worry about you again. I just think you really don't place enough value on your own time and energy."

Mei did not respond. In the boundless night air her lovely face, red from drinking, turned pale. Her luminous eyes sparkled as they glided round as though searching for some hope that she could only imagine but could not name. Her small mouth was tightly shut. Li Wuji's words had hurt her deeply. She simply could not fathom how this misunderstanding could have occurred. Was she to be forever alone, forever without someone who understood her? She refused to believe it. But if the day came when she had to believe it, she would not place her trust in anyone.

With these anxieties burning in her soul, Mei stood up straight and said with determination, "What's the use? I've been completely misunderstood."

"I assure you, I have not misunderstood! This is the way I see it: Here we have a young woman. Her brains and beauty are enough to infatuate any man. With her strong will she is also able to manipulate any man. Her penetrating thought has broken through all bonds. Her realization of her rights as a human being has led her to seek all of life's pleasures. She is a new woman, capable of opening up the most satisfying and most comfortable path for her life to follow. But she ends up of no use to anyone and hurting herself to boot."

There was no reply. Mei watched Li Wuji lean his head of long hair back on the trunk of the *wutong* tree as a strange ironic smile appeared at the corners of his mouth. Suddenly a patch of cloud blocked out part of the moon. Everything disappeared in darkness. The sound of Mei's charming laughter rose up and filled the air. Her light-colored clothes cut through the shadows as, like a flash of lightning, she rushed through the main gate of the school.

On returning to her room, Mei went straight to bed. As usual she leaned back on her pillow and read a few pages of a book before going to sleep. On this night it was a translation of Carpenter's *Love's Coming of Age*. The words bumped across Mei's brain like a small cart moving along a gravel road. It was extremely unpleasant, and within a few minutes her head ached. She threw down *Love's Coming of Age* and picked up another book. This time it turned out to be the famous *Three Musketeers*. Naturally this was smooth reading, but once again the meaning of the words escaped her. The only thing that made any impression on her was a series of names—d'Artagnan, Porthos, Aramis, the cardinal. In the end Mei even discarded the *Three Musketeers*. She blew out the kerosene lamp, closed her eyes, and prepared to go to sleep.

For a while a ring of yellow light shimmered before her eyes, then disappeared, only to be followed by all manner of noises. The wind blowing the fallen leaves against the window sounded like a driving rain. Mei could still hear Zhao Peishan puttering about in the next room. There was also a buzzing in Mei's ears, which turned out to be the indistinct sound of people talking. How annoying, these things that disturb a person's sleep. Quite angrily, Mei turned over and buried her face in her pillow.

A suffocating heat drove out the buzzing noises. When she uncovered her face to breath, she heard the clear loud ticking of the watch beside her pillow. She listened for a while, then suddenly thought of her beloved Negro doll with the small clock in his large belly at home in Chengdu. Who knew if this small object was still there? Perhaps it had met with the same fate as its owner! Her thoughts turned to other things connected with her childhood home. She thought of her father. But these memories of the not-too-distant past all seemed like relics of decades ago, leaving only faint traces, like a mist. Her present life was too busy, too changeable. Each day seemed like a year.

The sound of a bugle suddenly interrupted her ruminations. It became clearer and closer. Wasn't that "Quick March?" She saw the troops lined up in columns. Wasn't that Miss Yang tugging her by the hand? In her distracted condition she found herself in the sitting room of the Hui mansion, laughing modestly and refusing to cut off the chignons of the commander's second and third wives. The short, capable division commander sat off to one side strenuously pressing her on.

"I won't hold you responsible if you cut them badly. In the future, when I've bought the equipment, I want them to open a beauty parlor specializing in cutting off women's chignons. I'll ask you to be manager. Ha-ha. I'm not joking. This is what's known as killing two birds with one stone. On the one hand, it will propagate the idea of female haircutting. On the other hand, it will also promote careers for women!"

Then a large tuft of black hair fell from Mei's hand. Her hands felt very agile as the scissors went snip-snip and the hair piled up around her feet like thick layers of straw. She was trapped in a shower of hair! Black, blond, gray, short hairs shot at her like arrows, almost burying her. Mei struggled miserably to climb out of the mass of hair when something else flashed before her eyes. Arranged neatly in front of her were the snow-white heads of the two wives. Division Commander Hui and Miss Yang were stroking the two heads and laughing hysterically.

Mei awoke with a start, the sound of unrestrained laughter still echoing in her ears. It was only a dream! She breathed a sigh of relief and began laughing uncontrollably. Only dreams were that preposterous! That night at the Hui mansion Mei had indeed cut the hair of two of the division commander's wives, but not in such a wild and disorderly manner.

The cold glow of the scattered stars shone in the window. The wind was still howling. There was only the wind. All else was deathly silent.

Several bleak late autumn days followed. Mei began to look engrossed in thought, as though she had been hurt in some way. Her female colleagues—especially Zhou Pingquan—approached her with the same polite aloofness they had when school first started. Overnight, the harmonious atmosphere that had been built up in the women teacher's dormitory over the past few months once again became stiff.

But the exact opposite was true of the men. With the notable exception of Li Wuji, all the others were doubly eager to get friendly with Mei. First there was Principal Lu, who, because of the rumor issue, had a "heart-to-heart talk" with Mei. Then, in turns, Wu Xingchuan, Pockmark Qian, the Chinese teacher named Hu, and the teacher named Tao each sought out an opportunity to chat. At the faculty lounge, the recreation room, in front of the elementary school classrooms, or at the school gate, Mei was constantly being stopped for a few words of idle conversation. Three or four days later one began hearing new expressions such as "anti-Mei" faction (the women teachers) and "pro-Mei" faction (the men teachers), with Li Wuji, the male teacher with the disheveled hair of a girl, the only neutral.

This new phenomenon only disgusted Mei. Her usually gentle, pouting smile gradually took on a cold-blooded air. But she accepted these attentions with pleasure. She could not quite understand what the real motives of this "pro-Mei" faction were. How cowardly they were, this group of philistines. Not one of them dared express to her face how much he wanted her. It was as though they had so much time on their hands they had to form a "pro-Mei" faction as a diversion. Of course, it was even more the case that none of them could be said to understand her.

Nevertheless, the number of idle people increased daily. Even teachers from the so-called opposition at the county middle school joined in the discussions of this star of the city. After Principal Lu published a notice refuting the rumors, several teachers from the county middle school held a gathering with Pockmark Qian and the others to obtain the forgiveness of the other side, then began to "open social intercourse" with Mei. In the end they, too, felt compelled to join the new school of thought!

This sort of toadying behavior on the part of outsiders sparked an unexpected change of events. As though compelled to unite against an attack, Li Wuji could no longer be neutral and the female teachers abandoned their stiff expressions and renewed their contacts with Mei. When Li Wuji finally approached Mei after a week-long bout with his affliction, he was still full of concern for her well-being. Once again strange disarming words emanated from his lips: "I told you once that when the people at the county middle school claim to be adherents of the New Thought it doesn't come from the heart, but you didn't believe me. Now they, too, have an ulterior motive for trying to get close to you.

"Have they come to seduce me? I seem to recall that you once criticized me for refusing to be seduced!" Mei said cleverly, a gentle smile on her face. In her heart she pitied this disheveled-haired man, but she was also annoyed by his timidity and lack of ambition.

"Uh, uh. No. They've heard certain rumors, so they've come to make contact with you before anything happens."

"What rumors?"

"I don't know if they're true or false. But there are a number of people who are saying that it's already been decided that you will be named principal of the county middle school for next term."

Mei laughed hysterically. Could people possibly be saying such things? Gossips are certainly not lacking in imagination. The smile disappeared from her face as she said severely, "That was only a joke someone made in the drawing room of the Hui mansion. And they took it seriously! Let me tell you what really happened. That day—the same day you all met to argue whether I was an enemy— Miss Yang brought up the subject of the secret struggle between this school and the county middle school. Division Commander

Hui casually said something along those lines, and no one paid it any attention. Whoever thought it would turn into a rumor?"

"If it were true, what would you do?"

Mei stared at Li Wuji for some time, then without replying smiled and walked away.

Nevertheless, every day the rumors spread farther. As a result, Mei was burdened by even more socializing and was surrounded by even more flattery. As though buffeted by huge waves, Mei felt so jolted that she lost all sense of herself. The school even considered setting up a special reception room for Mei as there were so many visitors and invitations. Not only were there people from educational circles; there were battalion commanders from the army and section chiefs from the Daoyi Prefectural Commissioner's Office. There were even some unrelated ordinary people who could just as well have waited on the long benches of the Popular Lecture Society to hear Mei's twice weekly talk. During that period Mei wrote the following in a letter to Xu Qijun:

There's nothing I can do. Fate has pushed me to walk this ridiculous road. All I can do is accept my fate and go forward. But it is still the same old me: nothing has been added and nothing has been taken away! I am really not worried nor am I afraid. I am just a bit confused. Sister Qi, I simply don't know how I am finally going to get down off the tip of this cone. I also don't understand why no one else has come along who can move me like Wei Yu did. Maybe there is such a person. Maybe he is watching me daily. But my heart has already turned hard, turned numb. Maybe a hard, numb heart is better. This is the third thing I don't understand. I really believe that only if the flames at the core of the earth shot out and melted this world would that which is hard become soft and that which is numb come to life again.

It was particularly at night, when all was still and she lay on the bed limp from exhaustion like a soldier returned from battle, that these thoughts would rush into her mind and keep her from going to sleep. And each time her head would break out in a sweat, and the thoughts would be driven away by a hideous, contorted grin. Then, the next day, the wheel of life would roll on as before.

It was nearly winter vacation. The pro-Mei faction was becoming increasingly involved with the issue of who would be the county middle school principal when something suddenly occurred that diverted everyone's attention. Zhang Yifang received several anonymous letters. They did not seem to have been written as a joke, and the atmosphere in the women teacher's dormitory became unusually tense.

As it happened, during those few days Mei had been occupied outside of school. Except for returning at night to sleep, she spent very little time at the dormitory. Occurring at just this time, her activities naturally became a topic of conversation and the focus of suspicion. One afternoon Mei dashed out as soon as she finished class. She did not even notice Zhou Pingquan and Zhang Yifang standing to one side exchanging knowing looks. Seeing that Mei was out of sight, Zhou Pingquan scowled and said softly, "Look at what a hurry she's in. My suspicions can't be wrong." Zhang Yifang's expression changed slightly, but she still smiled, feigning indifference as she slowly replied, "But why should she? She has nothing to gain from it. Anyway, a few anonymous letters wouldn't be enough to stir up too much trouble."

"The trouble comes later. How do you know she has nothing to gain? On the outside she's always laughing; everyone is her good friend—wasn't she always saying, 'I really want to be your friend?' But in her heart . . . ! I've got her all figured out. She doesn't forget anything. During the county middle school incident we all opposed her behind her back. Do you think she doesn't know that? Someone must have told her already. She was born with good looks, so men like to be used by her."

Zhou Pingquan suddenly stopped talking and jerked her head as though she were pointing out a group of elementary school students playing ball nearby off to the left. But Zhang Yifang paid no attention to them. She glanced in their direction and said angrily, "Use? People are also using her." But when she turned back she was startled. Her face reddened. Standing before her was none other than Mei herself.

The lovely woman smiled candidly and handed Zhang Yifang a piece of paper. It was covered in mimeographed characters and contained one line in large print that read, "The romantic adventures of women teachers." Zhang Yifang's heart pounded. This was exactly the same as the anonymous letters she had received several days ago.

Silence blanketed the three women. Strange looks were all that passed among them. Finally, Zhou Pingquan patted Mei on the back and said affectionately, "Good sister. You've really gone to a lot of trouble. Did you find it somewhere?"

"The reception room is full of them! A pile this high. I'm told they were left at the school gate this morning."

"I saw someone up to something there! Everyone knows who it is. If he wants to make trouble, why doesn't he stand up and show his face? Why does he have to carry out his dirty tricks in secret?" Zhang Yifang cursed, ripping up the piece of paper in her hand.

"It's very common for a principal and a teacher to fall in love. Besides, it wasn't any big secret. Everybody knew already. Was it worth using it as a weapon? Mei, you must know who the trouble-maker is," Zhou Pingquan quickly interjected. Seeing that Mei was somewhat uncomfortable, Zhou accompanied her words with a smile calculated to make Mei even more uneasy.

Mei responded with a smile of her own, glanced quickly at Zhang Yifang, and said indifferently, "How would I know? In any case, all that matters is that he himself knows. It's no big deal. But if I should see any more of these, I'll bring them to you."

Mei departed, leaving one last laugh in her wake. Of course, she could see the expressions on Zhou Pingquan's and Zhang Yifang's faces, and the implications of what they said were very clear. Once again they suspected her. It was as though she were a totally evil creature. Whenever there was trouble she had to take the blame! The more she thought about it, the angrier she became. She was arrogant by nature. The more people opposed her, the more she opposed them. As long as people dealt with her honestly, she was willing to make sacrifices. But she could not bear to see her good-will abused like this. She was not willing to stoop to making expla-nations to get their forgiveness. As long as she felt she had done no wrong, she absolutely would not give in. She would resist! This spirit of resistance, this determination, excited her. The time for calm deliberation was past.

Bursting with anger, Mei hurried across the busy streets toward the Hui mansion. Division Commander Hui had wanted to hire Mei as a tutor for his children. The day before yesterday, when Miss Yang had come to ask Mei to say yes, it was agreed that she would go today and discuss the details. She had originally been considering the offer, but now she suddenly decided to turn it down. She thought resentfully, "They treat me like a thorn in their sides that they would like to squeeze out. They are not going to get away with it! If it will make them uncomfortable, I'll hang on, no matter what. I'll leave when I feel like it."

As though she had spit out a mouthful of noxious vapors, Mei was now able to relax. But when she arrived at the Hui mansion she was once again disappointed. Everyone in the mansion had gone to Longma Lake. The doorman said that Miss Yang had something to tell Mei and had requested that she join them there. An escort of bodyguards was waiting. After some thought, Mei decided not to go; she turned and headed back to school.

Not wanting to be viewed as timid or lacking in self-confidence, Mei deliberately made a circuit of the whole school. Although there was still a smile on her face, the flames of indignation were burning in her chest. She felt as though everything was going against her. Wherever she went in the school the atmosphere was as oppressive as that which precedes a thunderstorm. She saw suspicion in everyone's eyes, heard derision in everyone's laugh. At last she wandered into the newspaper reading room. There was only one person there. He sat in a dark corner of the room, a large newspaper spread out before him, obstructing his face. Mei picked up a newspaper and had turned over two pages before she realized it was a ten-day-old paper from out of town. She threw it down, stood up lazily, and was about to leave when the person sitting in the dark corner laughed, revealed his face and asked unexpectedly, "Miss Mei, what have you been up to—eh?"

Seeing that it was Wu Xingchuan but being momentarily unable to fathom what he meant, Mei smiled and did not reply.

"You know that . . . 'romantic adventures' thing. They've really been well distributed. They're everywhere. They were the biggest news in the city today. But Miss Mei, when you undertake something of such importance, you really ought to discuss it with your own people. All those fools at the county middle school want to do is use you."

Mei shuddered. What a strange thing to say. She really did not want to hear any more. But a curiosity to know exactly to what extent people were suspicious of her immediately calmed her down. With an equivocal smile, Mei induced Wu Xingchuan to continue.

"Let's be frank. Everyone is against that 'little fawn' and wants to drive her out. There's not one person who does not loathe that self-important manner of hers. If you're willing to do it, we'll all help you. There's one more thing, Miss Mei, a secret that I might as well take this opportunity to tell you. Did she know you before? No! But to us she talked as though you were old friends. Ha, what an odd creature!"*

A short silence followed. His strange words could not alter Mei's gentle and refined demeanor. At first she had listened carefully, but now she felt he had gone far enough. As he also seemed to have finished, she laughed slightly and replied, "Is that all? Thank you. But I don't know what you are talking about."

Mei began to walk away as she was speaking, hoping to make her usual graceful exit. But unexpectedly, Wu Xingchuan came up from behind, tugged at her sleeve, and said urgently, "Of course, that isn't all."

Mei turned and stared intently at him.

"How about us going to the Baohua Restaurant for a meal? I can explain things to you in detail there."

"Great. I already have a date to meet Miss Yang at the Baohua Restaurant tonight."

Wu Xingchuan's face suddenly turned pale. His mouth fell open and he unconsciously loosened his grip on Mei's sleeve, letting his hand drop to his side. Mei held back a smile as she continued, "Then we'll do it some other time—if you really wanted to invite only me."

Not caring whether Wu Xingchuan had anything more to say, Mei dashed out of the reading room and returned to her own room. Something peculiar pressed on her heart so that she did not know whether to laugh or to cry.

That night, when disturbing thoughts came to ravage her mind and left her head covered in sweat and throbbing with pain, biting her lip and forcing a hideous grin were no longer effective. These lingering random thoughts would not disperse so easily! The changes that had taken place in her life during the last few months passed across her mind like a military review, leaving her with one large question: why? She had no answer. But she did have a ready-made response to the question of the nature of her existence during the last few months. Chaotic! It was still chaotic, past and

---

*This is the first instance in the novel where the author uses the masculine form of the third person pronoun to refer to a female character, Zhang Yifang.

present. She felt that her environment would always be in conflict with her self, would never be able to match exactly. If she had found herself in her present environment two years earlier, how wonderful it would have been! Then perhaps she would not have been in such a confused aimless state. But now! Now she had been pushed forward by some invisible force until there was no way to reconcile herself with her present environment. She violently threw off her quilt, letting the cold midnight air pierce her flesh and enter her bones. Afterward, the questions and answers followed one another somewhat more logically in her mind.

"Why do I always feel so contrary? Because the pettiness, vulgarity, and cowardice of everyone here make me despise them. Couldn't I get by just by ignoring them? But their gossip, their suspicions, would always come to disturb my peace of mind. Then shouldn't I leave them? But I can't surrender. It would be as though I were frightened off, as though I had failed."

Mei laughed at herself. Suddenly she shivered. Instinctively she pulled the quilt back over her, tucked her arms and legs close to her body, and thought over and over, "I won't surrender! Must I fail?" She wanted to cast off these questions and get some sleep. But she could not. The question that now stuck in her mind and demanded an answer was the significance of not surrendering. But her exhausted brain could no longer provide a satisfactory response. At last she drifted off to sleep.

The next day when she awoke, the golden rays of the sun were shining directly on the wall outside her window. A warm breeze blew and the weather felt much like that of early spring. The maid brought in a letter from Miss Yang urging Mei again to become a tutor for Division Commander Hui. Sighing deeply, Mei paced the floor in her room. Unconsciously pulling open the door, she glanced out and noticed Zhang Yifang standing beside the walkway railing, her head lowered, lost in thought. Her worried expression immediately drew Mei toward her. Looking somewhat sheepish, Zhang Yifang laughed in the direction of the approaching Mei but said nothing. The two girls stood in silence for several seconds before Mei said, "Yifang, do you really suspect that I would make trouble for you behind your back?"

Zhang Yifang did not answer, merely staring at Mei with cheerless eyes.

"I don't want to argue. Someday you'll understand. But when I see how anxious you are, I think of how I, too, have suffered almost the same kind of embarrassment. I have now decided to leave here and become a tutor. In half a year here I've received nothing but a body full of scars. I don't ever again want to live a life where every day is like a war. Even more, I don't want to become the enemy of someone of whom I was originally fond. Yifang, if you trust me, I still would like to help you out of your present difficulty!"

By the time she spoke these last words, even Mei herself was feeling quite emotional. She grasped Zhang Yifang's hand and looked closely at her. A reddish blush rose in Zhang Yifang's cheeks. At the same time Mei felt the grasp on her own hand tightening. An intoxicating excitement spread over Mei's whole body. Quickly she resumed speaking: "I intruded into your group for no particular reason. Now I'm about to intrude into another group, and I don't know what strange future may await me there. Probably nothing good. Every day I hate Sichuan more. I hope to escape this place in six months at the most, to leave the bumpy paths of Shu* and walk the broad, free roads outside."

Mei spoke these last words softly, muttering to herself. As she stared vacantly into the distance, a smile appeared on her face. At the time she never suspected that she would still have to stumble along the bumpy paths of Shu for two or three more years. Nor did she suspect that in the position of tutor she would have to share the hardships of a hectic military career and that when Division Commander Hui became master of Chengdu, this job as tutor would make her the target of every opportunist seeking access to him. And most of all she never suspected that her good friend Miss Yang, who was now urging Mei to be a tutor, would someday pull a gun on her and that it would only be then that she would flee Sichuan to fulfill the cherished dream of today!

*This is the ancient formal name of Sichuan province.

Chapter Eight

By the end of October people began once again to forget the fear of artillery fire along the Shanghai-Nanjing railway.* It was a bustling Shanghai evening, already quite cold. Mei walked down the street wearing a thin, lined silk jacket. She had just come from the home of a new woman acquaintance and was returning to her own apartment. The autumn wind stroked her body like the icy hand of a goblin. Hunched over as she hurried along, she could not keep from thinking of Chengdu.

Ah, Chengdu! Only its warmth was worth recalling! In the cold wind of this evening, Mei's thought turned to Chengdu for the first time since leaving almost five months ago. A mood approaching sentimental attachment made her depressed. In the last few days a question she could not answer had begun to bother her again: if I don't go back, what shall I do? Her official reason for coming to Shanghai—attendance at that farce of a National Student League conference—was already over. At first she could still use as an excuse to stay here that the war between Hebei and Jiangxi made sailing the Yangzi dangerous. Now the war was over. Yesterday her fellow delegate, Mrs. Wen, had pressed Mei again for her return date. Ugh, that despicable suffragette!

Mei unconsciously turned the corner of Tongfu Street and entered a lane. The bone-piercing cold of the wind was absent here. The light of the street lamps behind her cast a willowy, dark

*The warfare referred to here and elsewere in this chapter was between competing provincially based Chinese military governors commonly referred to in English as warlords.

shadow of Mei on the ground. Stepping on it as she walked, a bitter laugh suddenly arose in Mei's heart. Lately this bitter laugh
had appeared often. It was no different from the laugh with which
she had scorned others in the past. To Mei, the dark shadow before
her was simply another self at whom she ought to laugh. This was
a new, second self that had emerged since her arrival in Shanghai:
a self stripped of self-confidence, an irresolute and hesitant self, a
more feminine self.

She did not know how this self could have become such a dis-
grace. Four months ago, when she had ridden the steamship *Longmao* down river through the Wu gorge, how proud and confident
she had been. She had expected Shanghai society to be vast, complex, all-encompassing, and fast-paced. Here she would find a suitable life-style for herself. She wanted to stand tall among this
boundless sea of humanity. Should she not have thought this way?
Since escaping from her "prison of willow branches," she had really
been quite successful: she had conquered her environment and
had also conquered the defects in her own character. She had attracted numerous men, and she had kicked them out of the way
nonchalantly, as though nothing had happened. No one could move
her heart, yet there wasn't one person whose heart she could not
see through. But in the more than three months she had spent
here in Shanghai, she had felt that the good life she had promised
herself was becoming more and more remote. Moreover, like a fish
out of water, since coming to this place, she had changed only for
the worse. Now all of a sudden there was even a second self causing
trouble for the original Mei.

Full of hate, Mei followed her shadow. She had already entered
an alley and was now standing before someone's front gate. Stopping instinctively, she realized she had taken the wrong road and,
without thinking, had come to the home of a friend. Hesitating for
several seconds, she finally pushed open the door and went in.

There was no one in the drawing room. The faint light of a
kerosene lamp revealed the vulgar decor of a petty merchant
family. The old fisherman with his mouth wide open on the good
luck symbol, which stood by the outermost wooden partition of the
house, seemed to be jeering at Mei. She heard footsteps coming
down the stairs.

"Is that Liang Gangfu?" Mei quickly asked.

Suddenly there was a gust of wind. A huge flame shot up from the kerosene lamp on the square table. Then, seeming to stumble and fall, it receded and died. As though she sensed some evil omen, Mei unconsciously retreated to the courtyard outside the window. She felt terrified for no reason at all. This was the first time she had come here at night, and, on top of that, there were no lights. It was only natural that in this strange house she would feel an even more intense fear of the unknown. She stood there in a daze, forgetting even to speak.

When the lamp had been relit Mei saw clearly that it was indeed Liang Gangfu, and she cheered up again. But the young man stood defiantly by the long windows in the drawing room and seemed unwilling to let Mei back inside. Although his back was to the light and Mei could not see his expression, she was certain that a cold, harsh gaze was focused on her own face. She tensed. She could not guess the meaning of his frigid look.

"So it's you. I can chat with you for ten minutes," Liang Gangfu said softly, turning toward her. Now Mei could see his face clearly. It was as elusively calm as ever. There was a wrinkle in the corner of his tightly closed mouth that resembled, yet was not quite, a smile. His strong, lanky body was infused with the vigor of youth. He was a likable, yet awesome, person. Mei laughed and walked into the drawing room. Gathering up her energy, she slowly replied, "Are you busy? I was only passing by and decided to come in and chat. It won't take more than ten minutes."

Liang Gangfu nodded, sat down in a nearby chair, and picked up and lit a cigarette, puckered his lips, and blew out a stream of pale blue smoke. He waited for Mei to speak.

"That Mrs. Wen came again to urge me to return to Sichuan. She said if I delay any longer, the water will be shallow in the upper reaches of the river, and it will be more difficult. . . . "

Mei spoke these words with deliberate hesitation so as to stimulate discussion. She looked carefully at Liang Gangfu, intentionally stopping on "more difficult," fully expecting to hear the words "Well, are you going or not?" in reply, but none came. She saw quite clearly that Liang Gangfu was still puffing leisurely on his cigarette without a sign of surprise in his expression. For a woman like Mei, who was used to having people pay attention to her, this was, of course, unbearable. Her dual personality suddenly re-emerged and she instantly reverted back to her original self. She shifted to a proud, sharp tone as she continued speaking, "Okay! I've decided to go back! Before I came here, at least I had some illusions about Shanghai, especially when I was on the boat. It's taken me three months here to realize it's not all it's cracked up to be. Of course, it's a cultured metropolis, but it's too vulgar for my tastes.

"People say it's the center of culture. Sure, the large newspaper offices, the large bookstores, and countless universities are all located here. But is that all there is to culture? I absolutely refuse to believe it! All this represents is silver dollars and loose change! The culture of Shanghai is money worship. People around here are all a bit vulgar. Look, you have the good luck symbol of an old fisherman hanging here. Yes, what Shanghai people worship is profit, and it's the profit of the old fisherman who doesn't earn it by his own efforts!* Chengdu may be provincial, but it's not this vulgar yet!"

Mei breathed a sigh of contentment. Once again she felt she was standing tall, looking down on everything, trampling on everything. Unfortunately, her happiness was short-lived. As she listened to Liang Gangfu's reply, her whole body instantly turned icy cold.

"I agree. You'd be better off going back. Shanghai is too complex for you!"

"I don't understand what you mean."

"It's too complicated. You'll get lost. You would even get lost in Chengdu. But at least you'd feel at home."

Mei had never been slighted like this before. Nevertheless, her rage was mixed with hurt. She stared intently at Liang Gangfu, turned on her heel, and left. He did not try to stop her. Watching her retreating figure, he smiled, blew out a puff of smoke, and closed the gate.

The sound of the heavy wooden gate slamming behind her dealt the final blow to the distressed young woman. Mei almost cried. Flying through the streets, she returned to her own building. Its

*The picture of a fisherman is a common one in southern Chinese homes, especially at the New Year. The association with profit derives from the picture's allusion to a pun on the word *youyu*, which means both "Have plenty" and "There are fish!"

owner, Provincial Department Chairman Liu, was in the midst of playing mah-jongg with some guests. Mei stealthily evaded their notice and ran up to her own room.

The reflection of her face in the large mirror looked pale. Like someone examining her own wound, Mei's whole body trembled and she collapsed on the sofa. The sound of tiles and cheerful conversation emanated from the floor below. She could distinctly hear the repeated groans of Mr. Xie, an expert in traditional learning, who was always playing the wrong tile. According to Mr. Xie, he and Mei's father had been "old family friends." Recently, this old master of classical poetry had written several books using vernacular Chinese.

Mei remembered that the first time she had met him here, and they had discussed his friendship with her father, he had made some insightful remarks: "Your esteemed father was too stubborn. Even if he was proud to be a true disciple of Jingyue,* he still should have worn a suit of fashionable clothes. For example, when he examined a patient, it wouldn't have hurt to carry a thermometer and have the patient hold it under his armpit to check his temperature. That would have been the approach of a traditional doctor who used Western learning for practical application.** Then he would surely have done a booming business, and perhaps his misery about his career would not have led him to an early grave.

"Or take me, for instance. The only reason I have been writing in the vernacular lately is that it constitutes a new suit of clothes. Of course, I'm still writing about the classics and the late Zhou schools of thought,† but these are now dressed in a new suit of clothes. People say I am collecting and collating aspects of our national heritage. I'm no longer working on the dregs of our past. Don't laugh. Haven't you been forced to wear a *qipao?*"††

*Jingyue was the courtesy name of the famous Ming period traditional Chinese medical expert Zhang Jiebin.

**This is a reference to the nineteenth-century Chinese slogan "Chinese learning for the essential principles, Western learning for practical application," which was used by late imperial reformers to justify the adoption of Western technology without abandoning the traditional political and ethical foundation of the Chinese state and social order.

†The Zhou dynasty ruled China from 1122 B.C. to 255 B.C.

††A *qipao* is a style of close-fitting dress with a high neck and slit skirt.

As she recalled this conversation, Mei unconsciously glanced at her own light blue *qipao* and began to think of her father, who had died last year, and others she had not seen for a long time. Confused, she asked herself, "Shouldn't I stay, after all? Of course, I would miss my hometown a great deal, but wouldn't I be better off making an all-out effort to get to know my new environment? But I can't continue to live in Department Chairman Liu's home. So where should I move?"

Mei was not happy with her present apartment because it had been recommended by Governor Hui. Everyone here most likely thought of her as the governor's mistress. Besides, the life-style here was so similar to that of Chengdu. She wanted to free herself from the debilitating anxieties of her past, to completely forget the disorder and confusion of her former existence.

But the wound that she had received at Liang Gangfu's home began to cause her pain again. She did not know what it was about her that he despised. In the three months since she had met this fellow provincial at the National Student League convention, had her behavior been so strange? Could it be that she was too friendly or that her frequent visits had made him dislike her?

Things had really changed. In the past men had only looked up to her. Whoever thought that things would now be just the opposite? Could it be that men were so unworthy of her esteem? Maybe not entirely. Liang Gangfu was a bit strange. It was not simply that his personality was cold and harsh. His actions were also unpredictable. It was in trying to deal with his stronger personality that she herself had become weak. It was also her inability to understand his inner mysteries that prevented her from catching hold of him and that left her scorned by him. This was why he was able to hurt her.

Once again Mei scrutinized her face in the mirror. It was still so pale. In her reflection she seemed to find her second self. Her original self cursed resentfully, "You should treat Liang Gangfu with more disdain! You should teach him a lesson and then cast him aside forever. Stand up proudly like you used to and conquer this new environment! Remember what old Mr. Xie said. All the people here have done is put on a suit of more fashionable clothes!"

With these words of encouragement, Mei ran hastily from her room to the drawing room. It was still noisy with the sound of people playing mah-jongg. Amidst the flickering lamplight and disorderly human shadows she had a vague sensation that the dark shadow of her disreputable second self was receding into the background. She ambled over to a large cupboard and took out a bottle of brandy. She gulped down two cups as though she were drinking medicine. Rose-colored clouds drifted before her eyes. She talked and smiled until, like a person floating in a mist, she could hold herself up no longer.

Two days later, on the pretext that she was remaining in Shanghai to study French in preparation for going overseas, Mei asked Mrs. Wen to return to Sichuan alone to report on the results of their trip. At the same time she moved out of Mr. Liu's building and took up temporary residence at the home of old Mr. Xie.

Mei could not locate a French teacher immediately. Therefore, she had nothing to do but while away her time each day visiting friends. Her present apartment was even farther away from Liang Gangfu than her old one. She had deliberately put some distance between them. She wanted to escape his intimidation and recover her self-respect. Mei had become a frequent visitor at the home of a new acquaintance, a woman named Qiu Min. There Mei felt very comfortable, not because she and this dainty, petite, and talkative woman and her considerably older husband saw eye to eye on everything but because Mei thoroughly understood them. On the surface they appeared to be a very loving couple. But Mei soon noticed that Miss Qiu harbored a secret anguish. Being an intelligent woman, Miss Qiu had never openly expressed it, but it was often revealed in the mixture of boasts and complaints that peppered her conversation.

One afternoon Mei had once again gone to Miss Qiu's house and had just pushed open the door when she saw the sober face of Liang Gangfu. This unexpected meeting left Mei speechless, but Liang Gangfu just casually nodded to her. Miss Qiu, who had been standing to one side, acted as though a family skeleton had been exposed and anxiously summoned Liang to the back door. There she talked to him in hushed tones for some time, then put on a terribly serious face and returned to entertain Mei.

"You don't know that person who was just here, do you?" Seeing that Mei wanted to change the subject, Qiu Min continued to press the question. Implicit in it was her fear that Mei might answer, "I know him."

Mei shook her head and smiled. She guessed correctly that Qui Min would now have more to boast about.

"Oh, you don't know him? You don't even know *him?* You and he are from the same place. His name . . . heh, everybody's heard of him. He controls half of Shanghai! He came over the day before yesterday. Ah, that's right, you had just left. It doesn't matter if I tell you. He came looking for Mr. Zhang to discuss important business, but unfortunately, Mr. Zhang has gone out. Luckily, I know a bit about these matters. Miss Mei, look how exhausted I am. First he came; then the children started crying. Phew, I'm going to be busy with this stuff until the day after tomorrow! Say, the day after tomorrow isn't the 7th, is it?"

Qui Min showed unusual restraint, but her eyes bulged as she stared at Mei. She often looked like this when talking enthusiastically. Mei suppressed a smile and, feigning an air of sudden realization, said, "I remember. I've seen him before in some alley near Tongfu Street."

"You must be mistaken. I know he couldn't live in that neighborhood. Liang. . . "Qui Min suddenly stopped, her eyes bulging even more than before.

"You're right. I was only joking."

Mei gently dispelled Qui Min's apprehension with a laugh and changed the subject. Nevertheless, aroused anew, her desires regarding Liang Gangfu gradually increased in strength. She could no longer escape them through idle chatter. Leaving Qiu Min's house, she decided to go to Tongfu Street. The secret she had just inadvertently uncovered was like a set of the latest military equipment for Mei. It helped her reestablish her long-lost self-confidence so as to prepare herself for a future victory.

This time Mei was not able to just push open the front gate of Liang Gangfu's home. She rapped on the door knocker for some time, but no one came out. Mei was about to leave in disappointment when suddenly a human figure flashed by from behind her. A face like a wildcat and a pair of somber eyes instantly evoked something in Mei's memory. Yes. Somewhere she had seen such a face, such a girl, before!

The cat-faced figure laughed first and said softly, "You're Miss Mei."

Time could not alter a person's voice. Mei instantly remembered. Wild with joy, she grabbed the other's hand and showered her with astonished questions: "Huang—it's Huang Yinming, isn't it? I haven't heard from you in three or four years! What are you doing here? When did you arrive? Where are you living now?"

Huang Yinming did not reply. Her somber eyes were fixed on Mei's face. She pulled Mei, bypassing the row of houses on that part of the alley, and entered a back door at the end of the lane. It was to the very building in which Liang Gangfu lived. There was no one in the drawing room, but Huang Yinming led Mei into an attic apartment.

They began chatting noisily. Huang Yinming seized the initiative and began asking Mei what had happened to her since they last met but gave her no opportunity to reply. Mei, who was gradually becoming excited, at first did not take notice of Huang Yinming's conversational strategy. But Mei's own curiosity had given rise to so many questions that they had to come pouring out. Thus, when it came to talking about recent developments in her own life, she turned and urgently asked, "Do you live here? How come I never saw you? Are you still in school? What about your brother?"

"My brother is teaching in Hankou. Ah, I should tell you about my sister-in-law. Since that year—1920 or 1921, I believe—when I brought her to Hankou . . . "

Mei interrupted what she suspected would be a long, drawn-out story and asked the question of immediate importance: "Then you're living alone in Shanghai? A week ago a man named Liang lived in this building!"

"I just moved here. I only rent an attic apartment. There's no one named Liang."

"Then who are you subleasing from?"

"I'm not too clear yet."

Mei smiled and glanced at Huang Yinming. Her answers were evasive, but Mei was already sensitive to her companion's vague way of talking. She could see that there were many small secrets concealed here. The Huang Yinming standing before her now looked a bit older than before. The mischievous, girlish behavior was gone. Her solemn round face revealed an unfathomable calm, not unlike that of Liang Gangfu. Although her eyes, full of experience, were still somber, there was also a glimmer of warmth in them now. In short, she was no longer the old Huang Yinming.

What had not changed were her habit of dominating the conversation and her sharp tone of voice. Mei stood up, turned around, and looked at the simple, crude furnishings of the small room. She then turned back to Huang Yinming, placed her right hand on the younger woman's shoulder, and exclaimed, "Who would have thought that I'd run into you again here, much less that in three or four years the young girl I once knew would have become a different person?"

"You've also changed. You're more beautiful and more charming."

"You're joking again. Yinming, I remember you once said that because you disliked pretense and because you deliberately tried to tear off the masks that people hide behind, you could not live in your father's house. Is that right? I think over the years perhaps this aspect of your temperament has also changed."

"First I want to hear the results of your observations of me."

"I suspect even this has changed. Otherwise, why lie so much to an old friend?"

Huang Yinming arched her eyebrows, then laughed and grabbed Mei's hand and squeezed it tightly, as if to say, "Really? Please forgive me." Mei did not smile. Feeling somewhat misunderstood, she pressed further: "I also remember you saying that you could not bear to have people suspicious of you for no reason, that if you were wronged, you would lose your temper, really lose your temper. I'm the same way. These past few years, everywhere I've gone I've aroused people's suspicions. You'd think I was a person who had nothing better to do than stir up trouble and foment discord. People would never tell me things that were important to them. But Yinming, we're old friends. Please be honest. Have I ever repeated one word of what you or your sister-in-law told me?"

Huang Yinming's expression also became serious, and she replied very sincerely, "Mei, don't look for trouble. I don't distrust you. But your questions are all . . . I have no way to respond to them."

"Don't tell me you 'have no way' to admit there is a Liang Gangfu! Aren't you violating your resolve never to put on false pretenses?"

"When it comes to my personal business, I will never lie. But when it comes to other people's business, or things that pertain to other people, I cannot divulge them to a third party."

"Even if you consider that party to be a reliable friend?"

Huang Yinming smiled but did not reply. After a while she slowly said, "Mei, it's best that you do not involve yourself in things that don't concern you. Someday I may be able to tell you everything, but right now I can't. Let's talk about my sister-in-law, okay?"

"Okay! Your sister-in-law. I gather that she, one, did not become a nun; two, did not commit suicide; and three, did not ask for a divorce."

"Right on all counts. On the way to Hankou I talked her out of all of them."

"Then let's not talk about your sister-in-law."

"But there are other things. . . . "

"But we still won't discuss them. Remember what you said. Don't meddle in things that have nothing to do with you."

Huang Yinming forced a smile. She scrutinized Mei's face, then stood up and shrugged her shoulders. Mei also stood up, bent over to smooth out the wrinkles in her dress, then raised her head and said, "I still have one more question. You don't have to answer if you don't want to. Do you know Miss Qiu Min? If so, what's your opinion of her?"

"I know her. Opinion? She's not a very interesting woman."

Huang Yinming put extra emphasis on the word "woman," as if she were not one herself. But it was a frank and sincere answer, so Mei appeared to be satisfied with it. She took Huang Yinming's hand, squeezed it tightly, and said, "Good-bye." While Huang Yinming went to open the back door, Mei took a peek into the drawing room. The good luck symbol was still hanging on the outer wall, but several chairs were missing and two large piles of paper, which appeared to be printed matter of some kind, now lay on the floor.

In her room at Mr. Xie's house, a letter was waiting for Mei. But as she made her way home, all Mei was hoping for was some sort of magic to lighten her burden a little. What she had just seen and heard pressed on her heart and forced her to recognize that she was despised. Although from her debased position she was able to catch a glimpse of the reality hiding beneath the facade people put forward, she was unable to look squarely in the face of the man she so fervently desired. In her entire life she had never before felt that people could not talk to her seriously, that people found her so untrustworthy. She anxiously asked herself, "Were they really all stronger than she—the feral Huang Yinming, the ghostly Liang Gangfu, even the not-very-interesting Qiu Min? She had some idea of what tricks they were up to and was certainly aware of the existence of such things. So why was it necessary for them to be so secretive and to guard against her as though they were protecting themselves from thieves?

"Fine. You shouldn't think so little of people! Two can play that game. Okay, let's see who is better. You can have your secrets and your activities, and we'll see who gets the upper hand." By the time this idea had made its second round in Mei's mind she was so carried away with joy that she began tapping her brown leather high-heeled shoes on the footboard of the rickshaw in which she was riding. The driver took this to mean that she had reached her destination and pulled over to the curb and stopped. Preoccupied, Mei stepped off, handed the driver the money she had been holding in readiness, and walked hurriedly along the sidewalk.

She continued to think of a way to be more independent so as to participate in the so-called activities of Liang Gangfu and the others. She began to construct castles in the air and then one by one she tore them down. She did not know how to go about this new undertaking. In the past she had never paid much attention to politics. Her past experiences had only trained her to manipulate slightly sex-crazed petty bureaucrats, small politicians, and low-level military men who dared not violate the old moral codes. From their facial expressions and their behavior Mei could read the inner workings of the minds of people like Qiu Min, but she could not sniff out the needs of society from what was reported in the newspapers.

Her steps slowed and she looked around helplessly. Only then did she discover to her surprise that the place where she stood was still one streetcar stop away from Pengju Lane, where she lived.

Mei entered her room still in this gloomy frame of mind. The first thing that she saw was the letter that had been waiting for her. She picked it up and glanced at it, then immediately put it down. It was a letter from Xu Qijun in Nanjing, a letter that had no power to alleviate her current depression.

Nevertheless, her thoughts turned to Xu Qijun, and Mei recalled their reunion more than three months ago when the steamship carrying her here had stopped in Nanjing. She particularly remembered the late-night conversation they had had at the Xiaguan Hotel. At that time the clouds of war between Jiangsu and Zhejiang were forming up and down the Shanghai-Nanjing railroad. On the streets of Nanjing everyone was speculating when war would break out. Even Xu Qijun was talking about the political situation. Hadn't she asked how the "anti-Zhili" clique had been able to secretly operate in Nanjing? And hadn't Mei said that she was not interested in politics and even made a flippant comment like, "Gentleman socialize but do not form factions"? But now her attitude had changed. Could it be that the dim sound of gunfire that she had heard two months ago had set her blood boiling?

Unable to suppress a bitter smile, Mei casually picked up Xu Qijun's letter and tore it open. How strange! How could this be! Mei rubbed her eyes in disbelief. She read the letter over from the beginning. There it was in black and white:

Yesterday I ran into that Li Wuji you once mentioned. You said you couldn't stand him because he used to pester you, right? Now he's changed. He's no longer interested in love. He says it's meaningless. Now he's involved in the political movement. Maybe this will make you hate him even more. But he knew you were in Shanghai and insisted that I give him your address. I'm sorry; I've already told it to him.

Mei tossed the letter aside and lay down on the bed to think. What political movement? Maybe he belonged to the same party as Liang Gangfu and the others. Could that prissy Li Wuji be one of them? Mei really felt that her idea of remaining independent was correct. The people she despised were all on that side. They all belonged to one group, and they all viewed her as insignificant and untrustworthy. That's how topsy-turvy and ridiculous this world was! But Mei's indignation emboldened her. Liang Gangfu, whom she had heretofore respected and loved, now became foul and contemptible in her eyes.

Gradually Mei worked out a program of action for herself. She would be careful to read the newspaper, make contacts with people in all political groups, and put on arrogant airs in front of Liang Gangfu and his crowd. Her feeling of repugnance toward them was very strong, so she considered this third item to be essential.

At dinnertime Mei discovered that there was a fourth item on her program. Mr. Xie had found her a French teacher, an old Catholic priest. Mei had no choice but to agree to give her mornings over to her French teacher. She had no idea, however, that this would also mean she could not go out at night. The old priest was much too strict. Every day he forced her to memorize new vocabulary.

Mei was so busy that all her plans went awry. But the days did pass more quickly. November was soon half over. Every day the newspapers reported calls for the opening of a "national assembly." Suddenly organizations no one had ever heard of began to spring up. Today someone would issue a manifesto; the next day someone else would send a telegram to the government. It was as though the heart of every person in Shanghai beat for the sake of the National Assembly.

Mei was no longer in the mood to practice her *le, la, les.* Initially, she lied about her intention to continue her studies and gave the old priest ten days off. As if to make up for lost time, Mei spent the whole of each day running around. She started by looking for Huang Yinming but could not find her. New people had moved into her building, all of them young people whom Mei had seen before but did not know personally. Moreover, a tin-plated sign had now been placed on the front gate that said something like "Provisional Office of the All Shanghai Alliance for the Promotion of a National Assembly."

The next morning, however, when Mei joined the people gathered by the pier on the bund at French Boulevard to watch the crowd welcoming the prime minister, she ran into Huang Yinming. This wildcat of a young woman was wearing a long gray cotton gown and distributing a thick pile of leaflets among the crowd.

"Yinming! What are you up to?" Mei edged up behind Huang Yinming and called out softly.

Huang Yinming looked startled and quickly turned around. Seeing it was Mei, she responded with a smile.

"It's been five or six days since I last saw you. Have you moved again? How come you didn't even let me know?"

"I haven't moved! Have you been to Tongfu Street?"

"I was there yesterday. There were quite a few people there, but everyone I asked said they didn't know you. I didn't go upstairs."

"Oh, they only rent the drawing room on the ground floor. They don't know who lives upstairs."

"Don't tell me their business has nothing to do with you?"

A round of applause suddenly burst forth from the crowd before them, interspersed with indistinct shouts. Huang Yinming did not reply to Mei's question but merely stretched her neck and squeezed ahead through the crowd. The sound of a steam whistle could now be heard. Very skillfully, Mei looked out through a crack in the forest of necks in front of her and saw a small steamship already edging up to the pier. By the iron railing at the entrance to the pier, the upper body of a man suddenly emerged above the throng of bobbing heads. He had a fat brown face and two pudgy hands sticking out of his large broad sleeves. He was holding a piece of red paper and shouting something in the tone of a government official. But all that could be heard were the words "Long Live."

Unable to endure the crush of the crowd, Mei fought her way out and stood on the south side of the street. When she looked back, several Annamese policemen were already dispersing the noisy mob. As the crowd broke up, people ran to the south side of the street. Mei let this human tide sweep her along with them. She had gone about the distance of one streetcar stop before she took a good look at the people pressing against her shoulders and noticed Liang Gangfu off to the left. The strange young man was looking at her, a smile on his face.

They walked side by side, neither of them saying a word. Before long they came to a fork in the road. Their route had already diverged from that of the crowd that had been dispersed at the pier, leaving only the two of them. Liang Gangfu turned to go his own way but looked back and said to Mei, "I haven't seen you for some time. I guess you've started going to school."

"No. I'm free every day."

"What are you planning to do right now?"

"Just walk around. Nothing special. But . . . I ran into Huang Yinming on the pier. In the crush of the crowd we got separated. I'm afraid she may still be there looking for me."

"She won't be looking for you. She still has things to do."

"Then shall we say good-bye? I'm sure you're also busy."

Liang Gangfu smiled again but did not answer. He lowered his head and walked a few steps, then suddenly said firmly, "Let's go to my place and sit a while!"

Mei glanced at him knowingly, and together they caught up with a streetcar that was about to start off. The streetcar was traveling west. When it paused at the next stop, some people threw a pile of papers in through the window. By chance they landed on Mei. She picked up a sheet to take a look. It was another leaflet about the National Assembly, and on the bottom was written the words "All Shanghai Alliance for the Promotion of a National Assembly." The building on Tongfu Street flashed across Mei's mind. She looked up at Liang Gangfu and noticed the trace of a smile on his lips, as though he had just greeted an acquaintance. The memory of the way Qiu Min had played up Liang Gangfu began tugging at her thoughts. Could it be that the lanky young man before her really was not to be treated so lightly? Mei had to consider how to deal with him.

Before she had finished thinking about this, Liang Gangfu called to her to get off the streetcar. They walked into a very clean, broad lane and stopped before a gate in a brand-new stone wall. Mei caught a glimpse of a wooden sign on the gate. Apparently the building inside housed the office of a lawyer.

Liang Gangfu lived in a side room upstairs. It was very tastefully, though somewhat extravagantly, decorated: Western-style furniture, a shelf full of books. There was no "good luck picture," but a copperplate etching of a naked woman, in an exquisite wooden frame, sat on the table.

"I've just moved in, so please have a look around."

Mei was surprised by the way he had broken the ice. Liang Gangfu had abandoned his usually cold, harsh manner and had become lighthearted. Moreover, at his instigation, conditions back home, which they had rarely discussed in the past, became the main topic of conversation. Gradually their discussion returned to Shanghai. Liang Gangfu lit his second cigarette and asked seriously, "If you're not going back to Sichuan, what will you do in Shanghai? Do you have any plans, any course of action, in mind?"

"I thought I told you. I've already hired a tutor to practice French, and I plan to go abroad."

Liang Gangfu laughed, raising his eyebrows. A look of disbelief appeared on his face. He inhaled a mouthful of smoke and said slowly, "I do believe you. But the illustrious Miss Mei hasn't become so wrapped up in her books that she has completely forgotten she is a member of the movement, has she?"

A faint blush passed over Mei's cheeks. She sensed that he was not finished ridiculing her, that at least he hoped to ferret out her true intentions. Therefore, she deliberately answered his question with another question: "Then is it your opinion that I am going overseas to study simply because I have nothing better to do?"

"Not entirely. But you can't deny that women who do so have ulterior motives—for example, to get a degree so as to become the wife of an ambassador one day or some sort of celebrity. But that's not your style. Maybe it's because you scorn such things. Maybe it's because you don't have the patience. Or maybe it's because you don't like to raise your hopes too high. In any case, this course of action does not go along with your present state of mind."

Mei replied with a long seductive smile, then withdrew the smile and said with apparent sincerity, "As long as you feel that way, I'll give up the idea. I'll just stay in Shanghai and watch all of you play this new game of yours."

Mei put special emphasis on the words "all of you," fully expecting to see the calm expression disappear from Liang Gangfu's narrow eyes. What she did not expect was the response which followed.

"You should be saying that you are going to join in our new game. Don't be so dispassionate."

Mei nodded frankly, sensing that it would be futile to rehash it all again. A diplomatically phrased explanation from Liang Gangfu followed. Mei distilled two main points from what she heard: Liang Gangfu's female friends, among whom was Huang Yinming, planned to organize a woman's association and were in the process of looking for members. Moreover, right now the most important task of the women's association was participation in the National Assembly movement. Therefore, they wanted women such as Mei, who had acquaintances in many different quarters and who were old hands at dealing with bureaucrats and politicians, to help them.

Seeing that Liang Gangfu had nothing more to say, Mei casually asked, "I gather Qui Min is also a member?" She meant nothing in particular by this remark.

"Who? Oh, Zhang Dacheng's wife? Yes, she's one. See, you already know two people. Later when you meet everyone, I'm sure there will be others whom you know."

"Okay. Until later then. Huang Yinming knows where I live. She can come and look me up."

Mei stood up as she spoke, glanced once more around the magnificent room, and left. It was nearly noon. The streets were alive with the usual hustle and bustle of a large city. Mei got into a rickshaw for the ride home. Along the way she saw two children, refugees from north of the Yangzi, who were grabbing each other's pigtails and fighting, trampling a large pile of papers under their muddy feet. A somewhat larger child stood to one side clapping his hands, laughing, and shouting, "Hit 'em. Stomp on it! Stomp it to bits. Nobody'll get 'em." Mei turned to get a better look. The papers seemed to be the same leaflets that were being distributed on the pier two or three hours earlier. Suddenly she became sad. A mood of depression stayed with her all the way home.

That afternoon, Huang Yinming came to see Mei. From the moment Yinming arrived she began talking about the women's association. Apparently already believing Mei to be an insider, Huang Yinming spoke in concrete terms about how to go about organizing, what activities to undertake now, what goals to pursue in the future, and so on. Her openness and enthusiasm made a very good impression on Mei but did not fully dispel the feelings of melancholy that had been aroused on her way home. Mei waited quietly for Huang Yinming to finish, then quickly brought up the scene she had witnessed on the road. There was an obvious tone of hopelessness in her voice.

"We anticipated this. We can't be overly optimistic, expecting that every seed will fall on fertile ground, take root, and sprout. Of course, there will inevitably be losses. Naturally some seeds will fall on sandy soil or will be pecked at by birds. We should bravely assess these losses," Huang Yinming replied enthusiastically. She had heard these words from Liang Gangfu a couple of days earlier, and now, as luck would have it, she had been able to put them to use.

Mei smiled without saying anything.

"You're with us, aren't you? I hope you'll check with Qiu Min tomorrow or the day after. She's in charge of this. I still have things to do so I can't stay. Good-bye."

Qui Min again. Suddenly a feeling of disgust arose from the pit of Mei's stomach. She really wanted to say, "Isn't she the one you called a very uninteresting woman? Why drag her in again?" But in the end Mei restrained herself and merely grabbed Huang Yinming's hand, squeezed it warmly, and, smiling sincerely, said, "I'm always willing to help out where you're concerned."

These quite ordinary words astonished Huang Yinming. She looked at Mei and slowed her steps as though she had something to add. But after glancing at her watch, she smiled and left.

As for Mei, she had absolutely no sense that there was anything startling about what she had said. Therefore, she had not even noticed Huang Yinming's momentary surprise. She was not merely paying lip service to these sentiments. The words came from the heart, and it was her own experience that made her think this way. Everything that had made an impression on her life had been the result of her helping someone or of someone helping her. Nothing had ever made her aware that beyond herself there existed "the group." Had she been aware of it, "the group" would have appeared only as something that oppressed her, the "Second Girl's Normal School faction" that she had run up against when she was a teacher at Lüzhou. Although like anyone else she had often spoken of society, of organizations, to her these terms had always referred to a particular school or government office. She was really unaware of the meaning of the word "group" as applied to them. Even though five or six days ago she had decided to do some group work, had planned to work independently for the political movement, had intended to pit herself against Liang Gangfu and the others, it was a momentary interest. It was an interest that grew out of arrogance, just like her decision in Lüzhou to oppose Principal Lu and Zhang Yifang.

Mei was equally ignorant of solidarity among women. In the past, women had fought against her and slighted her. Therefore, when she accepted Huang Yinming's invitation just now, it had only been because Huang Yinming had been frank with her and because Liang Gangfu had sought her help. Although this young man sometimes annoyed her intensely, more often she missed him and felt an uncontrollable love for him.

In addition, it was her nature to be active, to be forward-looking. She could not stand loneliness. What she had learned from the thought of the May Fourth Movement had been concerned with individualism, personal rights, and freedom of personal development. The little of Tolstoy's thought she had absorbed in the beginning caused her even now to maintain a yearning for the rational life, caused her to long for harmonious relations among people. It was this invisible force that had made her leave Chengdu and had forced her to charge forward with the spirit of a warrior. Her personality as well as the thoughts and experiences she had acquired during her lifetime had made it impossible for her to define her beliefs and had created for her a temperament that, while forever expecting an empty future, continued to charge resolutely forward.

In this complex state of mind, Mei pursued the mission now before her with great interest. She went to see Qiu Min and listened patiently to her half-complaining, half-boasting tirade. Mei also met with the other women. Finally, three or four days later, she assumed responsibility for part of the work.

Mei met daily with Qiu Min. The women's association had not yet formally been established, but Qiu Min had already given herself the title "general manager." No one knew where the title had come from, but she was certainly affecting the airs of a general manager, constantly trying to control the way other people did their work. Now that Mei was committed to the movement, she was not pleased with this phenomenon. Two or three other members felt the same way. Mei had once overheard a Miss Li talking with Miss Wu, "When I see how busy Miss Qiu is, it really upsets me. She's the only capable one. The rest of us are all stupid!"

"But she's a mess, too. Did you hear what she just said? It was totally illogical. It was so confused no one could understand it. I wanted to ask her a few more questions to get things straight, but when I saw how she was shouting herself hoarse, I felt too embarrassed to shoot off my mouth!"

"Oh, you're the one who's stupid. That's why you can't get things straight and think she's confused!" Miss Li said coldly. She turned to sneak a peek at Mei, then faced Miss Wu again and smiled. Obviously they considered Mei to be one of Qiu Min's clique. This was more that Mei could tolerate. A long repressed question fell from her lips: "Exactly who made her general manager?"

Miss Wu and Miss Li stared at Mei in amazement, then said in unison, "You don't know either? Then no one knows."

Mei detected the sarcasm in these words and felt extremely uneasy. But all she could do was smile and leave without saying another word. Mei had a vague sense that someone was manipulating this so-called women's association. She inferred this from remarks that Qiu Min had inadvertently let slip out, such as "This has already been decided," and "That has already been discussed." Naturally, Mei speculated that Liang Gangfu was probably one of the people operating behind the scene. She had once asked Huang Yinming, but that cat-woman replied with only a smile and seemed about to enjoin Mei once again "not to meddle in things that had nothing to do with her." Had Huang Yinming been willing to open up and tell her the whole story, Mei would definitely have added another question: "Why did they select someone as unpopular as Qiu Min?"

The doubts and suspicions that filled Mei's heart did not make her less active but did make her angrier. At the same time her contempt for Qiu Min increased, and a dispute gradually developed between them. Even though it was originally over an extremely trivial matter, Qiu Min insisted on assuming a serious attitude so as to demonstrate that she alone could handle the situation and that no one else would do. This was something Mei could not tolerate. She criticized Qiu Min coldly, whereupon she once again insisted on her own point of view. Her large, stupid eyes bulged like those of a huge goldfish. But after several words of sharp attack from Mei, they were transformed into the eyes of a dead fish, and she returned to a speechless state. All one could see were the red veins protruding from her temples like small earthworms. But rather than eliciting pity from Mei, Qiu Min's predicament made Mei detest her even more.

Despite all this, the work of the women's association continued to zigzag forward, and the time of its formal inauguration neared.

There were also rumors afoot that the masses themselves were coming together spontaneously for a meeting to prepare for the long-awaited National Assembly in Beijing. Of course, the women's association, which was still in the embryonic stages, had to send delegates to participate. But the most urgent task was to see that the association itself was quickly set up. For these reasons, several of the women met again at Qiu Min's home and talked for a long time. As usual, Qiu Min made the opening remarks, jumping around so that no one could make heads or tails out of what she was saying. This was followed by ambivalence from Miss Li and Miss Wu and a sharp and rapid rebuttal from Mei. Several of the others closed their mouths and smiled, and, as usual, the lack of results was interpreted as tacit consent.

As she left Qiu Min's house, Mei ran into Huang Yinming, whom she had not seen for some time. Unexpectedly, Miss Huang was dressed quite well and even seemed to have powdered her face. She called Mei over and chatted with her by the roadside; as they were about to part company, she looked back and asked, "You've progressed very well. I suppose you'll be holding the inaugural meeting soon?"

Mei knew this reference was to the women's association, and its mention rekindled her anxieties. She responded coolly, "If we push things I suppose we can get it off the ground. But how come all you did was sign up but never come over to do any of the work?"

"As long as you people are there it's all right, isn't it?"

"No, it isn't. It isn't all right at all!"

She said this with such seriousness that Huang Yinming had no choice but to turn around and await a detailed explanation. Mei gave a brief account of Qui Min's incompetence and finished up raging with anger: "Everyone is dissatisfied. If you'd come once you'd see. I've been wanting to tell you for a long time, but I haven't seen you. Okay, now you get the picture. In the future I'd appreciate it if you'd come and see for yourself. I'm fed up."

Huang Yinming pondered the situation in silence, then finally said, "You probably should talk to Liang Gangfu about this. It was his idea that Qiu Min be in charge. I don't have the time today. Let's talk about it more tomorrow or the next day."

Mei looked at Huang Yinming, nodded her head, and left. At least she had inadvertently answered one question, but it had given rise to others: If it was Liang Gangfu's idea, could he possibly consider Qiu Min to be a talented person? Could he be that lacking in perception?

The slanting rays of the sun shone on Mei's face, and the wind blew through her lined woolen long coat. As she walked slowly along her thoughts deepened until before she knew it she was home. As soon as she entered the house she heard the sound of Mr. Xie's laughter emanating from the downstairs anteroom that functioned as a drawing room. Mei peeked in, and to her surprise the person who turned around and smiled at her was Li Wuji. His hair was still long and disheveled, but his narrow eyes were more lively than before.

"Ha-ha. Didn't I say she would be back! Lucky for you that you didn't leave."

Mr. Xie tugged at his beard and started laughing again. He then exchanged random words of greeting with Mei and began to make small talk. When Li Wuji mentioned that he had been a newspaper reporter in Nanjing until a month ago, the conversation turned to the recent events along the Shanghai-Nanjing railway and the political situation in general. Mr. Xie suddenly frowned and said, "So, Mr. Li. What you say is entirely correct. What National Assembly? It's really a non-National Assembly. Take me, for instance. You have to admit that I'm part of this nation, right? But for the last month I've only been working on my own 'Critique of Li Bo and Du Fu'*—er, it will soon be finished. When it is, I'd appreciate your opinions. I never asked about the National Assembly and no one asked me about it. And even when my friends and I happen to discuss current events, we never mention this. Would you say that there were many members of this nation who were completely unaware of its existence? What National Assembly? It's nothing more than 'speculation.' 'Speculation,' Mr. Li. Your verdict was entirely correct, entirely correct!"

"Sir, you are absolutely right. That's why our *Lion* weekly is opposed to it!" Li Wuji said proudly, glancing sideways at Mei's face.

"Aha—your paper uses the classical language. Very good. You also print *lushi* poetry.* I haven't written those in a long time. Ah,

*Li Bo (701–752) and Du Fu (712–770) were two of China's greatest lyric poets.

*This is a form of eight-line poetry with five or seven characters in each line arranged in a very strict pattern of tones and rhymes.

but I have a few old ones. I'll get them, if you would be so kind as to evaluate them."

Mr. Xie stood up spryly; said, "Excuse me" several times; and hastened out of the room. Mei could not help smiling. It occurred to her that someone should sew a cloth bag to put that "old work" of Mr. Xie's in. That way he could carry it at his waist, and every time he felt he got along well with someone, he could take it out and ask him to evaluate it. But her ruminations were cut short by an unusual question from Li Wuji: "Mei, I hear you're very active. Is it true?"

Seeing Mei smile without responding, Li Wuji continued, "Just now Mr. Xie said you had been running around all day, so I guessed you must be up to something. Okay. After three or four years apart we have all awoken from our youthful dreams. I hope we aren't on opposite sides. What do you think of our newspaper?"

"What newspaper?"

"*The Awakened Lion.* The latest issue is out. There are several good articles in it," Li Wuji said seriously. He hadn't expected that Mei's impression of the title *The Awakened Lion* would be so hazy. Of course, she had seen such publications. But because they were written in the classical language and had old-fashioned punctuation, which she hated more than anything else, she had never picked one up to read. Now, seeing how Li Wuji was showing off, she could not resist teasing him: "Sorry, I've simply never read it. There is no fated bond between me and creatures such as lions."

Li Wuji was startled. He hastily thrust out his neck, tossed back his disheveled hair, and pressed her urgently: "Then what is your political position. What side are you on? We haven't ended up on opposite sides, have we? Mei, Shanghai is so complicated. Someone could very easily be taken in. There are people with their pockets full of rubles who are in the business of buying young people. They get others to do the work, while they hide out in three-story foreign-style houses and enjoy themselves. They particularly like to exploit women. Mei, maybe you haven't run into these fiends yet. But the time may come when you do, and I'm afraid you won't see their true colors because their faces are so handsome and full of smiles."

Mei impatiently cut off his eloquent argument: "Are you aware of such people? Do you know them?"

"Know? How would I know them?"

"You said their faces were handsome and full of smiles, as though you knew them personally."

"Oh, I was only inferring from the stereotype. People who like to use other people always have big smiles on their faces. Their method of dealing with women is to use love to attract them. Women have no opinions of their own. They'll become whatever their lovers are. So I urge you to go to Nanjing. Here—it's very bad."

Mei burst out laughing, making it impossible for Li Wuji to continue. Outside the drawing room the resounding voice of Mr. Xie chanting poetry could already be heard. He was holding a small volume printed on bamboo paper and bound with thread. Swaying from side to side, he entered and said cheerfully, "A mere plaything, a mere plaything. But simple plaything though it may be, within its pages may be found all the historical anecdotes of the latter part of the Qing dynasty."

Li Wuji now saw that he would not get another opportunity to speak. The sound of Mr. Xie chanting poetry flooded the room. After nodding and praising the poems a dozen times, Li Wuji had to leave. He handed Mei a small piece of paper: "This is my address. I should be in Shanghai at least ten days. Come see me when you have the time."

Dusk fell soon after Li Wuji left. Mei thought of going to see Liang Gangfu, but the talk of rubles, exploitation, love traps—all the strange words that had issued from Li Wuji's lips had failed to depart with him. Instead they pressed heavily on Mei's heart. Confused, she sat down and pondered until, as if suddenly awakened, she shook off the mildew of these random thoughts and decided to go see Liang Gangfu after all. But by then it was too late.

The next morning she had another French lesson. Mei suffered through the hour that she herself had arranged, then left the old priest's house, passing Liang Gangfu's residence along the way. The sky was covered with clouds. It was past ten o'clock. As Mei walked through the black gates on which was hung the lawyer's sign, she saw his maid press her lips together as she smiled perfunctorily at Mei. A sensitivity peculiar to women made Mei suspicious. Her steps became lighter and slower. Mechanically she climbed to the upstairs anteroom. Although the door was closed, she could hear the voice of Liang Gangfu: "You good-for-nothing. Is this what makes you happy—sneaking around, deceiving yourself, and deceiving everyone else?"

"I'll recommend someone to take my place, okay?" This was also spoken by Liang Gangfu. Just then Mei pushed open the door and walked in.

Mei was surprised to discover that the other person in the room was Qiu Min. At first she had given little thought to the words she had heard through the door, but now they suddenly took on a new significance. Mei felt her face tighten, unable to relax, and she looked once again at Qiu Min, whose eyes were bulging like those of a strange man-eating creature about to pounce.

Liang Gangfu was calm, as usual. Summoning Mei to sit down, he continued talking in a very natural tone. "Miss Mei, let me try something out on you. We have a problem here. Feudal thought insists that a woman not serve two husbands. Capitalist society recognizes each party's freedom to divorce and remarry, but prior to divorce, sexual relations outside of marriage must remain clandestine. We tend to look at this as one example of the contradictions in capitalist society, but there is another explanation based on the assumption of the uselessness of women. Even when they are excited by intense sexual desire, they do not have enough courage to get a divorce.

"Just now Miss Qiu was complaining that men were incapable of emulating Liu Xiahui.* She claims that women are highly emotional and cannot resist temptation. I am not a woman, so I cannot offer a judgment. What is your opinion?"

"I don't believe there is such a thing as an irresistible temptation," Mei said with assurance, her eyes focused on Qiu Min.

Perhaps this declaration was too bold or too wide of the subject or too individualistic because the room grew very quiet and no one responded for a moment. Finally, Qiu Min smiled and stood up, returned Mei's suspicious glance, and with a deliberate double meaning said, "The children are probably at home crying right now. I have to go. You two stay here and investigate the problem of temptation and resistance!"

*Liu Xiahui was a virtuous scholar of the Spring and Autumn Period (722–484 B.C.) who was known for his ability to resist temptation by women.

As though she had not heard these harsh words, Mei gazed out the window without moving a muscle. She was considering whether she should still tell Liang Gangfu about the mess the women's association was in. Small wonder that Huang Yinming said Liang Gangfu had done all he could to support Qiu Min. Forget it. "Don't get involved in things that don't concern you." Wasn't this what Huang Yinming was always telling her? Having made up her mind, Mei turned around just in time to see Qiu Min's retreating figure going out the door. Suddenly Qui Min stopped and turned back to the two faces staring at her from inside the room, slammed the door, and laughed as if to say, "That should make things easier for you!"

The room was silent for a while after she left. Liang Gangfu seemed to be searching for the right thing to say. By now Mei had already changed her mind and was considering how to present her case. At last, she began: "Did Qiu Min mention the women's association?"

"Yes. According to her, everything is going very smoothly. Is that true?"

"Of course, it's true. Qui Min is very capable."

"That's a surprise!"

Liang Gangfu's remark itself came as a surprise to Mei. She looked at him before continuing slowly: "Unfortunately, she has two skills she has yet to use: complaining and bragging. If she made use of these, everyone would be even more passive and things would get done even more easily."

"What? More passive? According to her, everyone admires her and is very willing to obey orders. Don't tell me it's all boasts and lies?" Liang Gangfu said as he rose to his feet. Although his voice was still calm, his expression had changed.

"She doesn't necessarily mean to lie. A while ago I heard you say, 'Is that what makes you happy—sneaking around, deceiving yourself, and deceiving everyone else?' Yes, Qiu Min's actions are consistent, whether she's playing around with love or managing the women's association. Of course, this has nothing to do with me. I really didn't have to come here and shoot off my mouth. But I thought I ought to come and let people know I'm not so muddle-headed that I don't know when I'm being used. Thank you for once warning me that Shanghai is too complex. You might get lost. Now

I've had some firsthand experience of that complexity. It really consists of no more than people sneaking around, deceiving each other, and deceiving themselves. To hell with it! Good-bye."

Her anger vented, Mei turned around to leave. She did not want to hear any abusive reply that might diminish her victory. She relaxed. At last she had exacted her revenge for the cold treatment and distrust she had received at Liang Gangfu's home a month ago and for the suffocating contempt that had been directed at her more recently at Qiu Min's.

But as she reached the door, Mei looked back and saw Liang Gangfu standing stiffly in the center of the room. A smile of indifference appeared on his face, without a trace of awkwardness or alarm. The feeling of victory in Mei's heart began to fade. Confused and unsteady, she descended the stairs.

Chapter Nine

It was three days later. The sun's rays came to rest lazily in Huang Yinming's small room as though they, too, were deep in thought. Having just finished a long conversation, the two young women looked quite weary. Mei lowered her head and gazed at the tips of her toes. Her heart was in turmoil. She could not tell if it was a product of pleasure or of excitement, but she did know that the anger that for no reason had come on her yesterday and the day before had dissipated. Now she felt that although Qiu Min was despicable, she was, after all, also worthy of pity. Weren't all people both weak and ambitious? Especially women! When by chance luck and opportunity came together and passion erupted, a woman could stumble blindly into a love affair with a man she did not really like. But at another time, when the same circumstances prevailed, she was just as likely to dig her claws into some other man in the hope of making up for the long absence of love.

Like a nagging itch, these thoughts drove Mei to distraction, until she was awakened by Huang Yinming's critical explanation: "Therefore, I feel that Liang Gangfu's attitude in this regard was not entirely unwarranted. Two years ago everyone was impulsive. The May Fourth Movement offered us two imperatives: to discard all the old dogmas and to rely on our own convictions to create a totally new system of values. But with our empty minds, what could we create? So all we did was follow the impulses of the moment. It was just such an impulse that gave rise to the complicated relationship between Liang Gangfu and Qiu Min two years ago. It was wrong to have kept it from Zhang Dacheng, but, Mei, just think about their state of mind at that time. Did Qiu Min really know Liang Gangfu? She was just tired of Zhang Dacheng's insipid middle-aged nature and hoped to find a little stimulation in a clandestine romance.

"As for Liang Gangfu, he recognized it as a momentary sexual fling. Of course, because he's neither a saint nor a superman, he couldn't resist the enticement of a woman. At the time they probably both felt as if they were in a dream. If it had ended there, perhaps my contempt for Qiu Min could have diminished a bit. But now Liang and Qiu are back together again. Liang Gangfu is no longer the man of impulse he used to be and has adopted a more meaningful way of life. But Qiu Min still wants to hang on him."

Huang Yinming suddenly stood up and took several paces. Her last sentence was spoken with more anger and more concern than would normally have been expected from a third party. Thus, one more complication was added to Mei's confusion. Her eyes followed Huang Yinming's movements, but she said nothing. Huang Yinming turned around, laughed, and continued: "Yes, she's still digging her claws into him. We can sympathize with her past actions, but now she's really becoming loathsome! She's regressing more every day. What a bore! Let's change the subject. You'll continue working for the women's association, won't you?"

Mei smiled and shook her head in reply.

"You still bear a grudge against Qiu Min, don't you? There's no need. The women's association does not belong to Qiu Min. You're not working for her. To take it one step further, it does not belong to you either. It belongs to a human collectivity bigger than any of us. Mei, if you would rather return to Chengdu and live the life you used to live, then it would be useless for me to say anything. But if you want to live a more meaningful life in Shanghai, you are going to have to get rid of these individualistic feelings and opinions," Huang Yinming said as she sat down. A faint red glow of excitement emanated from her somber eyes.

"I just fail to see what great significance there is in all of this for the human collective," Mei objected dryly. There wasn't a hint of dejection or weariness in her voice. On the contrary, it was quite vehement. She raised her long, thin eyebrows slightly, as though she had more to say, but she was cut off by a shout from Huang Yinming. "You say you can't see the significance!"

"That's right! No matter how you look at it, the association is just a bunch of petty housewives and young girls. They keep saying, 'Well done, well done, good, good.' But in their hearts they harbor nothing but sneers and criticisms. The girls and students are like wild rabbits. Not matter how you try to control them, they just keep leaping about. And the more they leap, the more disorderly things become. That's the situation. Even though our work is fundamentally important, it's no longer interesting. I don't like it. Besides, I'm fed up with working with young girls and housewives. I enjoy being active, not sitting around doing nothing. I like to take risks. I like to throw myself into what I am doing. When I was in Sichuan the road I walked was one of countless twists and turns. I never dreamed that when I got here it would still be the same."

"Things you can throw yourself into? That's for the future. The twists and turns you are taking now are there precisely to prepare for a happy future. You say the refined behavior of these young girls and housewives makes you impatient. But in China, where everything is backward, we can't set our hopes too high. In China, if a woman wants to make her contribution to society the only thing she can do is join the woman's movement. All she can do is patiently work to arouse the young girls and housewives."

"And you? Why haven't you joined in?" Mei pounced onto Huang Yinming's final words and refuted her harshly.

Huang Yinming smiled, looked carefully at Mei, and did not answer. Li Wuji's comments about "exploitation" suddenly leaped into Mei's mind. "It is also a form of exploitation," Mei thought, "to push the dull and boring work off on other people." Nevertheless, her intense curiosity prevailed over all the random thoughts that were rushing into her consciousness.

As if to drive these reflections away, Mei shook herself, walked over to Huang Yinming, and said, "I've decided to quit. Please understand. Until yesterday I felt that Qiu Min's methods were all wrong, but now I think she's going about it exactly the right way. Probably the only way to handle young girls and housewives who keep all their objections bottled up inside is to use Qiu Min's brazen authoritarian techniques. That hurried, impatient manner of hers is also well suited to dealing with girl students who, like these, leap about haphazardly like wild rabbits.

"Forget it. I take back everything I said before today. I also want to make a fundamental change in the way I've been living. Since coming to Shanghai I've become a mirror reflecting other people's ideas, not my own. From now on I want to decide things for myself, map out a new itinerary for myself. First I want to move. I don't want to live in the house of that old man from my home province anymore. It's been my experience that whenever I change environments, something new turns up. Yinming, let's look for a place to live together!"

Noticing Huang Yinming's hesitation, Mei pressed further: "You think I can't live frugally like you, don't you?" Huang Yinming smiled but said nothing. The door to the room opened a crack, revealing the face of Liang Gangfu. Mei, who did not see him, continued her questioning: "It's no inconvenience, is it? I've already looked at a place. It's very cheap. Tomorrow or the next day . . ."

Before she could finish, Liang Gangfu was standing coldly before them. Ripples of disgust rose within her breast. Only when they spread to her mouth were they restrained and transformed into an indifferent smile.

"You're just in time. We have a problem we're having trouble solving," Huang Yinming said in an exaggerated tone of voice as she looked at Liang Gangfu. She was very happy to have this opportunity to escape Mei's interrogation.

"Moving? It's a problem but not a difficult one."

"Not moving. Miss Mei wants to quit the women's association. I've just been trying to talk her out of it."

"And what I've just been urging you to do is move in with me," Mei hastily added, unable to resist a smile in the direction of Liang Gangfu.

"That's even easier to take care of. You can make a trade-off."

Smiling in return, Liang Gangfu leaned over, lay down on Huang Yinming's bed, and looked up at the ceiling. Huang Yinming, however, did not smile. She hurriedly reported the opinions Mei had just expressed before Mei could do so herself. Her eyes were fixed on Liang Gangfu like an elementary school student reciting in front of her teacher. Mei smiled and recalled what Huang Yinming had said about Liang Gangfu and Qiu Min's secret affair.

Suddenly her smile vanished. Once again there pounded in her ears Huang Yinming's angry remark, the one that had so exceeded what one would have expected of an outsider. "But Qiu Min still wants to hang on to him." Next, the image of Liang Gangfu sprawled out on Huang Yinming's bed flashed before her eyes. A strange feeling of displeasure, which she, too, as an outsider should not have had, enveloped her like a thin veil of smoke and separated her from the scene before her. She looked at Liang Gangfu's calm expression. She could see Huang Yinming's lips moving but did not hear what she said. Suddenly Liang Gangfu sat up on the bed. His loud, clear voice startled Mei out of her trance: "Great. You two can live together."

"By making a trade-off? You always say that. But this is one situation where the technique of trading conditions can't be applied," Huang Yinming instantly refuted.

"Of course, it wouldn't constitute an exchange of conditions. But as long as Miss Mei has decided on a change of environment, we should help her out."

At first these words sounded agreeable to Mei, but on reconsideration they seemed to contain the subtle implication that she was unsophisticated and lacking in ability. Her happiness dissipated. At that moment Liang Gangfu tossed out a weighty question: "But Miss Mei, what kind of new life did you have in mind?"

Mei pondered his question, unable to give an immediate response. She really had no clear goal. She had never mapped out the contours of her ideal future. She was also in an awkward position because she could not admit that she knew they had a secret and that one of her motives was to spy on them. But she suddenly recalled a long discussion she had had with Li Wuji the second time he had come to call on her. Without bothering to consider their meaning, she borrowed several sentences from that conversation to stall Liang Gangfu: "I can talk only about that in general terms. For example, in the past I opposed the forces of tradition. I ran away from my family, I lived on my own and, finally, I got a formal divorce. On the whole, everything I did was a success, but what earthly good did any of it do for the country? None whatsoever.

"In Sichuan I had no concept of country, but in the few months since I've been here I've gradually begun to understand what it means. The power of the foreigners here has made me feel that as a Chinese I should bear part of the responsibility for making China as wealthy and as powerful as foreign countries. I wish we had a stable government that didn't sell out the country and that our domestic affairs, foreign affairs, education, and industry were on the right track. Then I could put my mind at ease and do what I wanted to do."

Liang Gangfu calmly shook his head, but before he could reply, Huang Yinming's sharp voice cut in: "You expect the people in power to straighten out the country? It won't happen in a lifetime!"

"Of course, I don't mean to stand by with my arms folded and just wait for others to do it. We have to take some of the responsibility for it."

"But Miss Mei, you must remember that the gates to China are not closed. She cannot go about putting her domestic affairs in order in a free and unrestrained manner. Foreigners are constantly present, manipulating the situation. Moreover, if the government in power had not sold out the country, it would itself have collapsed," Liang Gangfu said slowly, knitting his brow and choosing his words with care.

"So if you're hoping for a government that is not made up of traitors, you're dreaming," Huang Yinming interjected.

"Well then, if there's no hope, why are you fighting for the National Assembly?" Mei retorted with emotion.

"Hold on, hear me out. You already know that the ultimate goal of the National Assembly is to establish a government based on the will of the people. If we could establish a true people's government, that would be different. But you can be sure that the foreigners will secretly act to assist traitorous governments, warlords, and bureaucrats and will not allow a genuine people's government to emerge."

"First overthrow imperialism!" Huang Yinming quickly interrupted, taking advantage of a pause in Liang Gangfu's discourse.

"There's one more thing, Miss Mei. You want China to be as wealthy and powerful as foreign countries. Good. If that could be accomplished, I would force myself to endorse it, but only in part. Do you know how the foreign countries acquired their wealth and power? You'll say it's because their industry is developed. You'll say we can also develop our industry. And who shall we call on to develop industry? Oh, we have capitalists. But you mustn't forget that China's capitalists are dependent on the foreigners. How can we expect them to have the courage to resist their foreign masters? They are capable only of relying on the power of the foreigners to squeeze China's common people. All they hope for is that they will be able to keep a few coins to build foreign-style houses in the concession area and take concubines. That is their highest aspiration."

"So if you expect China's capitalists to make a good showing, you're also dreaming," Huang Yinming shouted, as though drawing Liang Gangfu's conclusion for him.

No response came from Mei's corner. Deep in thought, she looked at Liang Gangfu's calm expression. She had not quite resigned herself to losing this debate, but having searched every fiber of her brain, she could not think of an appropriate rejoinder. The grand theories that Li Wuji had offered up to her on making the country wealthy and the army strong had not contained adequate material to refute Liang Gangfu. Her own repository of ideas had never been equipped to deal with these issues. Now all that came to mind were fragmentary expressions: a promising life, a happy future, the old Confucian morality, overthrowing idols, resistance, leaving the family, and going out into the world! But in the current situation, these phrases were clearly useless.

After a few minutes of silence, Mei forced herself to pick up the interrupted thread of the conversation: "In your opinion then, what should we do?"

"It's very complicated. Simply put, we must first expose the fact that the foreigners, our own government, the warlords, the bureaucrats, and the capitalists are all links in the same chain. We must do this to awaken the people. Once the people are awakened, they can become a powerful force."

Suddenly, Liang Gangfu began to hesitate, as though certain misgivings were making it difficult for him to speak openly. This did not escape Mei's sharp eyes. She used the opportunity to pull herself out of her dilemma by changing the topic of conversation. Laughingly, she quickly injected, "But your present activities don't seem to be restricted only to this sphere."

Liang Gangfu smiled, shot a quick glance at Huang Yinming, and replied ambiguously, "Who can predict the course of events? Society is a living thing, constantly in flux. We cannot stipulate rigid steps that must be followed. Neither our society nor our work stands on a blank page of history. There are innumerable visible and invisible forces all around us, dragging us in. As a result, we cannot freely choose when to act or what methods to use. In short, it's very complicated. I can recommend several books for you to read."

As he spoke, Liang Gangfu rose to his feet, apparently about to leave. He added seriously, "There's one more thing, Miss Mei. What made you suddenly think of living with Huang Yinming?"

"I didn't think of it suddenly. I was already sick of living in the house of that classical studies expert, Mr. Xie. I could probably move somewhere by myself, but I also hate being alone. If Huang Yinming is really not interested, then there's nothing else I can do. Are you still in favor of it?" Mei put particular emphasis on this last sentence. Her innate powers of observation had told her that Liang Gangfu had raised the question because of misgivings he had not thought of initially. "Absolutely!" he answered with equal emphasis, then smiled at the two young women and left. After a few minutes of further discussion, Huang Yinming consented to Mei's request.

That night Mei located the Qiqiang Middle School where Li Wuji was staying so as to repay his call and tell him that she was moving. Since returning from Huang Yinming's, Mei had been carefully considering what she and Liang Gangfu had said. Intellectually, she could not accept Liang Gangfu's point of view, although she could not think of any rebuttal. Nevertheless, for some unknown reason, Liang Gangfu attracted her, stirred the love that had lain dormant for so long within the deepest recesses of her heart. She was also aware that, when all was said and done, not only Qiu Min but even Huang Yinming seemed never to have captured the affections of this sober young man. And it was precisely his proud composure that Mei found particularly appealing.

There was no moon, but the light of the stars was brilliant. The street lights shone a pale yellow. At first the dark school building, crouched among rows of private homes that looked like pigeon cages, made a bad impression on Mei. She did not have to come here. The only reason she had made this special trip to report that she was moving was so that people would not suspect her of any clandestine activity. She had always been proud of the fact that she was open and candid.

At last Mei found the gatehouse. She waited for some time before Li Wuji cheerfully emerged, carrying a copy of *The Awakened
Lion*. "This is the most recent issue, the first one off the presses.
Allow me to give it to you so you might have the pleasure of being
one of the first to read it," he said seriously.

Mei accepted it with a smile. She rolled it into a tube, lightly
tapping it on her knee, and brought up the fact that she was planning to move. Without waiting for Mei to finish speaking, Li Wuji
jumped in to volunteer a place. "Very good. I was getting a bit fed
up with the old man's gift of gab. You don't want to go to Nanjing.
Then—okay, I have a couple of friends, a husband and wife, who
live on Beile Street. It's very quiet. You couldn't find a better place
to move to."

"Thank you, but I've already found a place," Mei responded
with a smile, tossing the rolled up copy of *The Awakened Lion*
down on the tea table.

"Will you be living there alone?" he inquired quickly.

"I'll have a companion."

Li Wuji's narrow eyes flashed strangely. As though his leisurely
technique of throwing back his head to get his hair out of his eyes
was no longer suitable in these critical times, he hastily pushed his
long disheveled mop back with both hands. Then he spoke hesitantly, almost to himself, "I suppose it's a girlfriend?"

Having received a cheerful nod of the head from Mei, Li Wuji
heaved a sigh of relief and continued more boisterously, "It's a pity
I'm a bit too late. Otherwise my friends' house would have been
perfect."

He proceeded to ask her the address and the name of the
girlfriend. Having told him, Mei stood up and was about to say
good-bye, but Li was bursting with things he wanted to get off
his chest. He pleaded with Mei to stay: "Look, it's only eight
o'clock. The students here have their own dormitory and the
faculty don't live on campus. So it's very quiet, not like South
Sichuan—for it to be this quiet at South Sichuan, it would have
had to be at least eleven o'clock. It's really still early. Stay and talk
a while, okay?"

Li Wuji spoke with enthusiasm. Unconsciously, he picked up
the rolled copy of *The Awakened Lion* on the tea table. Unrolling
it, he suddenly said with emotion, "Old friends have scattered like

the clouds. Who would have guessed that three or four years later and several thousand li away, I would meet you again?"

Mei could not refrain from sighing, as though echoing his words. The dimly lit guest room before her, the yellowing walls, and the disorderly, tattered furnishings all reminded her of the old school that had so resembled an ancient temple. And the man standing before her, imploring her to stay, was the same man who in the past had pursued her so closely. Was life really just a merry-go-round* twisting and turning but always ending up in the same old rut? Mei lifted her eyes slightly to look at Li Wuji. This tall, effeminate young man had changed. The deeply troubled look of a restless man who did not know what he was after had disappeared beneath his newly acquired wrinkles. And he now displayed the manner of a person who had found something, who believed in something.

Smiling unconsciously, Mei said, "Now that you're involved in politics, life must be much more interesting than when you were a teacher."

"Do you think so? But the person I was three years ago would not necessarily have liked my present way of life. It's true. I often ask myself, 'Is it because circumstances are different, or is it that my own way of thinking has changed?' I've come to the conclusion that it's the latter. It's because my way of thinking has changed that I find my present activities interesting. Mei, in the past three or four years we have both changed. You are no longer the person you used to be either!" Li Wuji said slowly, his eyes focused on Mei's face.

Ha, those eyes! In the moonlight, under the lamplight, how many times had Mei seen those eyes, so full of ardent hope. She felt something stir in her heart, but Li Wuji had already resumed talking, his tone somewhat more hurried: "I still haven't forgotten what you once said. You said that if we had met two years earlier, your answer could have satisfied me. You said it wasn't that you were interested in someone else but that the way you felt at the time—you wanted to make it on your own. So you gave me a simple 'no.' Now three years have passed and we meet once again. I'm certain that during these three years, even though our ways of

*In the original the analogy is to a lantern in which the heat of a candle causes a ring of horses to circle round and round. These were very popular during the Chinese lantern festival, celebrated at the first full moon of the new year.

thinking have changed, we have remained the same people, you and I. Mei, the way you think now, would you still want to give me a simple 'no'? I hope today I can get an answer that will satisfy me."

A deathly silence followed, but it lasted only an instant. Suddenly, Mei's loud, charming laughter shook the whole room and even more fiercely shook Li Wuji's heart. "Ah, again it's love!" she said through the laughter. "I seem to recall Xu Qijun's letter saying you despised love. You said it was 'meaningless.' Isn't that so?"

"Yes. I despise 'meaningless' love—for example, the love that once existed between Lu Keli and Zhang Yifang. But Mei, it's been three years. You and I are still single and now we suddenly run into each other. Think what that means!" Li Wuji spoke these words with great seriousness but also with a great air of mystery. He stood up and turned around as if looking for something. He then sat down again, his eyes riveted on Mei's face.

A slender thread of pity, a ripple of emotion, grew as it swayed within Mei's heart. At the same time the sober face of Liang Gangfu appeared to her in the darkness. Suddenly, with an evil smile, Mei drove them all away and attempted to change the subject: "Are you sure my way of thinking has changed? Even I'm not so sure. But when I get tired of something that I have become overly accustomed to, I do get a desire to look for a new environment. The day before yesterday you said a lot of things about politics. Afterward, quite a few questions came to mind. I don't think I can completely go along with your ideas."

"You don't agree? With what aspects don't you agree?" Li Wuji asked urgently, stretching his neck as though he had just been stabbed.

"I'd like to know how we go about developing industry and commerce."

Apparently not having expected the question to be so simple, Li Wuji laughed. "Oh, is that all? If the fighting within the country ended and if wealthy people invested and if the factories stepped up work for a while, production would increase and everything would be all right, wouldn't it?"

"And the money that's earned wouldn't land in the pockets of the foreigners?" Mei questioned in reply, unconsciously applying the theory she had heard at Liang Gangfu's.

"Who would be willing to give his own money to someone else? The reason millions now flow out of China is that she herself has no industry. It can't be helped. If we could produce everything ourselves, then wouldn't we be able to stand up to the power of the foreigners? Therefore, it's useless to spout empty words about resisting the foreigners. First we have to strengthen ourselves."

Mei smiled. Seeing Li Wuji's enthusiastic and offhanded manner, she couldn't help herself. What Li Wuji had said was not really new to Mei. She seemed to remember reading about such ideas more that ten years earlier in a book with a title like *Primer on Intellectual Discourse*. But they did raise another question, so she asked, "You are also opposed to foreigners, aren't you?"

"Of course! Our slogan is 'Resist the Power of Foreigners.' But we advocate the use of reasonable methods. We are also in favor of distinguishing between the good and the bad. We do not approve of those who oppose all foreigners."

A long discussion ensued. Li Wuji affected the manner of a lecturer, and the more he spoke, the more spirited he became. Mei, however, was beginning to feel somewhat weary. She waited patiently for a break in Li Wuji's fervent tirade and interrupted tersely, "Now I definitely must go. Tomorrow is moving day."

Li Wuji stood up uncomfortably and glanced at the clock hanging on the wall. He then turned back to look at Mei and said, "What time tomorrow? Afternoon? I'll come and help."

Mei tactfully declined Li Wuji's polite offer of assistance, whereupon he offered to escort her back to her apartment. Of course, she had no objections to this. But when they reached the door of the Xie residence and were about to part, Li Wuji grabbed Mei's hand and said with his last ounce of courage, "The day after tomorrow I'll pay a visit to your new home. I trust that in a new place, there will be new hope, Mei!" The light of the door lamp shone down on Li Wuji's face, revealing a slight redness around his eyes and a quiver on his lips. Mei smiled gently, for she could not think of any more appropriate way to react.

Two days passed before Huang Yinming finally found the time to move into the new house with Mei. In the courtyard they picked up a calling card left by Li Wuji. This ardent friend had already come to call the night before. After they had roughly arranged their things, Huang Yinming warned Mei not to make their address "too public." Mei stared in amazement. She hesitated for a while, then said, "It won't hurt to let one person know, will it? If you'd told me earlier that you wanted to keep it a secret, I wouldn't have told him. But now he already knows and he even got here before we did."

"Is he the Li on that calling card?"

Mei nodded, then asked, "Why do you want it kept a secret?"

"I'm just afraid that if we have a lot of visitors we won't get any peace and quiet."

"In that case, this Mr. Li has only come to Shanghai for a visit, and probably won't stop by more than once or twice."

Huang Yinming laughed with relief and dropped the matter. Nevertheless, Mei felt somewhat uneasy. She could tell that Huang Yinming's "fear that she wouldn't get any peace and quiet" had been blurted out without any prior thought. She was still unwilling to be open with Mei. At the same time she recognized that her own behavior could be regarded as indiscreet. "Why have I changed recently? Why have I become so muddleheaded, so lacking in precise plans?" Mei thought downheartedly. Numerous answers came to mind. Because she hadn't had any peace of mind lately. Because she was too eager to steal the spotlight. She wanted other people to look up to her. She wanted to demonstrate her own honesty and openness but instead had become indiscreet. Because she could not fit in with her new environment and the new people it contained. Because she was preoccupied with studying strange new things about the nation, politics, capitalists, industry, and commerce. Because . . . Mei stood up angrily and looked at the odds and ends scattered all over the floor, rushed over and kicked them as though they were the cause of all her troubles.

Mei had trouble sleeping the first night in her new bed. The soft cotton blanket felt like hog bristles, making her feel prickly all over. The wind howled. It was the first northwest wind of the year, the harbinger of the harsh winter to come. As Mei leaned back and listened, a sad and bitter feeling arose in her chest. Her thoughts were forlorn: "This is my twenty-third winter. I have already reached the end of my youth and have undergone many changes in my lifetime, but in the end, in the end, all that remains is my present loneliness! Will I always be alone? In what way am I inferior to other people, in what way have I let people down, that I deserve to be punished in this way?" The tears she had not shed these many years, the tears she had suppressed all the time she had been the object of suspicion and hate and men's attentions, came pouring out all at once.

Lying timidly on the bed, almost holding her breath, Mei could hear even the faintest noises. From downstairs came Huang Yinming's snores. The regularity, the soundness, of the other girl's sleep made Mei even more envious. And why shouldn't she be envious? Other people fit in anywhere. They could soar freely throughout this vast world. But Mei was helpless and alone. No one truly understood her, and no one was willing to try understanding her.

Suddenly the thoughts and feelings she had experienced during the day returned. The long string of questions and answers she had posed to herself once again intruded on her sad mind. In the end she cast all the answers aside. She had to acknowledge the painful truth: it was weakness. She had become weak. That was why she was muddleheaded, why she could not do anything right! She had become weak. That was why she could not restrain the nameless feeling of upheaval in her heart. That was why, although in the past she had been able to arrogantly ignore the men who had surrounded her, now she could not prevent herself from thinking constantly of Liang Gangfu.

As though she had discovered the hidden enemy, Mei became calmer. She no longer tried to sleep. Dazed and drowsy, she merely searched for the reason she had become weak. She did not find it and could conclude only that a new environment that was too complex, too vast, and too strange had swallowed her up, had been responsible for her feelings of insignificance and impotence, and had made her lose her true self. Since coming to Shanghai she had seen many new and, at the same time, incomprehensible things. Yes, incomprehensible! She was no inexperienced young girl. Her life had been far richer and more varied than that of most women. She had always felt she could see through the thoughts and personalities of the characters who inhabited this complex world. But now the woman whom this life of chaos and luxury had made of her could not understand the motivations behind the actions of those around her. Of course, she knew that Liang Gangfu and Huang Yinming were up to something, but she could not comprehend their dedication. What drove them to so earnestly risk their lives? What made such physically undistinguished people appear so extraordinary, so unusually attractive to her? Hadn't she thought again and again to stand tall and cast off the icy Liang Gangfu? When she saw that Huang Yinming was unwilling to live with her, hadn't she been able to convince herself not to beg? Yet an indomitable power had pressed her flat, had forced her to walk over to Liang Gangfu, had forced her to meekly plead with Huang Yinming.

Mei held her head in her hands and thought. One could almost say she prayed. "Ha-ha. You irresistible force, you strange invisible thing. Will you end up helping me achieve my aims, or will you drive me to defeat? All I can do is let you push me on, ever forward, ever forward. All I can do is surrender myself totally to you."

Mei raised her head in thought, in prayer, one could say. Drifting in and out of prayer, she lost all sense of space, lost all track of time. She was soon surrounded by vaguely familiar faces. People were pushing and pulling her. Places she had once visited appeared before her and she saw herself within them acting out a comedy of joy and sorrow, love and hate. Suddenly she heard the deep roar of a steamship and the solemn, hoarse cry of the Yangzi and saw the winding course of the Wuxia Mountains through which it flowed. Then with equal suddenness she was back in this messy room. Huang Yinming was pouting, complaining about Mei's loose tongue and impetuous behavior. How could she have rushed out and told people the minute they had agreed to move? Mei ran toward her to defend herself but tripped over a small suitcase on the floor and fell.

Mei cried out and opened her eyes. The rays of the sun shone down on her head. Through the clamor of the city, like a distant storm, came a strange *po-po* sound as though from a motor car passing right beneath the window. Mei stumbled down the stairs. Huang Yinming was not there. She had already tidied her room. A large piece of white paper spread out on the desk notified Mei that the new maid would be by around eleven o'clock and asked her to stay home to let the maid in. Mei picked up the note and crumpled it in a ball. Leaning against the desk, she picked up a book that happened to be lying there entitled *Marxism and Darwinism.* Both terms were vaguely familiar to her. She flipped through it for a while, then absentmindedly sank into a nearby chair. Her eyes skimmed greedily over the pages until she was distracted by the sound of someone knocking at the door.

The maid arrived and proceeded to monopolize Mei's time with questions about cleaning the rooms, buying the food, preparing the meals, and performing all the other miscellaneous household tasks that needed to be done. Just before noon Huang Yinming returned. After eating lunch, she hastily said a few words and left again. Mei was about to continue reading the book that had unwittingly fallen into her hands when the maid, standing like a shadow beside the door of the drawing room, said something quite extraordinary: "Young Mistress, is there another lodger living upstairs?"

Mei was startled. What a strange form of address, and what a strange question. She returned to her book and merely gritted her teeth and replied, "No."

"Then the person who just ate must be the young master," the maid said even more oddly, but this time with a tone of disbelief. Mei raised her eyebrows, looked up at the servant, and could not help but laugh. Huang Yinming's excessively short hair, her gray cotton-wadded long gown with its overly long sleeves, her somber, expressionless face, did all have the look of a man. Of course, she was Mei's "young master." Forcing herself to stop laughing, Mei answered seriously, "Right. That was the young master. His name is Huang. Just call him Young Master Huang!"

The maid nodded with bewilderment. Her lips moved, but Mei immediately added sternly, "Yours is the little room by the kitchen. Go straighten it up. You're not needed here." Her eyes fell once again on the book. After turning two more pages, she was still giggling to herself.

Li Wuji arrived as the sun was setting. The way the maid addressed Mei struck the young man as very odd. He chatted with Mei for several minutes, then said somewhat awkwardly, "A local publishing house is looking for a woman editor. The terms are pretty good. Mei, as long as you have nothing to do right now, could you please help out for a few days? Of course, if you'd be willing to stay on, that would be even better."

"I'm busy."

"With what? Are you still studying French?"

"I've already given up the idea of studying French. Now I'm studying to be a young mistress," Mei said, smiling gently. The look in Li Wuji's eyes and the tremor on his lips that night beneath the lamp at the door of the Xie house flashed once again before Mei's eyes.

"You're joking again!"

"It's true. Didn't you hear the maid call me Young Mistress?"

Li Wuji forced a smile. Then a look of uncertainty appeared on his face. But Mei had already resumed talking: "I was once a young mistress. Unfortunately, it was in name only. Now I want to learn how to do it for real. The last time we met you said that in the past few years everyone's way of thinking had changed. You can use what I said as a footnote. Very recently, I've begun to feel that there are many things I don't understand and many things that, though right before my eyes, I cannot see. I want to understand what I do not understand and see what I cannot see. I have to start studying everything from scratch. So as long as the maid is calling me Young Mistress, I might as well study that. Or, as another example, last time you talked to me of love. I want to study that, too."

Laughing softly, Mei walked over to the window and gazed up at the sky. A gray cloud floated quickly by, uncovering the red face of the setting sun. It seemed to be laughing, too. When Mei turned back again, she found Li Wuji already standing close beside her, his warm eyes even more aglow.

"I only want to study. When someone is in the middle of learning about something, he cannot answer yes or no. Of course, the study of love is no exception," Mei concluded gently but firmly. She then changed the subject, asking Li Wuji when he planned to return to Nanjing and whether he saw Xu Qijun often. Li Wuji looked disappointed. He replied with a tone of perplexity, never taking his eyes off Mei. Her face conveyed no particular emotion. She still had those same expressive curved brows, those same provocative but innocent eyes, and that lovable but fearsome smile.

"I hope that by the time I return to Shanghai your studies will be over and you can give me a definite reply," Li Wuji sighed and left. Back in the drawing room, the maid was again calling for the young mistress.

Two or three days later Mei began to feel that she was becoming a young mistress in earnest. Huang Yinming was very busy. She was out all day and half the night. Sometimes when she came back late, Mei even had to let her in. The maid frequently took three hours to half a day off, and it seemed logical that the responsibility for watching the house should fall on Mei's shoulders. Fortunately, she still had the book she had just come across to keep her from getting bored, and when she finished that one, there were many others. So she did not really mind if she was stuck in the house for several days.

These books opened up a new universe for Mei and enabled her to temporarily forget her feelings of aimless depression. She began to feel as she had four or five years ago when she first read the books and journals with the word "new" in their titles. She was even able to put out of her mind the pain of waiting to love but finding no one to give her love to.

Then one day Liang Gangfu came to call on the two women. He saw Mei immersed in the books, listened to Huang Yinming recount the joke about the "young mistress," and declared that reading alone was useless, that a philosophy of life and a worldview had to be based on revolutionary struggle in the real world. He also advised them to install a new-style spring lock on the back door, with three keys, one for Huang Yinming, one for Mei, and one for the maid, lest they all become slaves to the house.

Although she did not completely understand what Liang Gangfu had said, Mei found herself following his advice. She often went out walking, even though she had no place to go. Everyone seemed so busy and she was too embarrassed to keep bothering them. Finally, she thought of a way to while away the time. She would learn to ride a bicycle.

Letter writing also consumed a portion of Mei's time. Letters frequently arrived from Li Wuji, and to the end of almost every one was appended the question, "Your studies will soon be over, won't they?" Xu Qijun was not remiss either. Although she lived in Nanjing, her letters were full of news of Guangzhou. This was because her cousin, Xu Ziqiang, was in the military there.

All of this enriched Mei's leisurely life and prevented her from getting too bored. Like a person suffering from a fever who had already passed through the period of delirium, Mei now entered a state of sleepy calm. The curiosity that had prompted her to find out what Huang Yinming and Liang Gangfu were hiding had gradually abated as well. Mei encouraged herself with the words "What is the good of being a mirror that only reflects others?" Besides, she was already becoming aware of what Huang Yinming and her partner were up to. Lately Huang Yinming had not been as busy as before and, deliberately or not, had let on about her affairs while chatting. Mei always listened quietly without expressing an opinion. She was not yet able to formulate a judgment on these matters and was unwilling to treat them lightly.

Only Liang Gangfu's visits brought a feeling of uneasiness and a renewed mood of depression to Mei's calm but unavoidably dull life. Sometimes they would be alone, and just as the conversation was getting interesting, the voice of Li Wuji would suddenly sound faintly in her ears: "Would you still give a simple no?" She would look carefully into Liang Gangfu's eyes, hoping to find something different. But there was nothing. They had even discussed relations between the sexes. Liang Gangfu's eyes had brightened, and, as if joking, he had suddenly asked, "Miss Mei, why don't you tell me about your experiences?"

To Mei his words had an air of sarcasm and disdain. Her reply was very sharp: "They are neither unique nor carried out in secret, so I doubt they would be very interesting to talk about."

Liang Gangfu laughed dryly. He was not angry. Neither was he embarrassed. Instead he seemed to pity Mei for her narrow-mindedness. Mei felt immediate regret and wondered why she had expressed herself in such harsh terms. With the aching remorse of a young mother who in a fit of temper has hit her beloved child, Mei stared blankly at Liang Gangfu. After a few seconds, she sighed and continued, "Besides, I'm not sure that what I've experienced would be considered a tragedy. I was in love with someone, but he did not have the courage to love me. He said that if I really loved him I should stop loving him. I did everything I could to obey, but when everything was worked out he changed his mind. He was willing to take a chance. But it was just about that time that he . . . died of an illness!"

After a brief silence came the usual calm voice of Liang Gangfu: "You two would make a very good love poem. It's just too bad your story lacked any struggle to give it social significance."

Mei shivered. Such dry, callous criticism was more unbearable than a reproach. She bit her lip lightly and quickly changed the subject, picking something unrelated to get through the rest of the conversation.

Even after Liang Gangfu left, Mei still felt depressed. She hated this coldhearted man; she also hated herself. Why couldn't she forget him? Only a fool could not understand the meaning of the look in a woman's eyes! Liang Gangfu was alert and intelligent. Perhaps it was because he was too smart, because he already knew how strongly she was attracted to him, that he deliberately put on airs and toyed with the heart that had fallen into his hands. Perhaps he really was that cruel!

Without even noticing that she had dropped her book, Mei leaned back on her pillow and resumed brooding. The rays of the setting sun peeked through the dense clouds and shone on her face. She closed her eyes. Her body slid gradually down until she was lying flat on the bed. When all her hypothetical questions had been answered, the hint of a new source of consolation gently made its way into her muddled mind. Neither of them was a timid or bashful person. Neither of them had tried to manipulate the other in this affair. So, of course, neither was willing to grovel at the feet of the other like a lowly lap dog. No matter who was in love with whom, there was nothing to be ashamed of. It should be expressed directly. Why hadn't she told him? A clear demonstration was definitely called for.

Having come to this conclusion, a mood bordering on remorse carried her back to the conversation she had had with Liang Gangfu a short while ago. Mei still felt cold, as though an icicle were sliding down her back. She envisioned herself asking about the nature of "the social significance of struggle" and saw Liang Gangfu stand up sternly and walk over to her, a faint smile on his lips. Red stars exploded between them. As if pushed by an invisible hand, Mei threw herself into his arms. Their lips met. They embraced. Mei's body went limp. She felt intoxicated, delirious, suspended in midair. Then as though she had fallen to the ground, she found herself alone. Not far off, Liang Gangfu was slowly walking away. She caught up to him and grabbed him firmly but was greeted with a stern reproach: "What else do you want?"

"I love you."

"But I cannot love you. All I can give you is the pleasure you require."

Mei cried and wrapped herself around him like a snake. Suddenly a heavy fist fell on her chest. She collapsed. Red blood spurted from her mouth and dripped onto the floor.

Moaning softly, Mei opened her eyes, both hands still tightly clutching her chest. "Oh! What a nightmare. But it's not much worse than when I'm not dreaming," she thought, smiling coldly. Her face turned pale and she shed tears of heartbreak. Her reality was no better than a nightmare! She would rather die in her dreams! Her whole past came rushing back to her. She could not say that it was lacking in excitement, but it was so topsy-turvy. It was really much worse than a dream! She had already been loved by many men, but there had been only two whom she had loved in return. Two! The first did not dare to love her, and the second does not want to love her. And she was unable to make herself stop loving the second! Was this her fate? Such was the irony of her existence.

Before Mei's eyes, glistening with tears, there appeared the sad face of Wei Yu and the calm, smiling visage of Liang Gangfu. They quivered and expanded until finally they engulfed her entire body.

Outside the north wind howled. From the vast, pink, cloud-covered sky fell a light sprinkling of sleet about to turn to snow. The dark shadow of winter was already on the world.

Chapter Ten

Soon the white flakes of snow arrived, the water turned to ice, and the skies became gray and overcast. In the bitter cold, all fantasies and illusions disappeared. Only harsh reality pushed Mei forward. Even the force that forever disturbed the deepest recesses of her mind seemed temporarily frozen as well.

The rapidly developing political situation required even more young people to participate in political action. Mei, too, answered the call of history and passed the winter in a flurry of enthusiastic activity. But spring came again, as always, and, like all springs before it, called forth reflection, dreams, a looking back on the past with nostalgia.

One afternoon, the reflection of the sun off the streets emitted a heat that could not be ignored. A large group of tourists poured out of the station of the Shanghai-Nanjing railway. Mei jumped off the streetcar and wormed her way through this noisy mass of humanity like a water snake. Suddenly she stopped and stared to her right. In a rickshaw speeding north sat a tall, thin youth. From the back he looked remarkably like Liang Gangfu. "Has he returned?" Mei thought with surprise and joy, as she gazed after the rapidly receding vehicle. Unfortunately, the quickly flowing tide of people allowed her to look no longer. A panting figure, stinking of garlic, with a face like the shell of a crab, squeezed in front and blocked Mei's view, while the press of the crowd forced her to move forward.

The station was packed with people, all hurrying along with their heads down or looking about as though in search of something. Mei absentmindedly purchased a platform ticket and mingled with the throng that was pouring out of the train. She scrutinized each face as it passed her. For some unknown reason, the curves and wrinkles on each face seemed to resemble Liang Gangfu. November, December, January, February, March, April, May, she thought to herself. It was already more than half a year, wasn't it? He really should be coming back! The conference for the preparation of the National Assembly had already been held. A few days ago Mei had heard that he would be transferred back. The struggle here was expanding every day. A lot of people would be needed. So it must have been him.

Having come to this conclusion, Mei squeezed forward even more energetically. She was now on the platform. As she walked instinctively toward the crowd of people next to a pile of luggage, a smile appeared on her lips. Suddenly the smile vanished and her expression became serious again. Depressed, she thought, "He's back. But that shouldn't shatter the tranquillity I've been feeling these past few months, should it? The facts are clear. I must not stumble into that blind infatuation again! He is in love with someone in Beijing, the very same Beijing in which he has been for more than half a year and from which he is only now returning!"

Mei bit her lip and forced back the tears that were welling up in her eyes. Lowering her head, she walked more quickly. Someone grabbed her arm and a cheerful voice drove away her despair.

"We're over here, Mei!"

It was Xu Qijun, followed by a smiling Li Wuji. His eyes were fixed on Mei's face as though to say, "Your period of study should be over soon. Please give me a definite answer now!" Mei chatted away with Xu Qijun, avoiding Li Wuji's gaze. The station porter brought over five or six suitcases. Mei glanced at them and said, "So much luggage just for the two of you?"

"They're all mine. Mr. Li didn't bring any luggage. We ran into each other on the train."

"From the look of things, you may not be going back to Nanjing."

"Even if I wanted to go back, I couldn't!" Xu Qijun said with considerable feeling, then laughed and added, "We can't talk here. I'll tell you the whole story later."

The luggage was pushed along on a small cart, while the three followed behind, exchanging snippets of conversation. Xu Qijun wanted to stop first at the Mengyuan Hotel on Third Avenue to see someone. As she wanted Mei to accompany her, they turned the luggage over to Li Wuji and asked him to deliver it to Mei's residence.

The person Xu Qijun wanted to visit was her cousin, Xu Ziqiang. Mei had almost forgotten the mischievous adolescent, but as soon as they met, he treated Mei with the intimacy of old friends who saw each other every day. He had grown tall and strong, and his previously triangular face had filled out somewhat. He was a totally different person. Only his chaotic, unsystematic manner of speaking had remained the same, gradually awakening in Mei's dusty memory the amusing scene that had passed between them beside the river near the Zhiben Public School.

Xu Qijun listened to Ziqiang relate the events of his trip from Guangzhou, then turned to Mei and said, "I couldn't tell you the details at the station. This time I am really in trouble. I don't know why, but young Master Ziqiang here sent me a telegram saying he was coming to Nanjing on business and telling me to get ready. I don't even know what he wanted me to get ready. The telegram was a top-priority official telegram, sent from Guangzhou. The wording was unclear. Naturally, the garrison command came looking for me. All things considered, I was lucky not to fall into their hands. But I've already been in hiding five or six days. Cousin, what in the world made you send that telegram?"

"What? Nothing. I sent it for fun. Besides, it didn't cost anything," Xu Ziqiang replied, smiling impishly.

"Don't forget. It's a different world here!" Mei quietly interrupted, her lovely eyes turning slowly toward Xu Ziqiang's face. She thought of how this youth had chased after her, and she could not help but smile.

"That's why Guangzhou is more interesting, Miss Mei. Life is interesting there. There's something happening every day. You fight, you arrest reactionaries, you attend mass meetings, you shout slogans. And when the meetings are over and you're finished shouting slogans, you go to the Asia Hotel and take a room. . . ."

Xu Ziqiang stopped suddenly, looked at Mei, and laughed. The risqué ending to this sentence was already on the tip of his tongue, but in the end he was too embarrassed to finish it. Forcing himself to swallow the words, he laughed instead.

"Why did you come to Shanghai then?" Xu Qijun asked with displeasure.

"Oh, that. As I already had a month's leave, I figured I might do some sight-seeing. After winning a battle, who wouldn't want to take a few days off, put on a new suit of Western-style clothes, and have some fun?"

"But I must warn you to be more cautious. You have to take care not to make trouble!"

Xu Qijun's words were apparently too severe for the young officer to accept. He refuted her excitedly and offered a series of confused boasts about the number of "great deeds" he had accomplished. The more they talked, the more the two cousins disagreed. At last Xu Qijun, a stern expression on her face, left the Mengyuan Hotel with Mei. She did not even give her cousin her address.

Several "foreign cops" stood on the corner of Zhejiang and Nanjing Roads. Their hands were on their hips, their fingers pressed on the jet black barrels of their Browning revolvers. A fierce light flashed from their blue eyes, which they aimed at the faces of passersby. Even Mei and Xu Qijun were the recipients of these ferocious stares. Five or six "law-abiding city residents" were gathered in front of a stationery and tobacco shop, whispering to each other as though carrying on a discussion. They, too, looked suspiciously at Mei and her companion as they walked by.

Suddenly, there was a shout. Mei turned around and saw the large black hand of a Sikh* policeman brutally striking two or three people on the shoulder. The small group in front of the stationery and tobacco shop immediately scattered but stopped not far away to steal dumb glances at what was going on.

Two pairs of mounted Sikh policemen carrying carbines emerged from the west side of the street. They circled around in front of the main entrance to the Wing On Company for a while, then slowly made their way west again. Leaflets lay here and there among the turning wheels of the rickshaws and automobiles. The beautiful entranceways of the two department stores that faced

*The British used many Sikhs as policemen in the foreign-administered legation quarter of Shanghai.

each other on opposite sides of the street continued to ingest and disgorge group after group of customers: pot-bellied businessmen; strutting gentry; stylishly clad young wives, the greater part of their arms exposed but their necks forever hidden from the sun; and Western women in thin gauze dresses that, like long vests, left the tops of their bodies almost bare. Most notably, interspersed among this colorful tide of humanity were the foreign cops, the Sikh policemen and the detectives with their bellies protruding under their long black silk gowns, who were pushing and shouting as they patrolled the street.

The streets were bustling and peaceful, but it was the bustling calm that came after a storm. The unhappy faces of the people revealed displeasure at having been disturbed. When they reached the entrance to the Wing On Company, Mei whispered in Xu Qijun's ear, "Today is the second day the whole group has mobilized to make speeches to arouse the people of the city about the Gu Zhenghong case,* the supplemental censorship laws, and the harbor tax. Look how frightened the imperialists are of us!"

The two girls looked at each other and laughed, then strolled into the department store. Xu Qijun decided to buy some household necessities. So the two of them went to the third floor and then up to the fourth. There weren't many customers and the few who were there were browsing. The salesclerks leaned lazily on the counters chatting in groups of twos and threes. From the relaxed looks on their faces they might have been discussing the modern play with mechanical sets and a large orchestra that had just opened in town.**

Xu Qijun was in the clock and watch department looking at an exquisite little clock made in Germany. Mei ran up behind her and tapped her lightly on the arm. Just then, she heard the salesclerks, to whom she had been half listening all along, say something startling. Xu Qijun turned toward her companion and was about to ask her what was the matter when Mei's gaze was suddenly diverted in the direction of a distant row of windows facing the street. A door

*Gu Zhenghong was a worker killed by the foreman in a Japanese factory in May 1925. The protests against this incident gave rise to the May Thirtieth Movement, the second major anti-imperialist movement in early republican China.

**Plays of this type were popular in China during the 1920s. Two of the first to be performed were *La Dame aux Camilles* and *Uncle Tom's Cabin*.

leading to a balcony was open and leaning against it was a lanky young man, his back to Mei. A smile crossed her lips and, without signaling to Xu Qijun, she ran over to him.

When she was about five feet away, Mei verified that it was indeed Liang Gangfu. At that same moment, the young man turned around.

"So you really have returned! I thought I saw you at the corner of Baoshan Road," Mei said, smiling charmingly.

"I arrived yesterday. And Huang Yinming?"

"I don't know. She went out before me, at ten o'clock this morning. I think she was going to Qipan Street."

"Right. She was assigned to the area of Fourth Avenue and Qipan Street. Weren't you supposed to be with her?"

Feeling somewhat uneasy, Mei forced a smile and said, "No. I went to the train station to meet a friend. We just got back."

"Then you weren't there at the entrance to the Laozha police station? You don't know?"

"Did something happen?"

"Yes. Nothing particularly serious, but nothing trivial either. More than a hundred people were locked up at the Laozha police station. The police opened fire. Five or six people were killed on the spot. We're still not sure how many were injured. We lost one very good man. If Huang Yinming doesn't turn up, that will make two!"

His solemn words removed the glow from Mei's cheeks, but her eyes immediately turned red. Still calm, but with a hint of alarm in her voice, she asked urgently, "When did it happen?"

"This afternoon at one o'clock I was making a tour of inspection in this area and nothing had happened yet. At some time after three I got news in Zhabei that the bloodshed had already occurred. All right! The first bloodshed since 'Two Seven.' "*

An excited silence followed. Then Liang Gangfu smiled coldly and said, "Go home and see if Huang Yinming is there!"

"If she is, should I tell her to go to Number 240?"

Liang Gangfu nodded and left. Mei gazed blankly at the bustle on the street below. As she watched the people questing after plea-

*Two-Seven refers to events on February 7, 1923, that led to an anti-imperialist, antiwarlord strike carried out by the workers of the Beijing-Hankou railway and led by the Chinese Communist Party (CCP).

sure as though nothing had happened, the blood rose angrily to her face. By then Xu Qijun was already standing beside her.

After leaving the Wing On Company, Mei and Xu Qijun continued west on Nanjing Road. A pane of glass had been shattered in the window of the Tongchang Bicycle Shop across the street from them. Pieces of broken glass had fallen on the muddy sidewalk and were already being ground into a powder beneath the feet of passersby. Among the sparkling pile of fragments, a dark red pool stood out: blood! It was the blood of martyrs, of warriors. But the people who trod here so leisurely now wore highly polished leather shoes and boots with metal taps. Their gauzy dresses gave off intoxicating aromas and their faces smiled in absolute contentment, as though nothing worth noticing had happened on this spot.

Mei's heart ached with fury. She opened wide her blood-shot eyes and raced ahead. Everyone on the street became her enemy. Strong elbows jabbed violently into her soft shoulders, but she felt no pain. She continued to rush madly ahead. Yes, ahead. For ahead was the Laozha police station, the sacred hall of the martyrs.

But, when she reached the corner of Guangxi Road, Mei could go no farther. Mounted police, foreign cops, Chinese police, Sikh police, even merchant militia from the foreign-concession area, had been deployed in a tight military formation and were forcing all people traveling west to detour to the left or right.

There was no way to break through. Mei stood and watched. Suddenly, an equine head loomed before her. The mounted policeman's horse rushed onto the sidewalk. Mei quickly leaned over, mechanically grabbed the leather strap on the horse's bridle, and pulled forcefully to the right. The horse staggered about in a circle. Even the hefty black man sitting on him bounced up and down like a drunk. A disturbance erupted in the crowd. A Sikh policeman, grasping the handle of a gun, charged at Mei, his coarse black palm raised. Gnashing her teeth, Mei laughed fiercely, grabbed Xu Qijun's hand, and like lightning crossed into an alley at the corner of Guangxi Road.

By the time they reached home it was raining lightly. Huang Yinming was not there. The luggage had already been delivered, and Li Wuji had left a note saying he would be back that evening to talk. Mei snatched up the note, crumpled it in a ball, and threw it in the wastepaper basket. She then lay down dejectedly on the bed, without uttering a sound. The bloodstain in front of the Tongchang Bicycle Shop hung indistinctly before her eyes. The sounds of shouting and gunfire echoed in her ears, only to be replaced by Liang Gangfu's face and the exaggerated boasts of Xu Ziqiang.

"Mei!" Xu Qijun, who was seated opposite her, called out softly. She said no more but just stared at Mei. Then, as though she had already detected that something was troubling her companion, she smiled strangely. This did not escape Mei. She suddenly blushed and asked with embarrassment, "What? Tell me."

"It's nothing. It's just that a while ago, upstairs at the Wing On Company, I had to stand by and watch you abandon me, your friend, while you ran over to talk so intimately with that person." Xu Qijun dragged out her words, stopping on each one, in the same way that she had in middle school.

"That's because we had serious business to discuss and also because we hadn't seen each other in several months," Mei argued halfheartedly, unable to suppress a smile.

"Of course, you had serious business to discuss, especially as you hadn't seen each other for a long time! But I'm sure you must be aware that there was a special look in your eyes when you were with him. Your smile had a special radiance."

Mei's only answer was a gentle smile.

"Mei, I see now how well you've learned to keep a secret. You never mentioned him in your letters, and even when we ran into him, you didn't introduce him to me. Mei, tell me, should you or should you not be punished?" Xu Qijun asked, laughing loudly. She walked over to the bed and sat down. Cupping Mei's face in both hands, she examined it carefully. What a bewitchingly beautiful face. Curving eyebrows, bright red lips, eyes that seemed to smile even when they were angry. Xu Qijun looked at her avariciously, waiting for a reply.

Suddenly, a shadow fell over the beautiful face, the radiant eyes became moist; Mei sighed softly, as though swallowing something, and spoke: "Should I or should I not be punished? If I deserve to be punished, I am completely willing to be. Unfortunately, things are just the opposite of what you surmised. Sister Qi, how many times have I thought, if only you were here, I would put my arms around you and cry my heart out, pour out all my sufferings? If you knew my state of mind lately, you would probably tell me how much I've changed.

"Sister Qi, I've really changed. Just the way people used to fall madly in love with me, I am now uncontrollably in love with someone. But he is unable to let me love him, or perhaps he hasn't sensed that I want so passionately to do so." Suddenly Mei stopped and buried her head in Xu Qijun's bosom, like a grossly mistreated little girl seeking comfort by throwing herself into her mother's loving embrace.

Never having suspected that events had taken such a turn, Xu Qijun was temporarily stunned. After a while she said hesitantly, "Another Wei Yu, I suppose. But he doesn't look the type."

"He's not. He's the opposite of Wei Yu," Mei said excitedly, raising her head. She immediately leaned back dejectedly on Xu Qijun's shoulder and grumbled softly to herself, "That's me. Always wanting something I can't have. Back then, Wei Yu had another lover—his doctrine of nonresistance! I've come to the conclusion that this one also has a doctrine for a lover. But besides his invisible lover, he also has a tangible one, a flesh-and-blood lover. I would really like to meet her."

"Mei, be brave. Don't get trapped in a love triangle!" Managing to find some small way to console her, Xu Qijun gently stroked Mei's hair.

The driving rain fell on the roof like a shower of nails. Its tinkling sound filled the air as the room darkened. The clock on the wall struck six. As though suddenly awakened, Mei sat up and said, "Six o'clock? Oh, Sister Qi, I'm not afraid of falling into a trap. I'm even willing to get involved in a triangle. What frightens me is being in limbo, never knowing what to do. I'm determined to tear off this veil of confusion. I'm prepared to be disappointed in love. I'm prepared to give myself to a third lover—an 'ism'! It's six o'clock. I still have important things to do tonight!"

Mei stood up and called the maid to begin dinner, then outlined the bloody incident on Nanjing Road for Xu Qijun's benefit. At last she said vehemently, "Sister Qi, you've come at a good time. The most glorious drama of our age is about to begin in this Paris of the East, and we should all take our part in carrying out the mission of history. You must believe that the gunshots fired today on Nanjing

Road will kindle flames in every corner of China to burn from our necks the iron chains of imperialism and warlordism."

"But I'm afraid it will end up like 'Two Seven.' Didn't you notice those people coming and going in front of the two department stores? They were nothing but walking corpses. They live in a dream world where pleasure is their only concern," Xu Qijun hesitatingly expressed her lack of optimism.

"But what you haven't seen is that the real life's blood of Shanghai is pumping through the narrow, beehive-like groups of houses in Xiaosha du, Yangsha pu, Lanni du, Zhabei! Only the deep red, boiling hot blood of these areas can wash away the blood that is turning cold and dark on Nanjing Road! The times are different now. The oppressed populace has already been honed by experience. Besides, we are not sitting idly by, waiting for good fortune to fall from heaven!" Mei said with conviction. She turned and ran to the kitchen and, for the third time, pressed the maid to hurry up and start dinner.

The sound of the rain subsided, its patter now only a mournful sigh. As soon as they finished dinner, Mei went out but did not even take an umbrella. Xu Qijun felt very tired. Lying down on Huang Yinming's bed, she pondered the events of the day. Suddenly, Mei rushed in and said earnestly, "Didn't Li Wuji say he was coming over? Don't tell him what I'm up to." Mei then removed one of her slips. Wearing only a printed calico unlined *qipao*, she smiled and left.

The intermittent drizzle once again became a downpour. By the time Mei reached Number 240 her *qipao* was dripping wet and clung so tightly to her body that her high, pointed breasts stood out. When the six or seven young people gathered in the room saw Mei, rushing in like a nude mannequin, they emitted a simultaneous gasp of surprise. But when they noticed that there was not a trace of a smile on Mei's face, those who wanted to poke some fun shut their mouths and waited for a more appropriate opportunity. A moment later someone else walked unobtrusively in. It was Huang Yinming. The jests that were already on the tips of people's tongues gave way to questions and words of comfort and other serious matters.

"It was nothing. I sat in the police station for three hours. Then they brought in another large group. It was so crowded they had to let me go. They said they would go easy on the women. Ha. To-

morrow we'll show them how tough women can be!" Huang Yinming replied coldly. Her eyes fell on Mei and she could not keep
from laughing.

"It's seven thirty, Yinming. You're late—five or six minutes
late," a round-faced young man, who appeared to be a student,
said impatiently.

"True. You can punish me, but I have a reason for being late.
We had a meeting of the group heads at five o'clock."

"What's the plan for tomorrow?" Mei asked anxiously. Huang
Yinming did not answer. She glanced coldly at the group, then continued, "Let's start the meeting. Everyone here is aware of what
happened on Nanjing Road, so I won't go into it again. As our
group was assigned to Fourth Avenue, we did not suffer any
losses. . . ."

"We won't go to Fourth Avenue tomorrow. Nothing's going on
there. It's boring," a voice interjected.

"But the losses of the groups on Nanjing and Tianjin Roads
were great. Practically all of them were arrested. In front of the
Laozha police station we sacrificed an excellent comrade, Comrade
He. Let us observe three minutes of silence in memory of our departed warrior."

All heads were lowered. Not a sound could be heard save the
gentle patter of the rain. But when they raised their heads again,
several angry voices shouted, "Avenge our departed warrior!" "It's
time for a general strike!" "I'm not playing around on Fourth Avenue as a reserve anymore!"

Like the waves of an incoming tide, angry shouts followed one
after the other. The room was in turmoil. Suddenly, a tremendous
din arose from next door, exceeding the noise from the meeting. They could hear the shuffling of mah-jongg tiles, thunderous
peals of laughter, and dry coughs like the sound of ripping silk.
Through the uproar within and without, Huang Yinming spoke
coldly and with great authority: "Hold your comments for the
end. My report is not over yet. Now the arena of struggle has
widened. Our previous slogans are inadequate. We must put forward more general political watchwords. Preparations are already
being made for a general strike. A student strike will begin tomorrow. As for the shopkeepers, we'll have to see how successful
we are at organizing them tomorrow. We'll go out and lecture again
tomorrow.

"It's already been decided that we concentrate our efforts on the middle section of Nanjing Road, where today's bloodshed occurred! Maintain an attitude of nonresistance toward the armed oppression of the police. But as soon as someone is arrested, someone else must step in and take his place. We must continually have people lecturing, handing out leaflets, putting up posters, and shouting slogans."

"Good. To Nanjing Road. We'll rush in like a swarm of flies and suck up the blood we spilled there!" the round-faced young student immediately cried out in anger.

"But I don't understand why we have to adopt an attitude of nonresistance! People who practice nonresistance always hurt people and hurt themselves." As Mei asked this question, the timid face of Wei Yu once again appeared before her eyes.

"I agree with Mei," a cross-eyed teenager hurriedly added.

"There's no doubt about it. If we abide by nonresistance, we'll get arrested. I prefer to fight. I refuse to go to jail." Another serious voice emanated from a dark corner of the room, but no one could make out his face.

"We're doing it this way to avoid heavy casualties. Temporary nonresistance is not the same as defeatism." Huang Yinming first corrected Mei, then paused somberly to look over the faces of the group before slowly continuing, "It's good that you're willing to shed your blood. But we are not yet ready to allow needless bloodletting. The time for heavy sacrifices has not yet arrived. Our present strategy is to let large numbers of us get arrested, to use protracted warfare to arouse the consciousness of the city's people."

"Okay, let them arrest us. When we are all arrested, then what will we do?" the cross-eyed teenager shouted sharply.

"Keep your voice down! We will definitely not all be arrested! If no fresh troops enter our ranks, if we are unable to lead the broad masses to engage in struggle, then even if we all put our lives on the line, even if we all shed our blood, it will be in vain, insufficient to stir up a revolutionary upsurge. Besides, this attitude of nonresistance is only the strategy for tomorrow. We won't be practicing nonresistance forever. We won't be turning ourselves into believers in defeatism."

"Is that the plan you have decided on?" Mei asked, quite dissatisfied.

"That's it. Of course, there are still some aspects to be arranged, but you need not worry about them here. Comrades, tomorrow at one o'clock we will assemble at Nanjing Road. At two o'clock we will begin working. It's possible that the police station in the vicinity of Nanjing Road will set up a barricade. Charge through the barricade and march along the path red with the blood of today's warriors!"

These words were spoken softly but with unmistakable resolve. The eyes of the six or seven present glowed with enthusiasm. It was true. They could do something spectacular after all. Besides, this was an order, and none of them wanted to disobey an order. Seeing that there were no more questions, Huang Yinming handed out the next day's assignments and when she was finished, she told them to come at eleven the next morning to pick up paste, posters, and leaflets.

"Our destination is the corner of Nanjing and Zhejiang Roads. Our people will all congregate there. There will be last minute instructions after three o'clock, so pay attention!" She ended with these words. The meeting broke up, and, one by one, the people in the room slipped stealthily away.

The rain had already stopped, but there were strong gales. Mei's clothes were still soaking wet. As the wind blew on her body, she shivered uncontrollably. She hurried across a dark alley and turned into another lane. Suddenly she heard footsteps behind her. "Have I run into a 'mugger'?" she wondered. Slowing her pace, she quietly turned around to look. The street lamp shone directly behind her, and she could see clearly that the person approaching her was the cross-eyed teenager who had agreed with her opinion.

"Old Zhang. If you walk that fast, you'll make people suspicious," she said quietly, walking in front of him.

"But you weren't exactly walking slowly yourself."

"But my clothes are drenched and I'm extremely cold."

"But with your clothes drenched you're all the more beautiful."

There was no reply. They walked a few more steps. Old Zhang sidled up to Mei and said with a smile, "Mei, I really like you!"

"I like you, too."

Old Zhang smacked his lips and his eyes flashed in the darkness. He drew so close that he was nearly touching Mei's hair. She felt she could even hear the palpitating of his heart.

"Because you seem to be a revolutionary youth!" Mei added coldly. She hurried out of the lane, got into a rickshaw, and did not look back.

Early the next morning, Mei got up and looked at the newspaper. There was no commentary on yesterday's momentous events. She found a report on page three, but it played down the incident in one short paragraph. Mei threw the paper down with all her might and ran out to buy a copy of every newspaper in Shanghai. She flipped through them for some time, but their reporting of the incident was the same. Even where there was a commentary, it consisted of no more than a call to justice or a plea that the matter be left to the law to decide.

Huang Yinming had already gone out and Xu Qijun was writing letters home. Outside the window dark clouds covered the sky. All Mei could do was lower her head and pace the room monotonously as she waited with difficulty for ten o'clock to arrive so that she could go to Number 240 to pick up the leaflets and posters and drag Xu Qijun to Nanjing Road.

The streets were bustling as usual. The posters that were put up last night had already been torn down. What was left of them had been turned into a pulpy mass by the evening's downpour. Now they were as illegible and unenticing as the advertisements for medicines to cure venereal disease that were plastered all over town. Of course, last night's cloudburst also washed away any traces of the tragedy on Nanjing Road that had lingered in people's dreams. Now every good city resident was leading his normal, uneventful, contented life, running after money and wallowing in the mire as he always did.

Mei and Xu Qijun sat in the streetcar looking at each other and smiling but saying nothing. Mei's heart was filled with disdain and a raging fire of hate. Although she knew very well how to follow orders, deep down inside she did not approve. Nonresistance? Would this arouse the consciousness of the people of the city? How naive! These slaves, obediently raised on imperialism, were only worthy of being thrown into the Whangpoo River! She knew how to ride a horse and fire a gun. Why should she go around with these strips of paper and cans of paste? She glanced sideways at the package of paper under her arm and had a tremendous urge to toss them out the window of the streetcar. Right. She would select one of the puffy, round, complacent faces and throw them right in it!

She was already holding the package of papers in her hand and fingered them for a while before thrusting them back under her arm. Orders, after all, were sacred!

The atmosphere on Nanjing Road was similarly calm. There were a few foreign cops and Sikh policemen on the sidewalk. Five or six fully armed members of the concession-area merchant militia were lined up at the entrance to the Laozha police station, and mounted police circled the drive inside the main gate. The sidewalk leading up to the police station had been closed off. Perhaps because of this, the passersby momentarily opened their sleepy eyes. But Mei immediately understood the reason for all this activity: the foreigners were protecting their police station, guarding against trouble.

Going east from the Laozha police station toward the ballpark, the busy middle section of Nanjing Road, the street became more lively. Mei and Xu Qijun squeezed slowly through the crowd. In front of the display window of the shop specializing in foreign products stood several youths examining the brightly colored imported goods. Presently, they wandered over and stood in front of the window of the watchmaker's shop next door. Under their arms were packets of paper. Mei eyed them carefully, her heart thumping involuntarily. They were already all over the streets!

But it was only eleven thirty. Mei and Xu Qijun entered a snack shop. Here, too, it was unusually crowded. Here, too, there were young men and women whose mouths hid a smile and whose eyes glowed with excitement. They had all come to participate in this historic event. On each face was the same look; in each heart was a feeling of exhilaration that they would feel again only on their wedding day! Eating a bowl of noodles, Xu Qijun looked about her and suddenly laughed.

"What's so funny, Qi?"

"I was thinking about how the heroes of Liang Shanbo in *All Men Are Brothers* rescued their comrades at the execution grounds," Xu Qijun whispered, lowering her head to her bowl of noodles once again. After receiving Mei's gently laughing reply, Xu Qijun asked, "They are here to save their brothers or their leaders. What about us?"

"We are here to rescue the hearts of all Shanghai. We are here to knead these millions of hearts into one huge heart," Mei whispered a determined reply.

Xu Qijun raised her head and grabbed Mei's hand. She held it tightly and did not let go for some time. Suddenly there was a shout outside. An extremely angry voice yelled, "Citizens of China. Rise up! Rise up!"

Everyone jumped up and crowded onto the balcony outside the window. Mei rushed ahead of them all. Below was a sea of wriggling heads. Sticking out above the crowd, a Sikh policeman with a red turban wrapped around his head raised his stick and swung it wildly. A foreign cop seized the tall young man who was still shouting with rage. Suddenly, he flung his right hand and the leaflets he was holding flew into the air, greeted by thunderous cheers and applause.

The first shots of the day had been fired. Although it was not yet the designated time, Mei could wait no longer. She reached under her arm for the packet of papers, but it was not there. She had left it on the table inside. She took another look at her watch. It was only a little after noon. Much too early. The time for an all-out attack had not arrived. They could not act independently and give the enemy the opportunity to crush them one by one. Orders were sacred.

The two women hurried out of the snack shop. The crowd of a moment ago was already being dispersed. Several shop clerks held leaflets and read them quietly and attentively. The atmosphere was electric. People walked more quickly, as though they were being pursued by demons. Mei and her companion followed the road west. A group of three people brushed past them. At each shop they carefully paused and threw in some leaflets. One of them held a large paintbrush and smeared the glass windows with paste, after which another pressed on posters written in large scarlet characters.

"It must be time to act. Only a zombie would stand by and wait," Mei thought. She winked at Xu Qijun and opened the packet of leaflets. They followed close behind the group of three, nimbly and seriously handing out leaflets and pasting up posters. They met no obstruction until they had nearly reached the corner of Zhejiang Road. Here they could go no further.

The main artery near the "Sunrise Building" had become a battleground. Tragic, heroic screams mixed with enthusiastic applause swept over the crowd like roaring waves, so loud that they almost toppled the towering buildings in this part of town. The street was covered with a dense, oscillating mass of heads. The upstairs windows of the shops on both sides of the street were also crowded with excited faces. A long line of streetcars was stopped, and people were stretching their necks out the windows, madly shouting words that no one could understand. From the roof garden of the Wing On Company countless red, yellow, and white leaflets were being scattered and blown through the air by the moist wind. And, as though welcoming the leaflets, a resounding cry arose from the turbulent forest of heads below.

Mei squeezed forward with all her might. On the square, stone windowsill of the shop ahead of her stood a man who was spraying spittle as he shouted, "Down with imperialism." Suddenly, a foreign cop jumped out from the crowd, grabbed the speaker's collar, and raised his gun to clear the way. Two or three Sikh policemen also rushed over, brandishing wooden sticks. A crack briefly opened in the dense throng, but the shouts became more violent. Mei quickly penetrated the mass of people in front of her and rushed over to the windowsill. Holding on to a slender iron bar, she leaped up, filled the vacant "post," and began roaring, "See what is happening to our people! They are being arrested. They are being shot! Citizens of China unite! Drive out these bandit dogs. . . ."

Mei's voice was growing hoarse. Although she had been screaming at the top of her lungs, she could not be heard above the riotous, joyful responses of the crowd. She noticed Xu Qijun signaling to her from below and quickly turned her head. Before her loomed a tall Sikh policeman, charging at her like a ferocious demon. "Nonresistance?" The question flashed through her mind as she roared even more forcefully, "Citizens of China unite! Attack these murderous bandits—slave of the foreigners! Running dog!" Hurling these last two epithets at the onrushing Sikh like a stone, Mei quickly jumped off the stone sill, merged with the crowd and squeezed forward again.

No one was sure when the rain had started up again, it was now becoming increasingly heavy. Like a shower of oil, it only served to intensify the flames of anger in the hearts of the gathering crowd. The public square at the intersection of Nanjing and Zhejiang Roads was packed with so many shouting, outraged people that no vehicle could get through. This was their destination! The destination toward which everyone was converging! The battleground on which today's warriors would defy death and gather for the attack! Ha! They had already captured the field of battle.

The number six streetcar approached from the north. When it reached the corner of Zhejiang Road it was blocked by an angry, shouting throng. "Chinese people do not ride foreign vehicles!" "You are Chinese, too. Don't drive for the foreigners. Strike!"

All the passengers alighted. Someone threw a rock, breaking one of the streetcar's windows. The crowd clapped and cheered feverishly.

Mei managed to squeeze through to the entrance of the Sincere Company. She noticed the huge department store was packed with people, mostly dignified members of the gentry and fashionable women and girls. They all waited anxiously, total disapproval on their faces. A few of them sneaked up to the door to take a look, but as soon as they heard the angry uproar outside, they quickly recoiled. Small leaflets and posters that had not been pasted up slowly floated down from the roof. Mei looked up. The area between the Sincere Amusement Park and the road was filled with people. "Down with imperialism" was the only cry to be heard, incomprehensible shouts and curses echoing in reply.

Suddenly the crowd on the east side of the street shifted. There was a strange *gua-gua-gua* sound as a red fire engine loaded with merchant militia and police, its sirens still blaring, forged through the people and continued west, temporarily clearing a passage in the road. Immediately behind followed a long procession of streetcars, devoid of passengers, their sides and shattered glass windows completely plastered over with red big-character posters. From the far corners of Shanghai came the mighty sound of slaves struggling to break their iron chains and people fighting the heroic battle!

As soon as the streetcars had passed, the crowd reoccupied the street. Mei noticed a lanky man standing on the balcony of the teahouse on the corner diagonally opposite her. It looked like Liang Gangfu. He was waving his hand and hurling determined epithets. A new, louder round of cheers and applause arose from the crowd. As she joined in the shouting, Mei used all her energy to push her way into the street. She decided to go the entrance of the Wing On Company across the road and from there to force her way up to the teahouse. How happy she would be to stand high above the throng, on the balcony of the teahouse, shouting slogans by Liang Gangfu's side. Suddenly her delicate white arms felt very strong.

The moment she arrived at the entrance to the Wing On Company, the red fire engine returned from the west. The masses of people in the street screamed and drew back like a retreating tide. Mei realized that she would not be able to fulfill her plan to cross Zhejiang Road and make her way to the entrance of the teahouse. But what depressed her more was that standing on the balcony of the teahouse now were several policemen.

"Don't tell me even Liang Gangfu has been arrested?" As this thought flashed through her mind, another cry arose from the dense crowd before her. No applause followed. The crowd stirred and withdrew with an undulating motion in the direction of Zhejiang Road. Mei was pushed along for several steps; then suddenly her whole body felt cold, as though she had fallen into a pool of water. She unconsciously jerked her head to one side, and a spray of water hit her right in the chest, soaking her through to her underwear. The police were using water hoses to disperse the crowd. Mei was pushed along more than ten feet by the mass retreat before she could stop. In front of her stood a delivery truck that appeared to have been obstructed and unable to get through.

Disregarding everything, Mei jumped onto the truck and stared out at the scene before her—at the destination for the day and at the general situation on the battleground that her comrades had earlier occupied. Six or seven jets of water danced in the air. The dense crowd swayed, and the sound of their screams diminished, becoming weak and intermittent. But the powerful blasts of water could not disperse the crowd. All they could do was to make the people sway. Nevertheless, it was this buffeting about that was destroying the crowd's spirit and morale.

"Come on, comrades! Hold this front. All Shanghai has been aroused! The final victory belongs to us!" Mei shouted, carried away with anger. But she could say no more. A stream of water suddenly hit her in the face. She blacked out instantly. Her legs buckled and she toppled from the delivery truck into the crowd. Several muscular arms broke her fall, as a thunderous cry rose from every direction, merging in the shout "Okay! Charge ahead!"

When Mei was standing on the ground once more, five or six jets of water shot in her direction. The crowd again retreated south, carrying her along with it. She was already at Third Avenue before she could stand still.

Mei sighed and began to walk aimlessly. The atmosphere here was not as tense, but the electricity poles, the windows of the shops lining the street, and any other place where one could paste a piece of paper, were already covered with the day's posters and slogans. Excitedly, Mei walked and watched. Suddenly, she felt a chill. Her legs trembled uncontrollably, and she realized for the first time that her clothes were completely soaked. For some unknown reason, only her shoes remained dry. She was struck with a splitting headache and her legs felt as heavy as lead.

"Mei, where are you going?" Someone walked up behind her at the corner and shouted. Mei turned and discovered that it was Xu Ziqiang. He was wearing an attractive Western suit and the crease of his trousers was perfectly straight. He cut quite a figure. Meeting this young man suddenly reminded Mei of Xu Qijun and the fact that she had not seen her for some time. Mei's last impression was of her companion signaling to her from the crowd, but she could not recall where that had been.

"So, you had a taste of the water hose, too? You're soaked. Look, you can see right through your clothes. Mei, be careful or you'll catch cold. This is no joking matter. Come to my hotel and sit a while there. There you can have a glass of brandy and change clothes. It just so happens that I bought a new *qipao* to give to someone. Rest a while. I guarantee it will do you good. You don't want to get sick."

Without waiting for a reply, Xu Ziqiang grabbed Mei's hand and began walking. They passed a shop and were soon at the entrance of the Mengyuan Hotel. Mei was thoroughly exhausted. Her head still hurt, her legs still felt heavy, and now her back ached as well. Although her mind was still on Nanjing Road, she let herself be led into Xu Ziqiang's room. The young man rushed about looking for a bottle of brandy. He picked up a teacup, filled it to the rim, and handed it to Mei.

"I can't drink a whole cup," Mei said, taking a sip. She felt more comfortable now, sitting on a soft sofa in a room where the temperature was warmer than outside. Xu Ziqiang was rummaging through his large suitcase again. At last he let out a cheer. Pulling out a lined *qipao* made of shiny light-green French satin, he spread it over his outstretched arm for Mei to see, like an experienced clothing salesman.

"I don't want to change clothes," Mei said, shaking her head as she placed the remaining half cup of liquor on the table.

"You have to change. If it's undergarments you're worried about, I have those, too."

"But you must have another *qipao*. This one is too pretty. I don't want it."

"Only a *qipao* as lovely as this is worthy of you!"

Mei smiled, still shaking her head.

"Besides, I don't have another one. If you keep wearing those wet clothes, you are bound to get sick. The only thing we have to fear is illness. The responsibility for building a new China is on our shoulders. To let yourself get sick is counterrevolutionary."

His words were spoken with great emotion, and even Mei appeared to be moved. Without realizing it, the dislike that, since yesterday, she had felt toward this young man, was dissipating. She hesitated slightly, then slowly said, "In that case, I'll also need the undergarments and stockings."

Once again Xu Ziqiang went rummaging through his suitcase and finally came up with all the clothes. Placing them neatly on the *qipao*, he sat down on the opposite end of the sofa and lit a cigarette. Mei stood up and unfolded the clothes. After checking their size and deeming them to be suitable, she sat back down on the sofa and glanced at Xu Ziqiang as though waiting for something else. Sensing this, he blew out a puff of smoke, laughed, and said, "Do you want me to leave? Ha. Even the illustrious Miss Mei is a prude. Wouldn't behind that screen be all right? If you're really worried, I can go out."

Beside the glass doors leading to the balcony was a low screen. It stood in a corner and had originally been set up there to form a changing area. Mei said no more but picked up the clothes and walked behind the screen.

Xu Ziqiang focused all his energy on inhaling and exhaling his cigarette, never taking his eyes off the screen. The muscles in his face twitched. He uncrossed his legs but immediately crossed them again. He turned his head as though he had heard something, then flung the cigarette butt into the spittoon, jumped out of his seat, and walked over to the screen.

As he was about to reach the screen, he was startled by a sarcastic laugh so loud it filled the room. It was such a hair-raising sound that Xu Ziqiang involuntarily froze in his tracks. One of the panels of the screen suddenly swung open and Mei stood solemnly before him, dressed only in a camisole. She said coldly, "Ha, Xu Ziqiang. I see what's on your face and I can tell what's on your mind. This is not the Asia Hotel. Stop and think about it. Don't make a fool of yourself."

As she spoke, Mei unaffectedly threw on the new *qipao* she was holding in her hand, then walked toward the sofa and sat down on the nearby chair to put on the stockings. The *qipao* was still opened at the chest. The thin, white silk camisole tightly bound her full, round breasts, but two protruding circles of pink were faintly discernible.

Xu Ziqiang seemed dazed as well as somewhat embarrassed. He returned to the sofa, then moved closer to Mei. Bewildered, he said, "Heaven is my witness! Please believe that I was sincere. I only asked you to change your clothes for your own good. I had absolutely nothing else in mind. But Mei, you don't know how enchanting you are. Anyone who didn't want to take a peek wouldn't be human. I have always been your faithful comrade. When we met several years ago in Chongqing—I assume you still remember—I helped you most loyally. At that time I was still in middle school and you said I was a child. Well I finished my schooling and I've gone to war. I'm now a major and a company commander. I truly love you. You are the reason I go to war and fight in the revolution!"

"Well, excuse me. So you're a big-shot company commander. But one thing really bothers me. Why is it that every military officer I meet falls in love with me? When I was in Chengdu, army commanders, division commanders, brigade commanders, I seem to recall that they all said the same thing as you are saying now. But I never accepted their favors. I am still my own person." As she spoke, Mei picked up the other stocking and slowly pulled it on.

She then laughed, that same peculiar laugh that made Xu Ziqiang's heart tremble.

"They were warlords. I'm a revolutionary soldier,"* Xu Ziqiang pulled himself together and said indignantly.

"In that case, today, when all of Shanghai was rising up, why were you dressed so elegantly and neatly, strolling about in front of your hotel?"

"I didn't receive orders! If I had acted without orders, the commander in chief would have had me court-martialed."

Mei snorted but did not respond.

"Besides, the foreigners have guns. Yelling and shouting the way you do are useless. For a genuine revolution you must rely on the military."

"Fine. When you have exhausted the pleasures of Shanghai, then we'll have a revolution." Mei suddenly stood up and ran out of the room. Slamming the door behind her, she sped down the stairs. By the time Xu Ziqiang reached the top of the stairwell and yelled after her, Mei had already run out the main door of the hotel.

The rain had temporarily subsided. The sound of voices was still emanating like an angry tide from Nanjing Road. The overflowing joy Mei had felt earlier in the day had been completely swept away by Xu Ziqiang at the Mengyuan Hotel. Now, listening to the shouts of the crowd, her zeal was once again ignited. When she ran back to Nanjing Road, she found the street flooded with water and armed Sikh policemen and concession-area merchant militiamen patrolling both sides of the road. The sidewalks on either side of Nanjing Road were still jammed with people intermittently clapping and shouting slogans.

Many of the people walking north were turned back by the patrols. Mei continued to push ahead. Before her stood a foreign cop,

---

*Although the author does not specify Xu Ziqiang's affiliation, that he is stationed in Guangzhou implies that he is a member of the newly reorganized Guomindang Army, which was originally under the leadership of Sun Yat-sen and by this time was headed by Chiang K'ai-shek. At the time the story takes place, they were preparing for the northern expedition, which was undertaken in cooperation with the CCP to wipe out warlordism and reunify China. In the end the campaign fell far short of its goals, and the so-called united front between the CCP and the Guomindang ended in 1927, following Chiang's attack on the left after his conquest of Shanghai.

his arms outstretched. After looking Mei over he shouted roughly in crude Shanghai dialect, "Walk to the left."

At that moment the street came alive with the sound of rapidly ringing bells. Two or three bicycles approached from the east, their riders holding a small banner. Mei edged her way past the foreign cop and rushed ahead to get a look, catching a glimpse of the banner's bright red characters: "Storm the Chamber of Commerce!"

The clock on the lintel over the door of the Sincere Company across the way read a few minutes past three.

Postscript

The preceding ten chapters were written between April and July 1929. At the time I did not consider how limited was my strength. I wanted only to leave my mark on China's heroic history of the past decade. In August I lay down my pen so as to move. Later the pressure of urgent personal matters prevented me from taking it up again. Now half a year has flown by. The winters are long in this island country. At dawn a dense mist rushes in my window. In the evening icy rain falls on the eaves of my house. When the west wind blows I can hear the mournful tolling of the bells of a distant temple pressing in on me. It is all I can do to take hold of my brazier and nod off to sleep. Perhaps when the colors of the rainbow once again appear over the peaks of the mountains behind my house, I will finish writing this book.

Mao Dun, February 1, 1930

Compositor: BookMasters, Inc.
Text: 11/13 Caledonia
Display: Caledonia
Printer: Maple-Vail Book Mfg. Group
Binder: Maple-Vail Book Mfg. Group